The

SHAPING

of

WATER

Suspended In Space

1994

Marielise, strapped and trapped in her aeroplane seat, flew the little blue screen in front of her away from planet Earth into space.

Would flying as high as the angels grant her insight?

She zoomed back to see the close-up images of the actual curves and bumps of the mountain ridges on the earth beneath.

At this height, almost caressing the earth, was it easier to understand the world?

Pressing her face against the plane window, half-blinded, in spite of her sunglasses, by the clarity and brightness of the sky outside, Marielise stared and stared at Africa slowly moving southwards under her.

Mysterious and fantastic lives and deaths were being enacted on the extraordinary continent so far below.

What had she learnt while she lived down there?

What did she really know of those other lives?

She found her own life so mystifying that surely any rational knowledge of other people's lives was impossible?

Here she was, only a little older than the Apartheid regime whose end she had just celebrated, flying back to finish her doctorate at Cambridge. The struggle was over – or most probably only beginning. The world was changing again and so was she – again.

Marielise shifted uncomfortably. The plastic and metal bits of her bones did not like long flights and flying thrilled and frightened her. Atheist that she was, there remained that little niggle of fear, that flying would provoke the gods – or she grinned wryly – maybe just the Shades of Milimo Singani's ancestors, who lie drowned in the waters of Kariba Lake. Marielise loved the lake and delighted in its surprises and its beauty, but reconciling herself to the destruction that brought it into existence was another matter.

Well – the dam can't be undone – neither can I undo anything I have done.

It had taken her plane almost an hour to fly across the rainfall area that feeds Lake Kariba with water. If she could have diverted the flight downstream from the dam to fly over the huge flood plains and the great length of Zambezi River that the dam controlled, even more time would have been needed. Instead the Jumbo's flight path was well west of the African Rift Valley; that continent-long, ridged fault in the earth, an earthquake zone, with the Kariba Dam at the furthest flick of its curled tail.

Marielise's thoughts went from Kariba, to Milimo Singani and his mother Natombi. They had both been born in the Zambezi Valley and uprooted and impoverished by the dam's construction. She found herself smiling at their remembered faces. Was Natombi still the guardian of one of the Rain Shrines of the Basilwizi? What had happened to Milimo since he had left the cottage? The cottage where he had been the guardian of her happiest days. *Here I am,* Marielise said to herself, *between a lover who is alive and a lover who is dead; suspended above the country I lived in, and above the people of the valley whom I knew, while all that I have left of my life, work and friendships is stored on my computer.*

Marielise's mind slipstreamed away from the straight path of her plane.

Oh yes! The opposing forces of Good and Evil and the God I don't believe in, is only on one side.

2

The
SHAPING
of
WATER

RUTH HARTLEY

Matador
9 Priory Business Park
Kibworth Beauchamp
Leicestershire LE8 0RX, UK
Tel: (+44) 116 279 2299
Fax: (+44) 116 279 2277
Email: books@troubador.co.uk
Web: www.troubador.co.uk/matador

ISBN 978-1783061-990

British Library Cataloguing in Publication Data.
A catalogue record for this book is available from the British Library.

Typeset in Aldine by Troubador Publishing Ltd
Printed and bound in the UK by TJ International, Padstow, Cornwall

Matador is an imprint of Troubador Publishing Ltd

For my children in memory of lakeside days.

There was a 'Cottage', there is a Lake Kariba, the events are reasonably accurate historically, but all the characters and their lives and opinions are entirely fictional.

"Water is the best of all things."
Pindar (c 522 – c 438 BC) Olympian Odes.

"Manzi ni moyo"
Water is life
– Chinyanja saying.

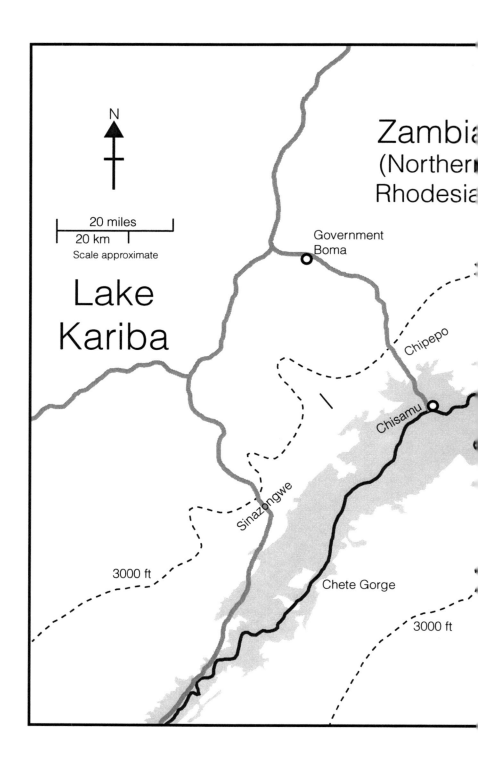

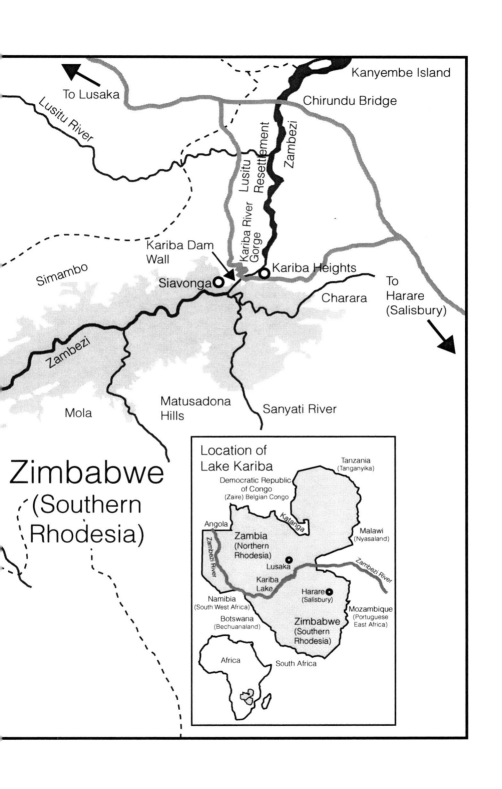

Map of Siavonga

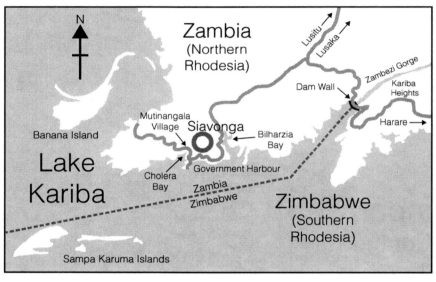

Her old friend, Father Patrick Brogan, had had no answers for her on that question, and perhaps, come to think of it, not that many certain answers for himself.

'Faith is the answer,' he might have said, shaking his head doubtfully.

At any rate, Marielise told herself ironically, hoping a stronger affirmation would make it more likely to be true, *I know which side is wrong and it is not my side. I know that my heart is fleshy and loving and so vulnerable, and I trust its rhythm – like the beat of the pop music in my earphones – the music that sweet Manda sent me with her warmest love while I was in hospital – my heart is good – good – good! The beat of my heart tells me that I am alive and good, but the syncopated beat of doubt, the counterpoint of uncertainty is there too, all the time.*

I am compromised and not just by my damaged body.

But this is now and that was then. There is no comfort in history, even my own short history. I meant well. I acted for the best. I tried to be good. I wasn't bad – well – maybe just a little under-informed.

Really – Marielise considered – *have I made any better moral judgements than my conventional Aunt Margaret and well-intentioned Uncle Charles?*

I am good aren't I? Marielise asked herself again without much certainty and then dozed over her wine and painkillers at lunch without concluding anything at all. After all she had no choice but to hang suspended in the atmosphere at 35,000 feet for another five hours and listen once more to k.d. lang singing with hope about waiting for and trusting in love.

3

Natombi

1947

I am Natombi.

I am ready now.

The elder mothers have let me leave the place where they have kept me secluded, my face hidden under a bead veil, while they taught me about the duties of marriage.

Tomorrow they will send for my husband to come and pay the bride-price and take me to his homestead.

All night on the journey to his homestead there will be drumming and singing. There will be beer and there will be dancing. By the first light of day I will enter his hut and be recognised as his wife. On the following night only, I will enter his hut to stay. Then I will be wrapped in garments that he must unwind before he can know me as a husband must know his wife.

My husband's name is Singani. He is the *sikatongo* who has the care of the Rain Shrine that brings us rain and good fortune. He is the inheritor of the shades of his ancestors who have taken care of the Rain Shrine before him. Singani already has a first wife. She is his ritual wife and I will be the junior ritual wife. At first I must work for this elder wife and do her bidding without complaining. When I have a child I may be allowed to have my own hut and garden and look after my own household.

Singani has worked many months in the fields of my mother

as payment of the bride-price for me. Tonight he will bring the goats and the gifts that were agreed for my family. Now I stand here wearing the beaded *insete* skirt that my mother has made for me by chewing the roots of *musante* tree and rolling it into many, many strings. My goat-skin beaded cloak and necklaces are presents from my husband. There are many beads of bright colours that are threaded into linked necklaces of differing lengths. I wear them across each shoulder and they rest between my breasts, which are still small and firm like unripe *mujenje* fruit.

I have been promised to my husband since I was six years of age. Now I have reached puberty and the time for my marriage has come. There have been twelve seasons of rain since I was born.

I am a child of the Basilwizi people who have always lived secretly in the Zambezi Valley where there are only paths for those who go by foot. The Basilwizi are those people who cannot be found when raiders come to rob and kill. We are the people of the river. Now there are changes that we cannot hide from any more. The white government comes more and more often to interfere with our people and our customs and our way of life.

I will be very sad to leave my mother and my sisters and go as a stranger to the house of another woman with whom I must share a husband. She has only one child and Singani is already a man of more than thirty years. I am afraid to go but I must not say so. I hope that they will be kind and that the elder wife will not be angry and treat me as her slave. I hope that they will share their food with me as is right and fair.

PART ONE
MARGARET

One

Impossible Dreams

1960

The steep hillside on which the cottage was built was covered by scrubby undergrowth without many big trees. The contractor simply cleared away the bush and any wood that the labourers could not find a use for was piled into heaps and burnt. He knew what his probable client would expect and he had terraced the hillside into giant steps using the rough rock left over from the road building on the site of the new township. The hillside was so steep that it was not possible to see the bottom terrace from the new veranda of the cottage, or to see more than the edge of the corrugated asbestos roof of the cottage from the place where there might one day be water. The future level of the water was guessed at by the contractor. Surveyors had been around the whole site taking measurements but, even so, mistakes about gradients and water levels were made by both the town planners and the architects.

The contractor did reasonably well with his estimates for his own design. It was a steep drive to the cottage and the plot was narrow. He chose to put the cottage up high on the plot and put 130 steps down to the lake – or where he hoped the lake would be.

Meanwhile the building of the actual township was on hold. Roads had been marked out and sites chosen for government offices. Until the road across the dam made easy access possible it had been difficult to get in building machinery and materials to do very much work. The cement for the dam wall was produced near Lusaka and previously it had to be transported across the Zambezi at Chirundu where there was a bridge, taken down through Makuti in Southern Rhodesia, and then back again to the southern side of the dam construction site. It was 150 kilometres from Lusaka to Siavonga but the cement lorries had to go almost three times as far. There were many escarpments that made precipitous barriers for road builders and then there was the Zambezi River itself. It could spread shining sheets of water across miles of flood plain or rise up in a savage flood, racing through perpendicular gorges. At the time of the building of Kariba Dam there were only two bridges across its entire length: one at Livingstone, the other at Chirundu, both between Northern and Southern Rhodesia, one the gift of the financier, Alfred Beit, the other part of the colonising strategy of Cecil John Rhodes.

The roads over the escarpment follow for the main part the old migratory routes taken year after year for millennia by elephants. Elephants, who for all those thousands of years would roam, not just around Zimbabwe, or just around Kenya, but all the way up sub-Saharan Africa from south to north and back again. Now human governments have decreed that elephants must obey human laws and stay within the bounds of national boundaries drawn by straight-edged rulers on maps. In the time before colonisation, a mere 150 or so years ago, elephants travelled where they always travelled, and they walked across mountains with consummate skill and ease, always finding the most direct routes through the least difficult of the passes. The people of Africa also wandered freely across the continent. They had always followed the paths made by animals and the elephant paths over the mountains always were the best way, as the European explorers were yet to discover. In the time before the elephants and the people were confined to national boundaries that cut their tribes and their herds into pieces, all the roads to Kariba and to Siavonga were elephant roads long before they became human roads.

The cottage was on the lake shore of the new township that would be known as Siavonga.

Siavonga was the name of the local chief and as was common with names of chiefs among the Tonga people, the meaning of the name had been lost. The reason that the first chief Siavonga had been given that name was forgotten. Whatever attributes, good or bad, that had earned him the name had vanished with the first chief. Whoever became the next chief took on the name of Chief Siavonga in a village ceremony and his own name disappeared. It was the same for Chief Chipepo in Gwembe and Chieftainess Chiawa beyond Chirundu. The only difference was that though local people said that this was the place of Chief Siavonga's village, there was no longer a village there. Villages along the Zambezi had the habit of moving as the river moved, each year the Zambezi would shift its banks as it settled itself into a slightly different place once the seasonal floods were over. Chief Siavonga's place was there but it could no longer be seen.

From the selected site for the north bank township that was to be called Siavonga, it was not possible to see or even hear the construction work of the great dam wall. The dam site was south-east of Siavonga and a short way down the gorge in a place known to the Tonga as Kariva: 'the trap'. It was called that by the Tonga because it was a giant reminder of the small rock traps they set in little gullies to catch tiny creatures. Little rocks carefully balanced across a gap on a thin stick to fall and crush an even smaller, scavenging mammal looking for grain. But this was to be the huge trap that was to catch the great Zambezi River.

Except that the Tonga knew that it would be impossible to trap the Zambezi.

At the place known as Kariva, the high ridges of mountainous hills rise up, almost blocking the path of the mighty river. It is able to continue its journey only through the narrowest and steepest of gorges. This huge and steep escarpment, one of the steepest in Africa, lies at the end of the Great Rift Valley, a continent-long seismic fault that stretches from the Red Sea through to Lake Malawi and Lake Kariba. It is a seismic fault that will, one day, split Africa into two.

Here near Kariva, 'the trap', in the middle of a wilderness, is a place called Siavonga, which is a name without meaning. It is a place that will be a town but a place that is not yet built. It is a place that is presently isolated by poor and inadequate roads and it is difficult to reach. It is in a country that is becoming another country, with another name. It is here that there is a plot where a contractor builds a cottage above a lake not yet filled with water. All this takes place in the newly created Central African Federation of the Rhodesias and Nyasaland that will be no more in a few short years. Two of these countries will change into independent states with different names when that happens.

It is an exercise in madness and dreams; in magic and megalomania, and the Tonga people know it to be impossible.

Two

The Priest

1957

It is the Garden of Eden, Father Patrick Brogan thought, then added to himself, *On a cool day at least.*

Today especially, it was so hot that sweat had soaked right through his shirt. Wearing sodden clothes made the priest feel foolish in front of the villagers, who were naked but with the unselfconscious grace and natural beauty that are integral to unobserved innocence. It was midday and the women and children rested flat on the packed earth under the grass shelters. It was still strange for him to see women who had no shame about the closeness of the skin of their bodies to the dirt of the ground. Sometimes their bodies seemed to him, too real, too physical, and too close to his own pale white boniness. He had to hold his own chest in, sucking air in secretly through his nostrils in case he inhaled some of their reality and had to submit to it. He however, liked the touch of the children. The feel of their hard heads and dry skin when they came up to him to grab at his strange outfit, provided him with an antidote of sorts to the immense desire in him to take his clothes off and lie down on the earth in the shade with the women. Nothing the women ever did had been suggestive or an invitation for him to join them. They simply ignored him, perhaps did not see him as a man, or even as human.

The heat crushed him too, but he waited. One of the men would perhaps arrive soon. Nothing did move however, except a dog shifting because a fly had bitten it. The dog whined as it was forced to cross a patch of burning sunlight. A woman gestured at the dog with a stick without raising her recumbent body from the ground and it took its bites and flies deeper into the shade of a winterthorn. Even the goats were absolutely motionless in the small shade offered by the overhanging roof of a hut.

The river was close by. He could hear the water's rapid movement against its banks, but the bush was dense and lush after the rainy season and there was no obvious path or direction to take in search of the men. In all probability the men would be on the river shore with their fishing nets, basket traps and their *bwato* – the dugout canoes they use to cross the river.

The rainy season was over otherwise his Land Rover would not have made the journey. The road was not so much a road as a gully for flood water, and until the water had dried up no one could judge the depth of its pot-holes. On the way down to the village Father Patrick had seen youths tending a few cattle, and some still green but mature crops of millet. There was no shortage of food for the Basilwizi in the Zambezi River Valley. River, gardens and the bush fruits provided for them all year round. They did not suffer the seasonal famine of those who lived on the dry plains above the escarpment, who were forced each year to hunt, or steal, to survive. While other rivers would run dry or sink down under the sand long before the rains came, the Zambezi itself would continue to rise throughout the cool, dry season as the waters from the Congo watershed made their gradual way towards the sea.

Father Patrick knew however, that in reality, this village in the valley was not the Eden of Christianity. There was child marriage, witchcraft, illness, superstition, unexpected and unexplained deaths from poison, snakes, crocodiles and wild beasts. Children would run away screaming when he appeared and some of the women too, were afraid. White people did not go into the valley very often.

To the people of the river valley, the strange skin colouration of white people meant they were ghosts – the lost shades of the dead who had not been appeased – the *muzungu*.

The priest waited a long hour. The sweat on his face could not evaporate and cool him but he did not try and wipe it away. There was no relief to be had that way. The tremendous heat made him wonder why he had agreed to come to add his words of explanation about the new dam to those of the young district officer in charge of the area. Father Patrick was only a teacher in a mud-hut school working in the valley as part of the outreach of Canisius School and the Chikuni Jesuit Mission in Monze. The district officer, Tom Holmes, had however, expressed concern about the increasing resistance by the Tonga to the plans for their resettlement.

"The governor blames the African nationalists," Tom had said, "but that's a small part of it. The Tonga don't trust us anymore. Why should they believe that we can stop the Zambezi flowing?"

He suggested that perhaps Father Patrick might be more convincing on the difficult spiritual questions of the shrines and the ancestors' graves. Father Patrick agreed to try. He was always curious to see more of the traditional life from which his students came. He did not admit to himself that he was also curious to see the women of the village.

Eventually one of the elder women called to a young boy – her voice sounded both harsh and casual, but authoritative. He heard laughter in it and his chest made a little thud of fear that she must find him amusing. She sent the child to tell the men of the village that the priest had come. He heard the men's strong voices talking and laughing before he saw them. They brought with them plump fish tied with fibres onto sticks.

The Headman greeted him and Father Patrick replied in ChiTonga in the traditional way.

Then the priest said, "I have come to try to answer your questions about the new dam the Federal Government is building down at the Kariva Gorge."

15

THREE

The Cottage

1963

The Guest Book, The Cottage, Siavonga.
June 1963
'To my dear Margaret,
So you can always remember your weekends at Lake Kariba,
With love from your husband, Charles.'

Charles had acquired the cottage, as he put it, for his weekend use and perhaps also for the relaxation of his senior banking staff. It was for Charles, who was not a self-serving individual, a curious and out of character arrangement, but he felt increasingly the need to 'get away from it all' at weekends. The break-up of the Central African Federation was imminent. The arguments, bitterness, financial problems and fears, generated by the demands of the Zambian people for self-government, and the resistance of the mining companies and Colonial Government, seemed to be incapable of resolution. Charles had chosen to believe wholeheartedly in the contract between black and white Africans that the Federation claimed to offer. Even as it collapsed acrimoniously, Charles hung on to the cottage, this one physical token of his faith in, and commitment to, a shared and progressive future for all races.

The bank established just before the formation of the Federation, had its largest office in the north of the country on the Copperbelt, where the mining companies operated. Head Office in Lusaka, where Charles was director, was close to government and diplomatic circles, but it was small. Few senior staff therefore, would ever choose to travel as far to the lake, particularly as the road to Siavonga was dirt from where it turned west off the Chirundu Road for the last 50 kilometres to the dam. In any case the cottage was without electricity or hot water or a swimming pool.

It consisted of two Nissen huts, one containing a kitchen and a combined dining and sitting room. The other contained two narrow bedrooms and shared a toilet and shower that faced towards the back. They were joined by a wide veranda across the front and the whole building was jammed as tightly back into the steep hillside as possible because the site was precipitous. Below the veranda the long, steep garden descended down to the point marked by a wall to where it was hoped the lake would eventually rise. The bricklayer who made the wall cut his name into the wet cement render:

'Mr Hitler Mulakata for Mr Beaumont'.

Mr Hitler Mulakata was proud of his work and his literacy. He had been born during the war.

The driveway to the cottage made two sharply-angled bends and stopped well short of the cottage under a huge *marula* tree. Still neither Charles nor Margaret had ever been obliged to carry anything heavy in their lives. Someone would always be available to carry down suitcases and provisions from the car to the cottage.

A modern township with a school and hospital was planned on the more level ground above. Roads, as yet unsurfaced, were in place. The township was to be built when the development of the second stage of the North Bank Power Station began. Meantime a

Catholic church was being built under the spiritual supervision of Father Patrick Brogan. The harbour had already been completed and a harbour master appointed. A small police station was in existence and the water storage and reticulation plant was ready. A few people from the resettlement areas, hoping for paid work, kept moving onto land near to the future township. They had to be constantly moved back to Lusitu, or just moved away. It was recognised that the new power station would need many unskilled labourers, but the construction company would be housing them in temporary buildings and dormitories at the turn-off to the dam and power station construction site.

Areas had been marked out for camping sites and hotels, and several risk-takers made, what they hoped, were shrewd purchases of land along the shoreline of what was one day to be the Zambian Riviera. One of these investors had built the cottage and a sister cottage further east towards the narrow twisting inlet that was to become known as Bilharzia Bay because of its stagnant water. This particular investor was a man with energy and a degree of taste. The Nissen huts were surprisingly not ugly and his costs were low enough to make the sale of them quick. Charles, as someone in the know, heard of them before they were finished and made the first offer on the one that had, in his opinion, the best situation and view. He wanted to see as far across the lake as possible to the most distant hills. He did not want to look back towards other people's villas or even to have to think about the dam.

Under these circumstances the Beaumonts were, from the start, almost the only people to want to use the cottage and it somehow became Margaret's special and sole responsibility and one in which she delighted. Clutching Charles's present of a 'Visitor's Book' against her pastel seersucker blouse, Margaret gave her husband a quick kiss on his cheek.

"Charles dear," she said, "I am not going to use this book only to list our guests – I am going to use it also as a diary of all the lovely weekends we will spend here at the cottage."

FOUR

Milimo Singani

1965

It was said that my mother, Natombi, became the priest's wife after the death of my father, Singani. This I do not talk of as I was a child at that time and therefore I was not told of it. That was also the year that began the resettlement of the Basilwizi and the year that was the start of our suffering and our hunger.

My mother said I was born three years after the white people stopped fighting with each other in their own land across the Overseas and came in greater numbers to trouble us in the valley. The year my father was killed it was 1958 and that year I was ten. This is what the priest told my mother my age must be, and therefore I gave 1948 as my year of birth when the record keepers of the white government asked me. Now it is what the new government of Zambia believes my age to be. So this is now my age. The Zambian government tells me that there are things that I owe them and that I must do. The priests at the church have also told me what I must do and what I owe to God. We learnt long ago not to trust the white government because it did not hear what we said. It seems now that our own government has also become deaf and, without hearing our voices, tells us what we must do.

It is said now that the white Catholic priests never have

married, and never do marry, but we, of the valley, know that a grown man must be with a woman at night otherwise he will become sick and weak. In those days we also knew that if a priest lived far from other priests and was not watched by them, he would do as all men do and as the Basilwizi do, and find a woman to cook his food and stay with him at night.

This is the story of how I came to live with Father Patrick and to know him for a good man who was hungry and needed a woman to explain to him how we of the Basilwizi live.

My father, Singani, was killed in the Chipepo uprising of the Basilwizi at the village of the Headman Chisamu in Gwembe. The uprising ended in many deaths and very many woundings. My father was buried near his village in the earth above the river. Now his grave is under the waters of the lake. The priest told me that my father lies 'full-fathom-five' in the middle of the great lake, very far from the Kariba trap that captured the waters and sent the floods rolling backwards and backwards, up and up the river in such an unnatural way that it rose over our homes and our shrines. I do not know too much what he meant by 'full-fathom-five', but he told me that it meant that there was as much water over my father as there is escarpment above the dam wall. He said that 'full-fathom-five' was a song about a drowned father that was made by a white poet in England long ago, and that the poet was an important ancestor for the white people who came to Africa. So maybe this British poet foretold the drowning of our ancestors and our valley by his people.

There were some priests from long ago who were buried in the valley near my father and whose graves are also 'full-fathom-five' under the waters of Lake Kariba. Therefore both the priest and I have ancestors whose graves are not tended because they are under the flood water.

We are therefore family in some ways.

My mother did not remain with the priest long. Her husband's brother came to marry her and take her back to Lusitu, the new place where we were all resettled by the British. When my mother left the priest, he agreed to take care of my education and I stayed with him at his school in Gwembe, and I was baptised, and I learnt how to be of the Catholic faith.

I learnt to read and write, to keep accounts, make rubber stamps and to serve in the church. When I became a man and I could no longer stay at the priest's school, he helped me look for work. Mr Beaumont is also a Catholic and when he was looking for someone to work at the cottage and help his wife, he asked the priest to find someone who was trustworthy.

That is how I am now employed by Mr Beaumont at the cottage at Siavonga.

FIVE

Concrete

The Guest Book, The Cottage, Siavonga.
June 1965
Charles, Margaret, Michael and Richard
*'We have finished furnishing the cottage at last and now I can
concentrate on the garden. Charles has employed a gang of local
workers, all Tonga, on piece work. All the grass is planted and
watered and they have dug the holes for the creepers and the hedge.
The ground is very poor and rocky so the holes are rather shallow.
I will bring down some oil drums, one to make into a barbecue,
and others to cut in half and turn into plant pots.
(Attached by a pin to the back page of the guest book is a list of plants
to be bought for the cottage from the government nursery in Lusaka.)'*

When Charles and Margaret bought the plot it was not very
beautiful and neither was the lake. The lake was rising steadily, but
slowly, across a devastated landscape stripped of vegetation by
bulldozers dragging chains and great weighted balls across the
bush. They could see in the distance the Chawara flats disappearing,
and the islands where drowning animals sought a temporary and
hopeless refuge. The valley was flattening out into featureless
horizons; it was becoming a watery desert. The sun, glinting on
the surface of the submerged Zambezi, reflected back a bright steel

light that hammered onto their sweating foreheads the fact that the temperatures in the valley, at over forty degrees, are unbearable for humans.

There is little comfort to be had at first, camping in a cottage without electricity or refrigeration, where drinking water has to be carried, and food cooked under paraffin lamps that invite the dancing attendance of every possible creature that flies, from insects, moths, heavy beetles, and flying ants to the many bats who come to feast on the insects. Those same paraffin lamps do not shed enough light on the ground to show the circling scorpions and spiders that hunt the insects on the ground that the lamps have also attracted.

"What do you suppose the land around here was like before the dam filled?" Margaret asked Charles, "It seems such a harsh landscape and quite bare of wildlife now."

Charles thought and then answered slowly,

"Of course there would have been baboons and leopard up here and probably duiker before we came – more animals during the rains than in the dry season, but you are right – this environment is very tough. We are high on the escarpment at this point. The valley would have been a very long way below and that would be where most wildlife would find food and choose to exist naturally."

"It seems strange to imagine that such vast areas of wilderness sometimes support so little animal life. Doesn't it seem like a waste?" Margaret wondered. Charles shook his head.

"I think it is enough that the trees and the grass breathe and grow. The escarpment provides shelter for the rich life in the valleys. You know how much insect and bird life is all around us – just listen to the constant rustles and the sound of crickets and cicadas."

"And of course – there are always snakes!" Margaret smiled.

Charles managed to buy at auction, and at a very good price, furniture from the construction company that had built the South

Bank Power Station. It had come from one of their guest houses. There were four single iron bedsteads and an iron bunk bed, two easy chairs, a dining table with six chairs and a couple of white painted chest of drawers, with a matching cupboard, and a substantial sideboard. There was also a full set of saucepans, crockery and cutlery, including glasses and table mats. The most expensive item was the brand new stove which used bottled gas. One of the original surveyors from Kariba South gave Charles the gift of a fridge that ran on paraffin. It was an antique monster even in those days, but Charles reckoned that paraffin was easier to buy than bottled gas, and a great deal less trouble to transport, so he was very grateful. They would, in any case, be using paraffin for lighting the storm lanterns on the veranda and in the kitchen. Candles would suffice in the bedrooms.

The furniture was trucked across the dam wall from Kariba South, to the road above the cottage, and then carried down by a team of labourers. It felt extremely thrilling to be driving over what still seemed a very new dam wall, so the whole family, Charles, Margaret and the two boys, Michael and Richard, chose to cross over the border and the dam wall to collect the furniture. They stood several hours in the pitiless sun to watch it being loaded into, and then unloaded out of the truck, by sweating black men, just for the reward of standing for another hour in unendurable heat on the dam wall. They had so much pleasurable excitement and such a vicarious sense of danger from being on the crest of the giant concrete arch with the knowledge of the lives it had taken and how the Zambezi had nearly destroyed it.

On the Rhodesian side, the construction site had been tidied up and planted with bougainvillea, but the bush of the Zambezi gorge far below still looked rough, untamed and scruffy, with raw, red tracks crawling alongside its river banks. The 300 foot drop to the Zambezi River in the gorge below the dam wall made Margaret gasp even while she cried out with pleasure at the swallows flying below her in its up-draughts. The great lake pressing against the other side of the wall made her hand go to her throat. The water was so dark and solid and dense with all the weight of Africa leaning on it and pushing it towards the sea. The God of Heaven and Earth, and all the Devils of Africa, must curse mankind for the hubris that led to this immense controlling creation in the middle of this virgin wilderness. How could the wall not simply fall down like a child's castle at its own overreaching pride?

Margaret restrained herself from telling the boys not to run about on the wall but she did hold onto their shirts when Charles held them up to see over the barricading walls on either side of the dam wall road. The dam offered such a provocation to a jealous Almighty that it was not improbable that He would demand the sacrifice of her sons.

The lake was so new and so unknown that they could barely conceive of it. As yet no one could recognise any of its coves and inlets. As yet its beaches were non-existent and unmapped, because the lake had not had time to grind the valley stone to white sand to lay down over its rocks. It was therefore not surprising that the family's focus had been concentrated on the engineering feat of the building of the wall. They stopped at every possible opportune crossing on the dam's curving wall to marvel at its size and height, and to gaze unbelievingly at the vast and deep waters that it miraculously held back. Only years later, after they were stopped by wars, and at gunpoint, from going near the wall, did they really come to know and to love the lake and the new world it had created.

SIX

Raw Earth

The Guest Book. The Cottage, Siavonga.
June 1966
Charles, Margaret, Michael and Richard

*'The boys have been collecting piles of Nile cabbage (Pistia
Stratiotes) from the edge of the lake. I believe it makes good compost
so I have asked Milimo to add it to the compost heap. Apparently
floating water weed, particularly Salvinia Auriculata, is a very
serious problem on the lake. There is so much of it that the
engineers are afraid it will block the power station turbines. The
fisheries' people say it will de-oxygenate the lake and kill fish and
everyone else says that it makes motor boating impossible. Charles
says that in places it is thick enough to walk on! I have told the boys
not to try. You wouldn't find them easily if they fell through a carpet
of Nile cabbage. The storms have brought rafts of weed with grasses
growing on them to the shore below the cottage. They are like little
islands. It seems extraordinary that such a huge new lake should so
quickly and thoroughly have been taken over by this plant.
We also found some water hyacinth (Eichhornia Crassipes) it has
a very pretty, delicate, mauve flower.'*

Even after the arrival of the furniture, the cottage remained
somewhat spartan in appearance, but Margaret made curtains, and

found sheets, tablecloths, deckchairs and a coffee table that friends in Lusaka no longer needed. In the end it was very simply fitted out, but adequate and comfortable.

To finish it off, Margaret hung a couple of her watercolour paintings of the lake on the walls dividing the bedrooms. On top of the sideboard in the dining room, she put a wood-fired black pottery vase containing wild grasses and a patterned Tonga basket full of the rippled winged fruit of the *mukwa* tree with prickly balls of seeds at their hearts. Her mother, Winifred, gave her a Swiss cowbell so that Milimo could be summoned from his hut. It was a relic of Winifred and Ronald's honeymoon trip to Europe.

Nothing could be hung on the inside of the corrugated asbestos roof. Even Charles could not devise a way to put up mosquito nets. The cottage had well-fitted screen doors however, that ought to keep out most insects and should keep out snakes. To guard against such intruders, Margaret also bought two mosquito pumps. Each consisted of a horizontal cylindrical tank that could be filled with liquid insect repellent or poison and a long handle with a suction pump that sprayed the liquid out through a nozzle. Milimo used them every evening in the bedrooms. Margaret and the boys thought they were more likely to be killed than to be protected by the evil-smelling fumes that they expelled, but Charles insisted on their use. Malaria in the valley was a real danger. Charles ordered that Margaret must live with the mosquito spray or cut down the vegetation she was planting around the cottage.

The cottage plot had the same stripped, desert-like, devastated ugliness of the lake in the valley. The raw, reddish-yellow earth on each terrace was divested of green growth; the rocks were harsh, grey, hurtful surfaces on which to graze knuckles and knees. The few scrubby bushes left were also grey and desiccated. The idea of making a garden on the plot was daunting.

Margaret and Charles had both had parents and grandparents who had arrived in Africa to face similar hostile environments and from them made farms and homes and gardens. There was no shortage of African labour to be found in the area and as usual it was cheap. Six men were employed on a temporary basis. Margaret put on her hat and gardening gloves, took her secateurs and baskets and started to organise her team of workers. They were first sent out to harvest the wild reclining *katete* green grass from the *dambos* and *vleis* because it makes such a tough, drought-resistant lawn covering. It was surprising how many armfuls of runners they gathered and how quickly it was planted. Then it had to be watered and the team of workers organised to carry the water in buckets from the standpipe at the cottage.

Margaret sat and thought, she sat and drew, she sat and made lists. She would have to bring down a hosepipe and watering cans, and a number of gardening tools and *badzas,* or hoes, for the men to use. She would probably have to bring plants from Salisbury the next time that she travelled south. In Lusaka, she would ask all her friends at the gardening club to give her slips and root cuttings, and she would make a visit to the government nursery in Woodlands. There were a couple of very good forestry men there, both *fundis* – experts on local and wild plants – and they would give her advice and help. Besides the plants there were very cheap indeed. She would ask them to give her some indigenous trees, either *Trichelia Emetica* or a *Khaya Nyasica*: both trees gave good shade all year round and in the dry winters too many of the local trees, especially the *mupane*, gave almost none. Margaret carried her huge hardback first edition copy of Coates-Palgrave *Trees of Central Africa* with her and knew almost every tree in it by heart. It was nevertheless, difficult to identify trees with any real certainty. In Africa every tree seemed to mutate into a sub-species in each slightly different environment.

The next time Margaret came down she planned to bring exotic plants, like Golden Shower and bougainvillea, to grow over the veranda; and Bleeding Heart and other creeping plants to grow up the terraces. She would, of course, plant some roses, though Charles said they would not survive. The first tree that she would plant would be a Rough Lemon. Lemons were of the utmost importance in the bush for all kinds of culinary purposes and for insect stings and gin and tonics. Margaret also planned to plant a hibiscus hedge between their plot and the neighbours' plot next door. She would make sure that none of the men working for her cut down a single tree on the plot. She had already identified a *mupane* and a *duiker-berry,* which must come to no harm. A *mupane,* if left to grow big and not mutilated by elephants, is an elegant tree though it gives little shade because its leaves survive by turning at right angles to the sun. The *duiker-berry* has small sour fruits that small antelope and other creatures will eat. She had also found a small fleshy bare plant only a foot or so high. Just possibly it might be a baby baobab.

Margaret reckoned that she would not need a team of workers for long. Once the grass was established, probably after the rainy season had begun, she would be able to manage with just one man to do the work. It would be good if he would live on the property too, so that he could look after the place and the equipment. In an area as isolated as this, spades and axes were very valuable and Margaret knew that the Tonga had different ideas about ownership of such objects. If it was lying about unused and they had need of it, they would see no reason not to take it for their own use for a while, maybe only until the next person established a greater need for it.

Charles, meanwhile, had been introduced to the local Catholic priest – Father something Irish – a Jesuit obviously – maybe he could vouch for one of the local men to be Margaret's gardener. Margaret would ask Charles if he could get a small house built for a gardener. She didn't really want a grass hut at the top of her drive. She knew from past experience that they had the habit of reproducing themselves and turning into little villages, and that these little villages would bring other kinds of problems and responsibilities. Charles, however, already had his eye on accommodation for his employee. The road contractors provided round huts constructed of sections of galvanized metal for their overseers. The road works had been completed for the moment and such a hut was available and cheap.

"Won't it be terribly hot?" Margaret asked doubtfully.

"He will live outside it – he's a Tonga," said Charles, "but it will keep his possessions safe."

SEVEN

Scorpions

The Guest Book. The Cottage, Siavonga.
July 1967
Charles, Margaret, Michael and Richard
*'Wild, windy night. Exceptionally clear night for July – did the
wind blow away the haze over the lake? The boys saw croc spoor
at Joe's Boat Hire but Charles thinks it was a large leguvaan. We
also found a huge black scorpion in the evening. Milimo killed it
by treading on it. It was at least as long as his foot. We measured it
against his sandal afterwards and the sting poked out by his heel
and the pincers by his toes.'*

Charles was up before Margaret as usual, though, as usual, she was
awake when he woke. As usual, Margaret lay still with her eyes shut
until he was shaved and dressed. Margaret had grown used to the
privacy and quietness that rising separately gave them and indeed,
had come to like it. Charles was a reticent man and intimacy did
not come naturally to him. Margaret knew that Charles was
particularly tired this weekend. In his capacity as a senior advisor
with long experience of banks and banking in Central Africa, he
had had some heavy meetings with official government boards
during the preceding week. His gentle manner, as Margaret had
learnt, hid a stern sense of morality and a determined will. He had
never risen late from his bed – not even on honeymoon.

Charles would however, be keeping a watchful eye on the two boys playing on the terrace below the veranda. The boys would have woken with the sun and gone outside before dressing themselves, even though dressing meant only putting on their swimming trunks. They would have begun by poking under stones with sticks to see what creatures they might disturb. Michael then would quietly construct a castle from rocks for his imaginary world, while Richard would be collecting beetles and ants in jars and tins and talking to them busily. Both boys knew it was safer to use a stick than to use their fingers in case their explorations disturbed the nest of a scorpion or the home of a snake. Charles had explained to the boys that big, black scorpions, like the one Milimo had killed, used their stronger pincers to hold their prey, but the smaller pink scorpions used an extremely painful injection of poison to immobilise their victims.

Margaret dressed herself slowly and carefully. She washed her face and neck in the cold water that was all that was available at the cottage. Milimo always boiled the kettle before Charles rose and left it just outside the shower room so that Charles could have a hot shave, but as soon as Charles finished, Milimo would take the kettle to boil water for the morning tea. Margaret had never seen Charles with stubble on his chin, not even when he was ill with malaria. She was grateful. Hairy or prickly kisses repulsed her and had done since she was a small child when a bearded uncle, who was too frequent a visitor, made sure to breathe in a blubbery walrus way all over her face whenever he could get close to her. Margaret chose a cool floral skirt and a simple blouse that buttoned down the front. It was too hot for a petticoat and the freedom of so few layers of clothes felt pleasant. It was lovely not to have to consider more clothes. She picked out her lightest sandals and wriggled her toes into them. She might put polish on her nails again this afternoon while resting away from the heat.

Margaret went first to say good morning to Milimo and see that all was prepared for breakfast. She was careful to approach the kitchen through the front of the dining room. The back door was Milimo's entrance to the cottage and that was where he left his *pata-patas*, those dented bleached rubber sandals that most Zambians used for footwear.

Milimo was cleaning the glass of the storm lanterns that had been out on the veranda the evening before. Seeing them Margaret asked,

"Have we enough paraffin for the weekend, Milimo? If not I will ask the Bwana to get us some from the petrol station at the turn-off to the main road before we eat at lunchtime."

EIGHT

Lusaka

The Guest Book. The Cottage, Siavonga.
August 1968
Charles, Margaret, Michael and Richard

*We all got sunburnt on our boat trip to Banana Island. Richard
saw a big tiger fish at least 24 inches long. Michael saw a pair of
fish eagles and some black kites*

*The mosquitoes are dreadful at night at the moment. The weather is
getting very hot and the lake is going down very slowly. We can still
jump off our garden wall straight into the lake. On our walk along
the lake we found great slanting slivers of black and white mica
which the boys collected. They were trying to see who could find the
biggest and most transparent piece to use for a window. Charles says
that mica fragments in the sand mean that it can't be used for
building because it makes the cement crumble.*

*The boys have captured some solifugids, or hunting spiders. They are
huge – as big as Michael's hand – and look as if they have ten legs but
the front two are actually adapted jaws which they seem to use like
antennae. They rear up in a very threatening way. The boys say they
will fight each other if put together but I have told them not to be cruel.'*

Charles and Margaret had an attractive house and garden in
Sunningdale, a desirable new suburb west of central Lusaka and

Government House. As usual for the wife of a business executive, Margaret was expected to entertain regularly and therefore had a staff of four in the house including a cook, scullery boy and two housemaids. Two men were employed to look after the garden and swimming pool. Charles had a driver who would have sat around most of the day if Charles had not made him available to do some of the shopping and errands for Margaret. The house was luxuriously equipped and the garden, mostly a flat expanse of lawn, had been planted with orderly trees, shrubs and roses. It was kept well-clipped by the overzealous use of secateurs and shears by a gardener who believed, with some justification, that taming African vegetation would bring him approval from white employers.

So the Sunningdale garden was not to Margaret's taste but she didn't complain. After all, one day perhaps, if Zambia's transition to independence did not go smoothly after the break-up of the Federation, they would return to Rhodesia to the old-fashioned colonial style home and hillside plot they had up on the Avondale Ridge. Margaret thought a garden should have secret paths, ups and downs, lush, over-planted borders that split onto the lawns, wild corners and plenty of birds like the one at her Salisbury home. The Lusaka garden pleased Charles however. It was an asset and it looked well-managed and under control. Dinner guests were impressed that a man, who understood business so well, knew how to organise his home life as well. Margaret was an asset too and Charles recognised that and was grateful and appreciative in his rather formal way. He did not forget birthdays and anniversaries. Margaret too, appreciated her good fortune. Other chief executives drank heavily or had mistresses and did not show the unfailing kindness of Charles.

The two boys, Michael and Richard, were still very young. Schools in Zambia were facing abrupt change and suddenly had to cope with hundreds of Zambian children eager for education. Teachers were in short supply even though there were programmes to attract volunteers from England for rural areas and training programmes for teachers at the university. Fortunately for the Beaumonts, some fee-paying primary schools had opened in the capital Lusaka. Charles said that these multi-racial schools were a good idea if one was to hope for a future in Africa and one of these schools would answer till the boys were old enough to go to boarding school. The schools needed to be the best if his children were to retain the advantages of their birth and culture and carry the liberal hopes of their parents into the future. Fortunately the school they chose was good and the boys were very happy.

To start with, Margaret was bored and alienated by life in Lusaka. She had to manage her staff and drive her boys to school and games, and of course do the shopping and decide on menus for dinner parties. That left her with tea and tennis to fill her days. It didn't feel very grown-up to her. It felt like the nutritional opposite of her boarding school days, a timetabled day with the meat of learning and companionship removed. Margaret was left with scheduled empty periods of time. How was she to make good use of it? She had been praised for her watercolour paintings and delicate flower drawings at school, so she found an art group with a teacher, and began once again to explore and develop her skill. Soon she had a reputation for pretty paintings of scenery, which always sold when she exhibited at the Lusaka Art Society. Now she had a bigger canvas to work on – the garden by the lake was her new project and at last Charles allowed her to do with it as she liked.

Charles too, loved the lake. Weekends there gave him the time to spend with his boys and to begin the task of teaching them how to be men. Charles had a .22 rifle that his own father had given him and he taught the boys how to use the gun safely, how to clean it and care for it and how to respect it. He also had friends who kept a yacht moored at the government harbour. Occasionally they were invited to go sailing. More often they were able to use the dinghy to potter around the inlets near Siavonga. On other occasions they would take a motorboat to Banana Island and go fishing or scrambling among its rocks. In those first years Banana Island was completely separated from the shore and the trip was an exciting expedition.

Margaret watched some of these expeditions with mixed feelings. It was good to see how proud Charles was of his two boys and to see the pleasure he had in spending time with them, but she noticed that Michael, a rather dreamy child, was often discomfited by competition and even disinterested in physical achievement. He always managed to sneak a book, or even a toy, into the car or onto the boat with him. To keep both him and Charles happy, Margaret made Michael responsible for her book, *Robert's Birds of Southern Africa*, and that seemed to provide a viable compromise. Michael could insist on sitting quietly to 'watch' birds and he did indeed become rather an expert for his age. He was an imaginative child, perhaps too responsible for his age, whereas Richard, a handsome boy, was confident and fearless.

Margaret occasionally thought as she looked at her sons, that she would have loved a daughter. The authoritarian hospital regime under which childbirth was marshalled in Rhodesia had tied her down in bed under stiff white sheets and made her boy babies prisoners in the nursery. Charles had barely been permitted to visit and most certainly was not allowed to cuddle his sons. Margaret had been made to feel as if she had served her purpose simply by giving birth, and could now go back to school. Charles would be bringing the boys up to be men. It was lonely at times being a woman in an all-male house.

Unable to admit to herself the extent of her dissatisfaction with Lusaka society, Margaret found herself dreaming of 'the little place by the lake'. It was somewhere she felt she was real.

That was a bizarre idea – selfish even – to not feel 'real' in the town; to not feel entirely happy in support of her husband and children. So many people would envy her life. So many people did envy her that she felt trapped by their perceptions of how happy and fulfilled she must be. Her existence was peripheral to the life that really mattered where actions were taken, decisions made and events happened. She couldn't quite get to grips with being alive when all she did was make preparations for other people to experience the world. All her time was spent in preparation for some future, but whether it was her children's future, or Charles's future retirement, wasn't certain. She did not feel fully human when the sum of her achievements was a well-planned dinner party menu and a well-stocked pantry. She found herself, fingers tapping on the paper-lined pantry shelf, staring at the rows of glowing glass jars of jams and jellies, pink guava, vermilion Rosella, purple mulberry, golden gooseberry and green tomato, with a feeling of insatiable hunger that was not for food.

What thrilled her, and made her feel alive, was managing with basic equipment down at the lake, coping without electricity, sitting in the dark instead of listening to the radio. The discomfort and shock of water that was too cold, and weather that was too hot. The storms that rushed out of the night, that banged doors and broke things, and left smashed up floating jetties marooned on the shore. The knowledge that there were crocodiles – prehistoric beasts – as quick as cats and as evil as Satan, who inhabited the lake. The simplicity of amusing oneself with rocks and water, of sleeping in the heat of the day, and of not sleeping in the heat of the night, those were real, and those were the things that Charles and her sons, Michael and Richard, enjoyed too. Then she felt really connected to her family.

Life at the lake was also private and personal whereas often in Lusaka she felt that she was someone else's property. Perhaps she was even an asset that belonged to Charles's bank? She felt at times as if she was disembodied.

Work mattered to Margaret too, hard work, real work; like the work of making a garden out of the harsh landscape and the unforgiving earth of the Siavonga plot.

There Margaret found reality and a home for her heart.

NINE

Spilling

The Guest Book. The Cottage, Siavonga.
June 1973
Charles, Margaret, Michael and Richard
We were able to see the floodgates of Kariba Dam opened. What a
truly wonderful experience! It made the dam wall shake!
It is too hazy to see the Matusadona Hills. Michael has seen a pair
of hornbills, and a golden oriole and two hoopoes. There was a
short wind storm but mostly it has been pleasant. The boys made a
fire on the beach and cooked their own boerewors.'

(In Richard's writing) 'Michael sosage was BLAK.'
(In Michael's writing) 'Richard's sausage was raw and bloody.'
(Michael had made a little drawing of a sausage stabbed with a
fork and dripping blood under his comment.)

Charles's friend from the Central African Power Corporation,
Peter Duncan, had called him up and told him to get down to the
lake pronto.

"They are going to spill. They are going to open the floodgates,"
he said, "If you all come down with me, I will get you onto the
wall in spite of the closed border, and you can watch the whole
business. You won't forget it." And he smiled and nodded, unable
to find the right words for what they would witness.

Charles explained to Margaret that the British contractors building the North Bank Power Station had gone into receivership, so the work was on hold. There had been major complications in the excavation of the Turbine Hall, a space big enough to contain St Paul's Cathedral in London. There had been rock falls, deaths and delays, and neither the contractor or the consultants would accept responsibility for the problems. New contractors would have to be found and new finances too. Charles sighed and shook his head over this difficulty. However, it had been decided it would be wise to lower the lake levels at this point to protect the coffer dams around the entrance to the turbines until the new contractors were agreed. Hence the decision to spill.

It was all rather short notice, but with great excitement all the Beaumonts, and Peter and his wife, Elspeth, assembled outside the barriers of the closed construction site on the approach to the dam wall.

Peter explained that the gates had to open with great care and one at a time.

"Maybe only one today," said Peter, "Yes. Everyone living down below the dam wall has been warned to expect immediate floods on the Zambezi but it is a big river and a wide flood plain – it won't be that bad. They'll open a crack first – have to make sure that everything is working well and in good order. Probably just one gate."

They waited, staring at the yellow-grey smooth curve of concrete. At its centre the dark rectangles of the gates looked as if they were rusted shut. Discoloured stains leaked down the wall under each gate. The swallows were still flying in the wall's up-draughts. Below the dam, the rocks were pink in the sun, dark-purple in the water. The Zambezi was clear and turquoise in the shallows, dark-green in its shadowed deeps.

"Look! Look!"

They saw the southern gate move. A black gap appeared. Then the white of the jet of water, a streak, became a surging, coffee-coloured, yellow-foaming cascade; climbing first, immense and curving, out, out, out, over the gorge. It seemed to take an eternity to reach its zenith and curve down, down, down, taking another age to thunder and crash into the valley. The sound of it deafened; the roar was tremendous. Margaret hardly heard the racket of the warning siren.

Margaret had held her breath as the gate opened, she found herself gasping.

The water levels in the pool below the dam mounted in an instant up its banks. The departing construction company had left wooden platforms and fences around the exits from the turbines. As the swirling waves smashed into them, they disintegrated into matchsticks, were flung high into the air and then swept from sight in seconds. There was soon a mist everywhere, like a soft rain.

"Look! Look! They're opening the second gate!" Peter shouted.

The wall was vibrating. Now it began to shudder steadily.

Margaret dared not admit that she was afraid and wanted herself and the boys to be off the wall and far away. So much power could not be controlled or contained. The Zambezi was an elemental force beyond understanding.

Margaret was silent as they made their way back to Siavonga. Elspeth never had anything to say anyway. Peter and Charles engaged in technical discussion about the dam's current construction problems. The boys, thrilled by the experience of watching the floodgates open, kept describing it to each other again and again. They planned to go off with the canoe as soon as they got back to the cottage.

"Do you know which construction company will get the North Bank contract?" Peter asked Charles.

"Probably the Yugoslavs will when they have finished the power station at Kafue Dam," answered Charles. "It means long delays before completion of course, but between you and me, the Yugoslavs are less concerned about safety and workers' conditions so they may cost less in the end."

41

"It's a mess," said Peter. "The contractors are rumoured to be suing the consultants because the original surveys didn't show that the geology of the turbine hall was unstable. They say it was mica schist in the gneiss rock that caused the rock-falls. The contractors are bankrupt anyway but there is a lot of bitterness."

"Well, lives were lost in the rock-falls," Charles said, "but there is no denying that the company did tender far too low for the job."

"At any rate Zambia got their way in the end," Peter laughed cynically. "They will have their own power supply at Kafue and who can blame them with all the politicking between them and Rhodesia. They are now fighting a war down there however much they deny it."

"It means there will be no development down here at Siavonga," said Charles, with a shrug of acceptance.

Peter and Elspeth returned to Lusaka after lunch, but Margaret kept thinking how central the dam had become to her and to Charles's lives.

TEN

Remembering The Past

"Oh, do you remember, Charles?" Margaret smiled at old recollections.

She was side by side with Charles on the dark veranda of the Siavonga cottage, under the smoky storm lanterns, while the fruit bats squeaked and the rapid waves slapped at the shore. Her two sunburnt, tired sons slept deeply in their bunk beds next door. In another few weeks they would both be going back to boarding school in Rhodesia. For now her whole precious family was still safe and in easy reach of her arms.

Once her childhood had appeared seamless, whole, complete, unbroken in its unquestioned rightness. Of course when she was a child, bones and hearts were broken and were mended. Friendships, often begun during infancy, were remade and then broken and very occasionally, though not always, remained broken, but the social fabric of their small society held together safe and intact.

That past seemed so different from the collapsing uncertain present.

"Oh Charles – do you remember – the first time you and Steve brought me to see the lake?"

Charles looked sideways at Margaret with a grin.

"How could I forget Maggie-Meg – I asked you to marry me

that weekend. Couldn't get Steve to take the hint and leave us alone for a while – I think he fancied you too!"

"It's so long ago!" Margaret said, reverent at the passing of time.

"It's such a short time actually," Charles contradicted then, reflecting further he said, "but such a lot has happened – so much has changed in fourteen years. No more Central African Federation, no more Northern Rhodesia – no more United Party."

"We were so hopeful then – weren't we Charles?" Margaret looked up at him. Perhaps even in that dim light she might read Charles's mind and see if disillusion and doubt had claimed him.

"Do you think it was all worth it? Was it right to come here to Zambia? Now when it is so new? Could we have stayed in Rhodesia under Smith and his illegal government? Could you have worked for them?"

"Oh no!" Charles replied. "It is better to be here trying to build a future for a new democratic country than back home fighting a lost battle for common sense and a multi-racial society, for people who don't believe in either of them." He squeezed her hand and fell to musing again.

Strange, thought Margaret, *sitting in the dark in this quiet meditative way, the world stops its onward rush and we are just here in our own time with the past and the present around us. As for the future – tonight it takes care of itself – I don't need to think of it. Tonight is ours – and mine.* And she linked her fingers lightly with Charles's.

So, thought Margaret, *all that planning, all that hope, all that talking and organising, and all of it for political control – it had come, it had gone, it was already forgotten. It was a great irrelevance that had dissolved even as the great lake was swallowing up the valley.*

Margaret had no glimmer of understanding that for Milimo, resting outside his hut on the terrace above the cottage, the great lake had not submerged the memories of the wrongs done to his people. Instead his drowned ancestors and their spirits spoke to him with every quiet wind shushing the lake's translucent surface, and with each tiny suspended particle of mica that glittered like a hardening tear drop in the water.

★

When Margaret was at high school, the Central African Federation had been all anyone talked about. When Jacob, her sister Sarah's recently-graduated and newly-opinionated husband, came to dinner, words were hotter than the dishes, and saltier than the gravy. Jacob, it seemed, had met and made friends with African graduates and even talked politics with them.

"These men know what they are talking about!" he insisted. "You can't ignore their opinions – they are intelligent, well-informed – they will not wait for the right to vote to be handed to them as a favour by our government."

Margaret could see that her father, Ronald, listened to Jacob and took note of his views even though he disagreed with him.

"The Federation is the answer to African advancement and ambition," Ronald counselled. "Africans can see the tremendous advantages and benefits that this provides for all its citizens. Wait and see. It will provide the social and economic answers we need.

We will lose the support of the white citizens of this country if we try to enfranchise too many uneducated black voters," he said, "We can't rush Rhodesians. People have too much to lose and no white leader can take them down that road faster than they want to go."

"It'll be too late," Jacob said. "It is already too late. The nationalists are already planning for war. They come out of prison where they have completed their second degrees and go for military training abroad."

"Yes – yes – to communist countries where they are duped and lied to! They are hostages in the Cold War we fight to save democracy," Ronald almost stuttered with anger.

"Africans understand the value of Marxist ideas!" Sarah tried to pinch Jacob's thigh at this, but his argument excited him more than her touch and she grimaced helplessly at her mother, Winifred. "Steam pudding for anyone?" Winifred offered as she rang for the cook.

Ronald was so infuriated that when Jacob suggested that he might go to listen to the lunchtime discussions at the National Affairs Board, he declined abruptly.

"It's the same day and time as my Club luncheon," he said, closing the subject.

"I'll go," said Margaret, sticking her neck out and looking at Jacob for support. "I can get permission from school now that I am in the Sixth Form."

Permission was obtained from Margaret's House teacher and once a month on Friday she walked from school across the park to the hall near the Christian Science Church where the National Affairs discussions were held. The first speaker she heard was a charismatic and sophisticated black man from Northern Rhodesia. He was very funny, very entertaining and very intelligent. Margaret had not expected to spend her lunchtime laughing. She looked around her. There were black men in the audience too, also laughing. Why was this situation so new and unexpected for her? How little she knew about Rhodesia and what the people in it thought about anything.

"Margaret – hello!" said a voice behind her shoulder. Margaret turned feeling shy and awkward. There was Charles and here she was, dressed like a child in beige saggy lisle stockings and her green school hat and uniform. Margaret had known Charles most of her life. They had played games together since they were tiny. She was not discomfited for long.

"Did you enjoy Mr Alick Nkhata?" he asked, smiling. "Did you know he is a close friend of Harry Nkumbula, one of the detained nationalist leaders from the Copperbelt?"

"Really! Gosh how amazing! I had no idea that all this was going on," Margaret answered. "Really, I sometimes think they don't teach us anything useful at school."

"If you are interested in politics," Charles said, "perhaps you'd be interested in coming to a United Party meeting? There are people who say the Federation will not last and we are organising a discussion group about it. Will you come to the next talk here?"

Margaret assented flattered and pleased.

At the next National Affairs discussion they sat side by side while Joshua Nkomo strode purposefully up and down the platform and warned his listeners that the African people of Rhodesia were angry, very angry with their wait for representation and the end of colonial rule.

"Soon it will be too late to talk of peace!" Joshua Nkomo said, turning to look directly at his audience.

Those few black men at the back of the hall applauded. An angry muttering rose from the seats of the white people as they got up and left.

Margaret's chest constricted and she had a stomach cramp. She was afraid. She was afraid that things would not work out for the best. That altruism and reason would not guide people to do what was right. There had always been in the background of her home, the solidity and reassurance of the 'menfolk': fathers, uncles, cousins, brothers and sons. Their certainty that they, the 'Europeans', were on the right track. If some at least, of the 'non-Europeans' had a proper education they would choose to join the Europeans' vision of the future. After Nkomo spoke however, Margaret began to doubt her parents' political wisdom. This time she and Charles did not share any laughter. Things had become far too serious even for young and serious people like themselves. Margaret suffered that odd sense of dislocation and anxiety that she remembered when the novel she was reading did not reflect the scratchiness of the dry lawn outside her bedroom window, where neither bluebells nor daffodils shivered under beech hangars in cool spring breezes.

Eleven

The Past Catches Up With The Present

"So the past is about to catch up with us in the next few weeks I understand." Charles leant forward to take a handful of salted peanuts. "Your dear sister's ex-husband has been here in Zambia for a while and never tried to get hold of us until now when he's about to leave."

"He probably didn't contact us in the belief he would spare Sarah's feelings. She was mortified when he went to jail under the Terrorism Act you know but she was also afraid for him and worried about the effect on Marielise.

It was dreadful for the child at the time – she was at school after all. Poor old Sarah. Jacob was a cross for her to bear – she was so afraid of being ostracised by her Jo'burg set. Luckily he wasn't in jail for long and left as soon as he was released – I think because he was born in Rhodesia it was not possible for him to stay in South Africa after his connection with the African Resistance Movement."

"Jacob would not be happy to be anyone's cross, especially not Sarah's," grinned Charles. "Where'd he go? Makerere University in Uganda and then here to Lusaka after Idi Amin's coup?"

"I think so, but now he has a quite prestigious professorship at Manchester or somewhere – he only wants us to keep an eye on

Marielise you know. She is the one with a university job here now and Sarah is worried sick about her."

"Your poor sister!" mocked Charles gently.

"Be kind!" admonished Margaret, "Sarah is a very good and loving sister to me and she really can't understand why you have dragged me off to live in an uncivilised country run by black people."

"Isn't it fortunate for your niece – our Mary-Elisabeth or Marielise or whatever she calls herself – that we do live here?"

"I don't know if it will be – we're unfashionable, old white liberals – no one young wants to know us these days."

Childhood had been easier for Margaret than it had been for her older sister, Sarah. Ten years older than Margaret, Sarah's childhood had been impoverished by the thirties recession and the Second World War. Life was tough while her father, Ronald, was away fighting during the Second World War. There was no market for the farm produce and Winifred, her mother, moved into a cottage in Salisbury with Sarah and lived on a small family inheritance. Sarah, intelligent but frustrated because she could not go to university, left school and took a typing job with a Jewish solicitor. Then to the horror of the solicitor, she secretly married his son, Jacob. When Sarah and Jacob started dating, Ronald was invalided out of the army with malaria but he was too ill to be of much help. When the scandal erupted onto the Rhodesian social scene, it was too late to change anything. Margaret's main disappointment was not to be a bridesmaid at her sister's wedding. She was too young to feel any of the disapprobation expressed at the local tennis club and she remained convinced her sister's romance must have a fairy-tale ending.

By the time Margaret was at high school all the excitement of Jacob and Sarah's marriage was over. Jacob was working as a social worker for the Salisbury Council. Sarah and Jacob had a new third floor flat on Jamieson Avenue overlooking the swimming pool and the central park, and Sarah was trying to decide whether to throw either herself, or her new baby, Mary-Elisabeth, or both together, off the balcony to alleviate her boredom. Fortunately for Sarah, Winifred was an indulgent grandmother with two spare bedrooms and once Margaret was away at boarding school, Winifred took on the weekly board and care of the baby. Sarah found herself employment as a receptionist for a divorced estate agent. He appreciated her looks and intelligence and the style she brought to his business. Sarah, in her turn, appreciated his business acumen and his generous and bulging pockets. They turned out to be a good partnership and set up between themselves a new branch of the business in Johannesburg. Jacob, surprisingly innocent, was pleased. He had been hoping to move to a job in a more interesting political environment and was offered a junior lectureship in sociology at the University of the Witwatersrand. The move went well and a couple of years later, when a divorce was agreed between Jacob and Sarah on the grounds that Jacob had had an affair with a female lecturer, the whole business passed almost unnoticed in Rhodesia. Winifred and Ronald were the only ones left grieving for the regular company of their granddaughter. Mary-Elisabeth however, made the sweetest flower-girl at Sarah's wedding and Margaret finally became a bridesmaid as, in that expected fairy-tale ending, her sister got married in church properly and for the first time.

When Margaret arrived back in Salisbury, her suitcase contained her bridesmaid's dress altered into a ball-gown. She went, not only to political talks, but also on dates with Charles. He had started work as a junior clerk in the local merchant bank, and she was aware of his rather broad shoulders, his charming, if diffident smile and the way he looked at her with interest. Margaret was about to enrol at the Teacher Training College in Bulawayo with other girls of her school year. Smiling demurely back at Charles on their final date, Margaret tipped her hips ever so slightly so that her full skirt swirled out over her hundred-yard petticoat, thereby exaggerating the narrowness of her waist in its constricting elastic belt. They agreed to write to each other and meet up in Margaret's holidays.

"We'll make a trip to the Zambezi Valley to see how the dam wall is coming on after all the floods they've had this year," Charles had promised, "Steve has a farm vehicle so he can drive us there and we'll ask if there is someone who can put us up safely."

Twelve

Choices

"I don't think I believed that the lake would actually ever come into existence. That weekend that we all drove down to the valley was such a strange time," Margaret said.

"When I saw the unfinished dam wall it looked as if it was being broken down, not built up. It was just a row of giant teeth sticking up in a random fashion across the gorge. The water looked so far away and insignificant – no bigger than the earth dam on the farm. I really didn't believe it would amount to anything much – nothing like this!" Margaret gestured at the lake before them as it lay glimmering under a glittering sky.

"All that stuff about there being nothing in the valley except tsetse fly – I don't think I believed it. Nothing seemed real to me. Least of all that there would one day be a dam. It all seemed impossible and unlikely, and yet – here we are," Margaret finished.

"I always believed in it," Charles laughed. "All those workers slaving away under the tremendous heat. What an achievement! All those hundreds of cement lorries churning up the dust on the escarpment road with poor old Steve trying to overtake them in our terrible old pick-up when he couldn't see one yard ahead."

"Mmmh – I was scared stiff all the way. The heat was unbearable, I thought I would suffocate from sweat and thick, sandy dust – and then when we got to the Kariba Heights Hotel and you had to rescue me from those Italian workers – I wanted to die!"

"You were so young and innocent – Steve and I didn't realise you had gone into the bar alone and the Italian men obviously thought you were – uh – a – well. We were pretty green also, Steve and me!"

"Really!" Margaret thought for a moment then smiled. "Of course that's what happened! What a fool I was – I had no idea then what a prostitute was, never mind that they lived and worked at Kariba. Is that why you decided to make an honest woman of me that weekend, Charles?"

"Something like that – something like that," Charles said. "I just wanted to keep you safe for ever – and to keep you all for myself too, before Steve decided that he was going to have you. Darling – I have finished my beer – let me get you another gin." And he bent and kissed her forehead on his way into the kitchen.

Margaret found herself fretting. When Charles returned she studied her drink, glistening temptingly in its tall glass while the ice clinked and the lemon fizzed and spun, then she turned to him again, wanting to be reassured.

"Charles – did we do enough? Did we try hard enough? Could we have done better? Politically I mean – and also as people?

Sometimes I am so ashamed to be Rhodesian. How did we fail so badly?"

"Of course we didn't do enough! Nobody ever does," Charles answered, glancing at Margaret and then falling silent for a few moments.

"Could anyone have changed the course of politics in Rhodesia? I don't know. I don't think so. You and I were caught between those whites who would not contemplate a future shared with black people and those who insisted on full rights for blacks at once.

"I'm not black – if I was – maybe I would have not

compromised either. I don't feel any sympathy for white people living in Africa who think they can deny black people votes for ever – or even for the immediate future. I have no sympathy for Jacob either – joining an organisation that was ready to use bombs. I do believe that communism is a dangerous threat to the liberty of us all in the west – at least we have freedom of thought and speech."

"Do we?" said Margaret very quietly. "Do we? They don't have it in South Africa."

"True," Charles acknowledged, "but Margaret – one thing I know – we don't escape the consequences of our actions – whatever they are – there is still a long way to go before anything is resolved in this part of the world."

"It's also been going on for ages," said Margaret, wanting everything to be better tomorrow just this one time. "Remember the Mau-Mau uprising and in the end in spite of everything, Kenyatta still becomes the president."

They fell silent, each occupied with their own thoughts.

*

The fifties, when Margaret was at school, were also the years of the Mau-Mau uprising in Kenya. The long and bitter fight for human rights against cruel oppression in colonial Kenya was seen in white Rhodesia as an atavistic murder spree, inflicted only on white people by a savage and primitive minority. The nineteenth century rebellions in Rhodesia against white domination were long over but once Rhodesians heard of the Mau-Mau, a prickling sense of fear and guilt kept everyone looking backwards over their shoulders. At school increasing levels of hysteria and prejudice on all matters to do with race and politics led to arguments and persecutions among the girls. School meals at the boarding house were served up by African waiters who also did the domestic work and gardening. To the white schoolgirls, they were nameless, worthless skivvies who were mostly ignored, but were verbally abused whenever their presence brought them close enough.

"While I am a prefect no one on my table will call a waiter *'kaffir'*."

The words came out clear and firm. Margaret's elocution was good. She was well-taught. Still she was surprised that she had managed to speak those words and that she was audible. She also expected an immediate rude response but the girls in her charge were taken aback. So surprised in fact that no one questioned her or challenged her, or insulted a waiter while she was on duty again. Margaret would be called a *'kaffir-boetjie'* behind her back from now on but she had realised, in that instant when Leonie jeered at Simba, that she had to take charge or give up forever and listen in misery to the daily diet of racism that was dished out to the men who served her food.

Simba, a tall ungainly man with huge feet, was standing at Margaret's table holding a tray of banana and jam sandwiches when Leonie, a child of fourteen, said to him,

"Hey *kaffir* – take the dog food away!" Then she had laughed.

Simba wanted to kill Leonie. The blood roared in his ears. He turned and walked back to the kitchen, blind and deaf with rage. Afterwards he was not sure what he had heard Margaret say though another waiter, a young boy called Thomas who was the same age as Margaret, said it was true. Simba did not care anymore. He was filled with hatred. It was devouring him. At night the girls above in the dormitories heard him shouting at the other workers in the servants' quarters. He raved in ChiShona about raping white girls. They understood the hatred in his voice but not his words, nevertheless it stopped them sleeping. Simba knew he frightened them. He knew if they complained about the noise he made he would lose his job, but he was growing tired of the sickening taste of bitterness. He would leave his job in the government school anyway. He would go to the mines of the Northern Rhodesia Copperbelt. They said the money was good there. They said the white mine-workers were the worst sort of racists – cruel bullies – all *'boers'* from South Africa but at least they would be men and he would not be ashamed to want to kill them.

The ill-treatment of servants took place at school meals every day. It continued at every table except Margaret's until she left school two years later. Then of course it began again and increased in viciousness. That was the year the right wing political party of Ian Smith began its campaign with a poster asking:

'DO YOU WANT YOUR DAUGHTER TO MARRY AN AFRICAN?'

It was printed over a photograph taken at an International Girl Guide Jamboree that showed children of all races running in a race together.

Nothing in Rhodesia was changed by Margaret's action except herself. She had crossed a line. She did not think that her action was political. She was not political. Politics was for men. Margaret had only done what her father would have expected of her. She had insisted on good manners. It was important to treat people well and with respect, especially if they had less power and less of everything that she did. It appeared to Margaret after that school meal, that the speed of political change in Rhodesia quickened and moved dramatically to the right. It seemed to her to be moving more and more towards a solution like that of South African Apartheid. Since that evening, nothing offered hope.

*

With a sigh, Margaret returned to the present, to the warm evening and the sound of the lake and Charles by her side. The boys, Michael and Richard, were asleep on the bunk beds, tired after a day spent swimming and fishing and scrambling along the shore in search of legavaans, snakes and scorpions.

It was more than five years since Rhodesia under its Prime Minister, Ian Smith, had made its Unilateral Declaration of

Independence. He had decided only six months before to shut the borders between Rhodesia and Zambia because, he said, of the support offered to dissident political groups like Joshua Nkomo's ZAPU by the President of Zambia. Margaret turned to Charles.

"Have you any guesses about what will happen next in Rhodesia?"

Charles very slowly shook his head once, twice, then again.

"Bloodshed," he said quietly. "There will be bloodshed."

Below Charles and Margaret the waters of Lake Kariba chewed ceaselessly at the shoreline, gnawing and regurgitating, smoothing and scouring, claiming an empire, reshaping an ancient geology with a million new forms of life as it explored the dam's creations of mud and crevice and beach and depth. On and on and on went the moving waters, invading, colonising, subjugating, populating and changing forever the largest valley in Africa.

★

Below the dam wall, in the deep cool shadowed night of the Kariba Gorge, there were a few quiet splashes on the river, a fish perhaps taken by a giant orange fishing owl; a stalking crocodile sliding its snout up onto the bank as a duiker or bush buck made its shy, delicate way to the water's edge for a drink. The shrilling of the cicadas seemed to make an unending chain of noise but to any experienced listeners in the bush there were momentary missing links in the sounds. There were abrupt silences where suddenly stealthy rustles could be heard as they shifted carefully onwards until the next cicada fell silent and the last one joined its racket to that of its fellow creature all over again.

Simba's young friend Thomas and his cousin Jonas, were making their way northwards into Zambia. They had come across the Kariba gorge to find the ZAPU encampments and join the liberation struggle. A Tonga fisherman ferried them over the

Zambezi in his *bwato*. The fisherman was wearing a traditional *mubeso* loincloth over his deformed and rigid hip. His teeth were filed into points. Around his neck was a *mpande* shell on a beaded string. He said that long ago a hippo cow whose path he crossed had almost broken him in half with one bite. He always laughed when he told this story. He had been young and foolish then but he had lived. He liked to be in his *bwato* as he found it hard to walk. His name was Mafwafwa: the one who has escaped death.

At the other end of the lake in the rapids of the headwaters of the dam, Simba was crossing back into Rhodesia with a group of guerrillas. They too were helped over the rapids by Tonga fishermen in their *bwatos*.

Simba had been recruited by ZAPU cadres while he was living in the Copperbelt. He had not wanted to join ZAPU but his rage against whites had never abated and he had not been able to keep any jobs in Zambia. The cadres took him to Tanzania and from there he was taken to China for three month's training. He was an intelligent, independent and argumentative recruit but he had good reason. The Rhodesian Security Forces were well established in the bush in Hwange district south of the Zambian border. Their kill rate for ZAPU insurgents was very high. Simba said that ordering regular army-style groups of the liberation army unsupported by the local villagers into this area could not win the war and they would all be killed. He and others guerrillas who said the same thing were right, as their leader, Herbert Chitepo, back in Lusaka would eventually have to admit.

Simba was going to his death at the hands of the Rhodesian soldiers. Before he died however, Simba would become a legend for his fearlessness and his rage.

★

Charles and Margaret and the two boys slept well that night. The weather was not too hot and they were at peace with their lives for the moment. Charles as usual got up at sunrise but half-an-hour earlier, a village Headman was banging on the door of the Siavonga Clinic. Before the bemused doctor from the power station construction company understood why he was wanted, he was being rushed into the bush in the direction of Sinazongwe. A group of local Tonga villagers had accidentally walked into the land mines laid around a ZAPU camp. There were four dead men and one who, apparently uninjured, was in shock and dying and would not survive the trip in the Land Rover back to the clinic.

No one ever did explain to anyone's satisfaction, who the land mines were set to trap and why.

THIRTEEN

The 'Other' Side

The Guest Book. The Cottage, Siavonga.
July 1973
Charles, Margaret, Michael and Richard

Piet du Plessis' small stone boating pier has been broken up by wave action. Piet says it happened gradually and not during a storm. The pier was needed to shelter his boat. Now that he can't use the boat on the lake he reckons he will use it on the Kafue River instead and not bother to rebuild the pier. Charles says that Piet must have used sand with mica in it so that the cement was too weak to survive the waves. It's really quite surprising how destructive these small lake waves can be.

It was quiet down here this weekend. People must have stayed away because of the trouble. The Zambian Army were out on the dam wall and there were roadblocks on the way down.

The harbour at Siavonga is empty. Everyone who owned a motor launch on Lake Kariba has moved it up to the Kafue Marina. All the sailing boats are at the Sailing Club also on the Kafue Dam. Nowadays that is where people go for picnics at the weekend.'

The southern border was closed.

It was no longer possible to drive directly from Zambia to Rhodesia. Either one went first to Botswana or took the longer route by far, drove to Malawi and then through Mozambique. It was not even possible to take a commercial flight unless one went the same way. Rhodesia had twice closed the border to threaten Zambia and then abruptly Zambia decided to take the initiative. With more luck than judgement the borders were shut when most of the rolling stock on the railway was inside Zambia. That was one advantage and the other advantage was that most people in Zambia were used to subsistence life and doing without. Imports stopped. Life became difficult because there were shortages of every commodity, from fuel to flour and medicines. Zambia had a weak infrastructure and few commercial crops.

The reason that Rhodesia had first threatened Zambia was in a vain attempt to make it give up its support for the liberation fighters of ZAPU with whom Zambia had traditional and historical links. Guerrilla camps were to be found all over the southern half of Zambia. At the time they were not very effective as a fighting force and engaged in small random terror attacks mostly against soft targets like local chiefs in Rhodesia who, living under threat from the Rhodesian Security Forces as well, were doubly compromised and were equally terrorised by both parties.

At first the guerrillas used horrible methods of intimidation against frightened village chiefs caught between the warring parties. They would gouge out the eyes of those chiefs and torture them. Accounts of these atrocities made Margaret sick but she knew also of the increasing violent racism and discrimination of the Rhodesian government from her visits home to see her family.

Once she had hoped for the transition to a multi-racial electorate that the Federation had seemed to promise. Now it was difficult to see what would happen. Of course there would be a black government in Rhodesia one day. There were black governments in Kenya, Ghana and Zambia already. Both Margaret and Charles still believed that progressive ideals would win out. They were in Zambia working for a future that will encompass all races but their hope was increasingly being tested.

Margaret found it curious to be seen as 'the enemy' because she lived in Zambia. Old friends and relatives asked her,

"What's it like there?" as if she had chosen to live in some kind of dirty slum. They did not believe her when she said it was pleasant and she was okay. They thought she must have formed dubious alliances.

When she said that she had a lovely house with a pool, they nodded sagely because they knew that all the terrorists were living it up in similar places and then asked her how she could bear to live near them. Every description and explanation she offered was met with disbelief and Margaret could not shift their preconceptions.

Margaret had more intelligent questions and a shrewder appreciation from the black teacher she gave a lift to once on a journey home to visit her parents. Margaret was ashamed for her country folk when he asked if she was English as she treated him like a person:

"You treat me like a human being. Oh –" he said "– it must be like that for everyone in Zambia."

And indeed, Margaret reflected, it was for the most part. There were times when Zambian officials were obstructive and difficult and wanted to demonstrate that now they had the power to revenge themselves for past discrimination, but most people just behaved – well – like people – in a friendly, good-mannered way.

Now, however, she was driving to the cottage and must pass several army roadblocks at strategic bridges and crossroads on the way. The soldiers always set out to be intimidating and waved guns around but generally they were fine once she had produced her Zambian identity card and greeted them in Chichewa. It was a strain though, and she was always relieved to turn down the steep drive above the cottage and be greeted by Milimo's smile of welcome. The cottage was home in a way Lusaka could not be. In Lusaka she felt there were so many conflicts and ambivalences between the people with whom she lived and worked. It made life interesting but occasionally was hard to navigate.

Some white Zambians were as racist as white Rhodesians and were just as suspicious of her 'progressive' ideas. Then there were the expatriates from England and America who thought they were progressive and that she, being a white Rhodesian, must be a backwards backwoods racist. Most people she just had to get on with because all together the Lusaka community was small enough for everybody to know or connect with each other, even if only by hearsay and gossip.

Margaret enjoyed most of all the company of the small circle of friends who worked for the wildlife society. It was here that her drawing skills were put to use illustrating an educational magazine for school children. Everyone in the group seemed knowledgeable and enthusiastic, but more importantly they were positive about Zambia, positive about its people, positive about wildlife conservancy, and positively working to make things work. This was a place that Margaret could be herself and also laugh a lot. How important that seemed. Zambia in other ways did seem beleaguered and unsurprisingly it was becoming paranoid.

At first Margaret busied herself with the unpacking and putting away the food. Milimo was pleased to have bread. There had been none at Siavonga for a week he said. He unloaded the sack of mealie-meal that Margaret had brought for him.

"How has it been down here in Siavonga?" Margaret asked Milimo.

She wanted to know if there had been a repeat of the July 1972 incident when a government edict was made to the effect that 'aliens' could not live or work within 20 miles of the border and the army was ordered in to round up people without proper identity cards. It was an attempt by the Zambian government to conform to the international pressure not to allow Rhodesian 'terrorists' to make their bases along the border. There were rumours of land mines going off in the villages near Siavonga and there were deaths. It was impossible to find out who was involved or who was responsible. It was also impossible to know what was going to be done with the 'aliens' when they were rounded up. Basically they were taken to a point beyond the 20 kilometre exclusion area and then left to do whatever they wanted to do, which was usually just to walk back to where they had been. The round-up had taken place on a Sunday morning at sunrise. Everyone in the township, expatriates, labourers, visitors, holidaymakers, servants and villagers were woken by soldiers and marched at gunpoint to the soccer field near the Boma where they stood all morning. Absolutely nothing happened and without explanation everyone was released. Charles heard all about it in Lusaka from the irate director of the construction company building the North Bank Power Station. He was furious at his treatment and had lost two days work on the site as a result. Charles was sympathetic but could only shrug. The guerrilla war was increasing in ferocity. Milimo being a local Tonga had not been bothered and he and his family had spent a quiet day at home out of the way of the soldiers.

"Ah!" Milimo said in response to Margaret's question, both smiling and shaking his head. "There was big trouble here last week. Shootings."

"Really?" Margaret encouraged him. "What happened – when?"

Milimo indicated the lake with his chin. "There was a boat here – below."

"Really!" Margaret repeated. "I thought all boats were banned on the lake?"

"It was not a Zambian boat," Milimo explained, "there was a Rhodesian man in it with four crates of beer. It was a fast boat – open on top. He came past slowly, slowly, looking, looking up here to see what was here. The police thought that he had come to spy on Siavonga and so they opened fire on him from here over our heads." Milimo pointed backwards with his head to the police station on the hill behind them.

"My goodness!" Margaret's eyes opened wide. "Was he hit? Was he hurt?"

"No Madam, he went very fast back to the other side – back to Kariba South. He was a spy."

Margaret did not suggest that a spy would probably not be operating in the midday sun with four crates of beer in his boat and that there wasn't much to spy on in Siavonga that the Rhodesians would not already be well-informed about. Milimo was exact about the number of beer crates however. Beer was in short supply in Zambia and beer crates were in shorter supply, as they had so many other uses in a village economy and were never returned to the brewery.

It was obvious that the boatman was simply lost and had fetched up at Siavonga by accident.

Margaret was glad he had not been wounded but the incident was a frightening escalation of fear and irrationality – what would happen next? Would it even be safe for her boys to go down onto the shore by themselves?

Around the lake's shore beyond the camping site was a small holding that belonged to Piet du Plessis, an Afrikaner who had lived and hunted most of his life in Zambia. A second Rhodesian boatman had made the same mistake as the first, then had engine trouble and been forced to make a landing in Zambia. He was fortunate – Piet du Plessis was a good mechanic and he didn't fear anyone. He fixed the engine, gave the chap some fuel and sent him on his way back home. Piet didn't talk about it but then he didn't say much ever. He would have told you if you had asked. He didn't have much time for Rhodesian politics but why give the chap a hard time when he meant no harm and had just been unlucky?

Everyone spoke of the 'Other Side' in reference to Rhodesia and very quickly a concept developed in people's minds that Zambia and Rhodesia were on opposite sides of the lake and so far from each other as not to be seen. In fact they were invisible to each other, not only because they inhabited – as they perceived and experienced – different and opposed worlds, but because they were side by side on the lake separated by Kariba Gorge and the dam wall and hidden by hills. The distance between them over the lake as the boats sailed was short. The distance by land over hills and through valleys was about 20 miles.

It was true that they were each on different sides of the Kariba Gorge but both looked in the same direction up the lake and towards the Matusadona hills. They had the same geographical view but different cultures. In fact it was quite easy for a boatman, dozy on a crate of beer in the midday sun, to pass the narrow entrance to the dam gorge with his eyes fixed on the distant hills opposite and then become confused by the landscape around him. It was after all the same country and the same bush and the same valley. The boatman would probably have been surprised to see substantial houses in the 'poverty-stricken north' and imagined that he was still in Rhodesia.

FOURTEEN

Other Ways To Cross The Border.

The Guest Book. The Cottage, Siavonga.
August 1973
Charles, Margaret
*A different part of the lake! We were actually at the
Lake Kariba Regatta, Kariba South.'*
(Margaret made this entry the next time she came to the cottage.)

There were other ways to cross the border.

Charles knew, through his work, the senior management of the company who were building the new hydro-electric power station on the North Bank of Kariba. The situation was very complex as, in spite of the hostility between Zambia and Rhodesia, the whole affair was managed by the original Central African Power Corporation, CAPCO, formed during the Federation and still based in Rhodesia. Crossing the border could still be done if absolutely essential for those individuals employed by CAPCO. Even so things could go wrong. Only a week ago an engineer, who had legitimately ventured onto the dam wall, was deemed to have taken one step too far by the Zambian soldiers on duty. He was seized and very badly beaten before someone in control managed to have him released to the South Bank Hospital.

Among Charles's friends was a CAPCO electrical engineer

called Peter Duncan, who had his own small plane in Lusaka. He was allowed to fly into the airport at Kariba South for the various CAPCO meetings. These flights were always discreet but as usual, even in complex situations, air traffic control had ultimate authority.

The big sailing event of the year on the Rhodesian side of the lake was the annual 'Around the Lake Regatta', which was to take place in August. Charles's brother, Steve, was taking part and wanted Charles to crew for him. August was the month when the lake waters would still be high but it was also well before the huge thunderstorms of the rainy season due in October.

Charles and Margaret would have had to make a journey of over 2000 kilometres to the regatta when it was in fact on the same lake where they spent their weekends. Peter Duncan, however, always affably helpful and always looking for an excuse to get in his plane, offered to fly a delighted Charles and Margaret to Kariba South for the occasion.

It would be a treat for Charles to see Steve and spend time with him, especially as they both loved sailing. Steve remained a wild bachelor, still farming on their father's Eastern District farm, still refusing to put up the security fences that Rhodesian farmers were advised to install against the 'terrorists', and still taking every opportunity to rush away on a sailing trip on Kariba or off the Mozambique coast.

The flight to Kariba was short and sweet. Plenty of dust and smoke in the atmosphere at the end of the dry season meant that they did not have a good view of the countryside from the plane but it was better than dodging around the huge thunderheads that massed over the lake later in the year. They flew twice over the runway at Kariba before landing to clear it of the antelope that liked to graze its mown borders. Peter was met by his CAPCO colleagues at the airport and Steve turned up to collect Charles and Margaret. Steve had arranged accommodation in a cottage at a lakeside motel.

"This cottage is *mushi* – better than the Heights Hotel – that's full of the Yacht Club committee and their wives having cocktails," Steve said. He did not go in for ceremony. Margaret and Charles laughed and looked at each other.

"I bet the hotel will have an African band that plays that Miriam Makeba song 'Malaika'," said Charles, "Margaret and I have listened to it in Malawi, Zambia and Rhodesia."

"I do love the song," Margaret said rather wistfully, "but it is funny that it's always the same song whatever the politics of the country."

"The regatta is to be shorter this year," Steve said, getting back to the important business.

"We are not to cross the bloody border – imagine – though what the Zambians could do to us I can't think. I don't suppose they even have binoculars to watch us and how could they see if we were over this mythical line, God knows – anyhow, those in power reckon that the narrows at Chete island are too damn dangerous because of lower water levels and the dead trees in the lake. So only five days on the lake instead of seven. Only four nights camping on the shore under the stars. Anyhow for sure we will have a *lekker* sail – hey Charlie! Glad you could spare the time."

The brothers laughed. Margaret saw Charles visibly relaxing and felt herself do the same. It felt as if she was shedding years of worry and layers of over-dressing. The blouse and calf-length jeans made her feel like a schoolgirl again. There were no social pressures here to constrain them. The shopping had been done by Steve: steaks, beers, salads, bread and even mushrooms, Inyanga cheese and white Marandellas wine. There were no shortages in Rhodesia. Nothing to do but chat, have a swim and later go to the Yacht Club party. First all three of them set off to the harbour to check out the boat and the provisions, and to meet the third crew member, Ben, a young farm assistant from Steve's district, new out from England for some farming experience before going off to agricultural college. He had sailed with his father on the Solent and was expecting the lake in Africa to be easy and calm.

"Plain sailing for you," grinned Steve, "just a doddle around for five days getting sunburnt and eaten by crocs." Ben grinned back. He didn't mind being teased but he was beginning to learn that when Steve made a joke there was an awkward reality somewhere and a steep learning curve.

Ben hadn't bothered too much about the politics of Rhodesia before coming out. The South African boycott and not eating South African oranges seemed pointless to him back home. He knew the Mau-Mau in Kenya had been 'bad' but not much else. The white Rhodesian farmer who employed Ben, together with his family had been very hospitable and kind to him on his arrival. He had found no fault with what they said about the policies of Ian Smith and the Rhodesian government but since he had spent time sailing with Steve he was being introduced to a different perspective on the situation. Perhaps there were after all, some injustices inherent in the situation?

"Well Charlie my *broer* – what of Zambia and all those *terrs* you are sheltering? What's going on in Zambia?" Steve asked.

Steve was increasingly vociferous in his denunciations of Rhodesian government policy. He was much more of a rebel than his quieter, more circumspect older brother but they shared a liberal upbringing and an intelligent, pragmatic concern for 'facts' and the 'truth'. All they had read, discovered and learnt convinced them that the way forward in central Africa was to give Africans the vote – Charles inclined to a gradual power-sharing approach and Steve to an immediate universal franchise for all Rhodesians black and white. Steve was an admirer of Garfield Todd, the Rhodesian Prime Minister who had advocated it and lost the next election as a result. No one suggested giving the vote to African women which was so small a surprise to Margaret that she didn't comment on it. It was a general belief that people who had not been to school could not be trusted to vote. Rhodesians pointed out the mess that they believed universal franchise had brought to Zambia.

The brothers of course were not alone in their views in Rhodesia but they were in a minority that was diminishing. It was hard to be optimistic about the outcome, especially given the way the security situation was changing. The hard-liners seemed to be the only whites who stayed on. Sanctions didn't help and the war was getting very ugly even if the press did not report it very accurately. Instead the grapevine operated and distorted the news further for everyone.

What Charles thought and experienced was important to Steve, who listened avidly. Margaret listened too, though many of Charles's opinions were known to her. Largely she agreed with them but the little group of wildlife and educational activists she had come to know provided her with other insights.

Margaret had been brought up by liberal parents too, but very conventional ones. She had learnt as a girl to listen to men and not give her opinion. Lusaka dinner parties required tact and both she and Charles had become more silent, even with each other. Under the warm enthusiasm of Steve however she began to give her own thoughts and recount her own stories.

She told the brothers how she had been talking to Henry Chishimba and confessed to him that she thought white people were uncivilised. Then she had been embarrassed because white people always use that ridiculous argument about Africans not being civilised. Margaret meant the story to be funny but she wasn't practised at telling funny stories so she let her voice fade away. Charles and Steve were amused however.

Charles mentioned that he had met a man called Mark Watson – he had come in to see Charles wanting a loan for a business plan for a project in Gwembe.

"I sent him to see someone else – I think they helped him but I am not sure. The man is rather an adventurer I think. He was born here in Rhodesia but crossed the border somewhere without going through immigration. He may have been avoiding conscription."

"Good for him!" said Margaret and Steve together, and clinked their wine glasses.

Charles said mischievously to Steve, "He's a damn sight more radical than you Steve!"

"He can't be," said Steve smugly. "Wait till I am banned or arrested."

"They know you're mad. You're safe!" Charles said, reaching over to clip his brother's ear affectionately.

That evening they went to the Yacht Club party and talked about the safer subject of wildlife and game preservation, and listened to the many recountings of the saving of the wild animals from the rising waters of the new Lake Kariba.

FIFTEEN

Regatta

Charles and Steve spent a little time in discussion about the weather.

"It looks like we may get rain later. Surprising for so early in the year," Steve said. The clouds were massing up over the Matusadona and though it was August, they threatened not to disperse. The day felt rather humid for the end of the dry season. Margaret, watching, felt a trickle of sweat under her dark glasses.

"Damn nuisance for sleeping if it rains at night," Charles answered.

They were down at the harbour with Ben making last minute checks on the boat equipment. Steve's boat was an ancient twin-hulled catamaran but fast, light and reasonably stable – not bad for the conditions that prevailed on the lake. Steve had sailed it on the Indian Ocean and was happy with its performance. There were a good thirty boats setting out for the regatta. The start line was some way off, close to an island. Each day they would race to a selected bay on the shore and camp overnight. A team of motorboats had been sent up the lake making sure that each site had firewood and drinking water and a stash of fuel for emergencies. They would have three nights on a more circuitous way west up the lake but should be back after two more nights on a more direct route back to Chawara Harbour. The whole regatta was planned so that it took place in Rhodesian waters. The border with Zambia followed the original bed of the Zambezi River so that at times it came close to the Zambian shore. This explained the incidents with the lost boatmen recounted by Milimo and Piet. Only near Chete Island did the border with Zambia approach the Zimbabwe bank. No boats therefore should easily make the mistake of crossing over the border into Zambia.

"Right – we're off then. Come on chaps!" Steve said decisively.

Charles kissed Margaret and gave her a smile, then unexpectedly he hugged her close and whispered in her ear – "Take care dear Maggie-Meg."

"You take care too, Charles – and look after that poor Ben too – don't let Steve rag him too much." Margaret held Charles very tight for a few moments. It was so pleasant to feel him in this relaxed and happy mood of enthusiasm.

"Love you!" she whispered back and then they were gone.

Margaret did not watch the start of the race for long. It was quite a distance away. A pleasant sight at first, the white sails against the grey-blue hills and the bright blue water, but they gradually vanished up the lake with the morning winds behind them.

Margaret was going, with a school friend, Anne, whose husband was also sailing in the regatta, to spend a few days at a safari camp and nature reserve on Spurwing Island, a place made famous in the days when volunteers rescued animals from the rising lake. She wouldn't hear about the regatta till she returned on Thursday evening by which time the sailors would be on their way home. She would of course think about them all the time whether they were flying across the water in the wind, cooking themselves a dark red while becalmed, or sleeping in the dark in the trampoline slung between the cat's hulls, while crocodiles sulked under them and mosquitoes whinged around them.

Anne and Margaret arrived back from the Spurwing Island in very good spirits. They had seen elephant, hippo, antelope and many birds. On trips to the mainland shore they had glimpsed a leopard and had even seen rhino. Margaret's sketchbook was full of notes and drawings, enough for a full year's worth of ideas and illustrations for the wildlife magazine. Anne was a quiet companion but very knowledgeable about wild bush foods, flowering plants and birds. Margaret would be able to share her new knowledge with her Lusaka friends at the magazine. It would be good to brag a little and contribute a bit more. Anne and Margaret had also chatted about children, schools, universities, husbands and hopes for the future. The holiday had been a rejuvenating experience. There would be much for Margaret to tell Charles on his return, even if he had also seen some game when he camped. She had used up all the film she had bought in Kariba and would now have to get more to snap the men when they sailed back into harbour.

One night there had been some of that grumbly thunder that goes on and on but without there being much rain or a cooling wind. Anne and Margaret agreed it was probably a very local storm and the men out on the lake would probably not be affected at all. On Thursday morning the lake was up in those short hard lake waves that went on and on, breaking on the shore without any driving wind. Again, and as usual, the waves relaxed their monotonous chopping at the beaches by lunchtime and the boat trip back to Kariba was smooth, swift and hot.

The two women went round to the Yacht Club which was very quiet. Wives and families of sailors were by the hotel pools or sunning themselves on the beaches. A few were out sailing in the smaller dinghies that were available or had gone water-skiing or boating and fishing. The first overnight camps had been packed up and the boats brought back with news that the race had gone well for the first three nights. Everyone had turned up and been checked in at the camps before dark, except of course for Margaret's wild brother-in-law.

"Always a bit of a chancer, Steve is," said the official with a smile, "they got in a good hour after dark the first day. I think they were showing Ben some elephant on the shore and missed the wind for a while. Probably 'up the creek without a paddle'," he laughed. "Guess they had to row a bit."

Margaret thought that sounded highly likely.

"Not sure about last night yet. Steve and Charles were late again I think. There was one hell of a big storm further away. Anyway the team will radio in tonight probably. It is all going very well. A great regatta."

Margaret went back to the hotel cottage and flopped on the bed with her eyes closed. She was tired physically and a bit sunburnt from her days on Spurwing but that felt good. The cottage lounge had been tidied up but it still had the feeling that Charles and Steve had just that moment walked out. Magazines, spectacles and bird books lay about. Margaret yawned. There was nothing to worry about, she felt sure. Steve and Charles were good at taking care of themselves. For all their disregard for turning up at the camp sites on time they were pretty safety conscious and despised the carelessness that put other people to unnecessary trouble or worry. Margaret had told Anne that she would have a quiet evening that night. It would be a pleasure to sit down and write long letters to their two boys at boarding school about all that she had seen at Spurwing. She would add some quick sketches too. The boys liked that. She wanted them to know that she had a life outside the home, one which they could respect her for having. Margaret fixed herself a toasted sandwich with bacon, cheese and tomato and poured out a glass of the Marandellas wine. It would be nice to bath instead of showering tonight and then indulge in a long lie-in in bed the next morning and read a book. She was reading Doris Lessing's *Four-Gated City* series with enjoyment, but had not recommended it to Anne. Lessing was not well regarded as a writer in Rhodesia. Lessing's ex-husband had been a communist and Lessing had written a book about the strangest of relationships between a white farmer's wife and her black manservant.

By Friday lunchtime the atmosphere at the Yacht Club was rather more tense. The team had radioed in rather late the night before with news that the lake conditions had been very bad during the day on Thursday. It hadn't rained but the waves and wind were extreme as, surprisingly, tideless lakes can be. A strong wind from the south-east sent huge choppy rollers up the lake for almost a full day. The boats had had a scary run to their furthest camp site with the wind behind them, most only using their jib sails or genoas and all sailing close together for safety. Two boats did not arrive at all. One boat had given up early and turned back to the Wednesday night camp site by mid-morning before it was closed down. It waited there out of the wind until the waves dropped and then simply motored back to Kariba on engine power, eventually arriving back late Friday afternoon with the news of the wind and the seiche. The other boat was Steve and Charles's cat, which no one had seen as yet, but the motorboats were out following the regatta, radios were fully functioning again and there was still one more day before the race was over. As yet there seemed to be no real cause for alarm. The lake was, after all, vast and Steve and Charles were experienced sailors. Anne and Margaret were invited out for a meal at Kariba Heights and then there was a film to watch in the hotel lounge. Margaret put her mind into automatic and refused to think about anything but the present moment. It was most likely that Charles, Steve and Ben would sail in tomorrow along with the rest of the flotilla.

On Saturday Margaret got up as slowly as possible, taking her time over her breakfast and sorting out the clothes and suitcases for their flight back to Lusaka with Peter Duncan on Monday afternoon. She then climbed into Steve's pick-up and drove down to the harbour to see what was happening and to put her mind at rest. The euphoria generated by her few days on Spurwing had dissipated somewhat and she found herself feeling isolated and actually rather alienated from the expectant families waiting for the sailors to arrive.

What had happened to the Rhodesia that she had grown up in and loved? Where was the generosity of her childhood, the positive optimism of her youth, the determination of the generation that she had worked with to make a better world for all the people of Rhodesia? Feelings had run high and arguments erupted over the break-up of the Federation. Ian Smith's Unilateral Declaration of Independence had been a very low point and yes – things seemed to become sour and nasty. She increasingly encountered suspicion even from her own family because 'you both live up north with them' as if whites somehow led a completely separate life from Africans in Rhodesia, while she and Charles shared with blacks in Zambia in ways that were complicit. Now she looked around her and saw that she did not recognise these people as fellow Rhodesians. There were new English immigrants with accents she could not identify but she recognised their behaviour as ignorant and rude towards the African workers at the harbour. Margaret saw with a shock that a couple of men wore red tee-shirts with 'White Power' emblazoned across their chests. When she looked for the Rhodesians that she remembered, those civilised – if that was the appropriate word – those hospitable, outgoing and helpful people with whom she grew up, she saw that they too had changed. She saw that men had gun belts with pistol holsters and when she glanced into an open car as she passed, she saw the shotgun resting on the back seat. The thing that hit her hardest however, was the words that came out of everyone's mouths – even out of the mouths of the sweetest looking children.

'*Munt*' they said and 'slopehead', '*kaffir*' or 'bloody Af' and they said the words with forceful venom or disparaging sneers. There was no context, that Margaret could see, that required such words or such disgust in daily usage. Even when they were not engaged directly with an African worker, Rhodesians still seemed to need to discuss them loudly using these words, and the words were solid, hard missiles that battered at Margaret's ears. It was true Rhodesia was fighting a war against terrorists, but the war did not yet seem to be much visible inside the borders of the country. It was also true that many men were engaged in the fighting against the guerrillas even if only as reservists in the towns. What could Margaret expect?

Rhodesia was her home but how could she ever come back to live in it? It had become ugly and fearful.

In Zambia there were people exercising new-found powers who would threaten you if they felt offended or if they thought you were racist, and bureaucracy and officialdom could make life difficult and troublesome but mostly people reached out to a smile or gesture. You were all human together and that was hopeful. The trouble was that in Zambia, she and Charles were only temporary visitors on work permits.

Suddenly Margaret was painfully and desperately nostalgic to arrive at her cottage and see Milimo's welcoming smile. The cottage was just 20 miles across the dam wall but it inhabited another world.

The day passed and was not without interest and pleasure. The boats came into the harbour in groups and singly – every crew laughing, friendly, pleased with themselves and with stories and adventures to recount, but Charles and Steve and Ben did not appear. Towards the end of the day, the commodore began glancing in Margaret's direction more frequently. Anne's husband had come in among the first and Anne came over to wait with Margaret.

"Stewart didn't see them during the last two days," she said. "Are you okay?" To which Margaret of course said she was.

"It's typical, Charles and Steve," Margaret answered. "They turned their mother's hair grey before she was fifty. Honestly I don't know why I am not grey too – but they will be all right. I am not worried yet!"

She wanted to deflect all concern away from herself. It was easier to cope with her anxiety if she and everyone pretended that it would be all right in the end. Margaret knew that the motorboats had been back up the course checking and there were a couple of light planes out for pleasure that would have been tipped off to keep an eye out for a lone catamaran somewhere on the lake. Someone from CAPCO was delegated to phone his counterpart at the construction company site at Siavonga, to find out if there had been anything unusual reported by the Zambian police during the day.

At sunset there was a consensus that there was no more to be done till the next morning. The commodore was calm and serious but careful to be optimistic. The harbour guards were told to keep the lights burning and to stay awake all night but as the skipper said: "Charles and Steve won't be sailing in the dark. They will be hungry by now unless they packed more food than they needed but that won't be a problem for those three – they'll be fine."

Anne and Stewart persuaded Margaret to come out to the end of regatta barbecue. She agreed because it would be dark enough for her to avoid being stared at as the woman whose husband was missing, and she knew she wouldn't sleep and the night would be very long if she went back to the chalet on her own. She didn't want to think about her two boys just yet either but found that every adolescent boy at the barbecue wore their faces – at least until he spoke and those ugly, racist, sneering words came off his tongue.

Oh please God! prayed Margaret, *Don't let my boys turn into racists too. Please God bring Charles home safely!*

★

As is so often the case, after a night of worry and sleeplessness, Margaret fell heavily asleep at first light and then woke feeling tired and rushed. She disciplined herself again not to hurry down to the harbour but naturally the commodore was already there and he came straight up to her.

"Margaret dear girl, relax! They have been spotted by someone from the flying club. It appears to be a problem with the rudder so they are limping in. The pilot said that three people waved at him from the cat and they all looked fit. The motorboat has gone out to give them a tow in."

"Oh God! Thank Goodness!" said Margaret, feeling as if the sun had just risen. Part of her prayer was answered – was it the most important bit of the prayer?

"Have some instant coffee," said the commodore, smiling, "and sit down, do."

SIXTEEN

The Enemy

Charles and Steve had made a detour off the course on Wednesday in order to take Ben closer to his first sighting of a herd of elephants. They then had a minor problem with the rigging and one way and another they camped that night on their own.

"After that everything went haywire," Charles explained to Margaret. "The seiche was one of the worst that we've seen on the lake let alone had to sail in."

Steve had explained to Ben the particular conditions on Lake Kariba that created a seiche.

"If a strong wind is blowing up a long stretch of water like Kariba, it pushes all the water up to that one end. Of course water can't stay piled up so it flows backwards against the strong wind and against the water blowing the other way. The result is you get these very high, steep waves very close to each other that are so tough for any kind of boating."

Steve said with a grin, "It was better to have the wind behind you and not to have to attempt to tack into it."

"You couldn't have sailed into it," said Charles, "we would just have sat the day out in some bay somewhere."

"At least it was only like that for one day," contributed Ben.

"Yip!" Steve said, "But in those conditions you can't see those damn petrified trees and I guess we must have hit one."

"Maybe," said Charles, "but it could have been something floating in the water – one of your 'big crocs' Ben."

Ben could not believe the size of the lake crocodiles and soon had seen more than the other two men.

"Anyhow," said Steve, "the rudder was damaged. We were sailing on a half-furled jib sail and at first couldn't understand why the cat was so unresponsive, we just couldn't keep her on course – she just wanted to take Charles back to Zambia and ditch him there – useless old bloke!" And he gave Charles an affectionate shove. "When we began to think that the rudder was the problem we just looked for a cove – any cove out of the wind and so we fetched up on the 'buggery isles' well – the shore. We were grateful that we were close to any shore – if we had been on the widest part of Kariba we could still have been running before the wind for weeks!" Steve exaggerated

"That felt really bad," said Charles, "We knew it must be Zambia and as Margaret and I know, the soldiers are trigger-happy – but we reckoned we couldn't be near any settlements and it was very unlikely that the Zambians would have a camp there."

Steve went on, "We had a soft landing on a reedy beach – perfect for crocs, hey Ben – and quiet, thank God, but the then the wind and waves make a frightful din so we probably wouldn't have been heard crunching up on stones. We just got on with seeing what was wrong – and seeing if we could fix it – the wind was dropping anyway but we kept pretty quiet – didn't know what might be around, hippo or elephant. In fact it felt rather deserted by animals – you have that sense that the animals have quit an area. Ben was on croc hunt – weren't you Ben? – and he found a dead antelope, half-eaten of course – the problem was it had been shot. Well if there were Tonga around and it wasn't good resettlement country – they wouldn't have guns. So we got quieter and more careful."

"One of the rudders was damaged," said Charles, "not too badly, but the lower pintle was broken. It kept kicking up so was giving us no steering power."   "We had to be pretty inventive," said Steve, "Ben was quite a useful chap to have around. We just about got it all sorted and then we heard the gunfire. Boy-oh-boy-oh-boy! Didn't we just about –"

Steve waggled his brows to explain what he had almost done.

"Steve knew it was Kalashnikovs that we could hear," said Charles. "The Zambian Army don't have them so that just meant one thing."

"We were washed up," finished Steve, "on the *'buggery isles'* – we knew we were right next to a ZIPRA camp. Ben knows what that is now – the armed wing of Nkomo's Zimbabwe African Peoples Union."

"So Steve had to go and have a look," said Charles. "Necessary but very risky."

"Too right!" went on Steve, "On with my old *veldskoens* and I sneaked up over the ridge as carefully as possible. They weren't worried – they had no one out on sentry duty. I didn't try and get close – just wanted to see what we might be up against – you know – numbers and equipment and so on. They had some boats down there – just banana boats, not bad for crossing but the lake isn't wide there. Then I heard women's voices and saw campfire smoke and then they had a bit of a party."

"We didn't get much sleep," said Charles. "Steve wanted to stay up on the ridge and keep watch and we all needed to sleep but it was a bloody uncomfortable night. There was a little thunder and a little rain in the night – all to the good as we hoped that that would keep them at home and we hoped they would be sleeping off the party. The night was dark which was to our advantage – they would sleep better than at full moon. It wasn't too good an idea for us to sail off in the dark as we didn't really know the terrain. Steve pulled out the maps – we wanted to know exactly where we were now that we had bumped into these guys.

"Anyway we left just before the sun rose – it was very calm and we had to row very quietly before we could catch any wind. Getting off the reeds was reasonably quiet and Ben didn't tread on a croc, but of course we didn't have the main sail up because we might have been a very easy target that way. That was Thursday of course but we had to spend two more nights to get back because we kept having such problems with the rudder that we had to go slowly and make use of the oar to supplement it. It was very tiring – very tiring. It felt great when the motorboat arrived and gave us a tow in."

Ben said, "I can't believe it but I don't think they'll ever know we were there."

"Oh yes they will!" said Steve, "Unless they have already left the camp they will have a big surprise tonight when the gunships arrive over their heads."

"What?" said Ben. He hadn't considered that eventuality.

"Yes," said Steve, "first thing I did was tell the big man about our trip. If our guys are too late to get them in the camp, they'll pick them up on our side. It's over for them."

Ben said nothing for a bit then he asked:

"You mean that the Rhodesians are fighting inside Zambia?"

"Yes," said Steve, "all the time – and inside Mozambique too. It's a goddamn awful war and will achieve nothing for us white Rhodesians."

"But you still told the army about them?" said Ben, now utterly bewildered.

"Yes," said Steve sombrely. "What else could I do? It is not a game."

Margaret and Charles looked at each other in silence. Then Charles bent his head and shook it from side to side again and again, as if his head was waterlogged.

"Come on," said Steve to his brother, "let's go and – drink! Come on Margaret, come on Ben! Let the good guys go and be bad!"

Seventeen

Debriefing

When Charles, Steve and Ben came ashore from their extended sail, they said nothing about their close encounter with the ZIPRA camp. Steve muttered into the commodore's ear unnoticed in the commotion and relief of their arrival and as the commodore was a senior army reservist in the Kariba Section, he only nodded and stayed silent. Steve then slid away to make a phone call or two while Charles and Ben allowed themselves to be ribbed about what useless sailors they were and how it was time they did some basic maintenance on their old catamaran. Steve had a pretty extensive debriefing with someone military that same night and maps were produced and studied in great detail. Charles was called in too. Ben was clapped on the shoulders a few times and asked not to speak of the ZIPRA camp again, though of course he did and was sometimes believed and sometimes not. Behind his back his friends said he was a Pom who was full of 'bull-dust'. Nevertheless his stories fed the general sense of outrage and fear.

Margaret could see that Charles was very unhappy about this meeting even though his expression did not change much. Back in Lusaka he told Margaret that he had been asked to provide information for the Rhodesian Security Services but he had refused saying he would not compromise his family or his work.

"I won't do it! The trouble is that it's not safe to be an informant and I don't know if it's safe not to be an informant. Who and what would I be protecting?" he said to Margaret, "But then I think of you and the boys and our plans for retirement and I think it is all such a mess – what is right? I ask – and I don't know! I don't know! Could you stand to live in England?"

"Charles," said Margaret, putting her arms around him, knowing he couldn't stand to live in England. "We did not choose this war, we must stay out of it. We do not believe it is right!" But she knew he was torturing himself.

"I won't speak of it again," he said with such a long face that Margaret almost smiled. She decided she would give him time and then see if she could cheer him up.

When he left for a game of squash and she was alone again, she found herself shuddering and hyperventilating: what madness on her part to offer comfort to Charles when she herself was sick with fright. If Charles and his brother had been discovered by the ZIPRA men, they would have been tortured horribly and killed, but, like Charles, she could not allow herself to dwell on it and of course she must not speak about it here in Zambia.

At least Charles was off to London soon for business meetings. That would cheer him up and he would come back as always with some gifts and some purchases of both essentials and treats for their store cupboard. Margaret would spend the week down at the lake with her bird books and sketchbooks and she would be busy planting all the new plants she had bought for the garden there.

EIGHTEEN

Guests And Relations

The Guest Book. The Cottage, Siavonga.
September 1973
Charles, Margaret.
Henry and Petronella Chishimba.
*'Many grateful thanks for your kind hospitality to ourselves and
our children, Mumbi, Musonda, Chanda and Kunda.'*

Charles and Margaret had invited one of his Zambian colleagues
to come down for the weekend. Henry Chishimba arrived in a suit
and tie and his wife, Petronella, and children, Mumbi, Musonda,
Chanda and Kunda, in their best and most expensive clothes. The
children were beautifully mannered and obedient but they had
been told not to play or run around and sat on the veranda kicking
their legs back and forward while the adults sweated over
Margaret's cold meat and salads. It was a very hot and not a very
successful weekend. Margaret had been especially to the Lake
Delicatessen in Longacres to buy jars of lumpfish caviar and French
cheese. She selected Brie from the cold cabinet after testing its
quality with her thumb to see if it had survived its long air journey
but none of her efforts had helped her guests relax. It did not at
first result in any deepening of their acquaintance or even in a
return invitation to dinner. Indeed Margaret felt rejected by

Petronella and somewhat hurt, though why should Petronella want to be friendly with her after all? In the end she admitted to herself that she was the one who wanted the connection and the friendship. Why was it easier for Charles and Henry to be friends at work?

Oh well, thought Margaret, *I don't mind keeping the cottage just for us but still – it would be nice to have the right sort of company sometimes.*

Margaret decided to ask her niece Marielise to come down to the lake with her for company. Charles was not keen on Margaret going anywhere alone after his experience on Lake Kariba and Marielise's arrival in Zambia was opportune. Marielise had just taken up a teaching post at the new University of Zambia and Margaret's sister Sarah, had asked Margaret to look out for her. Marielise was hardly a child – she must be just under thirty – but Margaret gathered from hints dropped by Sarah that Marielise was headstrong; "Political – you know what I mean," Sarah had said, clearly anxious about her.

"I wish she would find a good man," Sarah said.

Funny girl – Marielise – as far as Margaret could remember anyway. She had not even been christened Marielise but had chosen this Afrikaans version of Mary-Elisabeth for herself when she was about sixteen. Sarah had laughed about it a bit disconsolately.

"That's my daughter!" she said, "Impulsive and full of strange ideas. Heaven knows where she gets them from – Jacob probably – he's rather non-conformist." And she dismissed them both with a gesture. "Marielise said," Sarah continued to explain, "that the British had 'wronged' the Afrikaners and she wanted to acknowledge that. Honestly – how could anyone feel any sympathy for Afrikaners! They are so ignorant!"

Come to think of it, Mary-Elisabeth – or Marielise – had not even been christened. Her father was Jewish and had been divorced by Marielise's mother for lack of conformity, or had it been the other way around? Had Jacob divorced Sarah for too much conformity? Certainly they were not compatible. Sarah was ten years older than Margaret and Marielise about the same number of years older than Margaret's boys so they hadn't seen too much of each other as children. Sarah's second husband, a rotund self-satisfied estate agent and entrepreneur, had taken Sarah and Marielise with Sarah's new babies, a boy and girl, down to Johannesburg because everything was better down there – and safer, it goes without saying. He had provided Marielise with a good English education but Marielise may well have changed her name to annoy her stepfather. Marielise had never lost touch with her father, Jacob. He had eventually gone to live and work in England, driven into exile by his radical beliefs about the future for Rhodesia. Margaret had bumped into him once in Lusaka while he was a Professor of Sociology at the Zambian University. He had been made a Prohibited Immigrant there too because he had chosen, foolishly Margaret thought, to speak his mind about Zambian politics.

When Marielise turned up at the Sunningdale house, Margaret recognised her at once. She had Sarah's quick and pleasant laugh – it lit up her face with a smile, then bubbled for a moment before bursting out. It was always near the surface ready to appear. Marielise had a friendly, open face, her father's dark, thick wavy hair and intelligent brown eyes, with Sarah's full figure but she was her own person in every way and nothing she said or did recalled either parent's personality. Marielise had come by taxi.

"Really!" said Margaret. "I would have fetched you."

"Oh that's okay, Aunt Margaret!" Marielise said, looking relaxed. "I got one of the new Holden taxis with a driver in a suit and tie. Bit of an arrogant bloke but he chatted after a bit – I guess he was living up to the suit and tie." She smiled as she said it, as if that were natural enough for any man.

"I told him I was from England though. Everyone here is a bit jumpy around white Rhodesians and South Africans – understandable I suppose." She looked directly at Margaret as she said this, as if she was assessing her carefully. Her gaze was not unfriendly – just steady. Margaret was slightly discomfited. She had reached the age of being ignored by younger women or of finding them too well-mannered and considerate around her. Marielise's manner suggested that she wasn't aware of any age difference.

"Do call me Margaret please – I prefer not to be called Aunt."

Margaret continued,

"Charles tells me that the people in suits that he works with – both white and black – are inclined to stand on their dignity. Sometimes he says most of his committee meetings are about who is the most dignified and therefore the most important and authoritative person in the room – I guess arrogant might be a good description." Margaret didn't quote Charles's comments too often as they were meant to be private observations made only to her.

"Thanks Margaret," said Marielise, and again watching Margaret she added, "I suppose it's a change for blacks after all that colonial bossing about."

Margaret sighed, thinking of how diplomatic and careful Charles had to be all the time.

"Luckily," she said briskly, "I don't have to face that – the people I work with are just friendly and pleasant. We are a mixed team; men and women – white and black – and I do love it."

"We are pretty mixed at the university too," said Marielise, "but boy, are some of us opinionated! And most of us are convinced that we know best! Still I love it, even if it does get a bit heated." And she laughed her relaxed and natural laugh.

"What do you and your 'team' do? You must tell me all about it." Marielise began to ask but then turned to practicalities.

"First though Aunt – no, Margaret – tell me all about the cottage and what I should bring with me. Shall I cook? Do you want salads?"

NINETEEN

Fire And Water

The Guest Book. The Cottage, Siavonga.
November 1973
Margaret and Marielise.

This is the most beautiful and peaceful place in Zambia. There are so many birds in the garden. Milimo tells me that the one I heard calling is a 'gombe gofu' which I think maybe is a chinspot batis. I also heard 'monkey birds' making a clattering noise – that is what Margaret calls them. They are arrow-marked babblers! There is also a pair of peregrine falcons in the tallest tree behind the cottage.'

Aunt and niece enjoyed each other's company on the drive down to the lake. Margaret kept the conversation away from anything too personal. She wanted Marielise to know that she had not been primed by Sarah and that she did not have a hidden agenda. So after the essential polite inquiries about family, they both changed the subject. Marielise had lots of questions to ask about life in Zambia, though in fact she seemed well-informed and well-prepared. Margaret gathered that she had other contacts in Lusaka; people that Margaret had not heard of but that Marielise knew from studying in South Africa and England. Marielise only used their first names anyway, so Margaret felt able to venture opinions of her own to Marielise in the expectation that Marielise and herself wouldn't move in quite the same circles. She found it quite liberating to say something critical or funny about a diplomat or managing director who had bored her at dinner or whose wife had snubbed her at a cocktail party and made Marielise laugh. They had that family sense of humour and history that cuts across other differences. She also regaled Marielise with the stories of some of the extraordinary characters who chose to live down by the lake.

"There was a couple who lived under the corrugated iron roof of a half built warehouse with only wooden boxes and tarpaulins for walls. It is so cool in there," Margaret said. "They have the most wonderful collection of found objects, stones, bones and junk from the harbour and so many stories to tell.

"Then there is Father Patrick the Jesuit, who sometimes stays next door. Oddly the cottage next door to us is owned by another priest – and I thought they were all sworn to poverty.

"And Piet the Afrikaner, who is so kind and gentle. His parents live with him and they are so old – his father used to hunt crocodiles in the valley below the cottage before the dam was built – in the 1930s I believe. And then of course, as you would expect, there is the alcoholic couple near the campsite who are always fighting. One day the police were called and thought that one of them had finally killed the other because the toilet was full of blood and meat, but apparently it was just the meat order from the butcher which the wife had stuffed into the toilet pan when her husband asked her to cook supper!"

"And the Zambian population?" asked Marielise with a sideways look at her aunt.

"Mmmh," said Margaret, she was eating a biscuit, "At the moment the Yugoslav construction workers live in the housing that will one day be for Zambians. The local workers are housed on the way to the construction site – I'll show you where when we pass it. One of them has built a traditional double story Tonga house on stilts – it's used for protection against lions I think – though all the game seems to have vanished from around here.

There is a traditional mud hut village in the valley beyond Siavonga called Mutinangala that keeps on growing and growing but it is supposed to be an illegal settlement. We have met the district commissioner and his staff from the *Boma*, and of course we know the customs officers and the police. The hospital has a Yugoslav doctor and Zambian nurses."

Marielise was interested to hear about the lake itself and about how and why Margaret and Charles had come to own the cottage.

She said, "When I was about eight years old I won an iced cake at the school fête. It had a sugar picture of the Kariba Dam wall on it; I made a scrapbook of newspaper cuttings about the building of Kariba and the floods in '57 – was that the date? The icing shell was so hard that we had to turn it upside down and dig the cake out. We were left with a hard sugar shell that wouldn't even dissolve when it was sucked. The picture of the dam wall broke in bits. I remember wondering – the way kids do – if it was an omen or some kind of magic about the dam itself."

They both laughed.

Margaret said, "Well here's hoping the wall will last – at least for 200 years – I think that it's designed for some period that doesn't sound too long in any context – or is that the 200 year flood that it's supposed to resist?"

"Actually," Marielise admitted, "one of my university research projects will be to look at the resettlement of the Batonga when the dam was built."

"Heavens!" Margaret responded, "You definitely won't be able to do that. The whole of this area is under guard one way or another. There's Zambian Army on all the roads and bridges and river crossings – you'll see on the way down – and the bush is supposed to be full of ZAPU and ZIPRA guerrilla camps. All the Batonga villages in that area will be really dangerous to visit."

She was silent, remembering not to talk about Charles and the ZIPRA camp and a cramp of fear like menstrual pain gripped her. She swallowed hard and shifted her driving position to ease her back.

"You can talk to Milimo I suppose – he grew up in the Gwembe Valley – and to Father Patrick Brogan, I know he worked there among the Tonga. He had a connection with the Canisius mission school at Monze."

Then they turned to the subject of the cottage and its garden.

"Would you like to use the cottage on your own sometimes and bring your friends down Marielise?" asked Margaret. "We don't get down nearly often enough and I would love other people to have the pleasure of using it. So many people are put off by the roadblocks and quite honestly the cottage is a bit rudimentary, no hot water and no swimming pool. The government ban is still in place so no one can go boating on the lake. Charles and I swim in it but some people find that frightening. It's definitely not everyone's cup of tea but it is just so lovely there."

Margaret remembered the less than successful visit of Henry and Petronella Chisanga.

"It is strange really," Margaret said, "us white Africans want to go back to nature, enjoy wild animals, and slop about in old clothes, while modern Zambians seem not to care at all about their natural heritage – they want to live city lives and go shopping."

Marielise raised an ironic eyebrow and grinned.

"White people care about antelope not Africans. There was all that money for the Noah's Ark volunteers to save animals from the lake but, in Southern Rhodesia, not a penny for the resettlement of the Batonga – just a free ride into exile. Do you know the figures? It cost about a thousand pounds to save one animal – admittedly with donations from white people – while the then colonial government in Northern Rhodesia spent about eleven pounds a person on resettlement and on top of that they underestimated the number of people they were moving. That could be a good reason for the Batonga to kill wild animals for food and income don't you think?"

Margaret was silent. Wildlife education in Zambia had begun with the work of Noah's Ark in saving drowning animals from

95

Lake Kariba. Was wildlife conservation starting from the wrong place?

"We have made an awful mess in Africa haven't we?" she said finally, "and I don't think we are helping much now."

"Yes! We have and we are!" Marielise was silent for a few moments too.

"But," Marielise said, "it was not a Garden of Eden before we arrived either. We need a completely new social contract for humankind and…" Then she stopped and was silent again and for longer.

Margaret glanced at her niece, what was it Sarah had said about her daughter – that she was a 'Marxist' or something? Best not to ask what that new social contract would be then. Still, on reflection everything did seem to be an awful mess and getting worse every day – perhaps there could be an alternative solution. What could it be? Kaunda was determined on his socialist Zambian humanism, something he had dreamed up with a white Anglican priest, she had been told. He had started nationalising everything and changing the education system too.

That was causing even more headaches for Charles. Margaret sighed.

"I do love the lake," Margaret said after a while, "it is so very beautiful and it looks so peaceful and so natural, as if it has always been there. It does my heart good.

"But again –" she turned to Marielise with a chuckle, " – I feel that as it is made by humans, it must be fragile and I imagine the dam wall bursting and the water draining away and taking me with it – whooshing down the Zambezi to the sea on a great flash flood!

"Michael, my eldest son, says that if that happened, the whole valley would be full of thousands of stranded crocodiles all looking for something to eat!"

Marielise laughed too.

"Michael must have a sense of humour!" she observed then continued,

"Mm – all vainglorious projects must have their downfall – that kind of idea – yes – and human guilt for the harms we have done. Do you think someone could blow the dam wall up?"

"No," said Margaret.

"No," said Marielise, "and anyway Margaret, you aren't responsible for all of the wrongs we have done in Africa and neither am I."

Margaret drove her car carefully down the escarpment road and they both commented on how exceptionally dry the bush was.

"We had very poor rain this last season," said Margaret.

The sight of tall, white-barked trees standing out above the leafless scrub caught Marielise's eye. Knobbled, flower-shaped seed pods and a few bright lemon, hand-shaped leaves still hung from their branches.

"What are those amazing trees?" Marielise asked.

"*Sterculia quinqueloba* – African Chestnuts," Margaret answered, "Aren't they strikingly beautiful."

As they made the final descent into the Zambezi Valley, they both gasped with shock. The whole of the flood plain was either burnt, or still burning. Even the earth had changed its colour to black. Smoke drifted up from the ash-white skeletons of hundreds of fallen trees. The fires had spread as far as they could see and curving lines of orange flames snaked their way through any of the short, dry scrub that was not yet entirely consumed.

For a moment Margaret wondered if she should turn back. The air was thick and dirty from the fires. They were in no danger of catching alight, but Margaret couldn't see ahead of her or see any bush that was not destroyed. She wondered if they would be able to breathe in the heat and smoke.

"It looks like we are in hell!" said Marielise nervously, "Can the bush recover? It doesn't look possible! How did it start?"

"I honestly don't know," said Margaret, "I have never seen such an extensive bush fire. What on earth has happened to all the birds and animals – and people too. Sometimes they say fires start by themselves when it is tremendously hot."

For a while they journeyed silently, staring around them, subdued by the intense heat of the valley. They did not know if the sun, or the fire, or both, were responsible.

It was a relief to leave the blackened plain behind them and climb up the Kariba escarpment. At last they reached Siavonga and the cottage, Margaret zigzagged the car down the narrow drive and parked under the *marula* tree.

"Leave our bags. Milimo will fetch them," Margaret said.

Marielise pulled a secret face, but she obeyed and followed Margaret down the slasto steps to the cottage, shaking her damp tee-shirt free of her sweaty back as she went.

They stepped onto the level terrace by the cottage veranda and Marielise glimpsed through the lush greenery of trees and climbing plants, the pale reflective lake under a thinly-veiled sky. The rich, hot smell of wet African vegetation enveloped her together with the sound of birds and the quiet, misty shush of the fine spray of water from the hose that Milimo was holding.

"Oh Margaret!" Marielise said, "What a beautiful place!"

TWENTY

Adapting The Past

The Guest Book. The Cottage, Siavonga.
February 1974
Henry and Petronella, Mumbi, Musonda, Chanda and
Kunda Chishimba.
'*Grateful thanks for a lovely holiday weekend.*
Milimo looked after us well.'

Henry and Petronella did visit the cottage again but not with the Beaumonts. The next time they went down to the lake on their own. To Margaret's surprise, they readily accepted Charles's offer to use the place one weekend when the Beaumonts were not in Zambia. By then Margaret had deepened her friendship with Henry and begun to understand why Charles and Henry were such good friends. Henry was relaxed and funny in company.

As Henry explained, "Us Zambians have a lot to laugh at – we provide ourselves with constant entertainment because we screw up so often at running our country and our lives."

"The cottage wasn't quite what you expected was it?" a rather nervous Margaret had asked Henry.

Henry laughed easily. When Henry and Petronella returned from their weekend with the Beaumonts, they had shrieked with laughter for a good hour while Petronella did a rather good impression of Margaret jumping up and down from the luncheon table every few moments to wait on her guests. Neither of them was unkind about Margaret but the reversal of the colonial role was amusing and ironic.

"No," Henry said, "We thought it would be rather more upmarket I guess. We really didn't know you then Margaret. It's a very nice place but not what we expected."

"Oh." Margaret was uncertain if this was criticism or praise.

Henry chatted on.

"It's not that we want to escape the simple life you know – the fact is we have to separate ourselves from some cultural aspects of growing up with it to make the new Zambia function at all. Me – I go back to my father's village every now and then and sleep on the mud floor. It's good for me – gives me a sense of grounding that I like.

"For Petronella it's not the same. Her life in the village as a girl was hard work and sometimes she suffered abuse. She would still be expected to fetch water and wood if she went home whereas I am waited on. Petronella is not going back to that. She has a different way of helping with her family.

"At Independence you know there were only about a hundred Zambians like me – men who had a university education and had maybe travelled to Europe.

"We were all head-hunted and offered top jobs of course – some of us had already married Zambian women from the village at home and found that didn't work too well for them or for our new bosses. Some came back with women they had met while studying abroad. All of us found it harder than we expected in the new Zambia.

"I am really fortunate – mine is the best arrangement. I have found a Zambian woman who is my equal. Petronella has a degree – very few Zambian women do as yet."

Henry shook his head, laughing again.

"In Zambia you don't marry a person – you marry a village. Those of us with good jobs after Independence found we had a village, or maybe two, to support, educate, house and feed. In Zambia you have to share your good fortune with all your relations.

"Look at David Chona – his wife fled back to England when she found out that everything in her wardrobe and kitchen was shared with her husband's family. Possessions that she replaced just vanished the same way each month.

We Zambians are very village-minded!" Henry said with a broad grin, "It sure as hell makes hard work and success unattractive!"

Margaret kept nodding and smiling in an attempt to prove her sympathy and understanding while her mind whirred and wondered. How had it happened that she had only learnt about village life in her fourth decade of life in Africa?

"Petronella and I are from different tribes. We think that's good – especially for our kids. Petronella runs a business where she trains young Zambians – among them are a couple of relatives of ours. It's a pay-off that works for the village community but it requires firm handling. Petronella is good that way – thank God! She works bloody hard – all hours!

"I get to employ some relatives at my house – too many of course – but we live and learn. Anyway," Henry smiled again and this time Margaret joined in, "this time at the cottage, Milimo cooked us *nshima* – maize-meal porridge – and the kids cooked our steaks on the barbecue. It was an excellent compromise between village life and Lusaka life."

Margaret was unable to confess to Henry that on their last trip to Rhodesia they had been to see a brand-new tourist attraction at the Victoria Falls. The facsimile of an African village, complete with half-naked natives faking a traditional life untouched by colonialism, had been constructed on the edge of a Tribal Trust area. It was part of an initiative by the Rhodesian government in imitation of similar efforts in South Africa. It pretended to honour the 'culture' of the indigenous population while exaggerating a 'civilised' and 'primitive' divide that supported policies of separate development.

"This feels rather prurient," Margaret had whispered.

Charles too had been very uncomfortable.

"How does it feel to work here – this is a job and not a life surely?" He had hissed back.

Nevertheless they had both been fascinated by what they found in the artificial village.

"I had no idea!" Margaret kept repeating while Charles had suddenly needed to ask the so-called villagers many pertinent questions. Both of them had been surprised by the elegant simplicity of the life of the village and the detailed craft work and manufactures of the people.

Their last stop in the village had been at an *nganga,* or witchdoctor, who threw the *hakata* and then told white tourists of the good fortunes awaiting them in a future Rhodesia. Margaret had not been sure if he had a malign eye and had cursed her or if it was her own sense of guilt that had made her feel so bad.

"How could they treat people like creatures in a zoo? Even wild animals in a safari park are allowed more dignity!"

Twenty-One

Bread

The Guest Book. The Cottage, Siavonga.
March 1974
Charles, Margaret, Michael and Richard
*We saw a kudu and a pair of tumbling bateleur eagles on the way
down to the cottage. We stopped to collect some fresh elephant dung
dropped on the road. It is supposed to be very good manure for roses
and the garden. There was still water in the Lusitu River and the
flats were covered with green grass. It makes a difference driving down
this stretch now that it is tarred. We saw the pair of peregrine falcons
behind the cottage again – perhaps they are nesting there. We also
watched a really large shoal of small fish being driven onto the shore
by Tigerfish or something similar. They looked very pretty as they
leapt from the water. Charles thinks they must be lake sardines or
Kapenta, which they are now fishing in Rhodesia. Apparently they
were introduced to Kariba from Lake Tanganyika. They were put
into forty-four gallon oil drums and flown down here in a small
plane but naturalised themselves in the shallower waters of Rhodesia.'*

Margaret often went to the cottage ahead of Charles, taking the two
boys with her if they were home for the holidays. Charles would
follow on the Saturday, Friday night being a traditional night for
club meetings in Lusaka where business was discussed and drinks
and dinner mandatory. They both preferred to travel during daylight

hours because on the last stretch of road across the Zambezi flats it was still possible to see herds of elephant and antelope. Margaret and Charles always hoped to see wild game on their trips to the lake and the two boys spent the last part of each trip hanging out of the car windows in case of a sighting. Charles would not agree to Margaret travelling in the dark on her own in case of something unexpected. There had recently been an accident involving an elephant and an army lorry loaded illegally with local people needing a lift. The driver placed too much confidence in his elephant-sized vehicle and when he unexpectedly encountered real elephant on the road beyond Lusitu he mistakenly thought he could drive on through the herd. The largest bull elephant charged the vehicle and damaged it sufficiently to end its journey. The women and children in the truck were thrown about, heads, arms and legs all battered and broken, and the tiny clinic at Siavonga was stretched to its rather inadequate limits. The bull was stunned and then unsurprisingly killed – perhaps shot by soldiers in the following vehicle – at any rate the tusks vanished for a time and then were found again or other tusks were produced when someone in the government insisted that they belonged to the state. It was all ostensibly very moral as Zambia was a signatory of the Convention on International Trade in Endangered Species at the time.

On one such occasion, Margaret realised she had left the bread for the weekend behind on the kitchen table. There was no phone box that she could call from to ask Charles to collect it so she pulled off the road at a store just outside Kafue and went in on the chance they might have some left. Bread had once again become either unavailable or short. Political problems meant that flour imports were frequently held up. Luckily for Margaret, her cook was an expert bread maker and she could always get flour from friends in the diplomatic service. She was not hopeful of finding any in the roadside store but as Charles and the two boys could eat a loaf between them at breakfast she decided it might be worth the trouble.

The store was dark inside, its windows shuttered and barred. Margaret stopped and waited for her eyes to adjust. There were few customers inside. The owner was measuring out cheap fabric for two women at the far end of the counter and nodded at her to wait. A large, youngish white man leaned on the counter laughing and talking animatedly in Chichewa to two Zambian men. A small girl was using his hand to swing herself in half circles around him. He deftly stopped her from falling without apparently watching her and she concentrated happily on her movements, obviously used to amusing herself while her father chatted. Margaret was impressed by his ease with Chichewa and a little jealous of his pretty, dark-eyed, curly-haired daughter. She looked towards him smiling and he noticed her with a lifted eyebrow.

"*Muli Bwanji* and hello," she greeted him and his companions and then, turning to the child, she said hello to her too. Margaret was a naturally friendly person, and she greeted everyone with the same smile unlike most white Rhodesian women who had different expressions for different races.

The Asian storekeeper came up to see what she wanted.

"Good morning," she said, "Am I going to be lucky today – have you got any bread?"

"You have just missed," the storekeeper waved his hands over the crumbs on the counter.

Margaret shrugged.

"Such is life! *Zikomo*. Thank you anyway."

She turned to leave but the young white man stopped her.

"I can give you a loaf – how much do you need? I've just bought the two dozen loaves for my workers. Salim did me a favour by keeping them for me," he gestured at the storekeeper.

"Really! That would be kind. We are down at the lake for the weekend and I always take some if I can to Milimo who looks after the place for us."

"No problem – wait a mo'."

This time he controlled his daughter's playful game and

continued to swing her all the way up into his arms, then he strode out to his pick-up truck where he deposited her on the back seat and pulled two loaves out from under a tarpaulin.

Margaret dug in her bag for the right amount of *kwacha* but he waved it away.

"You're too kind – I should pay in gold! It's ridiculous that the price is so controlled when it's become such a rarity," Margaret said. "How about an exchange – look – I have a children's wildlife comic that your daughter might like – the *Chongololo* one. My two boys have been reading them on the way down. They're much too old for the magazine these days."

The young man hesitated but Margaret insisted.

"It's free. I get several copies for myself because I do some of the illustrations. Honestly I would be so happy for her to have it."

"Well…" he said, "Okay – I'll enjoy it too. Bonnie, you'll read it to me won't you sweetie-pie? I'm Mark Watson – " he offered his hand to Margaret, "– We live down towards the Gwembe Valley. Are you all right going through the roadblocks on your own?"

"Fine," Margaret smiled. "I carry spare newspapers for them and the soldiers have had the wildlife comic before now too. We get by."

"They've not got much to do anyway," Mark said. "The so-called Freedom Fighters just hang around the taverns drinking beer – they don't try too hard to take the fight across the border to Smith's men."

"Is that so?"

Nobody Margaret knew in Lusaka would have put things that way to her and she responded with platitudes to most of the predictable discussions about the Rhodesian situation, but to this stranger she found herself saying something that she would hardly have allowed herself to think.

"I do wish they would get on with the fighting if that's the only way we can progress. I want it to be over so we can start to treat each other like humans and share a properly elected government. It's not sensible – this – this racism! Why can't we just be civilised – I mean –" Margaret thought how complicated it was to express ideas if you didn't practise expressing them.

Then she laughed.

"I suppose I don't think us whites are very civilised – oh dear – it's exactly the opposite of what we think we are – oh dear –"

Mark's wife must be African – she had expressed herself so badly – would Mark misunderstand her? But Mark laughed quite kindly.

"Well, perhaps when it comes down to it none of us are very civilised if we feel threatened."

"No," said Margaret soberly, "we aren't." She was thinking of her family and their response to the guerrilla incursions into Rhodesia.

"Well, it was nice meeting you Mark," she said. "Goodbye Bonnie – it was nice meeting you too."

The little girl squirmed an acknowledgement of sorts and carried on reading, absorbed in her new wildlife magazine.

TWENTY-TWO

Cousins And Questions

The Guest Book, The Cottage, Siavonga
July 1974
Marielise, Jo, Zanele.
*'Wild, windy night. Exceptionally clear sky for July, I am told,
because haze and dust should make it hard to see across
the lake in winter.*
*A big argument about whether it is crocodile or large legavaans
spoor at Mick's Boat Hire point. Swimmers won the argument by
insisting it was not a crocodile!'*

August 1974
Marielise, Zanele, Michael and Richard.
*'Hazy but warmer. Lake dropping rapidly. Large orangey-pink
centipede about 5 inches long with turquoise stings climbed up the
tent pole above Michael, who opted to sleep in the tent!'*

Marielise began to use the cottage at the lake soon after Margaret
extended the invitation to her. She was able to use it much more
frequently than Margaret was able to because her working hours
and holidays and half-terms allowed her to use the cottage midweek and for longer periods. This also meant that she could
arrange her time at the cottage at different times to Margaret and

though the first weekend they spent together had been pleasant and relaxed they both chose to avoid being there together too often. There were even a couple of weekends when business luncheons occupied the Beaumonts to the displeasure of their sons, Michael and Richard, and they were entrusted to Marielise's care for a weekend at the lake. The boys were away at boarding school most of the year and Margaret wanted them to enjoy the freedom of an outdoor life while they were on holiday in Zambia.

Margaret worried that Charles and Marielise might not get on together for more than the conventional hours allotted for an occasional lunch or dinner, and in any case she liked to devote her time at weekends to Charles. She didn't want Marielise to find her dull and boring in her role as Charles's wife. Marielise preferred not to let her family know very much about her life. She had many secrets to keep and just let them know news that was positive and that they would approve.

At any rate, Margaret and Marielise fell into the habit of communicating by telephone though Marielise happily took charge of some of the chores and errands associated with the cottage for Margaret. She made sure that the gas bottles for the stove and the paraffin cans for the fridge and the storm lanterns were never empty, and that there were adequate candles and insect spray for the bedrooms. She carried messages from Milimo to Mrs Beaumont and from Margaret to Mr Milimo Singani, and checked that the kitchen cupboard always had tea, coffee, salt, sugar and tomato sauce.

Margaret had invited Marielise to use the cottage whenever she wanted if it was free, and soon after, Marielise told Margaret that she would like to bring her boyfriend's child down to the cottage with her. She wanted to clear it with Margaret so that there would be no problems and therefore no questions to answer or to arouse concern.

"She does spend time with her mum," Marielise said, "but her mum is in and out of Chianama Hills Hospital with severe depression and Jo and Bessie aren't married so most of the time, since Zanele was about three, she has lived with me and Jo. She is six now and I love her to bits – she is gorgeous and so bright." Marielise wanted very much to use the cottage and bring her friends from the university down to it and though she had no intention of confiding too many details about them to Margaret, there was the visitors' book to fill in and there was Milimo too. He regarded Margaret with deep deference and respect and Mrs Beaumont's permission was needed for every activity that guests might undertake. Margaret allowed Milimo this authority knowing that there were always guests who took advantage of employees whatever the circumstances.

Margaret was pleased – it would be lovely to have another child enjoying the cottage and the lake.

"Do let her bring a friend with her," she said, "it is so nice for children to have companions."

"Thanks Margaret," said Marielise, "I will do that, but Milimo has children too and at least one of them will be her sort of age."

Margaret for a moment was taken aback. She had not actively discouraged her sons from making friends with the children of African employees, it had never crossed her mind that they might, but then she thought – why not? Times are changing. After all, she understood Zanele might be an African name though nowadays young people chose very unusual names for their children so you couldn't be sure of that. Then because she couldn't help herself and was curious she asked –

"Where is Jo from?" That euphemism for 'what race is he?' And 'what does he do?' which is a way of finding out about the class or status of another person.

Marielise smiled, she was used to fending off questions about Jo and about quite a few of her other friends too, but she knew what Margaret was asking.

"Oh Jo's a white South African. I met him at Varsity but his family have all moved to England. He has met my mum, though ages ago. His dad's a lawyer in London. He's an anthropologist so he is always travelling around Africa and never in one place very long."

That at least was part of Jo's cover story. The other part of Jo's cover story was Marielise herself. She had a proper job and a university flat and could run a car. Jo was her partner and Zanele was as good as her daughter. To a large extent Marielise kept a low profile. She had done history at 'Varsity' in South Africa and sociology at the London School of Economics at that most interesting period of student history in the late sixties but she did not enter into any great controversies in conversation. She wanted to be able to stay in Lusaka for as long a period as possible and be as useful to her friends, Jo and Luke, who needed to stay discreetly and cheaply, and move around as their work demanded.

People like her father, Jacob Wolf, who made known his opinions about Zambian politicians and the Zambian government's lack of support for the guerrillas, who protested too vociferously, simply got deported and that was not necessarily a good thing for the Freedom Movement. Marielise had been in the Freedom Movement long enough to have acquired some discipline. She no longer felt that the Movement needed her voice to be shouting loudly and uselessly at deaf ears. No. The situation had changed dramatically with Oliver Tambo's statement that now the Freedom Movement must move into its war phase. The fight was no longer underground but had to engage in military action to end the evils of Apartheid in South Africa.

Twenty-Three

Paranoia

On Margaret and Charles's return to Zambia after their adventures during the regatta week, they saw a noticeable increase of paranoia and suspicion in Zambia. The papers shrieked about the dangers of spies and invaders from Rhodesia. An apocryphal story went the rounds of the white and expatriate communities claiming that an innocent white tourist had been killed by mobs in Lusaka simply because he had a beard. Apparently the men of the Rhodesian Special Services all had beards and had been seen in every Zambian town. Margaret was glad Charles was clean-shaven and had refused to be an informant.

Sudden curfews were announced and the police went round houses demanding that curtains were closed and a complete blackout maintained. It was hard for anybody to know what was really going on. Down at the lake it was possible to get radio and television pictures from Rhodesia, all very one-sided. British newspapers came by post and there was the World Service from the BBC but their reporting of the early stages of the liberation war was minimal. People knew what they knew, hoped for what they had always hoped for, and believed what they were told by the people most like themselves. It was still possible to be reasonably comfortable in one's suburban bubble, surrounded by fences and servants with the important reinforcement of security that comes from never having your point of view challenged.

For Margaret, life had changed since Charles's experience on Lake Kariba. It was as if she had magically acquired access to information on a different wavelength and the ability to hear sounds on a different frequency. Curiously she noticed that Marielise was already using that frequency and naively she assumed that it was just the university crowd who had that knowledge because they were all more interested in politics. Marielise didn't venture information but if Margaret asked her directly she would say what she had heard without offering a commentary and look at Margaret with that steady assessing look as she spoke. Marielise's information expanded on the brief British reports with details that shocked Margaret and turned her heart to ice. Margaret was learning to uncover what people were really thinking about and what they really meant to say by listening to what they did not say. *Not believing anything that is written in the papers or said on the news helps I suppose*, Margaret thought cynically to herself.

Charles advised, "Look at the numbers, Margaret. They don't add up. How can so few white Rhodesians continue to fund this war or pretend that they can stay in control of the situation indefinitely?

Look at the numbers of armed ZIPRA in Zambia compared to the Zambian Army. Of course Kaunda has to be very afraid that there will be a coup against him."

Margaret no longer asked why they stayed put. From Zambia they could at least make the long roundabout trip down to Rhodesia to see their parents or go all the way to Britain to see the boys. Richard was still at school, but Michael was just beginning his first year at art school. Charles shook his head at the idea of retirement to South Africa.

"How can South Africa not follow the same path as Rhodesia?"

"Australia – Great Britain? Well –" he shrugged, " – I could not feel at home there."

Margaret and Charles's families did provide other pictures of the situation. Steve provided an alternative and critical point of view about the military decisions of the Smith government but the rest of the relatives expressed fear and anger, largely blaming Zambia and a few 'bad lots' for what they described as the 'unrest' along their borders. They said that 'their' Africans were peaceful, law-abiding and happy with the way things were. Look at the townships – there was no trouble there. For sure it was a problem now that their sons would all be conscripted into the armed services on leaving school but they all knew that they would win this war, after all, they had the backing and support of South Africa and its military. Yes – it was the Africans who suffered most – they died in greater numbers than the white soldiers or the 'terrorists' but that was the fault of the 'terrorists' and showed what evil and ignorant people they were and how easily they were seduced by Russian propaganda.

Margaret and Charles looked at each other in alarm when they thought of their sons being conscripted. What would happen to Michael and Richard when they left university? Conscription should and must follow but the two boys were old enough to have their own opinions and to want to make their own decisions. Margaret and Charles had sent them to an expensive, multi-racial boarding school in Johannesburg and then moved them to a sixth-form college in Britain. They wanted Michael and Richard to feel part of a future multi-racial Africa but both boys were Rhodesian-born and therefore citizens of a country run by racist whites. Though Charles thought it natural enough that his sons would spend some time in training as part of an army, he could not feel happy about the Rhodesian war and Margaret was very much against it. In any case, how could they have two sons in a Rhodesian Army that was making incursions into Zambia while they lived in Zambia's capital city? Charles said to Margaret that the war might 'all be over' by the time the boys graduated, but Margaret thought that was wishful thinking and neither of them could imagine what life would be like when it was 'all over'.

Twenty-Four

Easter

The Guest Book, The Cottage, Siavonga
Easter 1975
Charles and Margaret, Marielise, Jo and Zanele.
'Cool, breezy, bright weather.
The manager at the Siavonga Inn tells us the lake is rising and
water is still pouring over the Mosi-O-Tunya falls The drive
down was slow and dusty because of road repairs and deviations.
Zanele found an arthropod which Milimo calls a 'hamagutu' – it
looks like a scorpion without a tail or sting but quite scary
according to Zanele. (Later note – it is a whip scorpion or properly
a Damon variegatus order Amblypygi.)
We saw a fish eagle – and seagulls! (Here in the middle of
Africa – thousands of miles from the sea!) Kingfishers, hornbills,
and cormorants. Margaret says that is the most water birds she has
ever seen on the lake. They seem not to be established here in large
numbers yet. Will that change? The lake is deep below the cottage
though – so not good feeding for waders.

It was Easter and the long weekend. The best time to be at the lake
was always after the rains, when the lake levels were still rising and
the weather was not too hot, the garden would be lush and green
and there wouldn't be much haze or dust, the only problem would
be that too many mosquitoes and insects would also be thriving.

Margaret and Charles were at the cottage and Margaret had persuaded Marielise to come down with Jo, her boyfriend, and Zanele, Jo's child on Easter Sunday with the intention that they would stay on after the Beaumonts returned to Lusaka on their own.

"Are you going to be okay on those iron beds?" asked Margaret, looking up and down at Jo's lanky frame. "Charles is not too comfortable on them but you are even taller!"

Jo smiled, "I often sleep in much less comfortable beds," he said with real feeling. "This one is a treat by comparison."

He was thin with slightly stooped shoulders, as if he was always having to bend down to the level of other people. His hair was long and wiry and kept escaping from the elastic ponytail holder that his daughter had lent him and made him wear with very detailed instructions:

"First you put it over your fingers like that – no Jo – like this – see! Then you hold your hair – no Jo – with the other hand Jo! Oh LET me do it for you Jo."

Behind his John Lennon glasses his eyes were kind and bright, and when he smiled his cheeks wrinkled attractively. He looked very young to have a child. Margaret could see that Marielise adored them both. Her face had a glow of happiness when she looked at the two of them.

"I'm for a swim," said Charles, stretching and getting to his feet.

"How do you feel about swimming in the lake?" asked Margaret, looking at Zanele a little anxiously. "We feel that as no one but us swims at this point in the lake and as it is so rocky and steep there won't be any Bilharzia. Bilharzia usually needs stagnant reedy water."

"Not a problem," Jo said, "Zanele is quite a good little swimmer and she has arm bands."

"Don't you worry about crocodiles?" Marielise wanted to know. She liked to swim but didn't want to go into the lake if she was by herself.

"Same for them really," said Charles confidently. "The lake is vast – crocodiles from the original river would have been widely dispersed and, being shy creatures who hate being disturbed, they will stay away from places where there are people and houses. In any case this rocky, steep bit of coast here doesn't lend itself to basking in the sun which is what crocs have to do being reptiles. We are also close to the original river bed here so the lake is about as deep as it gets only metres away."

"So we're safe enough – as safe as we can be anywhere," said Jo. He picked up Zanele and followed Charles down the long path to the water's edge. Marielise and Margaret gathered up towels, mats, books and some orange squash. Milimo had already carried the deckchairs down to the bottom terrace. He met them on his way back.

"Thank you Milimo, we'll have a salad for lunch," said Margaret, "Please lay five places on the veranda and could you bring down the coffee at eleven o'clock."

Marielise smiled at Milimo, "Good morning Milimo," she said, "how is your wife?"

Milimo smiled. "Soon we will have another child."

Margaret said in a heated whisper when Milimo had gone, "That darn priest encourages Milimo to go on having children. What is to become of all these children? There is no work around here and only the most basic primary school. I have brought down the boys' books and some magazines for the school but I don't think they do very much with them.

"Are you religious at all Marielise?"

Marielise shook her head and smiled.

"I think I am best described as agnostic."

The water of the lake so blue from the cottage was greenish when they were swimming in it. It was warm and rocked gently. As Marielise ducked under the surface, a million tiny flakes of suspended mica reflecting the dispersed sunlight sparkled around her. The mica was pretty even though the water was not clear. She felt that familiar cramp of fright in her stomach as she thought of herself swimming hundreds of feet above the floor of the Zambezi Valley. The lake was so deep – so very deep. The water must get so cold and so dark near the bottom. Even before the valley was flooded the land below this rocky hillside must have been in shadow for part of each day. There was a lost and drowned wild world down there, mysterious and somehow still present. A world that had not chosen its changes but still was somehow alive and part of life. What was happening down there? What strange embryonic developments were stirring in the cold darkness of the lake?

Charles, resting in the deckchair, was watching Jo with interest as he played with Zanele on the beach by the water's edge.

"Look at that young man, Margaret," he said, "he is exceptionally strong and tough. I wonder what he does to get so fit."

Margaret, too well-mannered to comment on a guest, did not reply, but she had noted Jo's physique from under her hat and over her book. He had the dark, red-brown skin of someone who lives outdoors and, though thin, he had the beautiful curved muscles of an African labourer. Margaret had also noticed that he had a scar on his shoulder that gleamed as if newly healed and that he winced as if the scar still tightened when he lifted Zanele.

TWENTY-FIVE

Tea And Sympathy

The Guest Book. The Cottage, Siavonga.
June 1975
Charles and Margaret
'Let us cultivate our garden.' Voltaire's **Candide**
(quoted by Father Patrick).
*'I have been reading about this new way of growing vegetables
without using chemicals that has been started in Australia. It is
about growing mixed crops rather than monoculture so the same
crops can grow permanently. It uses very little water and it very
environmental. It sounds very sensible for this part of Africa.
Charles says that it sounds rather like traditional African
agriculture and will not be very productive. I will try and find out
some more about it. I have just finished reading* **Silent Spring**
*by Rachel Carson. They say that Lake Kariba is full of pesticides
and DDT and that it is in crocodile eggs and even Fish Eagle eggs.'*

Father Patrick sat in the deckchair on the cottage veranda drinking
tea with Margaret. She offered him some home-made biscuits
decorated with sugar icing. The tea was pleasant enough and he
could see that Margaret had made a big pot. At least there would
be second and third cups to be had. If he was still here when
Charles arrived perhaps he would be offered some cold beer. He
could hear the paraffin fridge humming and vibrating in the

119

kitchen and he had noticed when Margaret took the milk out that it was well-stocked with brown bottles of Castle beer. What it was to have good connections! No one could find beer in the stores in Lusaka but Charles probably knew the managing director of the brewery. Some of the Lusaka priests did well too. The brewery director was, after all, a Catholic and an Irishman.

Father Patrick was relieved that Margaret did not make Milimo wait in the kitchen to serve tea for them. He had known Milimo for a long time, since he was a boy of ten and his mother had come to stay with Father Patrick. He regarded Milimo as his son. In fact, Milimo was presently his chief server at the church in Siavonga. He took care of the missals and vestments, and saw that the church was cleaned and his wife, Mrs Milimo Singani, would bring in garishly coloured flowers, canna lilies, hibiscus, or bougainvillea when they were in bloom for the altar. Father Patrick had taught Milimo to read and write in the small bush school he had run for the local Tonga so long ago. Indeed Milimo's careful, clear writing was almost a facsimile of Father Patrick's own.

It was Father Patrick who had suggested to Margaret that perhaps she would like to employ Milimo as a caretaker and servant at the cottage. At the time the Federation was breaking up and jobs anywhere were hard to find for people without connections to the Zambian political parties of ZANC and UNIP. Here they were thirteen years later and Milimo was still gainfully employed at the cottage and Margaret and Father Patrick still saw each other regularly. Margaret, Father Patrick observed, was one of those women who believe it is their duty to help other people whenever possible. For a white woman from a colonial background, she wasn't bossy and that was a relief. She didn't tell people how to improve their lives as some white Lusaka ladies on charitable missions did, but she was ready to act when asked. Books, newspapers, magazines and second-hand clothes and kitchenware could be found in the boot of her car at weekends and would be given to Milimo or Father Patrick to distribute as needed.

On this occasion however, Margaret wanted to talk to Father Patrick about Milimo and specifically about Milimo's children and contraception.

"He already has three children and a fourth on the way. I know Catholics are opposed to contraception but I thought perhaps you would understand more than anyone the hopelessness of providing for a large family in Zambia at the moment. He might listen to you – if – " said Margaret, leaving unsaid that vast gap into which Father Patrick's doctrinal beliefs must fit.

Father Patrick sighed. "Have you talked to Milimo about this yourself – or to his wife?"

"I hesitate to," replied Margaret, "he is a man after all and his wife doesn't speak much English. Won't she have to do as he wishes? Charles refuses to talk about it with them."

"Well – " Father Patrick said, thinking Charles was fortunate to duck the issue, "Milimo is his own person – many of us priests would not encourage our parishioners to have more children than they can feed and educate but it is also Tonga tradition and beliefs that drive the having of so many children. Only ten years ago Milimo would have been lucky if half his children survived. It is a great honour for a man to have so many children and for them to live. The Tonga also have beliefs about sex – "

Margaret interrupted him. She didn't want to discuss her employee's sex practice with a religious man. It didn't seem right.

"It's Milimo's housing," she said, "It's inadequate and though we have provided another hut so that he has two rooms, they are both small and unbearably hot. Charles thinks that we can't go on helping out and creating dependencies. Zambia is independent now and Charles thinks that must apply to its people too.

What can I do?" It was a question that she did not expect to be answered.

"Probably not a great deal," admitted the priest, watching Margaret. He could see that she was bothered by the problem. "At least money is not the answer – even lots of it. Perhaps you can help Milimo make some savings for the future. I'll look into possibilities for you."

"That would be kind," said Margaret relieved, "Thank you so much."

Margaret did not know that during the week when there were no visitors, Milimo often sat on the cottage veranda. Sometimes his friends would come and sit with him. When there was no one around Milimo's children played in the garden. Milimo never went inside the cottage except to clean it and prepare it for guests.

Father Patrick thought perhaps it was time for him to go but something made him hold on.

"Any chance of another cup of tea?" he asked, "I do so enjoy a properly made cup of tea!"

Margaret looked straight at him for a moment and smiled, and he saw briefly the kind thoughtfulness and honesty of her nature.

He stirred his tea slowly and said, without looking too directly at her.

"It is hard to bear isn't it – this awful war across the border that crosses into our lives all the time."

"Oh it is – it is!" Margaret responded at once, "It is the hatred and the intolerance that everyone shows towards each other. I feel as if I am being destroyed inside. My family in Rhodesia have become so bitter and angry. It's as if they blame Charles and me for it because we live in Zambia. They were – are – good people: 'salt of the earth' is what my father used to say, but what they are doing is wrong – so wrong – and I can't see a way out for anyone. The things that people do and say in Zambia are also wrong and – well silly sometimes – but I don't blame them – or anyone.

"I wish I could say who was at fault – I wish I could see how things could be put right without any more killing – but how…" she faltered and was silent.

"It is easier to take sides," said Father Patrick reflectively, "but people like you who care about both sides are the people who will be needed in the future. There is so much good in people – and kindness – I see it all the time, even when there is ignorance.

"Each of us is a sinner needing forgiveness but when a whole country goes to war for bad reasons, it does seem like an insurmountable problem. Charles I know has some faith that God will give him the answers – but what about you, Margaret?"

Margaret gave him a desperate look.

"I can't wait for heaven to compensate us." Then she smiled again,

"Sorry Father Patrick, but I need to feel that there is something small I can do that makes a difference now!"

"You are doing that, Margaret," said Father Patrick quietly, "You are doing it Margaret: you are looking after Milimo, and your garden, and Charles and your boys – and you do these things well and with love.

"Have you heard of Candide? He is a character in a story written by Voltaire, a French philosopher, and his advice is that we must each tend our gardens. We can only do what we can do."

Father Patrick finished his third cup of tea and stood up to go. Charles had not arrived and the beer would not be forthcoming. He thought a moment then said,

"Oh I have an idea that might help Milimo, why don't you get him to apply to the council for his own plot and then encourage him to start building on it? If he works at it steadily over the next few years he will at the least have the security of his own home for the future – whatever that may be."

TWENTY-SIX

Earthquake

'When the lake was eventually filled in 1963, a series of particularly strong shocks occurred. Ten epicentres were calculated by the U.S. Coast and Geodetic Survey: all were situated in the deepest part of the lake, the strongest having a magnitude of 6.1, and one of its after-shocks having a magnitude of 6. Several hundred tremors occurred in September 1963, and seismic activity then decreased – although fifty shocks occurred in 1963; thirty-nine in 1968; and several in 1969 and 1970.'

Published in Chapter 9 of *The Social and Environmental Effects of Large Dams:* Volume 1. Overview. Wadebridge Ecological Centre, Worthyvale Manor Camelford, Cornwall PL32 9TT, UK, 1984 by Edward Goldsmith and Nicholas Hildyard.

The Guest Book. The Cottage, Siavonga.
July 1975
Charles, Margaret, Marielise, Jo and Zanele
'THERE WAS AN EARTHQUAKE!'
(Dictated to Jo by Zanele and then signed by her.)
*'There was an enormous earthquake that made the ground shake
a lot then the snakes came out because they were frightened too.
ZANELE.'*

*'Charles thinks the earthquake may have a magnitude of 5 because
we were not the only household to experience it. We did see a
snake afterwards – unusual as it was after the sun had set – and
Milimo said there were very many snakes seen in Siavonga.
Apparently snakes are disturbed by vibrations like earthquakes but
we have no way of checking on the stories or numbers.'*

The earthquake struck as they sat watching the orange sun
disappear into an opalescent, turquoise lake.

Charles had seen to the sundowners, beers for the men, gin
and tonics for the ladies and orange squash for 'the most special
lady of all' – Zanele.

As he sat down they heard a sound like a huge train racing
over the escarpment and down the drive towards them. Then
the shaking began. It lasted for less than a minute. Zanele was
on Jo's lap and at first was not quite sure if he had made the
noise and shaking as a game for her. When she saw the spilt
drinks and saw the white faces of the grown-ups she kept
screaming on and on. Jo held her tight, covered her mouth
gently with his broad hand and hushed her. Marielise and
Charles were on their feet; Margaret was trying to hold jugs and
glasses in place. The storm lanterns waiting to be lit by Milimo
were swinging wildly.

"Oh my God! Oh my God!" Marielise kept saying, as she went
to kneel at Jo and Zanele's side and put her arms around them
both while she kept looking up at the veranda roof.

"Everything's okay!" Charles said. He was looking around to
see what had fallen or moved. "I'll check the gas bottles are turned
off in the kitchen."

"The dam?" Margaret put her hand out to Charles, trying to
sound calm and not frighten the child.

"Don't worry woman!" Charles sounded irritated. "It was just
a tremor. Nothing big at all! You'll see."

Milimo appeared looking flustered. Margaret heard the shrill screaming of his children in the hut above. Perhaps things had fallen over there.

"Are you all right?" she asked, "I'll come up and see."

"Madam," he said, "my wife is afraid for the baby." And Margaret went straight up to see if all was well and to reassure his family. Once it was established that all had survived without harm in both places, Charles sent Milimo up to the police station to see what gossip and possible information he could gather.

Earthquakes were the topic of discussion while Charles and Jo cooked steak on the *braai*.

"You really mean that!" Jo kept saying.

"You really mean they built Kariba Dam on a seismic fault line!

"You really mean that everyone knew that there were regular earthquakes here before the dam was built?

"You really mean that the earthquakes have steadily increased since the dam was built – and they've got stronger!"

Every time Charles said that he did mean it, Jo broke out laughing.

"It is quite insane – why choose this particular place then?"

Margaret could see that Charles was feeling rather defensive. He had had nothing to do with the decisions about the location of Kariba, which were all made when he was still at school, but he had given his heart to the idea of a Central African Federation that would provide security for white Rhodesians and hope for Africans and some kind of justice for everyone. Though the Federation had broken up over a decade before and all the countries around seemed to be collapsing into chaos and wars, Charles still hankered after his lost dream. Its failure hurt him deeply and he had found nothing to replace it. He set out however to explain the reasons for the choice of the Kariba Dam site over the Kafue Dam site and why he still thought that the shared responsibility of providing power might help the region. Jo listened without criticism. Once again Margaret had a sense that Jo and Marielise watched and withheld in some way that she couldn't quite define. However she liked Jo for his politeness and lack of aggression in the discussion. Perhaps he was a teacher who encouraged his students to have their own opinions. Her sons seemed to value that quality in their teachers at sixth form level.

Changing the subject slightly, Charles and Margaret regaled Marielise and Jo with the tales of the politics around the building of the new North Bank Power Station which was soon to be commissioned. Zanele however was getting tired and rather bored. Milimo returned with news that there was no news. A few of the more fragile huts in the valley had been shaken to bits and badly stored equipment in the government workshop had fallen off shelves. A car left without its handbrake on had run a little way down the hill. No one had been hurt, only children and a few women were frightened; on the whole people were less bothered about the tremors the more frequently they happened.

It should be the other way around, thought Marielise, as she and Jo tucked Zanele into the top bunk in their room. Jo asked if she would like to be in the bottom bunk after the 'noisy shaky-shaking' as she called it but she yawned and said no. Marielise and Jo looked at each other. There was no way they could predict the next tremor so best to leave Zanele where she would be happiest.

Different kinds of earthquakes, human disasters, became the subject of conversation as they sat outside in the warm dark with beer and wine. Charles and Jo had exchanged the kinds of credentials that men did exchange, about fathers and work and 'where did you grow up' and 'who do you know that I know?' Charles felt that he and Jo had established enough mutual history and so he began to talk regional politics and events with him.

"What about South Africa, Jo? Do you think they will always support Rhodesia as they do now? I've been told," Charles said, "that there are South African soldiers in the Zambezi Valley on the opposite side of this lake right now!"

Jo looked across the lake to the Matusadona hills that could be seen clearly in the moonlight and shifted his long legs uneasily.

"Mmmh," he said reflectively, "there has been stuff written about how South Africa sees Rhodesia as its sixth state – but also about how South Africa supports Rhodesia as a buffer state against what it believes will be a future threat from the *'donker nord'* – 'the black north' as it calls it. There's a pay-off however. The South Africans want Smith to make a deal with black Rhodesians to end the fighting. Vorster doesn't care about Rhodesia unless Rhodesia protects South Africa. It fits with the theory of Apartheid to have Rhodesia as a Bantustan like Zululand, except of course Rhodesia would have a shared government of blacks and whites together. Smith won't buy it though – he's too stupid. It might be an answer for him in the end.

"The war in Rhodesia – actually the war in the region – does not suit South Africa at all. It is good experience for their soldiers but that is all really."

Charles took a while to digest these ideas. Margaret could see that ironically he found some hope in the cynicism of them. He might consider a life in the Bantustan of Rhodesia if there was no more war and he could retire to his beloved farm. Margaret wondered how long such a Bantustan might last but she left the men to do the talking. She looked across to Marielise, who was listening with interest. Several times Marielise looked as if she would speak and then seemed to bite her tongue. Margaret wondered what was going on in her head – she was not really a quiet type.

"Well," said Charles after a short silence, "I would love the war to end but you are right: Smith will not make that move and, well, white Rhodesians are very proud of their soldiers and their heroism and commitment – there will have to be many more deaths first."

Margaret felt her chest tighten and freeze. Just across the water, just down the Zambezi Valley to the east and west were hundreds of men secretly getting ready to kill each other in perverse and horrible ways. Could they themselves escape? She must try to get Charles to leave – they must take the boys and go somewhere – anywhere – safe.

"What effect do you think the death of Herbert Chitepo will have on the terrorists, Jo? Was it a faction who had killed him as Kaunda said – or was it the Rhodesians?"

Margaret shuddered. Chitepo had been killed outside his house in Lusaka by such a huge bomb that both she and Charles had woken up, even though they lived over a mile away.

Jo said that he didn't have an idea who might have been responsible but the outcome was bad for everyone. He thought that Chitepo was an intelligent and educated man who was a good leader.

"The only way forward for Rhodesia will be through discussion and talks," Jo said. "It goes on informally all the time anyway. Chitepo would have been a good person to talk to."

PART 2
MARIELISE

ONE

Birdwatching

The Guest Book. The Cottage, Siavonga.
September 1976
Marielise and Jo.

A good weekend for birds – there were several paradise flycatchers nesting in the Trichelia Emetica. They are a delight to see with their chestnut colouring, long tail feathers and blue heads. I also saw a grey woodland kingfisher further down the plot. Even better I heard a water dikkop in the early evening and first thing in the morning by the shore. And I heard an owl – probably a little Scops. A superb weekend. I also got a couple of chapters of my research written up. I have made a herb garden behind the kitchen and planted ginger, chillies and coriander as well as parsley and rosemary – Milimo will water them. Hope they survive.'

A brief scowl in the mirror, a splash of cold water, the same shapeless tee-shirt over the same old bikini, and Marielise was ready for the day. She stepped barefoot from the shower onto the dusty path behind the cottage and into the kitchen by the back door. Milimo was at the sink with last night's dishes. Six storm lanterns were lined up on the kitchen shelf, each smoky and blackened from the night before.

"Good morning, Milimo. How are you today?" she greeted him.

"Good morning, Marielise. I am well," Milimo said. At her request he no longer addressed her as Madam.

Marielise had first considered using his family name and title – Mr Singani – and asking him to call her Miss Wolf out of mutual respect but then made the opposite decision. Mocking herself, she said in a fake South African accent,

"Bleery 'ell no! Respect tradition is right – but change is right on! After the revolution we'll all be equal. Maybe. Whenever. Soon. Perhaps. Anyway this is my place for relaxing and letting the world be itself."

Marielise thought of Jo with an inward smile. He did not allow any of the comrades to express doubt about the revolution to him. "It's a necessary discipline," he said. "Good training." Doubts raised by comrades were discussed at political education meetings and were always resolved positively. Jo might let Marielise rib him about its certainty in private or in bed. She was his woman then rather than his comrade and discipline between the sheets was restorative for them both. It was a game and by the end it was not a challenge to his authority. Jo had promised to drive down later that evening to join her at the cottage but his arrival always had more of the perhaps and maybe about it than the future revolution.

Marielise walked through the kitchen onto the veranda picking up her notebooks on the way. There was a fresh and refreshing pot of tea waiting for her. Delicious and thirst-quenching. She dumped her pile of notebooks on the veranda table, poured herself a mug of tea and started down the long slasto steps to sit on the wall at the end of the garden above the lake. It was time to observe the rituals due to the gods of nature – to sit quietly and stare at the calm of Lake Kariba and the distant blue hills of the Matusadona, with her binoculars round her neck and her *Robert's Birds of South Africa* on her lap.

As she turned the pages, she thought of her cousin Michael, and wondered how he was getting on at art school in Britain. He too, loved to watch birds and his knowledge was far greater than hers.

Marielise had encouraged Michael to study art. He had a real gift for drawing and the desire and ability to apply himself. Michael had needed encouragement because Charles was not pleased with his son's choice. Art for Charles was artful and not serious. Pleasant enough perhaps, decorative maybe, and useful when Margaret educated young people about wildlife and conservation with her drawings. It was a good hobby for her that gave her a little pocket money. It was most definitely not something that a man would do. Charles could not justify to himself any adult male taking up a career in painting, let alone his eldest son. He might as well be a confidence trickster. Still, Charles tried to reserve his opinion and wait and see. He did not realise that Margaret, as well as Michael and Richard, could see how strongly he disapproved of Michael's chosen career.

Perhaps, Marielise hoped, *Charles will blame me for Michael's choices rather than Margaret. It is always easier for families to blame an outsider than to cope with divisions within the family.* At least she was carrying out Charles's and Margaret's wishes with regard to Milimo. He was getting on very well with making concrete blocks for the house he was to build. She had brought down two sacks of cement for him this weekend, and if Jo managed to get away, he would bring another two. Milimo wasn't doing quite so well on the business on finding a plot for himself. He worked very hard at making the blocks but seemed to feel no pressure from the possibility that one day the job at the cottage would go.

"There is no water, Marielise." Milimo appeared on soundless feet. "The council have turned it off again. I have already filled a bucket for the toilet – it is there."

"Damn!" Marielise said, "Well we'll have to live with less water then! Can we store some in a tank or something? I'll see what can be done. It's sad for the garden if you can't water it anymore Milimo."

It was Jo who came up with a way of solving the water supply problem when he arrived later that day.

Marielise had walked up the steps to meet him when he parked under the *marula* tree close to Milimo's hut when she noted with a smile that the whole history of the cottage was recorded in front of Milimo's home. Paint and paraffin tins, oil and food cans were arranged in a row each containing a flowering plant. Some plants were from Margaret's garden and others, probably medicinal, were from the bush.

"Wherever is Milimo's food garden?" she asked herself, surprised not to have noticed before.

She told Jo of the man-made drought affecting the cottage.

"Water can't be pumped from the lake – it's too far," he said. "Tell you what – Milimo can you dig a large, round hole on the second terrace below the cottage, line it with bricks and cement and we'll use it as a storage tank for the cottage. That looks like the only possible site without too many rocks. We can also take a dip in it too if it's too hot to go all the way down to the lake – not a swim of course and Milimo can water the garden from it afterwards. Margaret will love the idea of saving water."

"Mmmh," Marielise said, "Do you think Milimo could have his garden there too?"

"Can you believe," Jo said to Marielise afterwards, "we sit above this immense expanse of water and no one in Siavonga can turn on a tap. We are down the road from the power station and have no electricity! We are all mad! What is this government doing?"

"What can Zambia do?" asked Marielise, "It hasn't enough resources and doesn't have enough people who know what to do yet."

She grinned, "We are much better off here when there are power cuts. Imagine the people in their air-conditioned palaces on Bilharzia Bay, sweating in the dark of their concrete bedrooms – at the least we have our paraffin lanterns and the breeze through the mosquito mesh! This is the life!"

A little later Marielise remembered something she had wanted to tell Jo.

136

"Do you remember the wide sandy beach in the inlet on the way to the government harbour? The one that we walked across last time we were here? The sand has all gone.

The last time there was a very big storm over Siavonga the gully above the inlet became a raging cascade and washed it all away. The sand must have been two or three metres thick but now the inlet is bare rock with a little smelly water running through it."

Jo looked at Marielise in disbelief.

"Come and see," she said. "What does happen to all the earth and sand that washes into the lake? Will the lake eventually silt up?"

Two

Reporting The War

Margaret heard about the bomb at Woolworths in Salisbury first from her family by phone and then from the World Service. She could not imagine it taking place in the street she had been walking down only two weeks before. She had been on her way to Meikles Hotel to have tea with Anne, her old school friend. Salisbury had looked so familiar and safe, very staid in fact, so comfortably provided with every good thing. Not like a city in a country at war. The shops had plenty of consumables. By contrast, Zambia was the country that looked more and more as if it had been defeated. Shopkeepers in Lusaka stretched out single lines of bottles of bleach and scouring powder as a decoration of sorts on rows and rows of empty shelves. Shoppers glanced in from the entrances of shops and left knowing there was no mealie-meal, no flour, no rice, no bread and no beer.

Marielise heard about the bomb from a colleague at the university and then saw it reported in several newspapers. As usual she collated all the information, keeping the newspaper cuttings and writing up a summary of the reporting.

Then she waited for the inevitable reprisals, the first of which came three months later.

Unsurprisingly Marielise and Margaret heard from different

sources and at different times about the reprisals inflicted by the Rhodesian forces and the large numbers of deaths in the refugee and guerrilla camps in Mozambique.

The freedom fight in Rhodesia had in some ways followed historic tribal routes. ZAPU, under Joshua Nkomo, was largely from the Ndebele tribe and had moved north into Zambia across the Zambezi Valley, a traditional route for carrying out raids during the previous century. Here it had the support of Zambia under Kaunda and received help from the Russians in the form of training and weapons.

ZANU, under several leaders including Chitepo, Tekere, Tongararo and Mugabe, was largely drawn from the Shona people and had gone east into Mozambique, where there were related tribal groups and where it was supported by Frelimo, the new government of Mozambique, and by the Chinese who likewise provided training and weapons. Both ZANU and ZAPU were building up armies for invasion while sending small guerrilla groups into Rhodesia to create fear and destabilise it.

At this point in the war, the Rhodesian forces, which comprised black and white soldiers together, were well-trained, well-disciplined and had excellent intelligence and the high morale that accompanies all of those facts. They also had the backing of the South African Army and their intelligence services. White Rhodesians saw their soldiers as courageous heroes. They were hated by the guerrillas but also respected and feared as enemies.

In the townships of Rhodesia there was little obvious evidence of support for the Freedom Fighters but there was also an increasing resistance to the government of Smith by word of mouth, in publications and in the opinions of black Rhodesians.

The reprisals were conducted with immense efficiency, effectiveness and cold-hearted ruthlessness – or was it hot-blooded ferocity? Only a small number of black and white soldiers carried out the operations with the backup of helicopter gunships. The white soldiers, using black balaclavas to disguise their skin, pretended to be Frelimo soldiers; and drove directly onto the parade ground at the guerrilla camp of Chimoio. As Jo said to Marielise with amazement and even some reluctant admiration: "What unbelievable *chutzpah!*"

Using a loudspeaker, they announced that Zimbabwe had fallen to the Freedom Fighters. As hundreds of excited guerrillas rushed onto the parade ground they gunned them down. As the guerrillas fled into the bush, the helicopter gunships pursued them. Well over a thousand people died. All such large encampments included refugees and ordinary people as well as soldiers. That was the way of the war in the bush. There were women and non-combatants among the dead.

Marielise was sickened by the news, which she read in newspapers and heard on the radio, but also got from as many sources as possible including those journalists who visited the university. Many journalists had encamped in Zambia to report on the Rhodesian war and they got their information on the grapevine.

"And the beer-vine and the whisky-vine," said Charles cynically.

However there were journalists who actually did visit the bombed and devastated guerrilla camps and came back with horror stories, some of which never made the international press. It was, after all, the time of the Cold War and the Western press was anti-communist and economical with the truth. All black guerrillas were supported by the Soviets and their allies, and as a result, the reasons behind their cause could not be told.

Margaret and Charles had their news from the Zambian, Rhodesian and South African newspapers. In each case the reporting was one-sided. Charles and Margaret doubted and hoped: they doubted that the reprisals and the war would bring peace; they hoped that some of the reporting at least was true and that it was that simple – the bad guys versus the good guys with the good guys winning – but still they doubted.

South Africa and Rhodesia created an armed opposition movement to the Frelimo government in Mozambique. It included

Portuguese dissidents and mercenaries. It was small, well-financed, and had no social policy for the country excepting to cause mayhem but it was presented as the legitimate representative of rational anti-communist, anti-terrorist freedom instead of what it actually was – part of the Cold War between Russia and the West.

Marielise and Jo watched the increasing destruction of the fragile new state of Mozambique by this new force with horror.

Charles and Margaret thought that maybe it did prove that independent African countries would not be capable of self-government in the foreseeable future. They were told categorically that Renamo was proof of the resistance of most Mozambicans to the Frelimo government.

In spite of Renamo's so-called popularity, attacks inside Rhodesia increased. A bridge was blown up as a train crossed over it, the border town of Umtali was attacked, white missionaries and farmers in isolated places were murdered.

Marielise tried to maintain a sense of detachment from some of the murders inside Rhodesia. She could not imagine taking physical action against her own family in a war. In Rhodesia it seemed clear that it was a race war – blacks against whites. She was sure it would not be like that in South Africa. She personally knew so many whites who were engaged in the fight against Apartheid. She was glad that she had spent such a small part of her life in Rhodesia, she did not have friends there, and could not even picture the place; but then she did know Charles and Margaret and had met their sons and Uncle Steve once or twice at family gatherings. She could not help but see their anxiety and concern and feel for them. She discussed them with Jo, who agreed that they were decent people and would adapt better than most to a future black government in Zimbabwe. It sounded fine but Marielise had increasing doubts about most white people's ability to adapt.

When they have fought and lost they won't be able to forgive even if they were guilty. Is it possible for those Africans who endured injustice and suffering to forgive? she thought, *And if they don't – what then?*

She did not permit herself to think that it would be a miracle if those guerrillas without the training and conviction of a Social Materialist perspective on the Freedom Struggle could forgive the wrongs they had suffered. Few people in the bush wars knew what the Geneva Convention was, let alone applied it to their own actions.

For Marielise, politics was still theoretical.

It became less theoretical after the first Rhodesian plane was shot down.

Marielise came home from a student tutorial to find Jo in the dark in their bedroom with the curtains drawn. Zanele was having supper with the family next door – a last minute arrangement, Marielise gathered.

"What's wrong Jo?" Marielise was peeved to find him on the bed with his face in the pillow. How could someone so tough find an ordinary head cold so debilitating, especially when they were supposed to be joining friends for a meal in an hour? What else could be wrong after all?

"You heard about the plane being shot down?" asked Marielise, pulling back the curtains just a little. "It's a horrible business and very bad press for ZAPU."

Jo sat up. He said with difficulty, as if his cold had thickened sufficiently to make speech difficult, "My friends were on the plane. My friends – with their children – them – the ones who helped get me and other comrades out of Rhodesia with plane tickets."

Then Jo broke down and sobbed until he was hoarse and could not stop coughing. Marielise put her arms around him and was filled with a sense of dread.

It was a gruesome story. The plane carrying holidaymakers from Kariba South had been hit by a missile. Good flying by the pilot crash-landed the plane with eighteen survivors, some of whom set off to find water. The ZAPU men who had hit the plane followed up their missile hit until they reached the crash and then robbed and murdered those of the passengers who were still at the site. Among them were a family committed to political change who had generously provided airfares to refugees passing through Rhodesia from South Africa. Jo knew them personally and had eaten at their home.

Jo, passionate about his beliefs, was also passionately loyal to his friends. He was completely broken by the news he had received that afternoon and the dreadful contradictions of the situation he found himself in. Marielise was forced to face the reality of the political choices she had made. They would become more and more personal, but never, ever, any more, would they seem straightforward or simple. The conflict was crashing out of control and the fragments of that explosion caused such random damage that everyone was a victim.

THREE

Murder

The Guest Book. The Cottage, Siavonga.
October 1976
Charles and Margaret
*'Two crocs seen at Eagles Rest – 4 and 5 ft long by Piet. Hot, still,
clear skies, government harbour unusable as the slipway is well
above the water level. Lake still dropping.*
*Problems with the paraffin fridge. Piet fixed it for now but says we
are unlikely to get replacement parts as it is so old.'*

When Margaret heard the story she was down at the cottage with
Charles.

Piet, their neighbour from around the eastern bay, came by to
see if he could help Charles fix the old gas fridge at the cottage.

"Did you hear about the murder in the valley?" he said in his
rich, deep guttural voice. "That mad man from Zimbabwe with
his African wife? Do you know him?"

Margaret abruptly changed her focus from worrying about the
limp salads and melting ice in her cool box to what Piet was saying.

"Do you mean Mark Watson?" she said coldly. Mark had been
kind to her at the Kafue store when she had been trying to buy
bread for the weekend a while ago – perhaps a year or more ago.

"That's him. That's the chap. Dead now though. Horrible –

and his wife and their little girl – only ten years old I think."

Margaret felt sick and sweaty. She needed a drink of cold water and poured herself a glass from the bottle in the warm fridge. Charles had already asked Piet what had happened and Piet told them in some detail.

"Mark used to hang out in the tavern in the village near his home with some of those so-called ZIPRA fighters who never do go and fight." Piet pronounced tavern as 'tarvern' as Zambians both said it and wrote it.

"He said they were his friends – but he was a seriously aggressive bloke after a beer or two sometimes. He told them they were a bunch of useless cowards and why didn't they cross the border and go and face Smith in his own country. Well – the ZIPRA blokes didn't like that – man! – Hell no! The next night these ZIPRA bastards went round to his place and murdered them all: Mark, his wife and the little girl – they – " but Margaret had gone out into the garden and left Charles to hear the rest of the story alone.

She knew Piet had also suffered personally from the guerrillas. His son, George, was farming near Chisamba. Like his father, he was an affable, easy-going gentle person, stocky and muscular in build with giant hands and a sandy beard. He had been set upon on his farm by some ZIPRA fighters who hung him up by his heels and set his beard on fire. He was saved by the intervention of his farm workers from much worse treatment. They had argued with the fighters that George was 'one of us' and a good man. Eventually the workers' persistence prevailed and the ZIPRA men left.

"George told his men that they wouldn't get a rise for saving his life though," Piet grinned. "By God he was grateful though – killed a bullock for them."

After Piet had had a beer with Charles and gone back to his place, Margaret told Charles she was, "just going for a little drive to see the grass orchids on the way to Banana Island."

That was what she did.

She climbed into the car and drove to the high point above the island, where she stopped the car and shut all the windows in spite of the heat.

Then Margaret screamed and screamed and screamed.

Margaret screamed until she was breathless and deaf. She screamed until her throat was raw and her chest hurt. She tried to fill the car with such a noise that all thoughts and knowledge of what she had heard would be pushed away and extinguished. She screamed until she was nothing but a scream herself – a huge round mouth, an Edgar Munchian monster funnel of sound, shrieking and shrieking.

In quite a short while she had screamed herself out and was left sitting in the car, gasping for air, staring at the grass orchids spread like a blue mist under the trees. At a distance unnoticed, an old Tonga man in torn khaki shorts and a worn faded shirt, stood, with an axe in his hand, silently watching her. When she started the engine to drive home, he turned and vanished into the bush.

Margaret did not scream again in that way, even when her youngest son Richard, that brave and golden boy, was killed three years later.

FOUR

Flying

The war, however, continued and the borders between Zambia and Rhodesia remained closed.

Jo was travelling to Tanzania to join the new SOMAFCO school set up by the ANC to cope with increasing numbers of refugees from the townships of South Africa. First though, he made arrangements to leave his daughter safely in the care of Marielise. Zanele also needed to be near her mother Bessie, who was still in and out of psychiatric care in Lusaka.

Late in 1978 Margaret flew down to Salisbury in Rhodesia via Bulawayo. The Rhodesian aeroplane did not have a silver undercarriage. It was apparently harder for the guerrillas with SAM7 missiles to see planes that were not shiny metal underneath. Taking off from Bulawayo Airport required immense skill from the pilot. He flew into the airport at a height of around 18,000 ft and then corkscrewed the plane down to the ground in a tight spiral. Taking off was a reverse spiral that was just as difficult. The plane had to be flown as if it were a vulture riding a thermal but a thermal so restricted that the bird had to fly sideways to make the tight turns and rise high enough to escape being shot down. It was uncomfortable and frightening for the passengers.

The reason for this new safety measure was the shooting down of the aeroplane that had carried Jo's friends, by a SAM7 missile as it flew out of the Kariba South Airport.

Retaliation by the Rhodesian forces was to be expected but no one could predict when the inevitable would take place.

In October Charles had to make a business trip to London. He was gone for two weeks at the driest and hottest time of the year. Margaret found the heat particularly trying while he was away. There was always a tension in the month of October as people waited for the first rains but this, the political stresses in Zambia and the continuing hopelessness of the unending war in Rhodesia, made everyone restless and worse tempered than usual. Margaret got up early routinely but in October the early mornings and late evenings were the best time of day anyway and this morning she was up particularly early to go to the airport to meet Charles's plane.

The skies above Lusaka were a bright bleached blue, while at ground level a dusty red-brown haze hung over the streets. The flamboyant trees along Cairo Road stretched their flattened, flame-coloured branches over the pavements but made only a sprinkling of light, inadequate shade over the passers-by. Even the roadblocks en route to the airport were manned by soldiers so lethargic and indifferent that she had no trouble arriving on time. The plane from Heathrow was often half an hour early. At this time of year, when there was not even a head wind to slow the flight, it was surprising that there was a delay. Margaret noticed the beginning of a breeze perhaps – a small susurration in the atmosphere of the airport. A light excitement – a sense of worry even – something out of the ordinary was happening.

Charles, from his window seat, looked out over Lusaka. Lovely to leave cold London behind for hot Lusaka but oh – the problems of Zambia were more and more daunting each day. As he looked out the plane however, it began to ascend again and to swing away from the airport.

What the hell was happening? It was Lusaka – no other flights were expected – what was going on?

Down below there seemed to be a myriad of bush fires – vast columns of smoke were rising into the sky – extreme even for the bush fire season!

The pilot made an announcement – something about waiting for clearance to land at Lusaka? Clearance from Green Leader? Who – or what? They circled again and then perhaps twenty minutes later began their approach to Lusaka Airport. Everything appeared quite normal and ordinary. On the tarmac as they walked away from the plane, Charles thought the ground staff were shouting louder and seemed more animated. The baggage was unloaded a little faster than usual, customs and immigration cleared him quickly and then he was through and Margaret was hugging him in a way that was demonstrative and unusual. Then she swore, which was even more unusual.

"They bloody did a victory roll over the runway before you were allowed to land! The bloody Rhodesian pilots did victory rolls over the runway! Oh Charles!" and she hugged him again even harder than the first time.

The Rhodesian Air Force had taken charge of the sky over Lusaka, threatening to shoot down the Zambian Air Force while bombing a ZAPU camp on the outskirts of the city. They had prevented the British flight from landing while they carried out their half-hour reprisal.

By the time Margaret and Charles reached home the casualties were arriving at the hospital. The streets of Lusaka were lined with silent, shocked people watching the cars, lorries, trucks and any vehicles that could be commandeered, bringing in the wounded – hundreds and hundreds of them, burnt and maimed and dying, driven under the flaming flowers along Cairo Road from the flaming killing ground where they had been ambushed, to the over-stretched and desperate teaching hospital. The doctors and nurses treated those they could save and left the dying to die. Those they treated died later because there was no anti-tetanus treatment. There were not enough hands free or available to give people in shock a sip of water. It was slaughter.

The Rhodesian retaliation followed the same pattern as at Chimoio and Tembue and Nyadzonya. Ground troops arrived and called the guerrillas to the parade ground and then opened fire on them with machine guns. They were backed up by helicopter gunships, which also made their retreat and escape possible. It was exemplary special service warfare and it was successful. The guerrillas and, indeed, ordinary Zambians, became convinced that Zambia was full of white Rhodesian spies and attacks on suspects increased dramatically. Life in Zambia became very unpleasant for everyone for a time.

FIVE

Raid

Henry Chishimba pressed himself against the wall of his first floor bedroom just to the left side of the window frame. With great care he pushed the heavy lined curtain a fraction away from the rebate so that he could look out at the street below. He could make out in the dark two army vehicles, maybe Land Rovers, parked side by side under the spathodea tree that leant over his fence. The curfew was in force and the moon had set so the night was still very dark. It was not yet 4am. He could see a group of men, perhaps six altogether, who were disputing with each other in hushed, but forceful and urgent voices. They spoke in English. A couple of them appeared to be on guard. Those men stood facing out from the vehicles and swung their guns in abrupt arcs as they surveyed the road and houses around them. Henry's heart stopped and he pulled back from the window with an indrawn breath. What to do next? Would they look up and shoot him in the face if they see him staring down?

Nothing helpful suggested itself to Henry except to continue looking out carefully without being seen. Petronella and the two younger children were crouched in a huddle by the bedroom cupboard. It was a big heavy *mukwa* cupboard but wouldn't be much use as a hiding place. He could see Petronella's eyes fixed on him, white flickers of fear in the dark, hot night while she mouthed silent questions. She kept the children's heads down and covered so that they couldn't see what was happening or what Henry might be risking by being at the window. Thank God that Mumbi and Musonda were at university in Britain.

The whole family had heard the gunfire. It had woken them up at 3.10am and sent Petronella flying into the children's bedrooms to take them into some place of safety, though nowhere obvious seemed to suggest itself. They gathered together, arms around each other, in the master bedroom until they heard the vehicles coming down the road towards them. One of the vehicles was making a dreadful harsh scraping sound, as if it was being driven on the rim of one of its wheels and its engine seemed to be failing. It sounded like a car being forced to reverse away after a crash – a sound not uncommon in Lusaka.

Oh my God! thought Henry, *Let the bloody vehicle start properly and drive away!* He could see himself, Petronella and the children all being held hostage by the men below until a last gun battle killed them all. Being Henry, he took a moment to remind himself that that might be a good end compared to some others.

Bloody Zambian Army – probably running away right now – and could they rescue a cat from a tree or a cow from a ditch? They would shoot us by mistake as soon as save us.

Why did English similes come with the English language? English was the language they mostly spoke at home these days. It didn't seem appropriate at the moment but he couldn't think of the words his father might have used to swear in this situation.

Henry's cousin was in the Green Buffaloes at the barracks opposite President Kaunda's official residence just a short distance away. He had joked with Henry in the self-deprecating way that Zambians have, that the army wasn't that interested in fighting right now. Uniforms, housing at the barracks, made life comfortable but who wanted to suffer like the Rhodesians did? It was true he said that one of the generals had been looking at the president's State House with envy. This general was complaining about the president's support for the liberation war but Henry's cousin just shrugged at the idea of a coup. There were rumours, but they could be discounted, even as they gained ground among the expatriate community.

Henry shut his eyes for an instant, blinked a few times, swallowed hard and peeked very carefully out of the window again. The talking on the street below him had stopped. Only one soldier – he was a soldier in uniform Henry thought – was on guard now. Henry couldn't see what colour the men were as their faces seemed to be covered or painted but he thought from the pitch and accent that some of the voices were definitely those of white men – white Rhodesians – who else? They were now all transferring bundles from one vehicle to the next. One of the bundles looked like a dead body or maybe just an unconscious one. It also seemed heavier than the rest of their stuff – what was that? Loot? Booty?

All of them will never get into that vehicle with all of that katundu! Henry was willing them with all his might to succeed and to leave. *Please, please, go*, he prayed. *Go you bastards – go!*

At the first sound of gunfire, Henry had known with certainty that it was a Rhodesian raid on the house of the Zimbabwean nationalist leader, Joshua Nkomo. It was the only possibility.

Only a day or so before, Charles Beaumont had asked Henry what he thought about the likelihood of a coup against the president. In spite of this expatriate rumour doing the rounds of the Lusaka Club neither of them gave that idea much credibility. They agreed that the real problem was the inevitable raid on Joshua Nkomo's house. God knows why Nkomo had been given a house in this particular, quietly affluent area. Perhaps the president thought that Nkomo's proximity to his own State House would make him too difficult a target politically, though no consideration like that had ever stopped the Rhodesians' Security Forces before. It was clear that the ZIPRA soldiers posted on sentry duty around Nkomo's house were in daily expectation of an attack. They had become so jumpy and trigger-happy that their neighbours had begun to find it dangerous to go home. Everyone avoided that street if they could, even if it meant going a very long way around to get to the Lusaka Club for lunch.

There wasn't anyone to phone for help. What phone would be manned anyway? The gunfire and explosions had been brief but savage and intense, and there had been no response from the nearby barracks or the soldiers protecting the president. Henry thought of his servants and their families lying on the floor of their quarters holding their breath in terror. Poor bastards – what was it to do with them?

It's probably a small mercy, Henry thought. *A shoot-out in this residential area where diplomats and Zambian families live side by side would be an international disaster and end in a civilian massacre! But why are these racist buggers parked outside my home? Go on you bastards! Leave! Yendani! Yendani!*

Then Henry added rudely but very quietly, "*Choka! Choka!*"

The engine of the functioning vehicle had not been turned off. As Henry watched it moved forward several metres and stopped again. One man remained behind. Henry saw a bright flash and suddenly the damaged Land Rover lit up and exploded into a roaring fire. The flames obscured his vision. He could see neither the soldier nor hear or see the vehicle but he knew both had vanished up the road towards Lusaka. It was a matter of seconds only. His fear had lasted an eternity but the actual incident was over very fast.

Petronella, seeing the orange glow through the curtains, couldn't help herself any longer and she screamed out loud. Chanda whimpered in her arms, but Kunda stood up and ran to the window to look out. Henry restrained him and called back to reassure Petronella. The burning vehicle seemed far enough away not to threaten the house, but he wanted to watch it until it burnt out to make sure. It might have explosives in it after all. He could feel the heat from it. It lit up the garden and street and showed them to be empty of human and animal life. Henry sent Kunda back to Petronella. It was extraordinary that nothing and no one came to see what was happening. There was no movement at all – just the flames and the movement of the vehicle as its tyres burst and collapsed.

Thank God the other Land Rover had gone and all the soldiers with it!

Next, Henry, every sense alert, heard a short burst of automatic fire from the direction of State House. Someone was shooting at shadows. A dog yelped in pain and the yelping went on and on but fainter and fainter as the dog fled. Whoever fired the weapon did not bother to do so again.

Eventually they all climbed back into the double bed. The children slept at once, exhausted from all the excitement, but the same excitement made rest impossible for their parents. Their hearts were racing and their stomachs knotted. They went over the event again and again, speculating, analysing fruitlessly. What did they really know?

The solid, warm darkness of the night had been a physical pressure enclosing them in a trap all through the attack, now before the sun rose it became a cold, transparent grey though still without light and all over Lusaka the phones began to ring again. People called each other trying to establish who had been responsible for the attack, who had been attacked, and why. People were calling to reassure and to be reassured. Neighbours of Nkomo's house had stories about bullet holes in their walls. In fact Henry was apparently the only person to have seen anything. The ZIPRA soldiers who probably had seen it all were now dead, or had been kidnapped.

Next morning the blackened Land Rover was still outside their window. Nobody from the army or police had been to see it. The only witness was the *spathodea* tree outside Henry's house which had been caught in the soaring flames of the burning vehicle. The top half of it waved horrified charcoal sticks in a reproachful gesture over the burnt-out wreck. Some of its lower branches, those that hung over the Chishimba's' garden, had survived because the updraft of the inferno had taken the heat straight pass them. Their orange tulip-like flowers and lush green leaves danced blithely in the summer breeze. As Petronella remarked when she finally felt brave enough to go and look at the scene of the incident, the common name for *spathodea* is 'flame tree' after all.

Nkomo's house was a smouldering, collapsed red brick shell, piled high with ashes with a drift of acrid smoke lifting up through the original woodland of *brachystegia* trees surrounding it. The British High Commissioner had tipped Nkomo off weeks before about the probability of a raid and he had not slept there for some time. At the Bowls Club opposite the ruined building, a bowls match was in progress by nine o'clock that same morning. Both teams were white expatriates or white Zambians. Both teams agreed that Nkomo and ZAPU had got their just deserts and they did not spare the battle site a passing glance or have a moment's sympathy for the fallen Africans.

Six

Aftermath

It did not take long for some of the facts about how the raid was executed to be established. Charles told Henry that it was assumed that the Rhodesians had crossed the Zambezi by pontoon near Kanyemba Island with their Land Rovers, early in the evening. Later that night they had driven up the dirt track from Gwabi, through Leopards Hill, to arrive at Nkomo's house soon after 3am. One of the vehicles had rammed the gate – probably the one that was damaged and set on fire near Henry's home. Henry lived so close to the raid that he could recount what he had heard. They had also used explosive mines to gain entry. They did meet opposing gunfire but the fire-fight lasted less than twenty minutes and then they were in control. Apparently some prisoners were taken, probably wounded, as well as a number of files from the office. Henry had seen the transfer of a prisoner and some of the other objects. One vehicle had been forced to waste perhaps less than ten minutes' time, outside Henry's home while it was decided to abandon the damaged vehicle. Then the Rhodesians all escaped by driving north for some hundreds of kilometres and blowing up a main road bridge behind them on the way. Finally they rendezvoused with the helicopters, which were sent to pick them up at some farm to the north-east. It seemed self-evident that they had had help from inside Zambia from white farmers.

It was hard not to admire their immense nerve and skill. It was impossible not to hate them if you were African. It was a reprisal of course. Charles felt sick at the endless circularity of action, reprisal, reprisal and action, all seeming to be going nowhere and achieving nothing. Just weeks before a second Rhodesian aircraft full of civilian passengers had been shot down as it left Kariba. This time there had been no survivors. This attack on Nkomo's house had been an act of revenge.

The raid that took place was only a few months before the Heads of Commonwealth Conference that was due to be held in Lusaka in August that year. It was soon after the election of a new and untried British Prime Minister, Margaret Thatcher, a Conservative and a woman – what could be expected from her at this event?

Marielise, who was feeling increasingly negative about the duration of the Liberation Struggle, predicted the worst outcome on the basis of previous Conservative policies towards Rhodesia and South Africa. There would be pressure for change from the other Commonwealth countries, especially the independent African states and, of course, India and that did offer grounds for hope. No one, however, seemed able to forecast what might happen though it seemed unlikely that there would be any resolution of the war in Zimbabwe. The raid on the Nkomo house suggested that white Rhodesians were simply never going to be ready to talk to ZAPU and ZANU even though they now only had control of the central plateau of Rhodesia, an area which amounted to about one third of the country.

Charles gathered from his brother Steve, that many Rhodesians were still defiantly optimistic even while they were planning a scorched earth policy if the worst happened and they lost their fight. Steve said it was rumoured that bombs had been placed in the South Bank Power Station and the dam wall on Lake Kariba. Peter Duncan admitted in his laconic way that he had heard similar stories.

SEVEN

The End

Lusaka meanwhile, was overrun with journalists from every part of the world, all speculating enthusiastically about what would happen. Every High Commission and Embassy in Zambia was also working overtime to help or hinder in some way. Henry Chishimba though, had a very low opinion of the British High Commissioner. He told Charles that the man was an arrogant racist.

"You know those awful jokes that we laugh at together sometimes – I usually hear them before you. It's okay if I tell a joke against myself or against Zambia or Zambians but the circumstances and the company matter – you are okay Charles!

"Well – Petronella and I were at dinner at the High Commissioner's one evening and he chose to tell one that was about President Kaunda. There is no way I would laugh at such a joke on such a formal occasion where the other guests are all white. Petronella and I sat without smiling and in the end all the other guests were embarrassed and didn't laugh either. We chose not to stay long after coffee was served. I think the man doesn't understand either Africa or good manners!"

Charles agreed and said so. He didn't tell Henry that the High Commissioner had also made disparaging remarks about the Chishimba's following the incident when really he should at the least have held his tongue and not exposed his ill-judged behaviour.

No. The situation did not look good.

It was November and Margaret was driving home up Independence Avenue on her way to have a late lunch alone. It was very hot but once again it was building up for a mid-afternoon storm and the gathering clouds were full of the promise of cool release after rain. Margaret's car could only move at a walking pace as a crowd of people was moving ahead of her towards State House. As they walked they shouted: "We want war!" and the men leading them responded cheerfully, "Okay! Okaaay!" They weren't very noisy or enthusiastic considering their aggressive demand. In fact they seemed oddly cheerful and friendly, and smiled at Margaret in her car. Margaret supposed that the demonstration had most likely originated from State House and that it was designed to send a message to the British that the peace process must make faster progress and be put more forcibly to the Rhodesians. The demonstrators gathered outside the president's home and began to sing the national anthem. At the front were rows of happy school children, all smartly turned out in uniform.

Margaret found herself wanting to cry but she could not say what had made her sad or why.

Moments later a policeman directed her onto the wrong side of the dual carriage way so she could pass around the crowd and further on a second policeman pointed out her way home. In a few minutes she was in Sunningdale outside her gate and her gardener leapt up from eating his plate of *nshima* and relish to let her in. Immediately she knew something was terribly wrong.

Maybe there was something in the gardener's glance or swift action, though she could not say exactly what that was. She knew with an immediate dread that she would remember everything about that afternoon for ever. Charles's car was stopped rather than parked in the drive and a second car obstructed the car port. Neither should have been there.

"Charles!" she called as she entered the hall. A lump of solid cold was congealing behind her breastbone and under her heart. "Charles?"

Charles stepped towards her from the sitting room. He was grey and stooped as if he had been winded. His hands were shaking as he tried to reach out for Margaret but he failed and his hands wavered away.

"It's Richard," he said, "Richard's dead." And his wandering hands went up to his face and over his eyes and dropped again to his sides.

Peter Duncan was there behind him.

"Hello Margaret," he said unnecessarily and then, "I am sorry. I am sorry." Though it was in no way his doing.

"What happened?" asked Margaret, as the frost took hold of her heart and spread into her brain.

★

It was such a useless, unnecessary death. It was just an accident following, as it turned out, a momentary panic and nothing to do with the Bush War. Richard had been with friends who were driving to visit Steve on his farm. He had finished his exams in England in July and had planned to travel for a year, first visiting Rhodesia to see his grandparents and then joining his parents in Zambia for Christmas. There should have been no danger as there was a truce in place between the guerrillas and the security forces even though there was still no trust between the parties.

The young people with Richard were armed and competent in the use of guns. There were six of them travelling in two cars for safety. They left the main Salisbury Umtali road very early in the morning and were driving through a stretch of untouched bush near Ruzawi when there was a loud bang and the first car lurched over and crashed into a shallow ditch on a bend, where it came to rest on its side. Richard's friends tumbled out clutching guns and rolled and fell into defensive positions. They all thought they were being ambushed. The second car stopped, and then reversed back with the passengers firing high shots into the bush around the damaged car. Nothing happened, there was silence for a few moments and then the birds started calling again and they heard frogs in the *vlei*.

"*Jirre!*" someone said. "It's only a fucking blow-out, man!"

It took them a few careful moments to reconnoitre the situation, bent over low with guns at the ready. The nearest one to the crashed car kicked at the wheel.

"Fucking hell! It's a just a bloody puncture. Look at the way the tyre's split! Look at this!"

They were only boys just out of high school.

They stood around for a few moments talking themselves down from their panic and laughing at each other's fear. Then they realised that Richard was not among them and a different kind of fear made their hearts pound again. They found Richard slumped against the front pillar on the passenger side of the truck. They were travelling without seatbelts. There were none fitted. The lurch of the car as it hit the ditch had flung Richard so hard against the metal frame that his neck was broken and his temple stove in. There was not much blood on Richard but as soon as they moved him and his head flopped they gave up any idea of using their resuscitation skills.

It was an unlucky chance. No one else was hurt, they were only bruised. Somehow they fitted themselves all into the second vehicle. Richard was laid on the laps of three of his friends while the other three sat in front. They turned around and drove as fast as they could back to the hospital at Marandellas. Some of Richard's friends cried secretly as they rocked along in the car. Some cried when they were finally alone.

★

Peter Duncan was to fly Margaret and Charles to Rhodesia in his small plane.

"Not a problem," he said in answer to Margaret's question of how the flight was to be managed. "We make flight plans to land at Kariba which is legitimate as you know. As we approach Kariba Air Control we file new flight plans for Salisbury – it's done all the time. Right now there is no danger from SAM missiles. This time of year it will be a bumpy flight that's all – big thunderheads everywhere right now."

Charles and Margaret flew down to Salisbury the next day. Charles was alone in the front of the plane next to Peter, Margaret was alone in the seat behind; each with their separate storms in their hearts and heads. Even at midday the thunderheads were spectacular, constantly growing, reforming and re-massing, iron grey, indigo blue and pure white structures, frail as smoke and larger than mountains. The little plane went up and down, around and about, and in and out of those cloud formations it could not avoid.

It was very beautiful.

It was unforgettable.

Charles and Margaret's pain was exquisite.

EIGHT

Independence

The war in Zimbabwe-Rhodesia ended as abruptly and as surprisingly as a tropical storm, and the regional situation was capsized so completely that many people were left either stranded on an unknown shore or adrift on an uncertain sea.

Margaret and Charles, Marielise and Jo, all went to the Zimbabwe Independence Ceremony in Salisbury separately without realising that the other couple was there.

Margaret and Charles feared there would be trouble at the arena but all that happened was some smoke and a scuffle with demonstrators that was quickly cleared up. They were reassured and hopeful after Robert Mugabe's speech. It seemed that the whole African population was behind Mugabe. Feelings were intense but full of hope and joy. After the event, they went back to a friend's house in Highlands, a suburb of Salisbury. In the morning the black servant observing his usual routine, took the dog with him when he went to the local shopping centre to get fresh milk and the morning newspaper for his white employers. Life was apparently to go on as normal for the foreseeable future for the owners of the property.

It was to change for Margaret and Charles. Charles was to stay on in Lusaka for another two to three years but he would, from now on, be travelling regularly to Zimbabwe as well to help the local banks make the transition back to legality. Margaret would gradually pack up the house in Lusaka and re-establish a home for herself and Charles, first in a Harare suburb, but later on Charles's farm near Ruwa where they planned to spend their retirement.

Marielise and Jo joined their friends for a party of celebration. They were all wild with excitement and triumph. Soon, soon there must be the same overturning of the government in South Africa. They danced away the night. For the first time they felt it was safe to openly proclaim their hopes. The front-line of the war of liberation had moved southwards in one massive stride. Jo and some of their friends would eventually relocate to Harare, which had overnight become the diplomatic centre of importance in the region. Lusaka would be downgraded and would lose some of its vitality and energy, at least for the time being.

There were losers of course. Many white people were packing up to leave for South Africa or Australia or, if they could get visas, for America or Canada. They had been betrayed by Britain and had learnt to hate their 'mother' country over the years of the Rhodesian war so they would not go 'home'. A number of white people stayed on in Zimbabwe. Some had hoped for this change seeing it as positive, others had come to accept its inevitability, and there were many who did not want to leave their homes and farms or the graves of their sons.

The Zimbabwean armies of ZAPU and ZANU would return gradually and a role and a place had to be found for many thousands of war veterans. Those who had fought for the Rhodesian side in the Bush War, both black and white soldiers, had to make the biggest adjustments and find new and different ways of living with the victorious enemy now that they had become the defeated enemy themselves.

Among them were those who were deeply traumatised and unable to adapt. They found themselves as citizens of the new Zimbabwe, free to cross the border into enemy territory. They had crossed before many times, to fight and kill; now a few of the ex-combatants chose to walk among the people they hated, wearing civilian clothes and trying to find a reason to carry on. What shore would they fetch up on, where would they come to harbour?

Siavonga was just such a place.

NINE

Adjustment

The Guest Book, The Cottage, Siavonga
February 1982
Marielise and Jo.
'It's over a year since we were last here! So many changes! The border is open again. We can cross directly over the dam wall to Zimbabwe. Freedom! **Kwacha! Uhuru! A luta continua***!'*

Siavonga was a poverty stricken, run-down village that had been neglected in the last years of the war. Margaret and Marielise had visited the cottage only a couple of times in the worst years of the fighting between 1978 and 1979. It was simply not safe to visit because it had become a dangerous no-man's land where the Rhodesian Army or a group of ZAPU fighters might suddenly appear. The Zambian Army was trigger-happy and nervous.

Siavonga had become used to Rhodesian helicopter gunships flying overhead, one day however, a foolish Zambian soldier, stationed at the one-time Lake Inn and Motel, had fired at some departing Rhodesian helicopters – a hopeless gesture of frustration or perhaps he was drunk – at any rate he was dead in minutes. The helicopter gunship had simply spun around and dived over Siavonga, spraying machine gun bullets over the club and then raking the collection of grass huts that made up the village of Mutinangala in the nearby valley. A couple more Zambian soldiers lost their lives but the casualties were highest in the village where men, women and children had no protection at all.

Even before Independence Day in Zimbabwe, Zambians were moving back into the border areas to take possession of their homes and to look for opportunities to build up their businesses. A tentative start was made on a holiday and tourist business along the coast. The Zambian soldiers moved out of the Lake Inn and the Geordie entrepreneur who owned it moved back into the empty buildings. He cleaned the place up, reconditioned the swimming pool, put barbecues and tables around it, and started serving large steaks on the veranda and double tots of gin and vodka at the bar for the price of a single. He filled in the bullet holes in the chalets so that people could sleep easier but left those that were spattered across the wall behind the bar as they made a good conversation piece for his clients. He was a tough guy, and shrewd. Among his clients were local government officials who knew they were powerful enough to get free drinks, but Jacky knew his money would be made from the expatriate community and the hoped-for overseas visitors. He offered to give them reductions on lunchtime food if they came with their families. He told them that he was expecting important dignitaries from Lusaka to come for dinners and they gradually perceived that it would be better to go whoring in the bars in the seedier parts of the village.

The clubhouse however remained an extremely relaxed and casual place that was recommended as 'full of local colour and interest' in the new post-war guides to the lake. Jacky had the gift of being all things to all men. He sympathised with the Siavonga residents about the lack of local developments, agreed with the expatriates about what a mess Zambia was and how it was all the government's fault – "So different from the way they do things in Zimbabwe!" He nodded his head when the white residents complained about the ignorance of Zambians, and when the new generation of eager white backpackers arrived en route to Namibia and South Africa he would keep them riveted to the bar with his tales about crocodiles, tiger fish, Freedom Fighters and the waterspouts on the lake that no one else but him had ever seen.

So it was to Jacky's bar that Andy Martin came and it was there that he stayed for a while as a general handyman and help in exchange for accommodation. Andy had once been a Selous Scout – or so Jacky said. Andy said very little. Not much was known about him. His family name was never mentioned. Andy would sit at the bar, the muscles of his jaw rigid, his fingers tapping ceaselessly on the top of the bar, his right leg twitching and twitching faster and faster, until he had to get up and walk about the bar veranda. His eyes kept flicking over the structure of the place as if he were assessing whether it was defensible. Then he would come back to the bar and have another short dark drink and more beer.

Andy was at the bar on one occasion when Marielise and Jo arrived for a sundowner. They wanted to see some of the changes that had taken place since the end of the war and they went up to the bar to speak to Jacky. Andy's presence made them both wary and uncomfortable. They said hello to him and he nodded at them, his expressionless eyes running over them both as if he were a lizard watching flies. It was as if his subconscious was a calculating machine while his conscious mind was dead.

"What an awful looking zombie of a man!" whispered Marielise when they had carried their drinks down to the pool.

"Mmmh, he looks traumatised," agreed Jo, who had seen people in that state before, usually refugees or survivors of bombings, or township rioting.

"Probably an ex-soldier from the Rhodesia Army."

"Probably to be avoided then," said Marielise, watching Andy through her dark glasses while pretending to be almost dozy. "We had better quit."

Andy however jumped up abruptly and left without a goodbye nod at Jacky, so Marielise and Jo went for a second drink to the bar and asked Jacky as inconsequentially as possible who he was. Jacky was always happy to gossip and he had somehow elicited information from the silent Andy.

"Yeah, he's ex-Selous Scout you know. Really bitter about the war. Tells me he's here to get his revenge – doesn't say on who he's going to be revenged – doesn't say how he's going to be revenged – reckon he's got a gun or two hidden inside that crap vehicle he drives but I haven't seen them and I didn't ask. Just told him that it's strict policy round this bar: no guns, no knives, no weapons. Think he got the message! He won't stay long – too twitchy – I've seen the type before."

Marielise and Jo then spent an hour or so failing to answer Jacky' questions about themselves without seeming evasive. It was a game they both enjoyed and they made it seem very innocent. On their way back to the cottage Andy passed them in his beaten up pick-up truck. They noted its appearance and registration number just in case they ever ran into Andy again.

TEN

Squash, Dinner And Refugees

Charles met Nick at the Squash Club in Lusaka a couple of years after the end of the war in Zimbabwe. They were playing in a friendly and informal competition between local farmers and some of the new expatriates. Charles was feeling better about life that evening than he had for a long time. He and Margaret would be returning to Zimbabwe fairly soon and there was an astonishingly positive atmosphere about the prospects for that country. Aid and aid workers, economists and money, were flooding into Zimbabwe and disappearing from Zambia. Zambia was no longer a Frontline State and as yet, no one was mentioning where the new Frontline in that other continuing war against Apartheid might be.

Nick was playing for the local farmers' team, though, as Charles discovered, he was an expatriate who was working for the United Nations High Commission for Refugees. He was an easy and sociable young man with a sense of humour that kept everyone laughing, sometimes at his own expense. There are always some players who cannot bear to lose even in a friendly match, but somehow with Nick there, the evening went along in a better spirit than usual. Charles and Nick agreed to play together again the following week and go to the club for a meal afterwards with their wives. So it was that the four of them met for the first time and in spite of the differences in their ages, had a pleasant and cheerful evening.

Nick's wife, Manda, was a young, attractive, mixed-race woman, with fine features and expressive eyes. Charles could see that Nick was proud of her, maybe a little possessive. Manda too, was easy in company. She said she had studied business at college and found herself very under-occupied as an expatriate wife, even with two very young children. Margaret asked her if she would like to be a volunteer at the Wildlife Club but Manda said no – there was the possibility, just perhaps available, of working as a part-time administrator at a little art gallery in the centre of Lusaka. What was Margaret planning to do on her return to Zimbabwe, Manda wanted to know.

"Ah – " said Margaret, looking across at Charles who was talking to Nick, she hadn't co-opted him yet and didn't want to spoil her chances of persuading him that her plans were worthwhile.

"Gardening – " she said, " – but gardening for food together with different varieties of plants and by using as little water as possible. A new way of being self-sufficient really – and I want to teach it. People were corralled into protected villages during the war and new skills will be needed. This kind of gardening is called Permaculture – it was started in Australia. I haven't told Charles about it yet – it's still a dream."

Manda laughed.

"Oh gosh! It sounds fascinating. We all need our dreams – and – " she nodded at Nick, who was engaged in conversation with Charles, " – we need our independence and our own projects too – all this trailing around after men and their careers!"

Manda shook her head without any apparent bitterness.

"It's wonderful to be in Zambia. I was born here you know, though my parents moved around and worked in several African countries but it still feels like a homecoming even though Africa has changed so much and keeps on changing. Nick chose to come here because I told him how important Africa was to me."

Nick was happy to talk about his interesting new job.

"Do you know that refugee funding has become an important part of the economics of the region and particularly of Zambia? The amount of income provided by the United Nations for refugees is essential for Zambia to function at the present," Nick said.

Charles pulled a wry face. He knew too much about the economic imbalances that resulted from wars, refugees and aid, never mind the problems created by low copper prices for the mining industry.

Margaret had some idea of the numbers of people and of the amounts of money involved from Charles, but had not given the scale of the problem much thought. She had assumed naively that when the refugees and Freedom Fighters returned to Zimbabwe everything would return to normal, whatever normal was.

"I suppose," she said reflecting, "that Zambia would have changed anyway. There's never really been a normal in Zambia – if by that you mean a status quo."

Nick gave a half laugh.

"There's a surprising number of South African refugees here and they will stay. You should see the problems in Malawi where there are vast refugee camps of Mozambicans. The pressure on food and water is enormous. Deforestation is a real problem. People have cut down all the trees for fuel and that's resulted in terrible land erosion."

"Yes," Charles agreed, "the problems multiply – and the dependency of the government on foreign aid. It gets more and more difficult to unpick it all and find solutions."

"Well," Manda said, "it would help if the British government didn't so openly support the Apartheid government. Until Apartheid ends there will always be wars here."

The others looked at her in silence and Nick raised a warning eyebrow. Manda never did accept that much of Lusaka's expatriate society was extremely conservative and did not like to be challenged.

"Expatriates always form a *laager* – it makes them feel safer but it's false," she said dismissively, but later in private, to Nick.

Margaret looked thoughtfully at Manda, then steered the conversation onto another aspect of the changes happening to the country that was of special interest to her.

"The war did very different things to wildlife. In some places it was protected because there were no-go areas for hunters, in others there was poaching by ZIPRA for food, and in yet others there were and still are huge numbers of landmines. Wild animals keep being blown up right now."

Manda and Nick shuddered at the idea. Conservation of wildlife was an issue that was not divisive for white middle class people.

Nevertheless it was a successful evening and hardly surprising that afterwards Charles and Margaret suggested to Manda and Nick that they should come down to the cottage one weekend soon with their children.

"We haven't been there much lately," Margaret explained. "The war made that part of Zambia a no-go area for most people. What with the roadblocks and nobody knowing whether they were manned by Zambian Army or ZIPRA or even the Rhodesians – we just stopped going and the place has been neglected. We managed to get wages and mealie-meal down to Milimo – he looks after the place for us – with our engineer friend Peter Duncan, from CAPCO – you know – they run the power stations, and he went down regularly because he had to – brave man!

"As a matter of fact – the Rhodesians blew up the bridges on the way down to the lake – just about the time of the Lancaster House agreement that ended the war. It was an awful business. We started to believe that a section of the Rhodesian Army was going to implement a scorched earth policy and destroy everything that would make it possible for the new Zimbabwe government to succeed.

"Honestly – we did not know what to think or hope for at that time – but why common sense should prevail when there hadn't been much sign of it before."

Margaret stopped. She and Charles did not talk about this time in their lives. It was far too painful. She was not even sure what Charles thought any more. He had been very withdrawn and sombre for over a year but recently spent quite a lot of time talking to Father Patrick. She had seen that he had a Bible on his desk with a bookmark in it but when she asked him directly, he had laughed at the idea of becoming religious.

"Father Patrick's a wise old soul," was all he had said.

"He's no older and wiser than you," said Margaret tartly.

Now, to her surprise, Charles continued the story of the bridges.

"It's an extraordinary irony," said Charles, "but the bridges were defended by an unarmed white man who lived in the valley. He happened by misfortune to be in the area and he saw what was happening on one of the bridges – the Rhodesians had helicoptered in and were setting explosive charges – so he stormed onto the bridge and told them to stop."

"Good God! What happened?" Nick asked.

"The Rhodesians shot him," said Charles flatly.

Manda winced.

"How truly awful!"

"Anyway – " Margaret was worried that these stories might stop Nick and Manda from visiting the cottage, " – that's all behind us we hope! The cottage is pretty basic but the lake is beautiful and our kids used to love it. Yours do swim, I suppose?"

"Oh yes! What about windsurfing?" Manda turned to Nick with enthusiasm, "You've always wanted to windsurf. What about boats and water skis?"

Charles smiled.

"It's all possible again – they've lifted the ban on boats on the lake and people are talking about opening up the camp sites again and even building a hotel."

Margaret said, "We've shared the cottage with my niece who is at UNZA – the university here – but she also may be moving so we have to look for someone else to take care of the cottage after we go. We haven't got a date yet – the one place I will miss most will be the cottage."

ELEVEN

The Gun

The Guest Book. The Cottage, Siavonga.
June 1982
Marielise and Jo

*'Shortest day of the year. Cool evenings – sunny days, no wind.
Ants are everywhere in the cottage. We woke in the night to find
the moving shadow on the wall behind our bed was ants! The
septic tank needs to be emptied. Milimo says he can arrange for it
to be done. The tiny island opposite Piet's cottage has had a hippo
on it all weekend. It seems to be eating some water weed that
grows there. Even if there had been a breeze we wouldn't have
windsurfed in case we disturbed it. Dangerous beasts, hippo!
Here in front of the cottage the lake is eating away at the shore and
removing huge chunks of rock. Where does it all go?'*

Andy wanted to wipe out defeat. He wanted to destroy anything
that suggested that his years of fighting in the Bush War had
achieved nothing for himself or for what he thought he had
believed in. He had grown up with black kids on the farm at Sinoa
and had learnt to speak Chishona before he learnt to speak English.
He hadn't done well at boarding school and by the time he was
sixteen he was back on the farm helping his permanently sozzled
father manage his indentured labour force. He stood behind his
father's chair in the tobacco farm, one hand on each side of the

chair back so that he could prop his father upright if he started to lean too far over while he awarded pay or beatings to the men in front of him. Farm labourers who quit their jobs were brought back by the police and treated as deserters. Andy's father would tell the boss boy to tie the deserter's hands behind his back with wire until it cut into the *skellum's* skin and then he would be beaten with a hosepipe. A hosepipe didn't leave the same tell-tale marks as a rhino or hippo skin *sjambok*. It was also illegal.

At times like this Andy despised his alcoholic father. He understood exactly what the labourers said about him and his father and he understood why they wanted to leave their work and go off to bury their fathers or their children, or to see that their wives were not living with another man. He didn't explain that to his father because there would have been no point. He felt more at home with the African labourers than in the sour smelling house with shaded verandas where his family skulked.

The farm went bankrupt and the land was sold within months of the death of his father from liver failure. Andy's younger brother had a bank job, a wife and a home and Andy's mother went off to live with him. She never stopped saying what a wonderful man her husband had been and how he had brought her red roses every year on her birthday.

Andy got a job on a mine for a year and then the Chimurenga, the Bush War, began and he was recruited into the Selous Scouts. He spoke seven different African languages and knew the names of every tree and shrub in the local dialect. He knew what bush fruit was edible and what could be used to poison an enemy. He knew how to survive in the bush with only a knife in his hand and it was there, in the bush, where he felt at home. Andy's early life had more than prepared him for the harsh training undergone by the Selous Scouts. He was quickly and easily one of their star trainees.

The Selous Scouts carried out anti-terrorist operations almost to the day of the Independence Celebration. Then it was all over. Finished. Stopped. Gone. There was nothing for them to do unless they moved south to serve in the South African war. They were marked men because of the kind of combat they had been engaged in. You could see in their faces and in their eyes the horror and the thrill of their experiences. They could shave their beards off and leave Zimbabwe but they could never leave behind what they had become. They were hated and could expect no mercy and they all knew that it was not safe to stay home.

Andy's skin was marked with scars and welts. He was burnt black by the sun. His hands were calloused and his fingernails thick and hard. He was fit. He was strong. Only one thing bothered him: his upper gut nagged as if he had just been kicked under the ribs. But Andy ignored pain. He only ate meat and potato or meat and mealie-meal anyway. If he ate those before he went drinking he was okay for sure.

"No problem! *Hazeku ndaba* man!"

He didn't need to think. He still slept in snatches a few hours at a time then took a walk around to see what was happening. Action and instinct had got him through the war. He did fine now without making plans or beating himself up mentally. The war was a bright silent noise in his head. It was a sensation on the back of his neck, a tension that kept his spine tingling and upright. It was movement in the periphery of his vision and background noise near his left ear. He was a little deaf in his right ear from gunshots and explosions. His left eye could always see women and children running from the village before they turned into twitching human colanders leaking blood. He could see the dying babies cut from their watching mothers' wombs. He could see the girls raped by bayonets. He could see the terrifying hatred and hateful terror in the faces of his adversaries before they died. He could see the other Selous Scouts around him. He could hear them all.

He could not remember his own self or distinguish between his actions and those of his companions. He did not bother to remember the long and longer times of extreme heat, extreme thirst, extreme cold, extreme exhaustion and extreme boredom.

They were a brief-seeming prelude to violent and eternal death.

Andy knew the war was over. He knew that he could go south and carry on fighting down there but he knew that that war was also lost. The whites were defeated in Africa, so why drag out the misery? He would go north and kill as many people – black people of course – as he could and then they could kill him. He had lived in this expectation for ten years. He would welcome it. It was inevitable. He would look for the opportunity to kill, find it, do it and die.

He crossed the border into Zambia for the last time. It was easy and he did it legally. No boats across Lake Kariba, no pontoon across the Zambezi with an army jeep. Just himself, his beat up old pick-up and his guns carefully hidden inside the structure of the vehicle and a passport with his own name on it: Andy Martin.

He wandered around southern province for a while, revisiting places that he had seen during the Chimurenga. He was looking for 'hostiles', for aggression, for enemies, for arguments, for hatred, for reasons to kill but he couldn't find it among the Zambians. ZIPRA and ZAPU had gone home to Zimbabwe where the Korean trained Fifth Column was exterminating ZAPU supporters. The BaTonga continued to live as vulnerable people have always lived, quietly and independently, dealing with everyone they had to deal with and avoiding anyone who they thought threatened them. People smiled at Andy and greeted him as they had done when he was a child on his father's farm. It was not like the countryside of the Chimurenga where people fled from you, or lied or cried or hid, and never ever smiled.

Andy still hunted. He visited the village bars and the *tarvens*. Andy knew what most white and other employers of servants don't realise, that servants and workers have a vast fund of knowledge about the people they work for which they pass on as gossip, rumour and supposition. Survival in the underclass of servitude and employment relies on understanding as much about the dominant class as possible and that means watching out for small details of habits and behaviour. Apart from the value of these observations for humorous stories and information of a salacious and sexual nature, they occasionally might have financial value, as for example, to thieves.

Eventually on one of his evenings in a bar in Siavonga, Andy caught the edge of some gossip about a man from South Africa who visited Siavonga; a man who belonged to Umkonto we Sizwe, who had been seen in Chaisa Compound, outside Lusaka in another *tarven* with South African Freedom Fighters; a man who was staying now at Siavonga, in the cottage looked after by Mr Milimo Singani. Andy joined in the conversation, pretending to be drunker than he was. He paid for some more drinks, talked, laughed and asked a few more questions. The man was there now, Saturday night, with his woman, but would be gone by Monday morning. Mr Milimo would be there early but he would go to the Catholic church for mass after breakfast. The man and his woman would be alone. The man's name was Jo. After another hour and some unrelated chat, Andy left the bar and drove himself back to his room at Jacky's bar. He made sure his gun and his knife were in good order, folded up his belongings neatly and packed them away. He slept for exactly an hour and a half. At dawn he got up and into his *bakkie*, he spun a tale to the sleepy security guard at the entrance gate about having to go to the Copperbelt to see about a job on the mines and he left to carry out his planned murder.

Andy by now, and by habit, knew the layout of Siavonga very well. This was a very quiet weekend at Jacky's bar. There were almost no visitors from Lusaka in Siavonga. Andy would park his *bakkie* discreetly on the top road above the cottage outside an unused driveway while it was very early in the morning. He would walk down to the shoreline through an empty property a little way from the cottage where Jo and Marielise slept. As soon as he was sure Milimo had left for the church service he would walk up to the cottage. They would not be afraid of a single white man and he would be able to get right up close to them before he used his gun to kill Jo. He might even be able to do the whole business with his knife but he didn't want any screaming if he could help it. Two or three quick gunshots might be noticed in the village but would not be acted on in any hurry. Occasional sounds of gunfire were not so uncommon that curious people would rush to find out the reason. Cars did backfire after all. Sooner or later they would know what had happened but not at once. He would be sorry to use the knife on the woman but if he had to he would. She was probably just as guilty anyway. He would then just run swiftly up the hill, jump into his pick-up and vanish as he had always vanished – without leaving a sign of his presence. He must do the killing in daylight so that he could cross the border while it was open. There was no longer any other quick way across the lake.

Andy sat patiently on the bottom terrace of the adjoining property to the cottage. Trees and bushes screened him from the lake and from the cottage, but he did not appear to be in hiding, just relaxing casually. A dog came along the beach hunting but though it stopped briefly to sniff in his direction, it continued on without deflecting from the path of its hoped for quarry. Andy could hear cocks crowing and the early sounds of birds in the garden. The lake was suffused with an increasing light. It was very beautiful indeed and Andy thought of how much he loved the bush at dawn as the last cool smells dissolved into sunlight and the ground hornbills boomed in the distance. He remembered for the first time for ten years how much he had loved the sunrise on his father's farm, long before his drunk father could fall from his bed, when he was out in the fields shivering and alone with the sound of the labourers' voices approaching and scarves of early mist floating across the *vleis* and around the granite *kopjes*.

Then Andy heard the sound of children's laughter just above him on the cottage path. Some children had come secretly down the path on bare, soundless feet.

Andy turned his head and saw two of Milimo's younger

children, Mweemba, a boy of five, and Busiku, a girl of about six, each with bright smiling faces.

"Hello!" they called out, taking turns to greet him; the English greeting was new to them and they kept its use for *muzungus*.

"Hello!" they called again, laughing with delight. The little girl was both pushing her brother forward, and hanging onto his hand to drag him back, while hiding herself modestly behind him. Then suddenly and unexpectedly, she darted forward ahead of her brother and went right up to Andy. He was sitting down and she was above him on the slope so her face was close to his and she looked into his eyes with merriment.

"Who is your name? Hello! Come with me!" and she put her hand on Andy's knee for a brief second then whirled away back to her brother's protective side. Her brother did a little dance to show how clever and brave he was. They wanted him to come and play with them as Jo did. They thought that he was there as a friend of Jo's.

Andy stood up. He was not thinking any more. The little girl took his hand in both of hers and tried to tug him up the hill to the cottage. Andy looked at her. A child: a small, carefree, happy child, quite unafraid of him. He was still not thinking or planning or deciding. He was just there with the children. He said to the children in ChiTonga, "No. I cannot stay here. I must go to my home now."

He freed his hand from the child's and walked down the last steps until he was standing on the rocks that dropped straight down into the water. Andy took the gun from his pocket, he turned it over in his hand, feeling its weight and metal smoothness, and knowing it as he knew it, as a part of himself. He then swung his arm back and, with one beautiful over-arm throw, he sent the gun flying far, far across the water until it dropped into the lake at its deepest point.

The children watched with interest, clapping and laughing. They gathered stones for themselves and practised throwing them into the lake but none of their attempts went as far, as deep and as purposefully as Andy's had.

Andy turned and went swiftly back up the hillside the way he had come. He got into his aged *bakkie*, started the engine and drove back across the border into Zimbabwe and up into the wild bushes of the Matusadona Hills.

Twelve

Theology

Marielise had met Father Patrick several times on the campus before she remembered that he had been the priest in charge at the Catholic church in Siavonga. There were several occasions where they had encountered each other as adversaries during student debates of an ethical or political nature. After a while Marielise learnt that Father Patrick had actually worked in the Zambezi Valley during the resettlement of the Tonga people and she realised that he was a valuable, indeed essential person, to talk to about that time in the history of Zambia for her research project, so long delayed because of the war with Rhodesia.

Father Patrick was very happy to oblige her. Like all of the Jesuit Fathers he was an exceptionally well-educated man and even with his contacts with the university he was starved for intellectual debate on moral and ethical matters. They got into the habit of meeting for coffee and would sometimes visit the university bookshop together. It was quite an odd place at the time. Price control meant that any books on sale were likely to be very cheap but price control also made it hard for the bookshop to provide a broad selection of books. Marielise and Father Patrick would hunt through the shelves together, pointing out to each other some of the stranger books that came in but also recommending any bargains or books of special interest to each other that they saw.

Father Patrick wanted to hear about Judaism from Marielise. Though his academic knowledge of the religion was greater than hers, he wanted to know what it meant to her to be half-Jewish. Marielise was amused by this because her father had not been an observant Jew at all. Nevertheless her father was an intelligent, self-taught man, who understood what he had chosen to reject.

Their most protracted arguments were on the merits of Marxism and Christianity. Father Patrick insisted that it was not enough to be civilised and altruistic, that humanism and even socialism, must fail humans. He dug out, for Marielise, a battered grey hardback written by a Catholic convert before the Second World War.

"What did you think of the book, Marielise?" he asked, fixing her with an intense blue stare from between raised eyebrows and spectacles lowered to the end of his nose. Marielise wrinkled up her own nose then smiled at her friend.

"Well I guess I am a civilised and civilising Pagan according to the author's definition. Perhaps she is right and between material reality and human nature itself, all of us who fight – or work – for a better world must fail to an extent. Of course she isn't suggesting that we stop trying to get rid of racism and injustice is she?"

"No indeed! What of God, though Marielise? What of God?"

Marielise gave a deep sigh.

"Oh Patrick!" she said, "You know I don't know. If there was a God – if there is a God – then yes! It would be necessary to give him that total commitment. I suppose it would be a kind of totalitarianism."

She thought of her commitment to the Freedom Fight and of her commitment to Jo and sighed again, this time with sadness and to herself only. Was everything – knowledge, love, success – all partial, limited and uncertain? Then she countered, "Why is it that we can only describe God in human terms? I am a feminist you know. To describe God as male does, I think, diminish understanding. It makes him less real to me."

"Marielise – you do like to tease, don't you."

Patrick pushed his spectacles back up his nose and shook his head. Marielise bit her lip and refrained from joking that God was inconceivable because, without doubt, Patrick believed in the Immaculate Conception of the Virgin. Patrick had told her about his childhood and schooling in Ireland but he never disclosed any personal feelings or desires and Marielise remained very curious about him.

Marielise and Father Patrick really did like each other and their discussions always left them feeling more cheerful. Now that Jo had left for Tanzania and SOMAFCO, Marielise missed having discussions where she could safely air her views. She hoped that Father Patrick would treat what she said as confidential and not repeat them to anyone else. The truth was that Marielise was an independent thinker and had never completely toed any party line. She had learnt that there were occasions when group solidarity and cohesion overruled doubts or alternative viewpoints. In discussions with Father Patrick she could risk being the outsider making the challenges.

She was also lonely without Jo.

Sometimes she was more than lonely. Sometimes she was desperate and felt her choices were too hard to bear. She would have loved to have her own children and even perhaps a quiet academic life where she could expect Jo to come home every night to her cooking. He would want each evening to read the next new chapter of her prize-winning novel. Ah well, Marielise had no illusions about those dreams – but even that cynicism could not stop the pain of her loneliness and take away her desire for a baby.

Thirteen

The Luncheon Party

Charles and Margaret gave a big luncheon party at their Sunningdale house in Lusaka one weekend.

It was not an obligatory business function but for friends and family. In fact it was in honour of Michael who was visiting from England where he was now teaching. It was also the first time they had entertained for some years. More than anything they wanted Michael to enjoy himself and they wanted to demonstrate to him how happy they both were and how well they were coping after their bereavement. It was also in the nature of a farewell to Lusaka as Charles was retiring to Zimbabwe at the end of the year.

There were perhaps forty guests at the luncheon including children.

Marielise and Jo were both invited and, as chance would have it, were back from Zimbabwe for a conference or some such reason, and could manage to come. Marielise, who always seemed so reasonable, as usual, sounded vague about what was really happening in her life. She was however, looking forward particularly to seeing her cousin Michael again.

So was Zanele, who was also in Lusaka for the university vacation. Zanele had had quite a crush on Michael when she was small and they were all together at Siavonga. Marielise had taken the three of them, Michael, his brother Richard and Zanele, down to the Siavonga cottage when Charles and Margaret were busy with social functions for the bank. Michael was then about nineteen years old. He had spoken of his plans to go to art school in England in spite of Charles's disapproval. Marielise had encouraged him and put him in contact with her old friend and lover, Eva, who was a successful ceramicist and a lecturer at a London Art School. She was very interested to find out how Michael's career was progressing and if he was still happy with his choice.

In order to have a few guests of Michael's age, the Beaumonts also invited the Harveys, Nick and Manda, with their two children, and their old friends, Henry and Petronella Chishimba, together with their son Mumbi and his new wife Jane. Mumbi was now working at Charles's bank. Then there were several of Margaret's old friends from the Wildlife Conservation Club, some of Charles's friends from the Lusaka Squash Club and a couple of his old friends from the days of political wrangling about the end of the Federation and the building of the North Bank Power Station. Other long-standing friends included the pilot, Peter Duncan with his wife Elspeth, and even Father Patrick Brogan who was now chaplain at the University of Zambia.

It was a warm, dry day; the swimming pool, still a little too cool for the older guests, was soon full of small, screaming and splashing children who were carefully ignored by the men gathered around the bar on the pretext of finding drinks for the ladies. Margaret, and those women who were mothers or grandmothers, sat near the pool watching out for accidents while chatting about the current difficulties of life in Zambia. The young and single like Zanele and Michael pulled out rugs and cushions onto the grass and lay about talking about their plans to fly off to exotic and thrilling Zambian holidays in various safari and game camps. Zanele joined in merrily without giving any clue that such holidays were well beyond her personal or her family's resources. She enjoyed the way Michael was protective of her. It was fun to tease him by talking about the risks she took wandering around Lusaka on her own. She was older now and no longer had a crush on him. She did notice however that he kept glancing across at Manda, who was without question the most attractive woman at the party.

Well, Zanele thought to herself, *Manda and I are most interesting to this crowd I suppose because Lusaka is still so stuffy about people who are mixed-race – but we are also the coolest.*

Zanele was confident of her own charms.

Nick started off at the bar chatting to Charles and Henry and Father Patrick, but then he wandered across to the younger group who by now were talking about going on walking safaris in the Luangwa Valley. It was something Nick was longing to experience. On his way across he bumped into Jo and Mumbi, introduced himself, and started up a conversation in his friendly way. Soon he found that Jo and Mumbi shared his passion for rally driving.

"You'll have heard of our great Zambian rally driver – Satwant Singh then?" said Mumbi to Nick, "There are plans for a motor rally around Kariba Lake sometime."

Marielise, finding herself rather in between the guests in age and with quite different life experiences, came over to the pool to talk to Margaret and was introduced to Manda, whom she was curious about in any case, and whom she had noticed as being rather lovely. Also sexy-looking, Marielise thought, with that familiar and pleasant warming sensation in her belly that came with a new physical attraction. Manda was clearly new to Zambia, and Marielise wondered how she was adjusting to the mix of racism and multiculturalism that was Lusaka.

As usual Marielise watched and listened first.

Manda was aware of Marielise's slow, apparently lazy, gaze. Since arriving in Lusaka, she had been stared at rather more than usual at social occasions and she had developed the habit of facing the starer, who more often than not looked away awkwardly. Lusaka seemed to be divided on racial lines and mixed-race marriages, and mixed-race people still seemed to draw undue attention which surprised and irritated her. She turned to Marielise with her direct gaze but Marielise's eyes crinkled up; she smiled her warm, relaxed smile and started at once on a conversation.

"How is Lusaka treating you?" she asked, "It's all change here again. Old Lusaka is so thoroughly shaken up by the end of the Zimbabwe war that it doesn't know if it's coming or going."

Manda was disarmed. People usually asked where she lived and what her husband did first. She assumed that was so that they could easily pigeon-hole her. Marielise though, seemed to be interested in her as a person rather than in her status as a wife.

"Oh gosh!" she said, "Life is never what you expect is it? I didn't expect that expatriate society in Lusaka would be so socially competitive and so – well – so disinterested in economic development and politics, and I guess so racially segregated – though Margaret's friends seem different – "

Marielise laughed with pleasure. She thought, *I think I am really going to like this young woman.* She said, "Oh Lusaka is composed of so many different groups of people and there is more crossover than you think between groups. What are you planning to do with your time here?"

Manda grimaced. "I have learnt that I have to have a work permit and that that might be difficult – my kids are still small – James isn't at nursery school yet. Nick doesn't think I should bother to work – his words – but honestly, I think I will go nuts if I am at home all day."

Manda didn't want to say that the few times that she had been asked to have tea or coffee with other expatriate wives had been excruciatingly dull. Then she exploded.

"The women I have met only want to talk about their servants! Can you believe it – their servants – and where to get their consumer items! I couldn't credit it! One woman imports dog-food and diet coke through her embassy! Oh and they talk about burglaries all the time too. One woman told me that she buys top quality steak for her guard dogs and makes her cook feed it to

191

them. Apparently they need the best steak before they will bite thieves! I would be so ashamed! Her dogs probably cost her more than her gardener's salary! I hate to think what her cook eats but it won't be fillet steak!"

Manda stopped with a smile and pulled an abashed face. She knew that her husband did not like her to display passion. His own dark passions were a deep, buried secret, to both of them.

Without turning her head to see if Nick was watching, Manda said, "Nick says I get far too excited about social injustices! Forgive me. You can see why I need to be occupied." She looked at Marielise, "Tell me, what do you do? Zanele is your daughter? She is lovely."

"Ahh." Marielise had noted Manda check herself, but she settled down for an enjoyable conversation. "Social justice is sort-of what some of my work is about. I am a social anthropologist and teach at UNZA but I also do work in Zimbabwe. That's where Jo, my boyfriend, lives. Zanele is his daughter but I guess she has mostly grown up with me."

Soon the two women were talking and laughing and they began to weave the threads of their conversation into the fabric of a close friendship.

They had been chatting together for almost an hour when Marielise remembered that she wanted to talk to Michael. She looked up, caught his eye, which had rather often looked in their direction, and beckoned him over to join them.

"Hey Michael – meet Manda! She's new to Lusaka and finding it like Lusaka is," she said. "Manda this is Margaret's son, Michael. Michael – what is happening to you?"

"Well…" Michael said with his lop-sided, pleasant grin. He had grown from a diffident adolescent to a young man who used a gentle irony to hide his shyness. "Thanks to you, Marielise, my life is one enormous challenge – right now I have two full-time jobs. I am teaching at a sixth-form college in the day and working at night to put together my first solo exhibition at an East London Gallery.

It's hell on wheels – and I am loving it! It's not quite as confusing as Lusaka though," he nodded towards Manda sympathetically

Manda had been curious about Margaret's son. Meeting him she felt that his self-deprecating manner hid a determined intelligence and a sharp sense of humour that she rather liked.

Michael turned to his cousin, "What's happening to you, dear cousin Marielise – or does your work still remain a dark and deadly secret?"

Manda was disappointed to realise that neither Marielise nor Michael were resident in Lusaka. She felt that the company of both Michael and Marielise would have enlivened her life. Still – they were with her at that moment and the lunch party was one of the most pleasant of her experiences so far in Zambia. The cousins were unpretentious and disarmingly unconventional, ready to argue about some idea or other and then laugh about it too. Manda felt sure that her family would like them and that the feeling would be mutual.

"Damn!" she said, "I was already counting on the two of you to cheer up my life in Lusaka. Why don't you live here too?"

"I visit Lusaka pretty often," said Marielise, looking at Manda in her considering way.

"I have an exhibition planned for Harare at the Delta Gallery sometime next year," said Michael, "I'll be back to visit the lake at the least. Might try an exhibition here too perhaps. My mother would love me to do that!"

"We'll all see each other again," Marielise promised.

FOURTEEN

Cock's Crow

The Guest Book. The Cottage, Siavonga.
April 1983
Nick, Manda, Emma and James.

'Cool, bright, breezy weather. Good windsurfing and sailing. Our wooden post to record water levels has broken and the top half has washed away. Brought red and orange chanterelles from roadside vendors on the way down. They were delicious. Two rainstorms – one thunderstorm at night. Acacia tree blooming. Hot but cloudy, peaceful and green. Brought St Augustine grass to replace the thinning lawn. Arranged for bricklayer to do more steps below the wall to the water's edge.

The Yacht Club had a picnic on the beach near Banana Island. Good steady wind from SW until 4pm. Lake dropped 2-3 ft. The children collected rocks while looking for semi-precious stones. We saw paradise flycatchers and hornbills. Not too hot. Cloud and thunder.'

Down at the cottage Manda surfaced when the sun rose. Nick was already awake.

She could tell.

"Bloody cockerel! I'll get Milimo to wring its neck," he said.

"And the one next door and the one on the other side and the one at the police station," suggested Manda sleepily. The sound of crowing did not bother her. Cockerels had crowed through all her dreams since she was a child in most of the places that she had lived in. There were cockerels next door to their home in Lusaka too but the sound of passing cars and the security guards calling out as they changed shift by the street gate was even louder. Nick slept through all of that racket and Manda did not tell him that it was the quiet of Siavonga that really bothered him at night – that, and of course, the heat.

Down at the cottage they slept behind a screen door that was not a very serious barrier to little creatures like spiders, scorpions or mosquitoes. It fastened only with a small iron hook and eye but then at those hot season temperatures anything that might impede the softest movement of air had to be jammed wide open.

Back in Lusaka they had had to install heavy-duty burglar bars on every window in the house and a rape gate between the living rooms and the bedrooms. Manda found it hard to sleep when she was locked in. She insisted the security company make an escape gate for her family through the bars in the bedroom. Fine to insist on keeping the children safe in their beds but no, she refused to bar the living room windows and look through them at the garden as if she was a prisoner. Let the thieves – *kabwalalas* – take the furniture, take everything but not her sense of freedom. Yes Lusaka was changing – all the expatriate workers agreed it was for the worse. Burglary, armed robbery, rape and even murder were talked about at tea every day by the wives. An armed rapid response security service to protect expatriates was in operation. Of course the new black middle class were just as much at risk and Manda's friends and colleagues from the poorer out-lying townships told her that they also could not sleep for fear of robberies. The more you had, the more you paid to protect it. If you were poor and were robbed, you were poorer and you did without.

So Manda loved the openness of the ramshackle cottage with its basic, out of date, but practical equipment and complete lack of anything electrical. They ate on the veranda under the swinging storm lanterns that stunk of paraffin and went to bed by candlelight without any fear of harm. In any case Milimo and his family slept in the huts above the cottage and Milimo was a well-known person in Siavonga. If there were rumours of marauders, Milimo would have heard of them. Manda always had a niggle of guilt about depending on Milimo for safety. Why should he be taken for granted in that way? But Nick just shrugged and said, "He gets paid for it so why not?" That was always Nick's response to situations. It depended on its monetary value and usefulness. Pay what it's worth. Well, he was an economist: capital development and resources was his job.

The delights of dozing and dreaming in the relative cool of the morning were not for Nick.

"Bacon and egg for breakfast Miranda. Tea."

"Lovely," said Manda, wrinkling her nose under the sheets at being called 'Miranda'.

Nick wasn't asking a question but making a statement. Nick made breakfast at the cottage. He liked to be busy. The children were sleeping late this morning after a late night and barbecue: James sprawled in his travel cot; Emma cuddled up with the sheet over her head.

While Nick did what he liked busily, Manda slipped on her bikini and a thin cotton caftan and slipped quietly off the side of the veranda to explore her beloved, dew-fresh, early morning garden. There was the battered, fruitless lemon tree, the spiny purple bougainvillea, and the philodendrons spilling over the indigenous trees on the top terrace and reaching above them all the tall tree where the peregrine falcons roosted these last few years.

"Those are Mrs Beaumont's plants." Milimo would say proudly and protectively.

Milimo still insisted on doing everything at the cottage as Mrs Beaumont would have wanted him to but Nick liked to assert his will and, to amuse himself, he often challenged Milimo by making him do the opposite to Mrs Beaumont's wishes. Manda, however, liked to think of Margaret Beaumont making this garden from the rocks and dirt of the original site and she took care not to uproot anything she had planted unless it was already dying and needed to be replaced. She wondered if Margaret was making progress with her plans for a Permaculture Co-operative Farm. Rather taken with the idea herself, Manda had started a vegetable garden below Jo's water tank and Milimo had begun to grow a little maize there.

Manda wound her way down the east side of the property that bordered the neighbouring cottage, past the spreading pile of compost dumped by Milimo, and under the spindly tree-trunks supporting the Tonga sleeping platform that Milimo was constructing for the children's use. Manda tugged at the supports. Were they strong enough? The children would one day be swinging off them, hauling up buckets of books and toys, and the ground below was rocky.

With that sixth sense that children have, Manda's children set out to compete with Nick, knowing that he liked to be centre stage. That battle became more and more tiring as they got older and more demanding. The kids also had begun to squabble with each other. Emma, the eldest, had taken to flouncing off impatiently, or staring hard and stonily at James, little and trusting as he was. In response James would get violently and furiously angry and frustrated with Emma. Nick refused to intervene, adjudicate or take much interest and Manda felt helpless and a failure in every family relationship.

Sometimes Manda felt that she had not two, but three children, and that Nick, the biggest child, was the most jealous and difficult. Manda had consulted all kinds of friends, books and even mentioned the subject to Father Patrick at work, but the situation seemed intractable. Manda's darling children, so easy to deal with one-to-one, were monsters together.

"We made them, didn't we? Nick and I," Manda sighed but owning her share of the responsibility didn't bring solutions either.

Manda did not want to admit to herself that Nick could not see that he played any part in the behaviour of his children.

There were too many unspoken questions that she did not let surface about her beloved husband. At least here at the lake, Nick was very happy. Lake Kariba had become his main hobby and he read, researched and collected as much information about the lake as he could.

"It's much easier to get information about the lake in Zimbabwe than in Zambia," he said. "I know that they do do research here too but it's the apparent lack of real interest by the Zambian government in this major asset, and the fact that no one organisation of body seems really interested in collecting and disseminating it that makes it difficult to find out what is happening to the lake itself."

Marielise had brought Nick a couple of books about the lake from Zimbabwe and Manda took out a subscription to a Zimbabwean fishing magazine. Nick looked a bit askance at it at first.

"Fishing is not my thing is it?" he said

"Mmmh yes, I do know," said Manda, "but you are interested in what lives in the lake and fish are included in that. Also the magazine has the monthly lake levels in it and where in Zambia are you easily going to find those? Let's face it – our attempts to record lake levels are crude and the lake has washed them all away – one after the other."

"True enough Manda!" Nick said, smiling at her. "We'll have another go though won't we?"

"Expect so," Manda said, smiling back. "Get out the theodolite and the pile-driver and we'll put in a steel marker post that is accurate and that will last two rainy seasons!"

Across the lake, they could see the Zimbabwean islands of Sampa Karuma. Once they were floating green hills but since the drought they had become a fortress of scrubby-topped, bare red rocks, rising high above the water. Nick, looking over at the height of these rocky cliffs, estimated that the lake must have dropped 30 feet or more in the last few years. That was an immense volume of water that was not there.

FIFTEEN

Dry Weather

The Guest Book. The Cottage, Siavonga.
August 1985
Jo, Marielise and Luke
_'A much needed break after a stressful time. We just chilled out,
sunbathed and swam, ate and drank, and read anything that was
not to do with work!'_

The weekend began badly.

Everyone was strung out and scratchy with each other.

August was a dry, unsettled time with hot dust blowing everywhere in spiteful, irritating gusts. The sky was pale and cloudless. The rains were months away and the air too dry. Marielise's skin and eyes itched constantly; her hair crackled with static and stood up in a crazy halo around her head. The wind affected her memory, blowing her organised lifestyle to bits. She returned home to collect a forgotten teaching file and found it had split open and the assessment papers for her students were chasing dead leaves around the floor.

Jo was preoccupied. Bessie had spent a month in Zambia after being discharged from hospital in England. She was returning to England with Zanele, who at eighteen was going to study film and media at university. Jo would follow them on a later flight and then head off for Cuba and Grenada where he hoped to find money and offers of help for the liberation cause.

There was a sense of things ending and doors closing, without anything new promised. A general feeling of stasis and lethargy: a hiatus without hope. Luke had been working at the Lusaka headquarters for a while. Like Jo he would be moving on that weekend. For a time he had been one of the link men between the Zimbabwe Liberation Army and the South African Freedom Fighters but he had decided to throw himself wholeheartedly in with the armed wing of the banned communist party of South Africa. He would spend some time in Angola and then secretly enter South Africa to work there. Luke felt he had made a momentous decision but no one seemed to take account of the importance of it. Marielise was angry with everybody and trying not to show it. She was angry with Jo for being preoccupied, angry with Luke for sulking, angry with Bessie for being in such over the top, crazy high spirits, and angry with Zanele for being so eager to go to away to study when Marielise would miss her so much. Whenever Marielise stopped rushing about and tried to speak, her throat choked up and she needed to cough to clear it.

Zanele and Bessie caught the Wednesday night flight. At the last minute Bessie's high spirits deflated and Zanele, unexpectedly feeling lost, clung to Marielise and cried. Marielise had found a way to cope with Zanele's excitement over university, but she was so taken by surprise at Zanele's change of mood that she burst into tears herself and then felt she had let everyone else down. Bessie, she knew, was jealous of Marielise's relationship with her daughter and with Jo. It really had not helped to remind Bessie of how deeply Marielise had become involved with Bessie's child and one time lover during her long mental illness.

On the following Friday evening, Jo, Luke and Marielise drove down to the lake to take a much-needed break. They took two cars as Jo would be returning early for the Sunday flight. Jo took many flights in the course of his work. After the trauma of saying goodbye to Zanele and Bessie, he asked Marielise not to come to the airport.

"It's easier," he said, "Airport farewells are so public and so painful. Once I am ready to board I want to focus on what is all just work for me."

He and Luke drove down in his car as they had business to discuss but in fact they had not even talked much on the way down. The valley had already reached temperatures well over thirty degrees centigrade and neither car had air-conditioning. By the time they reached the cottage they were all limp and damp but instead of relaxing, they dragged themselves round to Jacky's bar where they had indifferent steaks, too many of Jacky's double Siavonga gin and tonics and stayed too late. Back at the cottage, they fell into bed without talking much to each other and then they all overslept the next morning.

The lake level was dropping fast, even faster than usual for the time of year. They had to scramble down further than before over rocks that were sharp and loose and when they finished swimming there was no place to sit. The morning sun was concentrated on the beach and there was no shade, even under the trees on the first terrace, so they climbed slowly back up the 130 steps, stopping in the shade at each level terrace to repeat to each other that it was the hottest they had been so far that year and it was unseasonal. Jo and Luke were each thinking that in the next few months they would have to endure even worse heat and harder physical conditions when they returned to their camps and Marielise was wondering how they coped with conditions in the bush. At last they attained the veranda, opened some cold beers from the fridge and eventually, in spite of Marielise's efforts to steer the conversation to lighter subjects, fell to talking over the old, and for the moment at least, the insoluble problems of the struggle.

"We should be doing what ZANU did in Zimbabwe," said Luke, "It's useless all this training in the bush in Angola as we can't yet confront the South African Army in that situation and win – even with the Cubans and the experience we gain, we are being pushed backwards all the time. The whole region is being destabilised to prevent African socialist governments coming into legitimate power. Instead we should be getting more and more cadres into the townships and villages of South Africa where they can lie hidden and gradually re-educate the people about how to resist."

"We are doing that." Jo was repeating an argument, "We are doing that as well. Look at all the recent bombings. The attack on the oil storage depots, the shops in Jo'burg, the police – but you do know Luke, that it is very different in South Africa to the way it was in Zimbabwe. The situation for each region is so varied and complex – there are informers and spies everywhere and people have been without information or any kinds of educational resources for so long. The migrant labour force is drawn from all over this part of Africa – it is simply not possible to recruit most of those people to our cause; they know their time in South Africa is limited and they are embedded in every community. Then there is the exploitation of tribal differences by power-hungry tribal chiefs as well as by the nationalist *boere* government."

"Sure thing," answered Luke, "but we lose the people who carry out these acts too often and too quickly, and then have to find and train new, often inexperienced people. They aren't getting local support. There was much too long a period of time when no information was getting into South Africa. There are now actually many younger people in the townships who have not heard of Mandela, or Sobukwe, or Sisulu. Bram Fisher is so long dead and buried – and he was white – and Afrikaans – that he means nothing to ordinary black people even though he died for them!"

"The trouble is that we are all upset by the news from the townships at the moment – all the killings, betrayals, necklacings – that we know are disintegrating communities and making it hard for people to trust each other," Marielise said.

'What do you two know, really know, of this township life?" Luke turned on his friends suddenly, "How can you criticise and analyse and train new cadres? Neither of you grew up suffering daily humiliations and abuse – neither of you have ever been afraid to raise your heads and look another person in the eye because they are white and you are black!"

"Bloody hell!" said Marielise, "That's not worthy of you, Luke. We have worked through this race stuff often enough before – we are comrades and we don't gain from these kinds of comparisons. So what if we have had wonderful childhoods, we are here – now! With you! Fighting the same cause and – and we are of some use too!"

"Come on Luke," said Jo quietly, "this is why we have had a political education – so that we can understand how all this divides and destroys us. It is our understanding and analysis of racism that makes us good fighters and political activists and makes us effective together."

"Oh – I'm not getting at the two of you specifically. Our armed wing is made of recruits of all colours now and that is fairly recent, but look how long we have been fighting: it's nearly twenty-five years of armed resistance. There are always problems with the new men and women from the townships; nothing in their lives has given them any faith in white people from anywhere and they know the Western powers are not on their side. Even those committed to the cause have no political education and no real knowledge about South Africa or its history."

"I know, I know!" Jo leant forward with his head in his hands, "I just go through these terrible fears that we won't make it before we are all dead! At the moment the stories coming out of Soweto are so god-awful that I can't bear it. I can't bear it that we are fighting each other instead of the *boere*."

"It's very difficult to judge the situation," said Marielise, "because it keeps changing so fast – and not just the situation in South Africa. Look at what is happening in Eastern Europe with the Baltic States – they are starting to demand independence from Russia. Thank God – sorry – thank old Karl Marx for the Cubans." Marielise's smiled ironically. "How the Angolan war remains such a well-kept secret is extraordinary but it must be because the Americans are holding the fence for the South Africans. We need to find a way to publicise what is happening there!"

"There will be a pay-off," Jo said. "The USA is determined to make sure that there are no socialist countries close to it in Latin America. Who knows how long it will be before they invade Grenada? I just hope that I get in and out of both Grenada and Cuba safely."

"It's another reason for rethinking what we are doing," said Luke. "Okay – I am a communist – but I am not committed to any Soviet idea of communism: we can't approve the repression of countries like Czechoslovakia and Hungary, we will have to find our own African forms of socialism. Instead we are looking at the destruction of African traditions of community inside South Africa and that will be a problem when we come to build the new South Africa."

"Look Luke," Jo reached across to touch his friend's shoulder, "you are proven as a good fighter who understands the bush war and doesn't waste lives. You will be one of our most important leaders and thinkers because, though you are young, you are very experienced at bush warfare and very well informed – you really do know what you are talking about. Right now we are having to learn about new situations daily and react quickly. It is tough and it does look very bad at the moment."

"My friends, my comrades," Luke said, "It is okay and we must not ever lose hope. There will be majority rule in South Africa. The people will win. Today is a day when we are all full of anger and frustration for those back in Soweto. We just need to let it all out."

"The war against Apartheid is still not in the world press as it deserves to be," observed Marielise, "but more and more we have to understand world politics and how all that is changing – it all impacts on our struggle here in Africa. Look at the role that the South African arms industry plays in the world: sending big guns it has built – that were developed in Israel – to Iraq. Sometimes I think we are all crazy – you couldn't invent this stuff – who would believe you?"

Eventually they each admitted that the heat and the cold beer made it a good idea to have a doze. Marielise and Jo went into their room and were soon asleep. Luke took a bundle of old *Life* magazines left by Charles, a couple of bottles of beer, and went down to the reclining deckchair in the shade. Soon he too was sleeping, though lightly as he was in the habit of doing when on a mission.

Jo woke first and went to get a glass of water. He padded around till he felt sure that Luke was far enough away not to return too quickly. Milimo he knew would only appear when it was time to light the storm lanterns and set up the charcoal brazier for the barbecue. He slid back into the bed next to Marielise, stroked her face gently and then her breasts and cleavage, all moist and sticky with sweat to rouse her gently, but Marielise was already stirring and reaching out for him. They made love quietly and they were as slow and tender as possible, savouring their own and each other's pleasure in the knowledge that it might be months till they were together again. Learning again what they already knew so well of the feel of the skin and the shape of each other's bodies, committing it all to that memory that is so strong and frail because it is both physical and spiritual love.

As the evening cooled, the three friends made their way down to the water's edge. Distant *kapenta* rigs glowed and their engines muttered steadily on the furthest reaches of the Zimbabwean waters. The waning moon, setting west of the Matusadona Hills, was too pale and old to leave a trail on the lake and the kite-shaped Southern Cross with its tail of the two Pointers tilted over slowly, as if released from the weight of the drowning moon. Luke and Jo went into the water briefly to cool off but Marielise watched them and shuddered, though she wasn't cold.

"I can't bring myself to get into the water when it looks so dark. I know there are creatures in it watching me."

"Probably wise," said Jo, sitting down beside her. "Your friend Piet says that he has seen croc *spoor* on the sand at the hotel beach, but that's a good place for crocs to bask in the sun. This isn't. I still think it's okay here for the time being – it will change though."

"This is what we will have to be planning for South Africa in the future," said Luke, standing up and waving a towel at the lake, power for industry. This lake was built to power the Copperbelt mines."

Marielise was amused.

"It's so ironic – all during the Bush War – Rhodesia and Zambia were sharing this essential resource of hydroelectric power but Rhodesia wasn't paying for what it used. There was a huge fuss made and eventually the white government was forced to pay to Zambia what it owed. I understand that one of the Rhodesian ministers actually wept when he was faced with that reality."

Jo and Luke laughed, then Luke said, "It's somewhat different in Mozambique, the dam there is owned by the Portuguese who built it to provide power to South Africa. But if you can believe this: the war that South Africa is conducting in Mozambique through its agents Renamo is destroying the electricity network – pylons are constantly being blown up – this racist war is also counter-productive for South Africa."

"Apartheid is counter-productive full stop!" agreed Luke.

"God – they need us to be in power!" said Jo, "We are the ones with the understanding of the real interests of the region and we are the ones with the diplomatic links to the rest of Africa!"

Marielise was shaking her head sombrely.

"You guys need to be so careful! They want you dead – you two especially – but all of you who are socialists. In the end they won't care whether the South African government is black or white, as long as it sells its minerals and diamonds cheaply to the world and buys expensive guns in return. You guys will never toe the line when you come to power; sooner or later they are going to assassinate you even if you have won the war. All the rest of the world want is to exploit Africa's resources. They want a passive government in South Africa – not you guys."

Jo and Luke looked at Marielise. After a moment Luke said, flicking his towel at her, "Hey woman, always the brilliant analyst, aren't you? Always the optimist! Come on woman, it's time you looked after your men properly and got them some supper!"

"On yeah?" Marielise grinned, "Tonight the men cook. You know the rules – you men invented fire? You men are cooking the steaks!"

The three of them made their way up the dark steps to the veranda and the barbecue for steak, wine and beer. The rest of the evening passed pleasantly and lightly until at last they ran out of the need for conversation and simply sat in the humming dark, watching the bats skim and swoop over the terraces. Finally Luke said he needed to sleep in a bed and not a chair and he disappeared into his room and almost immediately snored gently. Jo and Marielise pulled their chairs closer and sat a little while longer, holding hands before they too went to bed and quickly to sleep.

At first light, Jo and Marielise woke hungry for each other, moving from erotic dreams to sleepy arousal, and then to full and passionate desire and orgasm as lovers can when they know each other well. For a while they lay together, whispering to each other, then Jo got up to leave for Lusaka. He called Luke who was already up and brewing tea in the kitchen and the two men walked up to Jo's car, talking and planning as they went. Marielise stayed in bed with the sheets pulled up over her head, trying to wrap herself in the memory and the smell of Jo, trying to make time go back that one hour so that she could have Jo, and he could have her all over again and again forever. When she heard the car leave and Luke return to the cottage, she called out that she was going to lie in bed for another hour and there she stayed, breathing in Jo.

Sixteen

Breaking Down

Marielise and Luke were silent as they shared a breakfast of coffee and eggs.

Marielise still immersed in a dreamy state, was avoiding thoughts of the weeks ahead without Jo. Luke however seemed sullen and downcast. At last Marielise made an effort to break out of her spell and, if possible, cheer Luke up.

"Hey what's up with you Luke?" she began, thinking she might need to cajole him into telling her his problems; but Luke was more than willing to talk, and to talk in a way that Marielise realised he could not do with his male comrades, or even in the company of Jo. At first he didn't make much sense, sentences tumbled out in a random clutter of ideas and accounts of events. Gradually, as he repeated himself, he became more coherent.

"It was hell," Luke said, "the mutineers were imprisoned, beaten and finally executed. It was so confused and confusing. These guys really had a point – what the hell were we doing month after month training in the bush, scared of being attacked or bombed all the time? Nothing seems to be going forward in South Africa but similar kinds of horrors and punishments and fears in the townships – murder – necklacing of people who just disagree with you – they only disagree!

"Okay – one guy was shot for rape – another two for getting

drunk and killing civilians in the market – maybe that is necessary in a war – I don't know – I didn't have to pull the trigger or order the execution! But these mutineers had a point – they didn't think they were mutineers – they were wanting to be heard – to be listened to – and they were loyal to the cause – they were loyal to the ANC – they just felt that the leadership in Angola weren't leading – weren't taking the fight in the right direction – they wanted to go back into South Africa and fight there.

"Of course the leadership was paranoid – is always paranoid, with good reason probably – that the guerrillas were being infiltrated by spies and agent-provocateurs.

"You could see how it was all going to unfold – you could see the unavoidable mistakes coming from miles off; you could see the misunderstandings – the fears – the hurry to make decisions – but you see that there are guys fearful for their position – their status – scared that their leadership is under threat and so they behave so brutally. Where does that come from? Where is the foresight – the planning – the consideration for the fighters.

"The trouble is you daren't speak out even though you are ashamed yourself. You cannot risk speaking out yourself and then you have to live with shame. Everyone lies about what happened – everyone – how can it get better? The lies are worse even than the mistakes!

"God, I keep asking myself – are we all monsters? Them, the *boere,* and us, the guerrillas? I believe that ours is the just cause – the right cause – that we should and must win, but we will come to power with blood on our hands with shame in our hearts.

"We have to be better people than our oppressors – we have to be! But what I see is that the corruption of Apartheid has corrupted us too. I am bad Marielise! I am bad!"

Luke turned to Marielise in a passion, his face contorted, his forehead creased into ridges, his hands held out towards her with the palms up flat. Marielise already had an idea of what Luke was talking about. Jo had mentioned the stories with much discomfort.

210

A version of the events had been not only in the world press, but also in the left-wing press. She opened her mouth to say something to soothe Luke, though what that might be she did not know. Before she could speak, he shocked her into silence with his next words.

"I need to fuck a woman," Luke said, "Let me have sex with you now! I need to fuck – I want to forget!" and he took her wrists in his hands.

"No!" said Marielise in a calm, steady voice, "I don't fuck angry men – ever!"

Her mind raced as she considered what might happen in the next few hours, what Luke might do, what she ought to do. She had wondered briefly if she might end up having sex with Luke after Jo had left. Marielise and Luke had been lovers before, though never when Jo was around. The fight against Apartheid made personal sacrifices and discipline necessary and comrades often did without sex. Those in the armed struggle had to have their choice of wives and partners vetted by the leadership for their commitment to the cause. Life was tough for men like Luke. Marielise liked him so it was easy for her to be generous physically. Luke had been a good lover and considerate. In his present state of angry misery was it likely that might he rape her if she didn't say yes? Perhaps it would be safest just to allow him to have sex with her? Just to submit.

"No," said Marielise again firmly, unwinding her wrists from Luke's grasp.

"I will not have sex with you while you are angry. We have been lovers and I will not let you spoil that."

The sound that Luke uttered was a roar, a roar of anger and frustration. Marielise thought for a moment that he was going to pick up the breakfast tray and smash it over her head.

"Cunt!" he yelled, "Whore!"

Instead he picked up the chair he had been sitting on and tossed it up, out and over the terraces as if it was a Frisbee. For a moment he stood there, his arms still raised, looking at Marielise with hatred and rage then he turned, vaulted over the veranda railing, and made his way to the lakeside by leaping down over each terrace as if he was on a training exercise.

Milimo had heard the raised voices. He approached silently and watched Luke's combat-ready leaving exercises from behind a tree on the terrace above the cottage. Afterwards he quietly went into the kitchen and loudly rattled the saucepans from the previous night as he washed them up, every sense alive to the situation. As usual he left his *pata-pata* sandals outside the kitchen and came barefoot into the cottage.

Marielise just stood very still, trying to calm herself by breathing more and more slowly while she considered what next action to take.

She could just leave, drive home and let Luke find his own way back to Lusaka but she had a sense of duty. Comrades must stick together. Luke would manage to get back to Lusaka without her but it was always possible that he would be exposed to dangers on his own. They weren't really supposed to leave Lusaka without permission; there were roadblocks on the way home. Luke was definitely off-the-wall. Was he safe to be around or did his behaviour mean that she should look out for him? Was he just jealous of her relationship with Jo? Marielise didn't think so as they were such old friends. She would pack up and get ready to leave but she would also fix lunch and coffee and wait to see what Luke did – at least until late afternoon.

Milimo had decided to water the garden in front of the cottage as it was one of those few days when the Siavonga council had not turned off the water supply. She was glad that he was around, but was she safer with Milimo there, or would his presence just infuriate Luke if he came back? She could not see Luke anywhere; he might have gone for a swim or taken a long scrambling walk around the shore. Sounds were different in the daytime. There was some traffic on the road, loud voices carried across the lake for great distances but quiet noises were muffled by the sound of the quick waves below.

Marielise threw herself onto her bed for a few moments' respite. She felt tired, sick and hopeless but she did not want to cry. That would weaken her and she might need all her strength to get through the rest of the day. After a while she did as she had planned. She had a cold shower, packed, organised lunch and set out the tray for fresh coffee, then she went outside to see if Luke was anywhere to be seen. She reckoned that he had so much to deal with that he needed a long time to work through the conflicts in his life. The water had finally been turned off, but Milimo was now busy slashing at the longer grass on the edge of the plot. For a second Marielise was livid with him. Why did he make a point of gardening at weekends? Was it so he could be seen to work? It was clear that he maintained the garden and cottage very well during the week. What he a busybody? Was he being protective? Of the cottage being trashed? Of her?

Marielise exhaled deeply.

"Thank you very much, Milimo," she said, "We may go back to Lusaka this afternoon – I'll come and tell you when I know. Go and have lunch now."

"Yes Mad... – ah, Marielise," Milimo replied and he stepped into his *pata-patas* and walked up to his home.

Marielise decided inside ten minutes that she wasn't very good at waiting but she hung around for another hour. She couldn't guess what Luke's mood would be at the moment, had he had enough time alone? She had trusted him before but was that wise now? People who had been at war did go mad after all. She set off to walk slowly and carefully down the garden steps to the lake. There was no way she could outrun Luke if he decided to attack her. She knew she could survive rape, but she did not want to be beaten.

Before she reached the bottom terrace, Marielise saw Luke. He was sitting hunched over at the gap in the wall above the water. He looked wet through as if he had had a swim in his clothes, but was that just profuse sweat after exercise? How could she judge if it was right to approach him? Should she call out to him? She saw his shoulders heave up and sag down. Was he crying? Would he hit out at her if she got close?

Marielise looked back up the hill – could she get hold of a loose rock on the terrace fast enough if she needed to protect herself? Then she looked down at Luke again.

What the hell! she told herself, *I know what I want to happen. I want it to be okay.*

She descended the last few steps, crossed the rough grass and sat on the wall an arm's length from Luke.

"Luke," she said, "my dear friend. How are you?"

Luke crouched as if he was bracing himself for a plane crash; he made a ghastly inappropriate noise, like a snotty tearful child.

"Oh Luke, my dear!" said Marielise, and she knelt down behind him with her arms around his shoulders and gently rocked them both together backwards and forwards, backwards and forwards. After a while Luke turned around and, without raising his head, buried his face in Marielise's shoulder. For a long while they just sat together without speaking until Marielise was too uncomfortable and stiff. Then she clambered to her feet, shook herself to get rid of the pins and needles in her feet and pulled Luke upright. They made their way slowly back to the cottage where Marielise made coffee. Then she raided Charles and Margaret's private store cupboard for their bottle of Duncan Gilbey whisky and poured a generous amount on top of the coffee.

"Cheers Luke!" she said, "Here is to us and here's to us winning the fight for freedom! Long may we be the free thinkers of the Freedom Movement!"

She was rewarded with a grin from Luke.

"God!" he said, "Forgive me. I was so jealous of you and Jo! So stressed about all that's happening – I haven't known what to do – what to think – I am so angry – so ashamed – so bitter!"

"You should be sorry for your behaviour," responded Marielise, "but commitment does not mean giving up independent thought and autonomy. Discipline mustn't turn us into robots. You are right to feel as you do. The problem is how do you manage your dissent and your feelings usefully inside the Armed Resistance Wing? What are your options, because your survival is also essential? I don't want you shot for arguing with the leaders."

"I gave up on the Trotskyites because they wanted to control my mind – I will find a way through this too. I have got the option of moving to take on a different role in Zimbabwe. I don't think I can influence what is going on in Angola but I reckon that they know they can't keep on with what they do there any more – they must change too," Luke explained.

"Good," said Marielise, "that's sorted maybe – but I have to say – you frightened me this morning, Luke. I thought that you wanted to rape me. What were you doing?"

"I felt so bad – so ashamed – that I felt I was very bad. I thought maybe I was becoming an executioner and a murderer and – a – a – also a rapist. I felt like a killer and not like a Freedom Fighter!" Luke buried his face in his hands again, Marielise couldn't make out what he said but perhaps he kept repeating, "sorry, sorry, sorry."

"I liked having sex with you," Marielise said, "but I am not a whore, and don't ever call me a cunt either. Jo is my man. He is the one I love most. He knows that you and I have had sex and he understands and accepts it as part of how we all live at the moment. I make my own decisions about myself and my body until Jo and I are able to live together full-time. We have agreed that. It's the same for him."

Luke was leaning back in his chair, avoiding Marielise's eyes but looking more relaxed and rather sheepish.

"Any chance of another shot of Mr Beaumont's cheap whisky in another coffee Marielise? Look, I admire you and I admire the way you stand up for the rights of women and thank you so much for telling me where to get off this morning. I am so proud to have you for my friend and I am so sorry for the way I behaved. I wouldn't have raped you – really – you matter too much. I am not a rapist!"

Luke continued after a silence.

"Women's rights are not considered a priority at the moment. We give them lip service inside the movement – but outside it we treat women and our enemies in appalling ways. Will we get it right in the future? We had better!"

Marielise poured him another scotch whisky and coffee, and kissed his head briefly as she handed it to him.

"Do you want to stay here tonight or go back to Lusaka?" she asked.

Luke caught her hand.

"Please – can we stay here tonight – will it be okay for me to sleep with you tonight?"

"Maybe," said Marielise, "I'll come to you if I decide to – Jo's and my bed is just for me though."

Of course Marielise went to Luke's bed later that night. She could hardly have lain in her own bed thinking about him lying awake next door to her, thinking of her. She admitted as much to him after their first, hugely energetic and exciting, but too quickly over sexual encounter.

"Have you slept with lots of black guys before me?" Luke asked her as they snuggled themselves together on the inadequate single iron bedstead.

Marielise laughed. "I'm not bloody promiscuous Luke you know! Just because I have two ANC boyfriends – and a girlfriend back in England – I am very careful – especially here in Lusaka! Why? Have you slept with lots of white girls?"

"No." Luke squeezed Marielise's shoulders, "No. You are my only white woman."

"So far!" teased Marielise. "Is it different do you think? Does the difference make it more exciting?"

"Not that much after the first time maybe," Luke admitted.

"Now it is just about you – I think."

"Well I am a pretty hairy, Semitic, kind of a woman – maybe you would like to try a truly Nordic woman?" Marielise kept teasing.

Luke stopped her talking with kisses.

"You really get to me Marielise, you know. Is that love?"

"God – I don't know! For me the difference is exciting but I think it is the difference between a man and a woman that excites me most. It's your maleness first – no – first it is your mind. I love the way intelligent men think. It's tough and aggressive and clear – then I love the physical difference. I enjoy your blackness – I like the contrast between our skins – it seems so extraordinary and beautiful."

Marielise ran her hand over Luke's face, tracing his brows, his eyes and his lips.

"I love this about you: the curling of your eyelashes, the springiness of your eyebrows and this defining ridge of your lips. They are African maybe, but mostly for me, they are Luke. They are you – and I love them – and you."

"How is it with Eva then?" asked Luke. Again Marielise laughed but more gently.

"Oh I do love Eva. I find some women very attractive – there is the passion with a particular kind of caring but not the difference in the same way – but then who knows, maybe sex is always different and always the same?"

Luke was moving into arousal again.

"Hey, hey," Marielise warned softly, "have we enough condoms for a whole night together? Did you bring more? Shall I get mine? We may need quite a lot tonight."

Seventeen

Lusitu

The next morning began slowly because Marielise and Luke had both overslept. A late breakfast was followed by a last swim and then a final coffee. They were only on the road back to Lusaka just before lunch.

"Does it bother you what Milimo makes of you when he probably realises that you sleep one night with Jo and another with me?" Luke asked Marielise on the drive home.

Marielise raised an eyebrow and turned briefly to look at Luke.

"Come on Luke – don't all you comrades swap stories about women and sex all the time when you are together?"

"There's a lot of boasting and lies at the camps," Luke answered, "even when there are women among the comrades, the men talk about visiting prostitutes – and then how they think they are trash."

"Umm – not pretty! Well, Milimo belongs by tradition and practice to those who think that a man must have sex every night – if his wife is not available then another woman must be found and used. Orgasm is not so much a pleasure as a hygienic necessity. I expect Milimo thinks our behaviour quite normal and right and good for your health! Women are an essential convenience for men in this part of Africa so nothing new there."

"Really!" Luke grinned his acknowledgement, "Have you talked to him about this?"

"Mmmh, no. I think it's better to not ask one's employees personal questions. I did ask him to tell me about people who I could interview once, when it wasn't safe to wander around the valley during the war and he did introduce me to his mother, Natombi. She was one of the guardians of the Rain Shrines that were flooded when the dam was built. She is a very interesting person.

"How did you escape traditional sexual practice and attitudes yourself Luke?"

"My father was a Christian priest and we lived in towns. He was against polygamy and that kind of tradition and basically didn't talk about it. He was for marriage, one woman, and chastity."

They had been travelling along a dead straight road through dry thorn-veld and scrubby bushes. Occasional giant baobabs raised leafless branches above the acacia trees, dustily powdered with palest pink and yellow flowering tassels in anticipation of the rains. Abruptly the countryside altered.

"Here we are." Marielise slowed down the car and pulled onto the shoulder of the road. "I wanted to show you this place – this is Lusitu."

They had arrived in an extraordinary hot landscape of shocking-pink humped and clay hills against a blue sky, as bare of clouds as the land was bare of foliage. It almost hurt the eyes to look at the vibrant colours in the heat. Spindly-legged grain stores and rickety thatched huts marched over the slopes. In the deep eroded hollows a little damp, dark mud and a snail trail of green slime was the only evidence that rivers of water had ever rushed through them in the rains. Gaunt brown men and women, angular cattle, and scavenging goats jerkily searched for anything that wasn't pink. A flat-faced brick store with a shadeless veranda advertised in uneven painted letters that it belonged to Mr Mulenga. Near the store, what appeared to be three concrete beds for three different sized bears were in fact three graves left by a settler family many years past.

The only plants growing where the poisonous grey-green euphorbias that not even the goats would risk touching.

"This," said Marielise, "was the main resettlement area for the Tonga who were moved from the Gwembe Valley to make way for the dam. The land cannot sustain the population that is living on it. Since the dam wall was built the ecology of this flood plain has changed completely. After the rains this area would have been gently inundated with water that brought nutrients and topsoil and fish. Food crops would grow as the water receded. Now when it rains and the rivers rise, they rush through the valley taking topsoil away and are gone so fast that there is no time for anything to grow.

"The Zambezi River is a very long walk away but that does provide fishing. Life here is harsh, especially if there is drought and each year the environment becomes more and more degraded.

"The Tonga do not forget or forgive what was done to them.

"Can you believe this Luke: in the year following the resettlement, over a hundred Tonga died here in Lusitu for no apparent reason. Officials suggested that it was accidental self-poisoning because the local bush food was unfamiliar but actually no one knows for sure and no official wants to believe they died because they were forced to leave their ancestral homes."

"I believe one can die of homesickness," Luke said with feeling, "My first winter in London I wanted to die I was so alone. When the sun abandoned me as well I felt too weak to eat or sleep."

"I think heartbreak can kill too," said Marielise, earning herself a look of surprise from Luke. Marielise caught his expression.

"Don't look at me like that, Luke! If you can die of homesickness I can die of love!" She smiled and shrugged. Being too serious might open the door to the infection of sadness.

"Oh! Did you know that Milimo nearly died of sorcery a few years ago? It's an extraordinary story. He was saved by the magic of my Uncle Charles, of all the most unlikely people.

Margaret was away in hospital – for a hysterectomy I think – and Charles got a garbled message from Siavonga that Milimo was dying in the hospital in Lusaka. When he went to see him he found Milimo practically comatose, very thin and refusing to eat. Milimo was convinced he was bewitched and about to die. The doctor told Charles that it was more than likely that Milimo would die if he didn't eat or drink. According to Milimo, he had had a sudden excruciating pain in his leg with no apparent cause – no bite and no fall. A traditional witchdoctor had conducted an exorcism and removed a metre long snake from his leg, but that failed to cure Milimo. He soon became so weak that he was put in an ambulance by the Siavonga clinic and transferred to Lusaka.

"That's when Charles called me and asked me what to cook for Milimo. I, of course, said that chicken soup was definitely the best medicine according to my Jewish grandmother and I told him how to cook it – very slowly for the best results. Charles started off with a whole frozen chicken – his cook had been sent off for the night as Charles had had supper at his club. I think he kept taking the chicken out of the broth and hacking at it until it thawed. At any rate he spent the whole evening making chicken soup and phoning me up every now and then to report on his progress and what it tasted like. Next morning before work, Charles took a flask of chicken soup to the ward and spooned it into Milimo's mouth, telling him it was powerful magic. He did the same at lunch and supper for two days and then Milimo started to eat again, and a few days later was hopping about slowly on one leg and a stick – thank goodness!

"It's sad in a way, Charles believed in the Federation – he hoped that if the Federation survived, whites would get used to the idea of power sharing and there would not be a war of liberation. He was desperately disappointed and sad when the Bush War began. I think saving Milimo's life became Charles's positive action for Africa. He was so proud of his magic cure – he was so funny! He did not even think of it as a trick or a con."

Luke laughed and shook his head.

"That stuff was always around us too but my parents, being

Christians and believing in education, would not discuss it openly – it was always 'village people back home who believed'."

"Lusitu is also where Milimo's mother, Natombi, lives with her daughter," said Marielise, "I visited her here to ask her about the Tonga resettlement for my research. Natombi also told me about Chief Chipepo's uprising and how her husband was one of those killed in the fight with the police. She is only about fifty-five years old you know – she must have had Milimo when she was about twelve or thirteen. I'll tell you what she told me of her history."

It was a long story and took most of the car journey back to Lusaka.

Resettlement

1958

I am Natombi.

I am the inheritor of the shades of my ancestors. I am the one who must take care of the Rain Shrine and ask for the ancestors to provide the rain for our gardens.

Here, at Lusitu, the ancestors no longer help us. The rain does not come and the water that the rain brings does not stay for long. Each year the river digs deeper and deeper into the *dongas*, and each year it runs away faster. Now we are left only with dust.

Have you seen this place where we now live? The earth is bare and nothing is growing on it. Look here at my breasts. You can see that they are empty and lie flat against the bones of my chest. They are only dry bags of skin. They have no purpose anymore because I am old and my children are grown. My breasts are withered like the land that we live on here at Lusitu.

From here it is very far to the Zambezi River. It is too far to walk there and to walk back in the daylight. Here the Lusitu River is dry again. It has been dry for many months and it will be dry for many months still to come. There is no water here and there are no more trees left. We are without fuel for cooking and we are without water for our gardens. We are staying here by the road because only the road can bring us work and what we need to live on. Only the road can take us to the hospital.

When I was a young woman, when my son Milimo was a child, when my husband, the guardian of the Rain Shrines, also was alive, I tended two gardens on the banks of the Zambezi Valley. One garden was watered by the rains of summer and that gave us *sorghum*. In the winter there was another garden that we planted on the earth that the flood waters gave to us. We had crops twice a year and so we always had food to eat.

We are the people of the river. Our river, the Zambezi, looked after its people well. In the summer we had rain and the river ran low and quiet. In the dry season the river would rise up high and run quickly to reach over its banks to cover the land with water. When the river returned to its own place it left behind stranded fish and good, rich earth for our gardens.

All year round we could find the bush fruits that grow on the trees and the creepers because in the valley those fruits did not grow only in the rains but could be found at all other times of the year as well. In the season of the floods it was harder to catch fish but it was then that the men could go hunting because the animals would leave the dry places on the hills and come down to the valley to look for water.

We, the Basilwizi, the people of the Zambezi River, are the people who knew the places to bathe in the river that were safe from crocodiles. We are the people who know how to cross the river in our *bwatos* in all seasons, whether the river ran fast or slow, deep or shallow, quiet over sand, or angry over rocks. Therefore all the people of the plateaus, north and south, came to the Basilwizi when they needed to trade for food, for weapons, or for slaves, or when they needed to make journeys to other tribes and places. We were the people who could not be found when there was fighting or trouble, but we were the people who made all the meetings of strangers, of friends and enemies possible. We are the people of the river and we knew the male and female spirits of the river before they were separated by the wall of the dam.

Now the spirits of the river can no longer meet each other and make our lives fruitful.

For a time after the British came, life was better for the Basilwizi because the Ngoni raiders no longer came to kill us and burn our villages. The Ngoni raiders destroyed our shrines and stole our sacred objects. Because the British were here, the Portuguese traders also stopped coming up the river to take us away as slaves. Before that time, the mother of my grandmother was captured by two Portuguese men who were going to sell her so far away that she could never find her way home. The mother of my grandmother, like all the Basilwizi people, knew well how to run and to hide. On the first night that the Portuguese men stopped to camp on Kanyemba Island where the Kafue River joins the Zambezi, my grandmother's mother and her sister stole a *bwato* and escaped from them.

At that time, we lived deep in the valley where there were no roads and the only paths were made by wild animals. Very few white men came on foot to look for the Basilwizi. Those white men who did come were missionaries but they chose to live with us and not to steal from us.

I, too, have learnt how to run away and to hide. Some years after my son Milimo was born, I ran away back to my mother's village because Singani was unkind to me and beat me for spilling some grain. Singani came to fetch me back, saying that he had paid a good bride-price for me. He came together with his brothers and the Headman of his village. They sat and talked with my family for many hours but I refused to return saying that Singani was cruel to me. After some days Singani's Headman told Singani that he must not beat me for I was a good wife who had given him a son. My family said that I would return, but first Singani must agree to let me have my own hut and my own garden, and not work for Singani's first wife any more. As is the way of our village and our people, my family took care of me. All of this was agreed and after that my life was more pleasant than before.

After I returned to Singani's village, life began to change for the Basilwizi. More and more of the young men of our people began to leave the valley to find work in the towns. Even some went from my village. Some men went as far north as the copper mines. When each year, they walked back to see us, they brought wonderful gifts with them and many more extraordinary and strange stories. Some of the stories we did not believe though the missionaries told us that they were true. The young men said that the towns had sunlight at night time carried on thin ropes and that the same thin ropes made engines move. We had seen engines and lights before but they worked with paraffin and fire.

Today I know about electricity and that it comes from the captured spirits of the river and is made to travel along thin wires to the cities. We also want the power of the river spirits to give us electricity in our homes in Lusitu but the government has not yet provided it for us. That is why we have no trees left here. All the trees have been cut down so that we can have fuel for the fires to cook our food. There are now too many people living in Lusitu. The trees have all gone and there is not enough land. It is not possible for all of us to make new fields each year and the earth is too poor to grow enough healthy crops to feed us all year after year.

When we first came to Lusitu the countryside was rich in trees and in animals for hunting. The government of Northern Rhodesia made us many promises and gave us money when we were forced to move. We were given a school for our children and a clinic for our health. They also made some wells for us because we were no longer by the Zambezi River.

Resistance

1958

We did not come willingly. We were ready to fight the government so that we could remain in our homes but they were stronger than us and they had guns and trucks of police soldiers.

We came to Lusitu with such great sadness in our hearts that some of us died from it.

We came to Lusitu in mourning for those who had been killed in the war in Chief Chipepo's district at the village of Headman Chisamu.

The argument with the British grew slowly over the years.

They did not come to us or ask us about the river. Instead, one day they came to tell us that they were going to trap the river at Kariva and make the water rise up over our village and over all the villages of the Tonga people.

We did not believe them. They did not know the power of the river like we do. For two seasons the river fought with the dam that the white people were building and for two seasons the river won. It also brought its waters to us at Chisamu and we had to walk away from our homes and leave them to the river and the crocodiles for many weeks. But we could always return to our homes and our shrines and the graves of our ancestors after the floods went down.

We heard that the Rhodesians had made our relatives on the other side of the river leave their homes but we knew of many bad things that were happening in Rhodesia because of the white people.

On our side we had the men of the African National Congress come and tell us that we would soon govern ourselves and be free of the British. We listened and a very few of us believed, but most of us felt that we could trust no one – not the British and not the nationalists. Some of our young men told us that they had discovered there was some truth in these stories on their visits to the north, but we are not a people to change suddenly onto one side then to change again quickly to the other. We listen and we talk and we hide from trouble. The congress men did not persuade us to fight. We understood that the fight was forced on us by the British.

Soon the British brought more trouble right to our villages. We saw them bring giant yellow machines to the plains by the river. Then they used great round, metal rocks and long heavy chains and they pulled down all our trees as far as we could see and as far as we could walk in a day. Then they made huge fires and burnt the wood. We had never seen such terrible destruction and such waste of firewood. Those men among us who had travelled told us that this is the way that the white British people start to make their farms. From this we knew that the British were going to steal our land from us and we knew that the story of the dam was a lie to frighten us into leaving the land so they could take it for themselves.

But the British did not listen to us or understand that we could not leave the graves of our ancestors, neither could we take their spirits with us, or the shrines of our Rain Rituals. Without the spirits of our ancestors and without our shrines we cannot know when the rain will come for our gardens.

We decided that we could not hide anymore and that we should show the British that we would resist them by fighting if we needed to do so. Then it was that the men of the Basilwizi started to gather at the villages around Chief Chipepo's place and to collect spears and axes. We thought that when the British saw how many of us there were, they would go away and leave us alone. None of us had ever seen so many warriors gathered together in one place before. It should have been enough to warn the British to leave us alone. There were more than 500 of our men.

We thought that we had enough warriors to make the British leave us in peace.

Instead more of them came. They tied white paper marked with strange writing that we could not read onto the trees by the road to the village.

They came with their chief and all his advisors. The chief brought his music makers with strange drums and trumpets made from metal not horn. They stood and played dancing music but they did not dance. We were not invited to make our music. We were not invited to dance or to drink beer. We refused to make them welcome and to build a *Boma* for an *indaba* with their chief.

Instead our men had to sit for a long time while their chief washed himself in cooking water inside his own *Boma* so that no one could see his body. We laughed when we heard what he was doing. Then he dressed himself in a white suit and a hat with long white feathers like a warrior and came and sat on a chair in front of us while we sat on the ground.

After that we no longer laughed.

The British chief told us that we were the children of his white queen who loved us but wanted us to leave our homes.

He told us that we were children and not men and women.

He told us that we did not behave well because we had spears.

He, however, had brought many men with guns who set up their camp and took our wood to make their fires.

He told us that we did not have respect for the law.

We were insulted because we do have respect.

We were insulted because he did not have respect for us.

He said that we did not obey him or the queen and he was angry with us.

It is bad to show anger to people and to shame them publicly.

We knew it was because we were not white like him.

We knew that this treatment was because we were black people.

Some of our men became angry too. They left the *indaba* and went off to beat their drums all through the night.

The white chief left the next day. Again we waited, but the police soldiers did not go away with their chief and after a short time many more of them came in big trucks. Most of them were black men like us but from other tribes and other places, and they did not greet us or talk to us. They could not speak to us because they did not understand what we said to them. There were more than a hundred of the police soldiers and there were white soldiers with them.

They marched together in bands of thirty men, all in the same dress with strong boots on their feet and hats that were too hard to break. They carried guns and had pistols in leather bags on their belts and hitting sticks too. Their white leaders marched beside them shouting orders and they obeyed the white men without looking at them. Each night they made camp and each morning went to get firewood in their trucks.

Our warriors went towards them in a war-like way to show them how large our numbers had become. We showed them our spears and how we could use them. We showed them our strength and our determination not to be moved. Our warriors went running many times towards them to show the police soldiers that we refused to be moved.

Then we waited.

It was a bad time.

Women took their children and went to hide in the forests that were left.

Men left the villages to make separate warrior camps.

It would soon be the rainy season and we knew that after it had rained and the roads had gone the trucks could not remain in our valley.

It is hard to talk of this time.

We suffered much. Let me rest while I remember those days of sorrow.

Gunfire

1958

Now let me lift up my head again and tell you more of that day.

In the early morning, while it was cool and before the sun came over the hills, we heard the police trucks start their engines. Once again we thought that they were going to look for firewood. Soon we saw that they were all moving very quickly and all moving at the same time. They were coming to our village to make us into prisoners so that they could take us away by force. When the trucks stopped we could see they were going to surround the village. We saw that the police soldiers were getting out of the trucks and forming themselves into groups ready for battle. One of the white soldiers who was the leader held up his gun and it made a bright fire go into the air with a big bang. There were a few women and children left inside the village. When they heard the bang, they ran away to hide in the bush but Chisamu, our Headman, hid inside his hut.

Then our warriors came running towards the police soldiers to fight them. They were very brave. Our warriors were barefoot and only had shields of skin and wood and a handful of spears. Some had spears with metal heads; most had spears of wood. Some also had an axe.

First the police soldiers fired guns of poisonous smoke at our warriors but that did not stop our warriors attacking them. Then the police soldiers fired their shotguns at our warriors. Those guns made many painful wounds all over the warriors legs and feet and some of them fell over and some ran away.

Even then our warriors did not stop fighting so the police soldiers used guns that killed. After that our warriors ran away leaving six men dead in the grass by our village. One of the dead men was my husband, Singani.

The sun was still making long shadows in the early morning and it was not even hot when it was all finished and our life in the valley was over.

That is when I took my son Milimo and went to hide near the Rain Shrine of my husband, the *sikatongo,* Singani, because it was my duty to take care of the sacred pots and ladles.

PART 3
MIRANDA

ONE

Falling Backwards

The Guest Book. The Cottage, Siavonga.
October 1985
Nick, Manda

'The lake has dropped many feet. We have found a triangular, flat rock face several metres high and wide that is parallel to the water's edge, and we marked on it an estimated high water level for this year with the date. With Charles and Margaret's permission we have asked a bricklayer to make more steps down to the water's edge. It is now such a long trek to the water that it needs to be made easier. We are also thinking of putting up a shelter with a grass roof so we can get some shade down there for the children.'

"The dam wall is falling over backwards," Nick had said the evening before.

Nick and Manda were having dinner with Andrew and Jessie in their new house. It was the second time they had moved to a 'better' house with more bedrooms and en suite bathrooms. The other guests, Tim and Sarah, were new to Lusaka.

"You're kidding!" said Andrew in disbelief. "How can it?"

"Well," Nick said, enjoying himself, "this is the year they can't generate power from the South Bank turbines because the level of the lake is so low. That should give you an idea of the scale of the problem. Imagine that you are standing with your feet in the water

237

and your back to the sea and a big wave slaps into the back of your knees – what happens?"

"You fall over backwards!" giggled Jessie, looking at Sarah.

"Exactly. It is easier to stay upright with your shoulders braced against moving water," said Nick, "Kariba Dam is an arch dam and it isn't built into the rocks on either side of the gorge. It was designed to be held in place by the water pressure behind it and therefore it needs a certain depth of water to remain stable. For the past few years water levels have dropped low enough to release this pressure and the dam wall is now leaning over backwards."

Manda laughed at the expression on everyone's faces. Quite possibly they didn't want to be convinced by Nick.

"How much is it leaning over then?" Andrew asked cynically, "Feet or inches?"

"Centimetres I think," said Nick, also smiling, "but think what water can do if it gets into a hairline crack."

"Ouch!" said Tim, "What's to be done?"

"Pray for rain?" Manda asked, her head on one side.

"Not what they are doing in Zimbabwe apparently," Nick answered. "They have tried to plug the crack with cement – trouble is that it will prevent the wall returning to the old position when – "

"If!" Manda interrupted jokingly. Nick looked at her.

"When the water levels come up again."

"Anyway, Sarah and Tim," Jessie said, "it means that we will have more power cuts than usual this year – honestly – what a welcome for you. Can you believe this country? It's so backward."

"There you go everybody," said Manda, "and Nick and I are off tomorrow to enjoy the lake all the same – aren't we Nick?"

★

And here I go again, Manda said to herself the following afternoon, *at my favourite place – just a little stressed though.*

Manda felt the familiar tension across her shoulders. When would be a good moment to try and talk to Nick about the kids' holidays? When would he sit down and relax enough for her to hope for a decision? He was always under pressure at the moment. There was some big new contract to be finalised and the funders and the partners all had to be in accord with Nick as the main facilitator. Nick had such bags of energy and drive. His work drove him. He loved it more when it was challenging and when he was winning, and as he was so good at managing other people, he usually was winning for which Manda was grateful. They did have such happy times together then.

Nick took it so badly when things had not gone quite as he planned. Though Manda did not realise it, he gave no indication of this to his colleagues. He saved it for home. He would arrive looking dejected and Manda would give him a little time and then coax him to tell her about his day. It took skill, care and tact to manage Nick's moods and Manda dared not take anything for granted. It wasn't safe for her if Nick became depressed but the constant pressure on her was such that she was not fully aware that she managed Nick out of the need to protect herself and her children. She did understand, however, that if she herself was ever tired or downhearted, her marriage would start to disintegrate very fast, and an angry Nick would demand she leave. She still did not grasp that this was Nick's game to make her malleable. He had no intention of losing her. But he did all of this by instinct and not design.

Her own training and social ability meant that she had a very good grasp of what he was up against with regard to both the business and personal aspects of his work. She also had a sixth sense of the ramifications of the current politics and social intrigues of Zambia. This was a gift she had acquired from her parents and the varied countries and situations that they had worked in during their years in the United Nations. It was also a love and concern of hers that they had instilled in her. She cared about Zambia and she cared about Zambians. In spite of all its problems, poverty and corruption, she felt at home here.

Manda's Goan father, Francis d'Silva, known as Frank by his colleagues, and her English mother, Helen Cressey, both British citizens, had met and married while Frank was working for the United Nations Food and Agriculture Organisation. Their first child had died following a caesarean operation, which left Helen unable to have more children. In the late fifties, they were both working in Northern Rhodesia before it became Zambia when the Katanga crisis exploded. It was in Northern Rhodesia that they adopted Miranda and Sebastian. As Frank and Helen said, their own birth children would have been half-Goan and half-English, so Miranda and Sebastian both being mixed-race, would fit well into their family. They had early encountered the racial prejudice about mixed marriages that was common in Britain at the time and felt well able to cope with the challenges that their marriage and their adoption of two mixed-race children would bring. This partly explained the family's itinerant lifestyle. Frank and Helen felt that travelling gave their family a like-minded international community of people from many diverse ethnicities and cultures.

Manda had enjoyed her childhood very much and most of it had been spent in one part or another of Africa. Nevertheless at times she felt as if she was rootless and a person who belonged nowhere. Sebastian confessed to feeling the same.

"I guess the parents thought that we would encounter less racism if we didn't apparently belong anywhere and if we were with people who mostly were mixed up families like us or at least lived in a multi-racial world."

"I guess they were right," said Manda thoughtfully. "We haven't grown up being miserable and put upon because we're brownish."

"I'm black!" interrupted Sebastian, proud and swift. Manda was a pale golden-brown and Sebastian a darker brown-gold.

"You see, that's why I like gardening," carried on Manda, "I need to put down roots."

"That's why I am married to Gerda," grinned Sebastian, "She is just a 'grounded' person wherever she is. Gerda, his German wife, was immensely practical and phlegmatic; Gerda and her two babies never seemed to suffer stress.

Manda sighed. Nick did not make her feel grounded. She loved him so dearly and she didn't doubt he loved her but somehow there was something missing. Something she couldn't quite put her finger on – safety? A sense of trust?

No – that didn't seem right. Life had never been conventionally safe for her or her family – they had been in too many almost war-zones – but they did have that security and love with each other inside their family.

Nick had not had that kind of home or family. Manda knew that and with that rush of warmth and generosity towards anyone who had suffered, Manda had reached out and loved him for his intelligence, his cheerful humour, his social charm and ready wit and he had loved her in return, attracted at first by, what was for him, an exotic beauty and that sense of other wonderful worlds that she carried with her, but in the end for her laughter, her bravery, her generosity and above all her kindness and her trust in him. That trust had astounded him and finally captivated him.

Nick had had a cruel infancy and childhood. His mother, rich and spoilt, the darling of an older self-made father, had married too young because her parents wished her to, divorced too quickly even when they didn't, and then found an indulgent older husband as spoilt as she was. Nick was a nuisance, a yowling baby with nappies of stinking yellow sludge. A nursemaid was found but didn't stay because Nick's mother was jealous and Nick's stepfather miserly. Nick was often left to cry and if he cried loudly enough to disturb them of an evening, he was pinched hard until he stopped. When he was older and misbehaved, his favourite toys would be taken away or broken in front of his eyes. He spent long periods with his grandmother, who spoilt him as his mother had been spoilt.

Poor boy, he was indulged, punished and never cherished, but he was a clever child and he learnt to charm, as his mother charmed. He learnt to control in the same way his mother controlled her husband, though he couldn't practise it on her. He learnt to fear his stepfather and he learnt what made his stepfather a person to be feared. What he loved about Manda was her kindness, something he had not had much experience of in his family. He did not really like to share Manda's kindness, even when it reflected well on himself. He was secretly afraid it would vanish, and he would be left squalling and broken, as he had been so often as a toddler.

Nick and Manda's relationship at first had been so easy and natural. Manda wasn't the most ordinary of fresher students. She was used to being with all ages and all kinds of people and being treated as an equal. It hadn't seemed particularly flattering to her that Nick, a final year student, had been interested in taking her out, and that had further intrigued him. She liked Nick and they were both interested in the same things. Age didn't enter into it for her. They both belonged to the Anti-Apartheid group at university; they both liked the same pop groups, but also liked classical music – and squash. Before the end of Manda's first year and Nick's last year, they were in love and wanted to get engaged.

Manda's parents said she was too young but also recognised that she was old enough to choose for herself.

Nick's parents were simply opposed. They were extremely rude and racist too.

"You can't marry a coloured girl! No, never! I'll disinherit you," said his mother.

Nick had no expectations from his stepfather and that was confirmed after a very short meeting with his parents. Nick and Manda together told her parents all that had happened, and they discussed it over a meal one evening when the couple were in London. Manda's father rather hoped that the relationship would end. He hadn't met Nick's family, but it seemed clear that that would be a very bad idea to try and talk to them at the moment. In any case, Frank had a sense of something not quite open in Nick, something hidden very deep and in a dark, unhappy place. What Manda needed, in his view, was an open, equal and loving relationship. *Still, how can anyone really judge*, Frank told himself, *and there's no telling how things may work out.*

It wasn't really practical for Nick and Manda to live together or marry at that moment and so they reluctantly agreed that a physical separation would be wise so that Manda could continue her degree and Nick get going in his career. Meanwhile they could write and phone and see each other over the vacations. Manda went back to university and Nick started his new job. He did well from the first and was very successful and popular, but a cold jealousy entered his heart. He was angry with his parents but they were, as ever, impervious to his needs or feelings. He had to punish someone so he punished Manda. He started going out with one of his colleagues, an attractive and ambitious woman called Laura, who would have liked to marry him. He stopped phoning and writing to Manda. She was shocked and hurt by the lack of contact and then stunned when a mutual friend told her that Nick had a new girlfriend. What could she do? She wrote to Nick wishing him all the best and saying that she would not be in touch again. Nick did nothing for a while except intensify his relationship with Laura for a month and then he cut Laura out of his life completely, to her utter mystification and hurt, and rather to his own discredit with his new firm. Still he continued to perform well and a humiliated Laura chose to move her job, so shortly all was forgotten.

By the end of Manda's second year, she had not found a serious replacement for Nick. She didn't entertain going out with the mature and married student who pursued her for a while and she knew that the other young men were determined to remain single so that going out with them had to be for fun only – then out of the blue Nick came back into her life. He turned up without phoning or writing at the start of her third year. She came out of an engrossing seminar to find Nick waiting for her outside the lecture theatre.

Nick, of course, could not say he was sorry, but he flung himself at Manda in a rather puppy-like way, adoring, pleading and funny. Manda opened her arms, her heart was still full of love for him, and that was that – for the time being at least they were a happy couple.

Nick and Manda spent Christmas with her family. They were making plans to live together after Manda graduated when Manda realised that she was pregnant. The passion of their reunion had resulted in some hasty fumbling with condoms and some laughter. It was very many years later that it crossed Manda's mind to wonder if Nick had decided at that moment to make her pregnant, thereby ensuring his ownership of her, whatever his parents said.

Frank and Helen didn't want Nick and Manda to marry too quickly even under these circumstances, but of course they thought they should live together. The main concern for Frank was that Manda should finish her degree. Frank and Helen also insisted on meeting Nick's parents, and as soon as this was agreed, a not entirely unsuccessful meeting took place. Nick's parents had to admit that Frank and Helen seemed to be well-educated, well-mannered and well-off and Frank was even rather handsome and well-dressed. They had expected he would look flashy, which was, they believed, normal for social-climbing Asian men. Helen's father however, had been a Conservative Member of Parliament so that mollified them somewhat. Frank and Helen however, were downhearted after the meeting.

"They are the last family I would want our girl to have for in-laws!" sighed Frank. "There will never be any real warmth or kindness from them to either Nick or Manda."

"Nick seems warm-hearted enough doesn't he?" Helen wanted reassuring. Frank raised his eyebrows and his hands.

"He has chosen a warm-hearted girl," he said. "Judging from

his parents' behaviour towards him and Manda, he needs loving and he hasn't had it at home."

Frank was worried in spite of the happiness he saw in Nick and Manda. Manda's own choice had taken her into the heart of an unhappy and racist family. It seemed to them a dreadful irony that it was her uncomplicated and trusting nature that put her most at risk.

TWO

Sunburnt

The Guest Book. The Cottage, Siavonga.
January 1986
Nick, Manda, Mumbi, Jane, Andrew, Jessie and all the kids!
'Arrived in a rainstorm to a lake muddy from the run-off from the
hills. The Acacia came into bloom overnight. We saw Grey
Loeries or 'go-way' birds; they call out 'go-way' or as Milimo says
'kuwee' which is their Tonga name. We also saw a shrike, and in
the garden at night, fruit bats and fireflies.
I will plant petrea, julbernardia, cestrum and herbs – but forgot to
bring the fig tree to plant by the beach.
The road to Lusaka road is closed due to non-payment by the
government to the road builders. We drove down the old federal
road and edged past lorries stuck in the mud, denting our rims on
potholes. Milimo has found leopard orchids for the garden. They
grow on the bark of trees.
The rain has cleared the sky and so the sun has been very hot and
we all got sunburnt on the water.'

The day had been exhilarating. It was hot and bright but there had
been a gusty, changeable wind on the lake all day. Windsurfing had
been a real challenge. One minute you were flying fast across the
water, the next the wind dropped completely and in another

moment it rushed at you from another quarter and you were in the water shouting in surprise. Then back on the board leaning to pull up the mast and you would be spinning in an eddy of wind, wondering where it would blow from next. Now all six friends were resting on the lawn below the veranda on a stifling evening without a breeze, lazily comparing bruises and sunburn and windsurfing achievements. Mumbi and Andrew had been stars with the children taking them out in pairs in the sailing dinghy and even letting Emma, together with Mumbi's oldest boy Muna, have a go at being skipper. The children were all flopped about on the grass reading. The sun, the wind and the sailing had tired them all out.

"Hey Manda, you're getting really dark!" said Jessie stressing the 'dark' as she glanced over at Manda. Jessie was all sun-streaked golden hair and golden skin. Manda knew that too much sun took the bloom from her skin but to hell with it – life had to be lived and she loved windsurfing.

Nick glanced across and his eyes checked over Manda, but Mumbi, with his eyes shut, said, "Hey babe – you're gorgeous, Manda – getting to be a real hot Zambian chick. Soon be as dark as me and really beautiful!"

Manda laughed, she fished a dissolving ice cube from her gin and tonic and flicked it towards him. He caught it neatly without sitting up and in a swift movement dropped it onto Jessie's bare midriff.

Mumbi had a steady kindness that made him a reliable friend. Manda sensed he would always be her ally. There had been moments in her recent life when she contemplated a love affair with someone who would recognise her as a separate, whole and intelligent person, and not just as an appendage and possession. Mumbi could, perhaps, be such a lover. Mumbi would always see her as a whole person, but affairs were far too complicated. She could never bear to hurt Mumbi or his wife, Jane. In any case Nick was, somehow, not quite predictable. *Perhaps*, Manda thought, *marriage subsumes women? Perhaps all wives are less than individual people?* She frowned a little. Was her dissatisfaction mere ingratitude? The sex in her marriage was okay, even good. Why did she feel so constrained and why did she always have to be so careful?

Jessie had shrieked and squirmed at the cold ice and was still scowling at Mumbi. Manda got to her feet.

"Time for supper chaps – you're cooking! Come on you guys, light the *braai* – I'll sort out the meat – it's time for wine and more peanuts and olives," she jumped to her feet and went into the kitchen to replenish snacks and drinks and carry out the food for the barbecue.

There were six of them that weekend and four children. Manda kept the main cottage bedroom as a space for herself and for Nick and their two children. Without even realising that she was doing it, Manda always made sure that Nick was comfortable and protected and that they had some privacy. The two other men had agreed to sleep on the veranda and Jane, her two children and Jessie had sorted themselves onto the beds in the second room without any fuss or complications. After all, the cottage was thin-walled and the doors were only mosquito screens. The narrow iron bedsteads mostly made for rigidly chaste sleeping arrangements. In Manda and Nick's room the two beds had been pulled side by side by Marielise and Jo once it seemed unlikely that Charles and Margaret would make regular return visits to the cottage. Manda and Nick always began their nights at the cottage squeezed together on one bed, but sooner or later, one of them would roll into the other bed, as otherwise rest was impossible.

The sun had only just set and a full moon was rising. Across the lake they could see the lights of the Zimbabwean kapenta rigs fishing for the lake sardines that had become a staple food in the region.

Jessie, looking at the kapenta rigs, announced, "Andrew and I are going to take a houseboat holiday in Zimbabwe on the other side. It is ever so luxurious."

"A 'gin palace' on the lake – how posh!" Jane said and then gave a little shudder, "I wouldn't like it. They say that crocodiles have learnt to follow the sound of an engine because they know that there is food around boats."

"They have a strong wire cage that they lower off the back of the boat so that you're protected from the crocodiles if you want to swim," Andrew said.

Nick laughed.

"It's an uncomfortable thought, but every kapenta rig is supposed to be encircled by crocodiles. They hear the diesel engine and know that the light attracts kapenta and the kapenta attracts bigger fish like tiger. They lie just beyond the light of the rig so you can't see their red eyes. God help any person who falls off a kapenta rig. Crocs don't even make a swirl in the water when they attack."

"Do you know how much light those rigs create?" Andrew said, "When Jessie and I flew up to Lusaka from Jo'burg we thought we were over a town. The light from so many kapenta rigs around Sinazongwe can be seen soon after leaving Bulawayo and well over the escarpment – that is quite a spread of light pollution each side of the lake."

"We don't get dark nights here anymore unless it is too stormy for the rigs to be out on the lake," said Nick. "We're really grateful that the Zambian rigs don't come up here – the water's too deep at this point on our side – the best kapenta fishing is over shallow waters where the kapenta feed, that's why our rigs fish near Sinazongwe.

"Remember Manda, how we came down to try and see Halley's Comet and the sky was just too brightly lit?"

"The impact of the lake on the environment just goes on and on in ways that no one could have dreamed of," said Manda thoughtfully. "I am sure that the local climate is dramatically changed – that's another thing you notice flying over the lake – there is often no cloud over the lake even when there are huge storm clouds and thunderheads all around it."

"It always seems that it rains only over the Matusadona and never on this side too. Often the gorge below the dam will have rain when there is none above the dam wall – presumably the valley had all had the same weather once. Who knows?" Nick was fascinated by Kariba. "The ecology below the dam is quite different now. The Zambezi plain isn't regenerated by floods each year, instead there is – well – like a high tide on the river each night when they don't generate electricity. It may only be inches but it changes the environment."

Mumbi and Andrew looked interested but Jane changed the subject.

"How was Jo'burg, Jessie? Did you do lots of lovely shopping and eating out?"

"Oh yes! Fabulous. I got some really smart clothes at Sandton and cheap too. I also went to Woolies' for the standard stuff for the kids and Andrew – it's not bad quality at all – and we had a great meal at Antonio's restaurant in Rosebank. It is nice to be somewhere civilised you know."

Manda wrinkled her nose and grimaced in the dark where Jessie could not see her but Mumbi did, and he gave Manda a grin before asking:"Hey Jessie – what was the political situation like down there? How's my friend the main man Prime Minister Mr Botha – has he got any more realistic ideas about what to do with his unruly blacks!" Mumbi pronounced 'blacks' with a mock South African accent as 'blecks'.

"It's really terrible down there," answered Jessie with no sense of inappropriateness or inconsistency, "the people in the townships are just killing each other every day with this awful necklacing – you know – they put burning tyres over each others' necks – horrible!" and she shuddered.

"Now why would they do such a thing as that I wonder?" Mumbi started ironically but Manda caught his eye and shushed him. Jessie was a lost cause politically – they all knew that – but her lack of interest didn't necessarily make her a racist.

"She is a 'richist'," said Mumbi privately, "She practises 'richism' – she even likes me because – though I'm black – I'm rich, rich enough anyway!"

"Hey!" Andrew changed the subject yet again, "Is your name African Manda? There are people and places here called Manda – there's Mr Manda at the office."

"My name is Miranda actually," said Manda, "I just couldn't say Miranda when I was little. Manda was the best I could manage and it stuck.

I think my parents had a Shakespeare thing going because my little brother is called Sebastian."

"So Daddy is Prospero then," teased Andrew, "Ah-ha! What does that make Milimo then? Is Milimo your Caliban?"

Manda was surprised to feel a sudden and furious rage, she stuttered then stopped. At last she said coldly to Andrew, "If Milimo is anyone he would have to be Ariel because we never see him but he looks after us all in magic ways without – I hope – any of us treating him like a slave."

"Sorry," Mumbi was bland, "I didn't do much Shakespeare – so I don't understand. Who are all these characters?" and Jessie the ingénue, explained in a school-child sing-song voice.

"It's Shakespeare's *Tempest*. Prospero is a magician marooned on an island with his daughter Miranda. He has a slave called Caliban who is a particularly nasty, ugly creature. A good spirit called Ariel who does his 'bidding' – as they say – carries out his wishes by magic.

Prospero creates a storm to get well – revenge – and win back his dukedom, and of course get a husband for Miranda. Everything works out fine in the end –oh and Caliban's mother is an evil ugly black witch called – hmm – Sycorax – I think."

"Oh-ho!" Mumbi was laughing. "And so here at the cottage we have all the elements of the *Tempest* don't we? Slaves, witches, magic, dispossessed chiefs and evil black people – "

Jane held up her hand in front of Mumbi's face.

"Avaunt ye! Stop teasing us all. Enough of slaves and sorcery. We have had more than enough of all that in Africa. It is only a hundred years since the last beastly white European Portuguese raiders came up the valley to this point to trade goods for girls and take away lovely Tonga maidens as slaves."

"Slave traders wouldn't find it so easy to negotiate the dam wall," Nick said and filled up all the wine glasses again. "There are still African Mottled Eels in the lake you know but they may disappear as their route to the sea has been cut off as well."

"Hmm." Jane sipped her glass, then turned to the children, "Time for bed small people – off you go and we'll come and tuck you up."

When Manda and Jane returned from the bedrooms, Jessie was back on the subject that most interested her.

"Manda, why don't you and Nick ever go to South Africa? It's really difficult to get all kinds of things in Lusaka – you must really want to go."

Mumbi almost choked on his beer and then spluttered with laughter.

"Honestly Jessie – you have just commented on Manda's suntan – where do you think she and Nick would stay in South Africa?

Jessie was rather miffed.

"What do you mean? There are plenty of good hotels."

"Jessie," Manda explained gently, "in South Africa it is against the law for Nick and me to sleep together. We would be arrested and put in prison if we tried to spend a night together in a hotel."

Jessie was dumbfounded and disbelieving.

Jane explained, "They have a law in South Africa against miscegenation Jessie – that means that it is illegal for people from different races to have sex, children or marry in South Africa. Manda would go to prison for longer than Nick would because she is blacker than Nick. You may remember from history that the

252

same law was introduced in Nazi Germany to stop Jews mixing with Aryans."

"Oh," said Jessie and she was silent for a while, looking at Nick and Manda.

"I never really thought of you two as being different," she said, "but you aren't very black Manda, are you? Couldn't you just stay out of the sun and then pretend to be white?"

There was a brief silence. Mumbi and Jane looked at Jessie with such mixed up expressions of amusement, astonishment and anger that Manda began to laugh and then couldn't stop and went on and on laughing until everyone joined in.

Almost sobbing with laughter, Manda cried, "Jessie my dear – you have certainly proved how totally silly that law is!"

"It is also evil and causes terrible suffering!" Nick was laughing but also angry.

Eventually Manda caught her breath and she said, "They don't have any certain methods in South Africa for deciding what the race of a person is either, you know. Skin colour is a very poor indicator of the race you belong to unless it is very obvious. They do go on blackness and whiteness first. The next test though is the pencil test." Manda put her hand over her mouth as she began to laugh uncontrollably again.

"What the hell is the pencil test?" asked Jane, who though laughing was quite shocked.

"Oh God!" Manda said in between gulps of air and giggles. "I would definitely fail it! They put a pencil in your hair and if it doesn't fall out easily – then you are black! Jessie, my dear, I am a black woman and proud of it. I won't go to South Africa because of Apartheid!

I think I'll have another glass of wine and drink to it ending soon!"

Three

Satellites

Manda and Nick had only recently arrived in Lusaka when they met two more of the Bush War's flotsam and jetsam. These two people however, were very different from Andy, the one-time Selous Scout who had worked briefly for Jacky.

Jeff and Lauren were a very attractive and sophisticated couple with two charming, well-mannered children. Lauren was all long legs, elegant casual clothes, and golden blonde hair cut in a simple but stylish fashion. Jeff was exceptionally good-looking with an intelligent, handsome face and an easy charm.

Nick and Manda had met them at the Squash Club and then been invited for sundowners at their luxurious home. Outside the house was a giant parabolic sieve as high as the second floor and as big as the swimming pool. Manda's eyes widened and Nick smiled.

"It's Jeff's business to sell these huge satellite dishes," he said, "Don't know if they'll catch on – they are pricey and take up rather a lot of space."

Jeff and Lauren met them at the door and took them into the lounge for olives and tequilas.

They were Rhodesians – from an old farming family – but had actually been farming for some years in Angola because the boycott of Rhodesian meat and tobacco produce made farming in Rhodesia unsustainable. They had a good life in Angola – even a light plane of their own – until Agostinho Neto's attempt to overthrow Portuguese colonial rule. They hadn't had to leave immediately: "We couldn't sell the farm of course," said Lauren with a wry shrug, "We went to Holland for a while – but anyway – we're back in Africa – everything looks good for a new start and so we are here to do business."

Manda thought they were rather vague about dates and places but then she was no expert on the Rhodesian Bush War herself. She didn't feel entirely comfortable with either of them. Although they had been welcomed by the expatriate community as desirable dinner guests, something about the couple made her think of chameleons and of a matched pair at that. It was odd that they gave absolutely no indication that they had even noticed that she was mixed-race. It was the absence of even a slight difference of interest or opinion between them in her racial background that made her suspicious. Manda knew very well that many people, but especially white Rhodesians and South Africans, always registered her skin colour by the slightest of eye movements. She knew that often the women would be a shade more polite and friendly, while their men might look a little more awake and glance across at Nick before looking again at her. Jeff and Lauren however, were so cool, so careful, and so urbane that she couldn't quite trust them. They also appeared very well-off for a couple who had lost a farm in Angola. That she assumed must have been a hostile environment for white Rhodesians. There were other questions too. For example, why hadn't he come back to Rhodesia and fought in the Bush War? He didn't look like a conscientious objector or a pacifist, or for that matter like a coward, and she certainly couldn't quite imagine either Lauren or Jeff joining the Anti-Apartheid movement. She shook her head for a moment. She wasn't suspicious by nature so this doubt was a departure for her. Maybe it was her new friendship with Marielise that made her wary.

"What business are you going to be doing here then?" she

asked. "Lusaka can be a very challenging environment, can't it Nick."

"Those giant satellite dishes for television," said Jeff, "My firm in Zimbabwe has developed them from our own designs. They sell in South Africa but if you install one here you will be able to watch Zimbabwean and South African TV and get all the sport."

"Really!" Nick was immediately interested, "Watch world rugby here in Zambia! I would like that. What's the cost?"

So the evening passed pleasantly enough.

Manda and Nick invited Lauren and Jeff back for dinner one evening and that was arranged and agreed. Just as they were about to leave, Jeff offered to give them a quick glimpse of the South African syndicated CNN on the television from his satellite dish. Of course they couldn't resist the opportunity though Manda was beginning to worry about Emma and James, back home with the babysitter. They sat down again, this time in the television room where moments before the children had been watching a film on video. Jeff flicked and flicked at the remote until the screen itself blinked on and swirled into the publicity on CNN. They waited a few moments and then on came the endless circular repeating news – women talking, then men talking and then a reporter talking over a bloody bundle of flesh being carried away from a wrecked car by some black teenagers. It was Mozambique; it was the damaged body of the ANC lawyer, Albie Sachs, after the South African secret service exploded a bomb under his car. The report was repeated and repeated, the pulped body lifted up again and again.

Manda's head spun, she felt tipsy and sick. Albie Sachs could not hope to survive could he? Was this a danger that her friends Marielise and Jo faced? She did not know exactly what Jo and Marielise did anyway. Where was it Jo worked when he was out of Lusaka? Tanzania? Mozambique? What kind of people set these bombs? She looked at her host and hostess, their faces apparently indifferent to the images on the screen in front of them, though had not Jeff made a calculated glance across at her to assess her reaction to the gory scene?

It was Nick who said, as they drove home moments later, "I guess he was in Rhodesian Intelligence don't you? Probably sanctions-busting in Angola. Didn't the sanctions-busters fly Rhodesian beef and tobacco through Angola to Holland?"

"I guess you're right." *Nick could be so smart sometimes*, Manda thought.

"What do you think he is doing now?" asked Manda, "Working for South African Intelligence instead of Rhodesian Intelligence?"

Nick grinned.

"Let's get a satellite dish from them and see who we can spy on."

Manda smiled at the joke but the feeling of sickness did not go away.

FOUR

The End Of An Era

The Guest Book. The Cottage, Siavonga.
Easter 1987
Nick, Manda, Marielise, Jo, Emma and James
Siavonga 1000 Rally.
'Full moon – no kapenta rigs out fishing. Lake up and rising at
last. The hut that we built on the beach has washed away and the
roof of it would now be 10 feet under water! Too many ants. We
swam, fished, windsurfed. Weather hot! Visited the crocodile farm
and celebrated (mourned?) Zambia's withdrawal from the
International Monetary Fund and the 'End of an Era' with a
lunch party at Jacky's bar. There will be no May Day celebrations
and the president has parted company with the IMF. The
exchange rate been reduced.'

The Siavonga 1000 Rally was to take place over the Easter weekend.
The first one in the area, it would start and finish at Siavonga, go
along the dirt roads, over the escarpment, down to Sinazongwe
and back. There was no longer any danger from the land mines
left over from the Bush War; the roads had been in use for a while
without incident. During the Bush War the long distance motor
rallies had to be held in the north of Zambia. This event, for the
first time, would include drivers from Zimbabwe, though it was

predicted that Satwant Singh of Zambia would be the one who would win. He had famously completed a motor rally in Zaire on three wheels, by using his co-driver's weight on the bonnet to maintain the balance of his Opel.

Jo and Nick were both avid fans of motor rallies and fond of recounting the times they had taken part in local or student rallies in Britain. They had already started to compete with each other, comparing notes on driving in the bush, saying how close they had each been to disaster, and how in the nick of time, luck, and occasionally skill, had saved them from death. Manda and Marielise made irreverent, hero-worshipping faces and then went into the kitchen to stack drinks and food in the fridge. Manda was happy to have time with Marielise. They didn't see each other often, but Manda found Marielise's friendship a pleasure and an affirmation. Manda sensed that Nick didn't much like Marielise, but if Jo was also around, Nick was more relaxed and Manda felt freer to be herself.

Every camp, bungalow and hotel was full to capacity. Marielise and Manda had made arrangements to share the cottage, and a party of their friends would also be at the lake in various other company-owned or private cottages. Manda was pleased. Emma and James would be able to walk along the shore of the lake to the place where Mumbi, Jane and their children were staying with Jessie and Andrew. Jessie had said that really she was happier in a place with electricity and en suite bathrooms where she could see to put on make-up. This holiday villa also had a big swimming pool which would occupy them all happily for hours but would be a godsend for the kids. No doubt they would also want to sail or windsurf if the wind was right. It was as well however, to have the windsurfer and mirror dinghy moored at the landing where there was also a motor launch that could act as a rescue boat.

Changes had been forced on the cottage during the preceding weeks. Milimo had called Nick in Lusaka to tell him that there had been a robbery and things were missing. Cutlery, crockery, saucepans and other essential items had gone. The deckchairs on the veranda had also been taken. All the items were replaced easily enough but some of the magical sense of protection and safety that the cottage offered was lost. Marielise was the first person to hear the story from Milimo in person. Milimo said that the thieves had come up from the lake and carried the stolen goods away on a small boat. That was why he had not heard them break the locks, he explained. They could not have come down the hill past his home. There had also been a wind storm during the night. Perhaps they had come under cover of the noise of the waves. Marielise gave him a long look as he finished his account but she said nothing to him. Something of her doubts however, came across to Manda when Marielise repeated Milimo's story.

"What is bothering you about this?" Manda asked, narrowing her eyes.

"Don't tell Nick or Jo," Marielise said, "I don't want to get Milimo into trouble, but his version just does not add up. I don't buy the thieves carrying stuff down to a boat on the shore. I think that they simply put the screws on Milimo and he let them into the cottage. We all know that life is dire for most Zambians at the moment but there is another factor – and that is Milimo's son.

"There's no work for anyone at the moment. The local youths smash the glass insulators off the power pylons and sell them as fake diamonds just as they sell smashed traffic light glass as rubies and emeralds in Lusaka. I think Milimo's son is friends with that lot and therefore he is likely to be a friend of the local *kabwalalas*.

Milimo would always look after his family first. Of course I could be wrong and there would not be any proof and nothing much to gain from finding out."

Manda agreed, then she laughed sadly.

"Poor Milimo. What a quandary for him. I don't suppose that they will keep coming back to rob the cottage? There are much richer pickings at the other holiday villas in any case. Let's wait and see what develops. I won't tell Nick," she said, "I still trust

Milimo – even though that seems ridiculous – even if he did let the thieves in.

"We have the same problem at work in Lusaka. Employees, especially if they are women, are likely to be blackmailed or threatened into stealing from their work place. Everyone is desperately poor and many are starving."

It was an odd situation but it fitted the times. There was a strange atmosphere throughout Zambia that weekend. Rumours had been flying around Lusaka for weeks before.

The president was going to make a key statement. Something important was to happen. Decisions were to be made, and after they were made, Zambia would never, ever, be the same again. The company of friends who gathered down at the lake were all oddly light-hearted and upbeat. They knew that the jobs and projects might all be dramatically altered by events in the next few days, but what the hell – life had never been that certain in Zambia – or in any of Zambia's neighbouring countries. They were, in any case, fairly well-cushioned, even Mumbi and Jane had funds outside the country and could expect to find work elsewhere too. None of them was light-hearted because they didn't care about Zambia. They all, astonishingly, found it liberating to have no idea what tomorrow held for them. Of course they all knew they were not in any physical danger. Every time they sat down together however, they returned to the rumours and the speculation about what the president was planning to do.

"Have you seen this story in the international press?" Andrew asked.

It was lunchtime and everyone was seated around the table on the veranda eating salads and drinking white wine and cold Mosi beers. The children helped themselves from the buffet in the kitchen and came and went from the table as it pleased them. Emma stopped occasionally to rest her elbows on the table by Nick and listen to the grown-up conversation.

"It's pretty damning if it's true," said Nick,

"I don't believe it," said Manda, going against the tide of her friends' opinions. Marielise looked at her sharply.

"I think it's unlikely to say the least. How can any Zambian President be the richest man in the world? It is just not possible."

Marielise laughed and said, "If it is true, then it would be an amazing achievement for an African wouldn't it? How can we, Africans, be bad at everything, in every way, and still one of us can end up being the most fabulously wealthy individual in the world?"

"It's a reputable magazine," said Andrew, surprised at the opposition.

"Yes that's true," said Manda, "but the story still does not seem likely and the figures don't add up. It says the president owns a tanker full of Iraqi oil – well if he does – and what good is that to him until it lands – I don't see how that can add up to make him the richest man in the world. Okay I might buy that he's the richest African President – but even that I wouldn't be sure of."

Jo said, "Hey look – this isn't important is it – except to blacken him."

"You can't blacken him more," interposed Mumbi, "the man is already black."

They all laughed and groaned at the too-easy joke, but Jo persisted.

"It's because the president wants to quit the International Monetary Fund agreement that all this bad press is happening."

"Come on! Not really!" Andrew was annoyed. "Why would the international press lie about this?"

"When has the international press ever run a positive story about Africa?" asked Jo

"There are no positive stories to be told about Africa," said Andrew

"Hey!" Mumbi was angry, "I'm a positive story – Jane's a positive story. Why are any of us here if there are no positive stories to tell? Are we all cynical monsters just here to get rich?"

Someone coughed rather artificially. Marielise raised an eyebrow and changed the subject a little.

"I think it's a good idea to drop the IMF myself. Look what it's done to Zambia. Inflation goes up by thousands of kwacha every single day. The gap between the rural poor and the urban rich is unbridgeable. How can it be right to run any country on this basis?"

"There isn't much of a rural poor anymore," said Nick, "It's an urban poor now. Over 50% of Zambians live in the towns now because that's where the food is and there is no transport to and from the countryside."

"Yeah! 90% of the population exist on the black economy – for once that's not a 'black' joke!" said Mumbi, "Money remains in the hands of a tiny black elite and white expatriate companies."

"It's typical African corruption – " began Andrew, but Manda interrupted.

"Rubbish! Rubbish! It's not typical 'African' – it's typical 'anywhere-in-the-world' corruption when all resources, capital, people, technology, are scarce and exploitable in a developing country."

"Anyway, Jacky says that it's as good as the end of the world for Zambia," said Jessie, "that's why he is throwing this big party for everyone he knows in Siavonga on Sunday. Free booze and food. Should be fun!"

"It will be the same as it was when the president nationalised the mines," said Andrew, "that was an economic disaster."

Jo shook his head.

"That's to read only one aspect of the story," he said. "Take a serious, long look at the history of mining and colonial exploitation right round the world and you will have to come to a different conclusion."

"Colonialism is over – it's finished! No argument!" answered Andrew.

"No!" insisted Jo, "Mining companies are global conglomerates and outside the control of governments. They can call the shots in most places in Africa – and in the world."

"Except in South Africa," said Andrew

"Wait and see," said Jo and Mumbi together and they both laughed.

"Come on – let's go for a sail – the wind is getting up again!" said Nick standing up. He had noticed the garden parasol dip and swing in the freshening breeze.

The friends continued the discussion after their evening *braaivleis*.

"Why do African leaders stay in power so long?" Andrew demanded, "Look at Nyerere and Kenyatta and Kaunda – they have all been around twenty years or more. Are you telling me they aren't corrupt?"

"We're not telling you anything," Marielise said easily, "Okay, it isn't good I know, but here, the majority of the population are urban and rural poor with minimal education. Life is a struggle for most people. Believe me they will make political demands in time – but political involvement and organisation develops gradually and has to come out of need and experience. It will happen."

Mumbi smiled.

"It's an African tradition to respect one's elders but not always to listen to them. Central government seems far from most people's lives. Our leaders have sycophants and self-seeking foreign governments for advisors. It's true however, that ordinary people are very dissatisfied. They can see that the IMF has made poor people poorer, but then so can the president. I think that is motivating this possible break with the IMF."

"We should know by the end of tomorrow," said Manda. "Will it really make a difference?"

"Who knows," Nick shrugged, "but many things in Zambia are reaching breaking point. Inflation should not be allowed to go on at this rate."

"It's typical African corruption and incompetence," repeated Andrew.

"For God's sake!" Jo was driven to expostulate, "The whole of this region is part of the frontline in the war against Apartheid. South Africa with the connivance of the West has destabilised the whole region from Mozambique to Angola! That is where the corruption begins! With it comes disinformation – look at this story in this magazine! How can we get to the truth?"

"Why don't you get Milimo here and ask him what he thinks?" Andrew said.

"Honestly Andrew – what a dreadful idea. Do you think we should order him to give us answers as if we were above him?" Manda was again so furious that she couldn't express herself clearly.

The conversation was in danger of escalating into a serious row. For a few moments everyone was quiet until some organising of wine and snacks filled the silences. Marielise wondered if the differences were rooted in race or class or money. She sighed. Manda sighed too. Perhaps it was down to personalities and desired outcomes, or maybe it was an optimistic, as opposed to a pessimistic, world view about the human state. Jo wondered how any country or any people could be healed after the damage of their subjugation to colonialism, Apartheid, and armed conflict.

After a while he said, "Zambia has been fortunate. Colonialism didn't get its teeth into this country and destroy people's spirits as it has in the rest of the region. Individuals here have an enviable healthy self-respect."

Mumbi laughed aloud.

"That's a start! As a country we know how much we have to be modest about in Zambia!"

FIVE

Forgiveness

"What can you do if you can't forgive someone for something they have done to you?" asked Manda.

Father Patrick had not been expecting the question.

For a moment he thought that he might be the person that Manda could not forgive, then he realised that it was a nonsensical notion. The old guilt would never leave him no matter how often he made confession and tried to atone for what he had done. Something in Manda's expression unaccountably recalled the distant past to him. He blinked his eyes and tried to focus his mind back on the question and the questioner, but she carried on speaking and gave him a few more minutes' grace.

"It's not as if I don't need to be forgiven myself. I know I have done all kinds of things I am ashamed of but I do try to say I'm sorry and make amends. It's just – " she stopped, searching for the right way to explain herself,

"This – um – thing that they did to me is really bad and how can he – they – not know it's really bad. I don't understand how they could not know what they were doing – it must have been deliberate! It must!"

Then she almost cried out, "I can't bear how I feel about this person. It's driving me mad because I am so angry with him –

them – so, so furious and if I am to carry on I have to be able to forgive – or not mind – and I can't do either – and I can't understand why he – why it happened."

Manda and Father Patrick were sitting in the office at the new AIDS/HIV Education and Advice Centre. The last client had left and, as they sometimes did when work ended, they would have a cup of tea together before going home. That way they would miss the worst of the traffic rush down Cha Cha Cha Road at the end of the day.

"This sounds like a very important question Manda," Father Patrick said. "Do you want to talk to me about it – or maybe one of the counsellors here?"

He smiled gently to be reassuring.

"I can't tell if this is a religious question or a personal one."

"I don't know exactly," Manda reflected, "I think I wanted to talk to you because forgiveness is something that priests understand – I think – don't you?"

"We understand that it is hard to forgive and that we all stand in need of it – probably most of the time."

Manda sighed.

"I'm not religious at all – we weren't at home when I was a child you know – I would say I was agnostic, but I do see that religion helps people get through problems; it kind of structures things by using rituals.

"I really need help right now though Father, anything at all would be good."

Father Patrick could see that Manda looked tired and brittle. He knew she had recently recovered from malaria and he had decided that that was the reason for her sadness and depression. Again he was gentle and asked,

"Do you want to tell me who has done this to you and why? Would that help?"

Manda looked down and shook her head slowly and definitively.

"No," she said, "I can't. I can't."

Manda did not want to cry. She bit her lip hard then reached for the teapot.

"More tea, Father? I need some too."

Father Patrick tried to think what comfort he might offer this young woman without preaching at her.

"For us humans, there are no easy answers. Things happen that are terrible and are unforgivable. Forgiveness is sometimes beyond the capacity of ordinary people. You might find comfort in the love of God if you decided to look for it in him."

For a moment Father Patrick saw Manda smile rather sadly.

"I can't see myself turning to God for help Father, though right now, I would grab at anything that helped. I need to understand what made this person do this to me."

Manda gave the priest a desperate glance but then looked away. He could see that she did not want to divulge more. It must be some aspect of her marriage that was wrong, but what? He felt certain that Nick was faithful to Manda. He had seen how Nick and Manda watched each other, even when they were out with other people. Perhaps that wasn't right. Perhaps they were too focussed on each other.

"Don't blame yourself, Manda," he said and smiled at her in return. "Forgiveness is divine you know. Maybe you just need not to mind being human and failing occasionally. Perhaps this will pass too? I will be praying for you."

Why did he feel that he had had this conversation with this woman before, when he knew that all they had talked about previously was the work they shared at this centre.

"I'm always here if you need me you know," he said

"Thank you, Father," Manda said, "I'm fine – not quite over the malaria yet, I guess."

"Well – take care Manda," said Father Patrick, "I'll see you and Nick at the trust meeting next week. We are so grateful for the pro bono work he does for us here and we certainly could not manage without you, Manda, and your hard work as volunteer manager."

Manda locked the office and climbed into her car. She sat for a while, fighting despair. She still did not know what to think or feel or do. Perhaps she was still weak after her bout of malaria. So silly of her to have got it. She had missed one week of her anti-malaria prophylactic and then she and Nick had visited friends who lived outside Lusaka. Within days she had started to feel feverish, and then it all happened unbelievably fast. At lunch she had had the worst headache of her life and by teatime had not been able to lift her head from the pillow. She was barely conscious when Nick got back from work but had managed to whisper to him that it must be malaria.

"Please phone John," she said. "Please get him to come now." She did not hear or see Nick pick up the phone and as consciousness slipped away from her, she was aware that he was not moving. Nick was just sitting there watching her move inexorably towards death.

Manda had recovered consciousness forty-eight hours later in the Teaching Hospital. John, her doctor, was by her bed, checking her temperature and pulse. She felt empty and drained and very weak. Her hand was attached to a drip. Her head was still sore but light and pain-free by comparison with the headache she last remembered. Nick seemed to her to be still sitting where she had last seen him, though that was not possible as she was in a different place.

"Hello my darling girl," Nick said.

"She'll be okay now," said John, with a strange look at Nick, "Bloody lucky though. It will be a little time before you feel strong again, Manda. Take better care of her Nick."

At the time Manda had no idea what John had meant.

Nick had been sweet to her and very thoughtful and considerate after her illness, and she had recovered completely without any complications. This had been her first week back at the counselling centre in Lusaka and she was enjoying it while taking it slow. Then one afternoon John had turned up at the centre as he did occasionally to see one of his patients. He had taken Manda to one side.

"Is there something wrong with Nick?" he asked, "His behaviour was quite strange. We were supposed to have a game of squash the night you were taken ill. He didn't show and after I finished playing I called round at your place to see what was up. You were deeply unconscious and Nick was just watching you and doing nothing. He should have called me the instant he knew you were ill. With falciparum malaria, time is of the essence in treatment. Every minute that you are unconscious increases the probability of cerebral malaria and death. Nick knows that for God's sake! It is a miracle that you are alive, Manda. A bloody miracle."

Manda had been so shocked by this piece of information that she could not speak and just nodded at John. He was in a rush as usual anyway and Manda had been left to try and understand what Nick's behaviour meant. She couldn't understand it and couldn't take it in. Nick loved her and cared for her but he had sat by her watching her die. The disconnection between his emotions and his behaviour was total and bizarre. She hated him and could not forgive him but she still had no idea what to do herself and she still could not believe it.

She was, herself, becoming disconnected and insane. Living in Zambia had reduced her to the level of a kept woman. As an expatriate wife she couldn't work unless she had a work permit and they were only given for specific jobs so she had opted for voluntary unpaid work. The problem was that Nick seemed pleased with her dependence on him. Should she be grateful? Was it generous of him not to mind that she had no income to contribute to the family? It meant that she had to ask for everything she needed and she found that humiliating. It was no compensation that Nick gave her expensive, unasked for presents but never bought her the plants that she wanted for her garden.

She was losing her sense of self-respect.

Worse, she was losing her autonomy and her freedom.

Six

Guilt

The priest was unusually troubled after he had left Manda at the counselling centre.

Forgiveness and guilt? Well – they were old and recurring themes for everyone and not least for himself. Yes – he had confessed. He had atoned. A long, long time had passed.

Yes. He had sinned long ago but even one sin has a way of staining the whole of one's existence. One sin can't be isolated, wrapped up, sterilised, or even burnt and destroyed. Sins have consequences and those consequences have ramifications that are well beyond any one person's control. It was the consequences of his sin that worried him most deeply. He had done what he was asked to do by his order but had that really been the best thing to do? What was right?

God was useful – had Marielise said that? Or had he read or reread it recently? God is useful because he limits our responsibility for our sins.

Marielise would have grinned as she said: "If one takes too much responsibility for one's mistakes – errors – then you could never move on and do anything useful with your life – could you Patrick?"

He had agreed that she need not call him Father.

Father Patrick stopped, parked his car and climbed out.

As he did so, the remembrance of his wrongdoing struck him and the remembrance was so sweet, so poignant and so bitter, that he was paralysed. Memory returned with all the sharpest, dearest sensations of smell, of sight, of sound, dry dust, dry grass, wood smoke, fire, the smell of guns, of blood, of sweat – and all the perfume of her.

He leant back against the car with his head bowed. The recollection of that time dissolved the last thirty years of his life. He was back there in 1958 in the valley, looking at the ruined village of the Headman Chisamu.

Seven

Those Who Run Away And Hide.

1958

Thirty years ago there had been no vultures overhead that day, nor were there any on the following days. Perhaps there were no dead bodies to find.

The police and their officers were searching the whole area in case people were hiding or had run away and died of their wounds. The search would continue for several days. Nobody wanted to add deaths by drowning in the new Lake Kariba, to the deaths from the gunfire. The water was rising fast and the nature of the local geography was such that people would find the water circled around their villages, filling up the gullies between them and the safety of the road out of the valley. They would be cut off from the hills before the silt banks of the river were overcome with the flood. The water would approach unexpectedly from behind and not from the Zambezi itself. In any case the rains would soon be on them and the roads would quickly become impassable. There was perhaps one month left to find people who had hidden away.

The Governor of Northern Rhodesia was very deeply saddened and ashamed that his Northern Rhodesian Police Force had been responsible for the deaths of the villagers. He felt a father's responsibility for the Tonga and could not understand why they hadn't obeyed him as children should. In his obsessive fashion he was determined to get the correct figures of the numbers of dead and wounded Batonga so he could know the exact and tragic result of his decisions. He insisted that the district officer and his staff, together with the police, find every one of the dead and all the wounded.

Father Patrick had arrived in the afternoon after the gun battle. He was in time to see the first group of weeping, defeated women and children loaded onto the lorries for the eighty-mile long, bone-shaking journey to their unknown future home. He was taken at once to see the wounded in case any needed or wanted his prayers. Those most seriously hurt were already on their way to the hospital. The competent doctor had no need of the priest's help with his own ministrations. He was asked next to help check the identities of the dead. Among the bodies he saw that of the *sikatongo*, Singani: a little crumpled corpse with a bloodied head. He would be a great loss to the cohesion of his village. How would they manage without his knowledge of ritual and social order?

The priest had seen dead bodies before in the villages and known the grief of their relatives. It was his job after all, but the scale of this tragedy was outside his experience. He felt the shattering and destruction of the whole way of village life as if it was his own life as well.

There were not many villagers to see. Most of the men had run away, either during the battle or as soon as they realised they were beaten. Some twenty prisoners were under guard in a barbed wire *boma*. Headman Chisamu was in handcuffs in a police vehicle. A couple of huts were on fire and the grain stores had been broken open and were being emptied into hessian sacks. The smell of smoke and the taint of cordite and tear-gas hung in the air. The village chickens were already back underfoot but the goats were scattered at some distance.

The women and children, now cordoned off in the village after their return from the forest, had collected their pathetic belongings into piles. Some did not even have any means of fastening them into bundles. Their hopelessness, fear and grief, were overwhelming to watch. Father Patrick was of no help to them. Desperate to help and assuage his own misery at the situation, he began to look around him to see if he could recognise any of the village women. Had any children become separated from their mothers? Who was missing?

The priest had seen Singani's first wife on the lorry, her head in her hands, her children by her side. But where was the second wife? She was not to be seen. She must be hiding. Father Patrick had an idea where that might be. Singani had once shown him the sacred sites of the local Tonga. There was one very important Rain Shrine at a distance from Chisamu where the second wife had helped Singani with the ritual appeasement of the ancestors' spirits. She might be there trying to protect it, or she might be simply hiding. He would have to walk to it as there was no road, but first he would need the permission of the police officer in charge – that was if he could find him.

Father Patrick found the district officer, Tom Holmes, who was very distressed and angry.

"That bloody man!" he kept saying, "Why didn't he stay out of it? He made a bad situation so much worse! That bloody man! And they played comic opera at the *indaba*! Comic opera – Gilbert and Sullivan! Stupid! Stupid!"

Father Patrick did not ask who he meant. It was better that the district officer let off steam here in the bush than said something out of place about the Governor of Northern Rhodesia back in Lusaka.

In response to the priest's request, Tom stopped his rant.

"I don't know if it is safe to go off on your own. Oh God!" he shook his head sadly,

"These people are mostly gentle and kind – they know you – go carefully. I'll sort it with the commanding officer. Go on."

So Father Patrick Brogan, a young man still not thirty years old, set off to the Rain Shrine to look for the *sikatongo's* ritual wife.

275

She had been married to Singani as a twelve-year-old child. It had only recently become illegal to marry off children. At first, Father Patrick was not certain he would find his way, but as he walked on, the path became familiar. He felt as if the *sikatongo* was once again at his side explaining the significance of the Rain Shrine and he remembered the name of the second wife.

It was Natombi.

He saw the boy first and then thought he made out a second taller figure in the shadow of some trees. The boy immediately moved backwards out of sight and the shadows absorbed the taller figure. Father Patrick stopped. He called out a greeting in ChiTonga and then, feeling foolish because he did not know what to do, he called out an offer of help. Nothing stirred. It was pointless to go further. He sat down and waited.

After perhaps an hour, he rose to his feet and turned back. First he called again: "I will come back again. Let me help you."

As he walked back two police constables came towards him. Unaccountably he shook his head at them, indicating that there was no one hiding in that direction and the two men veered off northwards towards the thicker woods of the hillsides.

Eight

The Rain Shrine

1958

After a few days Father Patrick came back again to the valley. Tom Holmes was still sending out search parties but reckoned that all the wounded had been found and treated. He said the final count was eight dead and thirty-two wounded. He remembered Singani's younger wife and shook his head. As far as he could tell, no one had seen her get on a truck and leave the valley.

Once again the priest walked to the Rain Shrine. Again he called out greetings and an offer of help and then sat and waited. Again nothing happened. After a while he stood up to leave but first he left an offering at the Rain Shrine of some mealie-meal, sugar and matches.

He did the same the following week and again soon after. He saw no one. Each time his offering of food had gone and each time he replaced it. He knew the fourth time would have to be his last. It was the middle of October and by midday every day the rain clouds had begun to build up into thunderheads. He was sweating as he walked, as well as prickly with the electric tension generated by the promise of a storm.

When he arrived at the Rain Shrine, Natombi and Milimo were waiting for him. They stood together quietly: the skinny, barefoot boy in ragged shorts and the graceful young woman with a length of cloth, a patterned *chitenge*, tied up under her armpits and around her body. She too, was barefoot. At her feet rested the clay pots and wooden gourds and ladles from the Rain Shrine, together with some small, strange parcels wrapped in a dark fabric and fastened with beads, feathers and a curious, sticky, resinous gum. As he approached she bent and picked up the objects, indicating to the child to carry his share. Without looking directly at the priest, she greeted him.

"Let us go," she said.

Father Patrick Brogan had not thought clearly about what was to happen next. It was already late afternoon and Tom had left. The eighty-mile journey to Lusitu could not be made in the dark. He had avoided thinking about how he would transport Natombi to Lusitu because he did not dare think about what it might feel like to be alone for so many hours with a woman. Now they would have to stop for the night at the mud-hut school that the mission had made his responsibility. That meant he would have longer alone with her. Had that been his intention all along? What should he have done that was different?

Together they packed the objects from the Rain Shrine carefully into the Land Rover using armfuls of thatch from the derelict huts. The road back was bone and clay pot breaking. Natombi and Milimo climbed into the vehicle and sat on the bench seat next to Patrick. His skin came alive at once with his awareness of her. He did not need to turn and look to know her appearance. Natombi's arms and shoulders were young and round, her breasts softened with child-bearing. Her well-shaped head balanced on an elegant neck. She had the straight, thin nose of the Tonga and her cheeks were a smooth curve from her upward sloped eyes to her full lips. Her long, slim-fingered hands rested on her lap. She was breathing next to him and he was breathing in the dusty smokiness of her weeks of hiding in the bush. The inevitable hardness and swelling in his groin made him clumsy on the clutch as he shifted into four-wheel drive. He cursed himself again. She was a refugee, a widow of only five weeks, he could not, would not force himself on her. He was a priest for God's sake – there were actions he could not contemplate in any case – so why was he tortured? What was he going to do? Why were men made this way?

They reached the school-hut at dusk. Patrick's assistant came to greet them when he heard the approaching engine. Patrick asked him to find a sleeping place for Milimo with the other students in the classroom that doubled as a dormitory.

"We'll go to Lusitu tomorrow," he told both Natombi and his assistant.

He showed Natombi into his round mud-walled home. A curtain hung across it between his camping stretcher bed and his chair and table study. She was hesitant and addressed some words he did not follow to his assistant.

"Where is his wife?" she had asked.

"He has none," the assistant said and shook his head in disapproval.

"You may have the hut for your own tonight," Patrick said. He had a spare bedroll in the Land Rover. I'll sleep outside."

All the while his desire increased and his anger with himself grew greater.

Natombi took Milimo to the pump by the well so that they could both wash. She rubbed their heads and bodies into a white lather with cold water and red carbolic soap.

Patrick had a small, charcoal-lined, wire-mesh larder, its legs in four tin lids filled with water. Inside was a lump of smoked bacon, wrinkled tomatoes, pale cabbage and yellow oil which Patrick started to prepare for supper. When Natombi had finished her bathing, she came back to the hut and took over the cooking of the *nshima* and relish from him. When the meal was ready, she served him first then waited until he had finished eating before giving food to Milimo and herself. Patrick could smell the heat of her clean soap-scented skin.

The night was warm and sticky, noisy with shrill crickets and the insistent triple piping of tree frogs. Patrick's assistant took Milimo to the school hut and then went home himself. Natombi put the cooking fire out and left the pans outside for the chickens to peck clean in the morning. She looked straight at Patrick for a brief moment, then turned her back on him and went indoors to the bed.

Patrick lay on the raised clay *stoep* outside his hut. He prayed. He became resigned. Onanism is a sin too but there are worse. He was so tired and not very comfortable. The sky grumbled at him noisily. He drifted into sleep and then woke up abruptly rigid with desire. All he could think of was Natombi. *Oh God! This was hell.* He was hit hard in the eye by a huge, heavy drop of water. The sky threatened thunderously and this time raindrops the size of half-crown coins struck the ground and made the dust rise. Still it did not rain properly and Patrick's erection stiffened. *Natombi I want you!* The single raindrops turned to drilling rods of water. Patrick had to go back inside the hut. At least the storm and rain was so noisy that no one could hear him groan with lust. He rolled himself into his blanket to better wrestle with the devil.

NINE

Kindness

1958

Patrick felt a hand on his shoulder and unrolled himself in wild guilt. Who had come to shame him? Who?

Who but Natombi, come in kindness to be his wife for the night, not knowing that he would be damned to hell forever for her generosity. Oh it was wonderful. Wonderful!

Having relieved Patrick from a self-inflicted sin in too short a time while condemning him to eternal perdition, Natombi knelt to stand up and quietly to return to her own bed.

"Please stay. Please stay," Patrick begged. He wanted so much to love her and not just to have satisfied himself.

She hesitated and then she lay back down again next to him. He felt her surprise at the tenderness of his caresses, her realisation of pleasure increasing from his book-learned tutoring, her responses to her own growing desire. She was his Bible, black with richness and meaning, his Solomon singing of a wealth of luscious harvests. She was every poem of the many he had read of love and chivalry, of Eros and Thanatos, of life and death, of God and the Devil. She was everything for him that night and he knew that he too was everything for her that night. He had given her his perjured soul, which was already promised elsewhere, and she was from now on the guardian of his spirit. He was lost that

281

night. Not for sex, but for love. All in that one night! He had one more thing he wanted to do that night. He wanted most of all to hear Natombi laugh. The one thing he would do before the night ended was see her smile and share with her the laughter of lovers. That would be the one good act for them both that might earn him forgiveness.

The next morning had the freshness and beauty of every first morning after the first rain of the season, when every living thing is sizzling with renewal and every bird is singing its heart out in honey and music. Father Patrick knew he was at the end and the beginning of his life. Today was his first day too.

He should have left at dawn so that he could take Natombi to Lusitu and then return in daylight, but he had done nothing but wait. Milimo was with the other boys and as it was not a school day they ran and they played. Father Patrick wondered what Milimo had told his new friends about the fight at Chisamu's village. He could see that there was much talk going on by the well between Natombi and the other women.

It was two days later that Tom Holmes pulled his Land Rover up unexpectedly outside the school. He got out, and came straight over to Father Patrick.

"I have got Singani's brother here," he said. "He offered to come and look for Natombi and Milimo at Chisamu but we were told on the road that she came here a few days ago."

"Yes," said Father Patrick, getting slowly to his feet, "she is over there with the women."

So that is how the world ends, he thought, *with me whimpering by myself tonight.*

Natombi and Patrick did not touch each other again. It would not have been mannerly. They avoided looking in each other's faces too. That also was impolite. Patrick searched in his hut and in his mind for something to give her but could only offer promises already broken. Natombi, however, asked him to keep Milimo at the school and to give him a good education. Patrick agreed. He would sort out any problems with his superiors at the mission when he went for his next confession.

Father Patrick looked at Singani's brother and hoped that he would die soon and painfully. Natombi must go to be the wife of her dead husband's brother. That was the custom. What else could she choose? What else could he choose? It was over.

It was not over but what followed months later was out of his hands and perhaps had never been in his hands to decide.

That matter was looked after by the elder priests of his order.

TEN

Running Away

The Guest Book. The Cottage, Siavonga.
October 1989
(Written in Milimo's careful and tidy handwriting)
'Manda Harvey
Marielise Wolf
Nick Harvey'

Manda fled to the cottage. She needed to be by herself, somewhere where no one would come to bother her, somewhere where it would appear normal enough for her to be by herself without her having to invent reasons that she herself might forget. The stress had started to affect her memory and made her behaviour seem inconsistent even to herself. She told Nick that she wanted some time alone. It was odd that he didn't ask why or ask her not to go but she could no longer tell what was normal or what wasn't in their relationship. Emma and James were spending the weekend with Mumbi and Jane's two children. She knew they were safe and happy.

For months and months, maybe for two even three years, Nick had cut her out, had blocked her out. It was hard to explain how and impossible to know why. At first she joked, without believing it, that he was having an early mid-life crisis, or joked that he wanted but couldn't face the thought of planning a change of career, but no matter how she phrased these ideas – whether as jokes, questions, even if she came at them sideways as questions about her own future, or as questions about the children's future plans, or even if she asked him directly about the plans of his senior management back in Europe – she elicited no response from him. She could sit next to him on the sofa, across the dining room table from him, or chat to him over coffee after a meal. He was there in his flesh and he looked at her when she spoke but he made no effort to respond. He didn't seem angry, he didn't seem disinterested, he just did not respond. Manda thought that he must be hearing and thinking about what she said and that if she waited patiently he would respond later, but weeks and even months later nothing had changed.

Manda arranged weekends at the cottage for just the two of them. That had always been a relaxing and communicative time for them both. Sitting out on the veranda in the warm dark, with a bottle of wine between them, she would entertain Nick with scenarios about different lives, different futures, new and interesting places to go and visit, all in ways that were humorous or fanciful but with the underlying question – *what next for us, my love? What do you want to do, my love?*

These times seemed to have passed pleasantly but nothing developed from these evenings either. Manda began to feel like a ghost talking through a soundproof glass window. She began to feel powerless, as if she had walked through a syrupy fog that weighted her limbs down and dulled her senses.

Nick remained solid and immoveable. Several times when she lost herself enough to try to plead with him for an answer, he turned towards her and, though she couldn't explain how he did it, he somehow bulked himself up so that he seemed to threaten her simply by his presence. It was as if he leant on the air between them and that was enough to crush her lungs. There was nothing in his expression that changed; he was just using his size and his breadth to remind her not to go further. Manda backed down every time. She had long ago learnt that if she showed herself to be vulnerable, if she wept or begged him to be kind, it put her at risk from a blow or a piece of spoken cruelty that was hard to survive. Nick showed her no physical affection. He neither kissed nor cuddled her, though they continued to have sex.

Manda felt she was a fool; felt she had been a fool. She was a very tired fool though. Too tired to think at all. Too tired to understand what was happening to them or to resolve it. There was no way that she could know for certain that Nick was simply fulfilling the future that his abusive parents had created for him. A future guaranteed by his childhood of broken toys and solitary pain.

She had believed that he wanted their relationship to be good and to get better. It hadn't all been bad. They had had wonderful times together, been good friends and shared so much. Weren't all marriages the same? Good and bad in parts, rough and smooth, up and down, better and worse? Or was her marriage like the curate's egg, all bad and she was just lying politely about it? No one should walk away from a marriage easily – especially when there were children. In any case, walking away would not be easy. Zambia felt like home. Everything in her life was here in Zambia but expatriate wives are not citizens. She did not have a right to remain – and worse, she did not have a ticket out. She did not have a paid job to go to or a career to sustain her.

When at first things had gone wrong in her marriage to Nick, the first time he hit her for example, she had thought that she could persuade him to be different, that together they could rationalise their relationship and it would go on and on improving. All that happened was that it changed. He stopped hitting her and she stopped turning to him for comfort when she felt hurt or vulnerable. That made her feel isolated. It seemed better and safer for a while, but then as always, he found a new way of damaging her and of damaging himself.

It would always happen at the moment that she felt safe again and happy in the relationship: at the moment when things were going well. After a pleasant evening out or on holiday, when the kids were not there to see, out of the blue he would turn to her with that face – that face of stone with the frown cut into it and his eyes like rocks, and he would tell her it was over. She was to leave on the next plane, never see him or the children again. He was beating her, battering her, not with his fists, because she had told him not to do that, but with every cruel and hateful word that he could summon. She would reason with him, say she loved him, say that their marriage was still a good marriage, she would weep, ask him to say it wasn't true, and then she would go and pack her bags. A couple of times she went far enough to phone a friend for help, once she phoned Sebastian, and once her mother, to say that her marriage had broken down irretrievably, though she could not explain why and how it had happened so apparently abruptly because she had never said how hard it was before to anyone.

The next morning she would get up stiff with grief and exhaustion and so afraid, but usually before she could arrange a flight it was over. Nick seemed not to remember what had happened and he would not refer to it again – at least until the next time. Until the next time life would go on normally, happily, but without facing up to any decisions about where life was taking them.

Manda tried to suggest marital therapy, provided books or films that touched on relationship issues. Sometimes Nick read them. Sometimes he didn't. There was never a way to make a connection between the brutal Nick and the Nick who loved Manda.

Manda and Nick had created the illusion of a better than average marriage. Manda did not know how common her situation was because no one talked of such marriages.

Of course I would leave my husband if he was a wife-beater, but Nick isn't.

That was understood. What was not understood was that fear and abuse are not simply manifested in a physical beating and that entering the trap of such a relationship is a very gradual one, and well baited with rewards for goodness, love and kindness.

The trap does not catch victims or fools, it catches lovers.

Manda was sure Nick loved her. Well – she was sure that he needed her love – no he did love her. It was hard to tell – it was all so close up and important that she couldn't work out what was at the heart of it all – what really was their relationship based on? She didn't know and with time couldn't undo the knots and tangles of how they worked together. Everything that she thought was a good quality in her herself seemed to work against her in her marriage: her loyalty, her commitment to the relationship, her independence of mind, and her sympathy and understanding for a man so damaged and traumatised by his childhood.

The trap that was her prison was complete. She had colluded in its creation. All the problems of their marriage were secrets that no one could possibly begin to uncover. From the outside their relationship looked good, intact, perfect even. No one would understand what their life was really like. No person would ever believe her. The secret of their misery was absolutely safe.

Now Manda was tired; she was too confused, there didn't seem to be anyone to blame for how things were. She was left with a paralysing sense of guilt. How had this happened to her? How had it happened to Nick? What was it doing to the children? She must go away. She must go away and think. Must go away and find a solution to the problem.

So Manda went to the cottage and tried to find somewhere in herself a clear space for thinking and planning how to leave Nick safely.

Where would safety be for herself, for Nick and for the children if she left him?

If she was allowed to go by Nick.

Eleven

The Cottage

Manda was not expected at the cottage. It was strange to arrive and find the doors locked and barred, and the deckchairs and table not out on the veranda. Milimo was not far away and one of his children went to fetch him. Milimo's wife gave Manda the keys and she started on the business of removing the padlocks. They were of course stiff and awkward and Manda scraped her knuckle. Sudden panic overwhelmed her.

What the hell was she doing down at the lake on her own? Why did she feel so afraid? Why so lonely? As she stood at the barred iron door, irresolute, the cottage changed from a delightful, calm refuge into a shabby, inconvenient, stale-smelling, isolated hovel. She wouldn't be able to sleep there on her own in the dark with only a box of matches and candles to protect her. She was already in a panic.

She was often on her own. Manda never thought anything of flying to England and taking a flat on her own for a month. She was competent, independent and practical but why had she come down here? Why was she now afraid?

Manda was even more surprised to feel uncomfortable when Milimo appeared. Perhaps she had greatly inconvenienced him by arriving without phoning him first? He did look taken aback when she said she was alone and she realised once again, that she knew nothing about this man. Not how old he was, or where he was from, and certainly she had no idea of his opinions or thoughts. She had been a considerate and responsible employer she thought. She had even allowed herself to think that she was fond of Milimo and his family; that maybe he liked her – well – that was a question that she couldn't answer even if it did matter. Milimo had always simply been part of the cottage.

Here they were on the veranda looking at each other in surprise as if for the first time. Manda saw a man of about forty who was a little taller than her, slim and fit, simply dressed in clean shorts and a tee-shirt with *pata-patas* on his feet. He had a calm, intelligent expression and a gentle face. Milimo saw a dark-skinned woman, in shorts and tee-shirt, her hair hastily pulled into a knot at her neck. She looked tense and tired. She looked worried and sad. She looked just as his mother had looked when his father had died so long ago at Chief Chipepo's village, before there was a lake in the valley.

Manda recovered and took charge of the situation. She greeted Milimo and asked after his family

"I'll only be staying for one night," she said, abruptly changing her plan to stay all weekend. "Please can you get the fridge going for me and get the barbecue ready – and make the beds – only the first bedroom."

"We haven't got charcoal or cooking oil," Milimo said, "but I can get it from the market. Will Mr Harvey be coming down later?"

"No, he won't, and no, Milimo," Manda was wanting to flee, "I'll go to the market to get the charcoal and oil – I'll see if they have some vegetables too. Is there anything that I should get for the cottage? Is there anything that you and Mrs Milimo would like me to get?"

Manda went back to the car, unloaded the cold box of food that she had brought, and the fruit trees that were her excuse for being there. Milimo could take them down to the cottage for her; her overnight bag was already waiting outside her room where she had left it. She reversed the car around carefully in the small space under the *marula* tree and drove away from the cottage, around past the church, to the scruffy little market above the low cost housing.

Manda did not hurry. She did not want to get back to the cottage before Milimo had finished with all his chores, which she knew he would complete carefully and thoroughly as usual. He would sweep and dust, unlock the cupboard with its store of bed linen and loo paper. He would put bottles of boiled water to chill in the fridge where it would, at first, warm the fridge. *Dammit!* Why hadn't she phoned him first so it was all waiting for her? She hadn't foreseen his presence slaving away in the background while she actually was staying there. What she did love about the cottage was that Milimo had always done all the work before they arrived, then he would slip away like Ariel, a magical facilitator of the illusion that the cottage was a refuge that existed without exploiting any other human. That was why she loved the place so much, even though it was without electricity or air-conditioning. Here in Zambia, as in all Africa, there was so much exploitation, so much inequality, and here at the cottage she could pretend otherwise and not feel responsible for any part of it; as if the lake was not itself an enormous, wonderful and beautiful proof of the exploitation of Africa.

The marketeers were cheerful and helpful. Manda bought a couple of plastic bags of charcoal. She normally bought a whole sack in Lusaka where it was much cheaper, but this would do for tonight. She found tomatoes and mangoes, and some okra for Milimo's wife, then she idly turned over some of the second-hand clothing that was supposedly brought in as aid for distribution but found its way into the hands of private traders – the biggest and most successful import of business into Africa – had Nick said that? She had only been a few minutes away from the cottage and needed to kill more time. The sun had warmed her and so had the smiles of the marketeers but thoughts of Nick made her feel wretched again. Where could she go for an hour or so? Certainly not to the motels where she might be recognised and greeted and have to make small talk.

She turned her car westwards and let the road take her very slowly around Siavonga. She passed the grand house built by the government minister next to the grand house built by the businessman, each with their guards and security lights, their slasto-paved patios with swimming pools and imported plants and non-indigenous palm trees. Here the tarmac gave out and the road surface broke up into gullies and boulders where goats sauntered and chickens scratched. She passed Mutinangala, the grass and mud hut village tumbling down the hillside along the stinking sewer of a stream that disgorged itself into Cholera Bay and she heard Nick's voice saying in her head: "*Cholera has only recently arrived in Zambia. It has been gradually finding its way down Africa from the Mediterranean.*"

At last Manda drove up onto the wooded hill that overlooked Banana Island. The dry season was ending but the weather had not started to get really hot as yet. Banana Island curved out into the bay with its tail of half-submerged and still sinking granite rocks joining it onto the mainland. Manda pulled the car off the dirt road onto an even smaller track. Without knowing it she had found the exact place that Margaret had stopped at when she screamed and screamed at the death of Mark Watson.

What was Manda going to do? Screaming was not her way. Crying perhaps? She seemed to have cried rivers in the last few weeks. Today she felt all dried up, drought-stricken like the bleached grass around her, barely moving as the light wind swung around from blowing off the lake all day to its evening of blowing off the land. Manda climbed out of the car and looked around her. Then she saw them.

She saw all around her the blue dreaming haze of the grass

orchids; their pale and delicate stars an unlikely miracle in a world that was drier than the dust of bones. Their brave beauty made her gasp and then her tears began to fall, without sobbing; she wept and wept for the loveliness of them and for all the goodness and hope that was disappearing out of her life forever. Still with the tears running down her cheeks, she turned her eyes to the sky and she saw above her the birds – hundreds and hundreds and hundreds of them – spiralling upwards and upwards for thousands of feet in a vast thermal, not storks as she first thought but black kites, *migrans migrans*, setting off on their annual journey to the other end of the earth.

Manda was watching, spellbound on the hill above the lake, a breathtaking sight over her head, a fragile beauty around her feet, and her shattered heart breaking into pieces, with still no way of knowing how she could take a step forward into the tomorrow she must choose.

She stood and stood, her head tilted back staring at the circling raptors, until she heard the soft purr of an approaching car engine. *Damn!* Would it carry on past her – surely it wouldn't stop? It stopped so quietly that Manda wasn't sure if it had. *Damn again!* Manda smeared the tears off her cheek and turned round slowly, wondering how to avoid whoever was in the car – could she pretend to be out for a walk? – she heard light footsteps coming towards her and then a voice:

"Manda!" a woman's voice said, "Manda – hello! I've come out looking for you."

Unbelievably, it was Marielise.

Manda turned right around and stared at her.

Marielise looked at Manda standing alone among the orchids under a vast sky swirling with flying birds, her face shining-wet with her grief and she opened her arms and held them out to Manda.

"Ahh Manda, poor, poor Manda!" she said, "Come here and tell me all about it."

TWELVE

Refuge

In the early morning before the sun rose the next day, Manda and Marielise made love. It began with an innocent kindness and a gentle soothing that was only tender and caring. Then sudden desire and passion overcame them both. Manda felt that she had come home again. Home to a place where she belonged and was safe, to a loving person whom she too, could love. She felt that she owned herself again and was able to give herself as she chose.

They talked most of the night before that happened.

At first, after Marielise appeared so unexpectedly, Manda cried. She cried so much sitting in the car with Marielise, with Marielise's arm around her shoulder and a box of tissues on her lap, that she couldn't talk very clearly, except to keep repeating nonsensically that she didn't want anyone to see her like this, she didn't want Milimo to see that she had been crying, and Nick must never know.

Eventually she composed herself enough to feel up to the short drive back to the cottage. She followed Marielise who said that she would go first and see that Milimo was reassured and the coast was clear of people who might see Manda's tears.

"Only be ten minutes behind me," she said, "or I'll come out again looking for you!"

Marielise confessed that, like Manda, she had taken a chance on the cottage being empty because she needed to stop over to get some sleep on her way from Harare to Livingstone. She didn't say why she was going there.

"When I arrived Milimo was positively upset. He said you were already here by yourself and he didn't know who else was coming and you had told him what to do etcetera, etcetera. You know how fussed he can be about Margaret's cottage, so I said not to worry – I would go and find you and see if it was okay for me to stay also. Actually, I did wonder as you were down here by yourself without Nick – I wondered if you had a secret assignation – or a lover – honestly that's how my mind works – sorry. So I thought I had better ask your permission not to ruin your love affair," and Marielise gave her delightful, warm, chuckling laugh and squeezed Manda's shoulder. Manda put her hand over the arm holding her and pressed it tighter against herself. It was so comforting to be held in this warm friendly way – like a blessing. She could feel the stress easing and lifting. Maybe she would be able to think again instead of just fret.

"Oh God, it's not a love affair – if only! It's my marriage that's the disaster!" said Manda, feeling ready to collapse again.

"Tell me about it – if you would like to, that is," said Marielise. "I'm a good old agony aunty as I have been through all kinds of love and shit myself!"

So they talked and talked, first of all about Nick, and then about Manda, and then about Manda and Nick and inevitably the children, and then back to Manda and then Manda and Nick.

"I sort of know about this stuff," said Marielise surprisingly. "I put in time at the first Refuge for Battered Women in London in the seventies when I was in the Women's Movement. Of course I wasn't there as a victim – but as a counsellor. I learnt quite a lot from the experience though. Battered women are not necessarily beaten all the time but they are controlled by fear and threats and it's because they love their partners that they don't just leave.

Usually they don't have enough money of their own either. Financial control is fundamental to the control of women by men – that's how it's mostly done.

"What do you think you want to do, Manda? I must warn you that there is no possibility that you will be able to change Nick. It doesn't work like that."

"But he loves me!" said Manda, starting to feel afraid again, "And I love him!"

"Of course you do. You aren't the kind of person to settle for less are you?" said Marielise. "Besides, it sounds as if you aren't really an easy victim yourself and you gave him so many opportunities to sort things out for himself and as much help as it is possible to give. The trouble with abusive relationships is that while the abuser may not be able to help himself, the person who is abused is not necessarily a masochist looking to be a victim just – I am afraid – a loving woman looking to be loved and loving.

"Look," Marielise insisted, "Nick picked a good woman for himself. Don't think he doesn't appreciate your good qualities – without you he will have trouble with his own self-hate and his need for self-destruction. Don't measure yourself as a failure because of this relationship."

"I can't leave him! What will he do without me? He needs me!"

Marielise was silent a while, looking at Manda and thinking of Jo's daughter Zanele, she was as lovely as Manda. Marielise still missed Zanele very much, even though she was now a young woman of twenty-one years studying film in Britain.

"Manda," she said, "you need to save yourself first. You are drowning now too. If Nick is drowning it is what he has chosen for himself – but you – you cannot go down with him. You are becoming sick and ill with misery and stress and you will be no use to anyone at all soon."

They had started before sunset with a large pot of tea, which was Marielise's prescription for replacing tears after too much crying.

"One must always be able to cry," she said, "otherwise one cannot heal one's sadness."

After sunset, they opened the new bottle of gin and sliced into the lemons Manda had brought. By nine o'clock, Marielise said that they must eat before they got too drunk and she dug in her cold box for the piri-piri chicken she had brought with her from Harare.

"I learnt how to prepare this dish in Mozambique years ago, it's garlic, coriander and fresh green chillies," she said. "These are left over from a lunch party we had yesterday. I made too much as usual, there is green salad, yellow Malay rice and a bottle of green Portuguese wine. A perfect meal! My favourite!"

So they talked, ate and talked some more.

Manda wanted to hear about Marielise. Marielise as usual muttered a little about her present job, that it was a bit boring.

"What about the Women's Movement then?" Manda asked curiously.

"What about it then?" Marielise said with her ready laugh. She looked sideways at Manda and grinned, raising a dark eyebrow. "Are you asking if we were all lesbians or just me and Eva?"

Manda smiled, leaning back in her deckchair and beginning to feel very relaxed.

"No, I don't suppose you all were. No I suppose that I have always felt sorry that I was too young to know what was going on. We did have some women talk about it at school. That was the day that the boys were allowed to go to watch the football cup and the girls had to stay at school. As one of the women said, the school had clearly demonstrated the issue of women's liberation to us that day anyhow."

Marielise laughed and Manda sat up a bit more and turned to her.

"Actually – you are bi-sexual aren't you, because you told me Eva was one of your lovers? I mean can one change over one's life? Without being forced to I mean – just be – whatever sexual orientation one wants to be?

"I know it seems an odd question – but well – here I work with people with HIV/AIDS. Here it's a heterosexual disease, but naturally I have done some research about sex and AIDS. I have been so under-informed about homosexuality – I have been thinking about it more and more."

Marielise looked at Manda seriously for a while.

"You know," she said, "I think that the differences are mostly nonsense – I think we are, most of us, just naturally sexual creatures ready to be physically loving with any other gender or the same gender, if only we weren't so afraid. At least that is what I have found to be true. I don't think of myself as anything but a sexual creature."

Manda allowed herself to get a little drunk that night. She wanted to give up on adulthood and responsibility for a few hours. She wanted to float away across the lake and up into the sky and be free and daft and young, then come back to earth the next day ready for whatever she had to do, which was probably leave Nick – which was definitely leave Nick.

She didn't want to face it, but she had known that there was only one solution to the problem of her marriage. She had thought of it with dread, unable to imagine that there would be anything good on the other side of such a terrible alteration in her life. Talking to Marielise had given her hope because she had, at last, accepted the reality of her situation. Marielise had a way of laughing about tragedy, which did not in the least diminish the tragedy, but seemed to place it inside the context of all human effort and failure, of the hope and despair that all people suffer. To see her particular unhappiness as different, or worse, or better, than the unhappiness of any other person, was to make her own life harder, while to have a sense of that shared pain, offered her a kind of balm. Previously, Manda had chosen not to confide in any of her Lusaka friends because they were also Nick's friends and that would be disloyal. It meant that she had felt lonely to the point of desperation.

Somehow Marielise had come to her rescue with such warmth and friendship and – and – Manda almost could not say the word – Marielise had come with love – and that was a miracle.

Marielise had admitted to herself years ago that she was attracted to Manda. Attraction, Marielise knew from experience, was never simply physical. Marielise had seen the grit in Manda, had seen her independent way of chewing over an idea and coming up with a thought or an opinion that was all her own, original, constructive, disinterested and without meanness. She had watched Manda when her face lit up with pleasure, with humour and with love and she had wanted Manda to love her too.

Of course Marielise loved Jo most of all. She also loved Luke and Eva and she loved Zanele as if she were her own child. The life she had chosen meant that she could not own them, or hold onto any of them for very long and yet she was constant to each of her loves and the constancy she saw in Manda was a quality she admired and valued in her own loves. She was glad to be spending time with Manda, sad that Manda was so sad, aware that Manda would move on too, but for the moment it was enough to be with her and for their friendship and affection to grow.

At last Marielise decided to be frank with Manda, telling her about herself and Jo, and their work for Umkonto We Sizwe: the armed wing of Mandela's ANC. Marielise knew Manda well enough to have gauged that her attitudes and views would be supportive and confidential. That in itself was not enough for Marielise to divulge any secrets under normal circumstances, but Marielise also had a highly developed instinct about people acquired by necessity over many years. She knew Manda would tell no one about Jo and herself. The bond between them would not easily break, even though they both understood that their lives would immediately start to go in different directions. They knew that this intimate time together was an interlude, that their friendship would last but they would not stay lovers.

"What do you think you will do next?" Marielise asked

"Go back to England and get a job if I can," answered Manda. "I will ask Nick for a divorce, but I think it may be safer and easier if I don't tell him that right away but do it in stages. I still can't bear to hurt him, but talking to you has made me realise how afraid I have become of what he will do to me. I can't say what I am afraid of – only that I am.

"You know, I have never lied to Nick – it always seemed that lies would poison a relationship – even white lies do not come easy to me. Now I must just play a game of pretence that will get me out of this marriage quickly, and without any more hurt.

I can't tell how much it has meant to me to be with you, Marielise, and how much I love you – I hope that we'll see each other again – I hope so!"

"I love you," said Marielise very quietly, "and I always will."

Then she added with her warm laugh, "You will always be one of my top lovers with Jo and Luke and Eva, but we both know that this time together is not the central relationship of our lives."

"Right now I wish it could be," said Manda, "but today I must go home and start to work out what I am to do and how I am to do it. I know I have to leave Nick – escape him somehow. I wish I could do it without hurting him, as that has dangers for me – but our relationship is a trap for me and not a life I can survive any longer. This time with you has given me a key to the way out I think."

The two women put their arms around each other and held each other for a while.

As they tidied up the cottage after morning coffee, they heard a car on the drive overhead. Manda recognised the sound of the engine and panicked.

"My God! My God! It's Nick – what will I do?"

"I'm here," reassured Marielise, "I'm here."

But Nick was quite calm when he appeared, he seemed almost dulled.

"Oh it's you, Marielise," he said almost indifferently. "I did wonder. I didn't recognise the car."

"It's Luke's car. My car's in need of some work. Yes – very bad of me – I apologise again! I took a chance on the cottage being empty and rather spoilt Manda's quiet weekend – but I have to fly – I have to get to Livingstone before dark tonight. It's a long drive and the road is dreadful I am told."

Marielise looked at Manda, her back to Nick, and signalled with her raised eyebrow.

"Okay if I'm off now Manda?"

Manda nodded. She would cope as she had always done.

"We were both just leaving Nick."

"I came down to see if you were all right. Manda. Not really happy about you being alone down here you know, as nothing locks. If you are coming back right now there's no need to stay. You go ahead. I'll grab a cup of coffee and follow in a minute."

Marielise looked at Manda and then at Nick, as if considering whether or not to speak.

"Look," she said, "I have bad news – I wasn't sure whether to tell you or not, but you will hear soon enough anyway. Margaret and Charles have finally decided to sell the cottage. They haven't been here in almost seven years and it doesn't make sense to keep spending on it. They asked me if I wanted to buy it, but honestly I have no capital and we expect to be back in South Africa in the next few years. Charles is writing to you to ask if you would like to buy it. You'll get a letter soon. Milimo doesn't know yet so we must get him to make more effort to get his own land from the Siavonga Council. So sorry Manda. So sorry Nick. I know we all love this place."

Manda and Nick could only shake their heads and shrug.

So they talked inconsequentially for a few minutes more and then Marielise kissed them both and parted. It was an ordinary enough farewell on the surface but something in the tenderness that the two women showed each other aroused a sharp agony in Nick. He was incapable of showing Manda that tender love, and though she had always given it to him, he was overcome with a bitter jealousy that almost stopped his heart. She had no right to show love to an outsider. It had been hard enough for him that she loved their children as well as him, but this – he could not let this happen.

Nick did not try to understand his own feelings because he feared that he could never be able to contain them. He could only deny them and bury them or ignore them but somewhere deep inside him the desire was born to find a way to kill Marielise and that need began insidiously to eat at his guts.

Marielise had gone a half-hour since. Manda's car had reached the top of the drive and turned home to Lusaka. Nick glanced round the cottage. Milimo was busy with the bed linen and the broom.

"Mr Nick," he said, "do you want this paper?" and he handed Nick a scrap of thin blue paper. On it were the words: 'Zanele filming Maripodi Camp. Jo will be there. He says to come and join them.'

There were dates on the paper for the following week.

On the drive back to Lusaka, Nick decided to stop on his way home. He would call at Jeff and Lauren's house and see if Jeff was up for a game of squash that evening. If he wasn't free perhaps he would still offer Nick a drink. The scrap of blue paper was burning a hole in Nick's pocket and the thought of Marielise spending time with his wife was burning a hole in his heart.

Nick could not bear Manda to have intimate friendships, even with other women.

He had to have total control of her for his own life to be bearable.

THIRTEEN

Love And Hope

Marielise was happy. Delightfully, wonderfully happy. She was spending time with her dearest and closest people and they too, were happy to be with her. It was also work of course, but then they were all workaholics, and being busy added to their happiness.

Zanele was there with some friends from film school to make a documentary about the ANC camp outside Livingstone. They had managed to fund their own travel, and beg and borrow equipment for their filming. Towards the end of the Bush War in Zimbabwe, events seemed to be speeding up for the Liberation War in South Africa. Nelson Mandela had received hospital treatment and been moved into a more civilised prison. It was said that the South African government had opened talks with him and with other leaders of the ANC and Umkonto We Sizwe. It was now much easier than it had ever been to get good publicity for the Liberation War. Zanele's documentary was guaranteed airtime in America and all over Europe. Possibly even in Britain as well. Of course there was great uncertainty and many doubts, but it was clear that things were changing and now they could hope for a future, and not just endure the present. The documentary would show how forward-thinking the Liberation Movement was, how positive, how humanist. It would show that they were winning and it would show what good leaders they would be in the soon-to-be-born new South Africa.

Marielise had thought of her friend Manda often as she drove to the camp. She thought of Nick too. He was outwardly so likeable and did such good work. It disturbed Marielise to think of how damaged Nick's psyche was. She did feel compassion for him, but also anxiety for him, and anger. Why could he not decide to overcome his damaged past whatever had been caused of it? Marielise had devoted her life to the belief that people could recover from suffering and repression. What other hope was there for all the damaged and violent people, both black and white, who were to be the legacy of Apartheid? The desire must be there to make things better. Was that desire not human nature? Surely, surely, it must be possible for damaged people to want to be healed and to search for that healing for themselves? Marielise shook her head over Nick with sadness and doubt. She was worried for Manda, but her own raised spirits and hopefulness made her feel sure that she too, would find a way forward into a better life. Nick, however, seemed likely to remain his own insoluble problem.

Most of all, Marielise delighted in seeing Zanele, so confident and intelligent, so creative and so comfortable in her relationship with her tiny film crew. Jo's pride in Zanele was even greater than Marielise's and together they took much pleasure in her company. Jo was well, fit, strong and confident about the future too, and he and Marielise had much enjoyment in being with each other and in the thrill of once again being indulged and indulgent lovers. They knew that they couldn't be together very long, so they relished every second they had.

Zanele had other ANC camps she was off to document on film. Jo was expecting to be at some very high level strategy meetings in Botswana in the next few weeks. There was even the possibility for him of openly moving to South Africa. A number of the ANC senior executives were planning for this to happen soon. The problem was that even though there were peace talks under way, there were rather too many maverick racists in South Africa who would continue to hunt and kill Freedom Fighters for anyone to feel safe. At the camp they continued to all look over their shoulders and follow the routine security procedures they had been trained to use as second nature.

It was midweek. Zanele had gone ahead to set up her day's filming at another site in the camp. Jo and Marielise luxuriated in bed together for a few minutes longer than usual, then rushed a cup of coffee and some toast. The car that Marielise had borrowed from Luke for the trip was parked at the side of their bungalow under a lean-to garage. Jo climbed into the driving seat, car key in hand when Marielise suddenly leapt out of the passenger seat.

"Dammit, sorry Jo," she said, "I'll just get my camera – I left it on the table by my coffee cup."

Marielise swung open the door of their square breeze-block accommodation and stepped back into the kitchen. Her one single light movement seemed to collapse the whole building around her. She had no sense of the blinding flash or the noise of the explosion that had blown the car apart and killed Jo. She thought only that she had become Alice in Wonderland and that she was struggling to free herself from under a pile of furious picture cards. The pressure from the angry cards grew and grew and crushed her into the ground till at last, everything around and about her disintegrated into choking black dust.

FOURTEEN

Balancing Act

The news of Jo's death did not make the Zambian press or TV. The assassination was reported in the British press but without giving the names of those killed and injured. Since the weekend when he had found Manda and Marielise together at the cottage, Nick made a point of watching for stories about attacks on the ANC camps. As a result he heard that Jo was dead and Marielise seriously injured before Manda had any idea of what had happened. It was a dreadful dilemma for him. How was he to tell Manda? How could he not tell Manda? At first when he heard the news, he felt a curious stirring in his lower body. He couldn't decide if it was a pleasant or uncomfortable sensation. Was it the start of diarrhoea in his bowels or sexual excitement in his groin? He ended up sitting on the toilet and spending more time thinking than was normal for him. The bombing had happened so soon after he had spoken to Jeff, that common sense told him that there was no causal link. He couldn't reach a conclusion about how to tell Manda though, so as was usual for him; he pushed the thoughts deep into his subconscious and tried to forget them.

Before the weekend Manda had been tired and fractious. Since the weekend she seemed tired but calm. They didn't talk about the reasons for her going off to spend a weekend alone but Nick didn't find that reassuring. Eventually Manda commented on the report about the reported bomb at the ANC camp with a worried frown.

"Wish I had the full story about this," she said.

"Shall I try and find out about it for you?" Nick offered. Manda looked surprised and hopeful.

"Really! Would you? How though?"

"I've got my contacts," Nick said, "both at the High Commission and at work."

He still did not know how he would cope with Manda's reactions to the news. As it happened he didn't have to say anything. Zanele managed to get through to Manda from Harare. Marielise was in Intensive Care there and would probably be moved to Britain for further treatment as soon as it was felt she was out of danger. Zanele was at her bedside most days. Zanele still could not bear to speak about what had happened to Jo, but she got the bare fact of his death over to Manda in a few words.

When Nick got back that evening from work he was met by a pale and determined Manda. She told him that she was going south to Harare to be with Marielise and give Zanele a break. She had packed her case and the car was full of fuel. She would leave early the next day.

"I hope that's okay with you Nick," she said. "You'll be all right won't you? There's nothing very important that I need to do here in Lusaka and Zanele needs help. If you take the children to school in the morning, Jane will have them in the afternoon. I will be back inside a week."

Nick could only agree.

"Oh and Margaret Beaumont has a flat in Harare where I can stay. Zanele is there as it's empty at the moment."

"Make sure you phone me and give me the flat phone number when you arrive," Nick said.

FIFTEEN

Harare

It was a long drive south to Harare in Zimbabwe. Manda had made the journey before and, though accustomed to it, she never found it easy. The passage through customs on the Zambian side was always busy but the officers had become more relaxed with time. The same could not be said for the Zimbabweans. They were much more likely to search your car or nitpick about some detail on the customs form. If one managed to show unfailing patience and good humour one would get through eventually. This time Manda was on edge and tired. She explained that a friend was very ill in hospital and was treated with sympathy, but even so the crossing through Chirundu was very hot and tedious.

At last she could settle down to drive steadily onwards. Journeys, Manda had found in her years in Zambia, were good for thinking and resolving problems. She was worried about Marielise but that was not productive thinking. She needed to concentrate her mind on Nick and her marriage.

She was too close and involved in it to arrive at a useful perspective on her situation on her own. Marielise's assessment had both shocked her and at the same time confirmed what she did not want to admit. Nick was not going to grow and learn emotionally and his way of managing his feelings was to be abusive and controlling. With the same kind of care and positive politeness that got Manda through the customs barrier, Manda could make her marriage work. True there were times when it did seem to work spontaneously and happily for them both but those highs were always followed by dips into profound lows. Manda recognised that she was probably right in her judgement that Nick's childhood had left him damaged and depressed. She had begun to realise that he chose not to understand himself and did not want to re-experience the past. He simply transferred his feelings of self-hatred and doubt onto her whenever they troubled him.

Did the good times offer a sufficient credit balance to make the bad times bearable? Once Manda would have thought so but now she could see that the bad times were damaging the children too and she herself was losing both energy and courage. Her spirit was wearing out. She was starting to wither and die. Slowly perhaps, but certainly. She needed to save herself. After nine years of marriage, it seemed incredibly selfish to think of herself first. Even if that was the first thing to do, how could it be achieved? The further Manda drove from Lusaka the more she began to feel fear. Nick was not going to let her go was he? He was controlling and he did not want to lose her. How could she make her escape and how could she protect her children? For the moment she had no idea.

She arrived in Harare without reaching any conclusions.

It was time to focus on Zanele and Marielise and the loss of Jo.

Zanele was apparently coping well. She had plenty to focus on. Her grief for her father would swallow her up totally in a few months time but now she was busy looking after Marielise. Jo had been buried hastily in Livingstone. It was planned that he would be given a proper funeral and a memorial service at some time in the future. Zanele had not been there at the burial. Marielise could not be there. Jo's parents could not get there either.

Zanele had accompanied Marielise to Harare within twenty-four hours of the assassination. Zanele had made her film crew carry on filming throughout the aftermath. The first rushes they had filmed had been on the world news but Zanele was determined that a documentary would be made of Jo's life and she was already trying to set up a team to do that. Zanele told Manda that it was thought the bomb had been aimed at Luke because the car was his.

"It makes no difference," she said, "they wanted Jo dead anyway. It's terrible for Luke though. He feels such guilt."

"What about Marielise?" Manda asked, "How much does she realise?"

"Oh everything," answered Zanele. "She welcomes the physical pain I think because the loss of Jo is not to be endured."

For a moment Zanele seemed on the point of breaking down herself and her voice quivered but then she was back organising.

"Marielise is to be moved to a Birmingham hospital that specialises in bomb trauma," she continued. "Her injuries are not life-threatening any more – they want to limit any disabling damage if they can. She was lucky it seems, the door frame protected her head and upper body from the weight of the concrete blocks as the front of the house collapsed, but her pelvis and left hip were crushed. Luckily nothing internal was perforated. She will be okay and walk with a limp perhaps.

"I don't know how she will manage without Jo though – they were such soul mates."

Again Zanele's voice broke and Manda put her arms around her.

Manda spent her days at Marielise's bedside though Marielise was still mostly asleep or dozing. It was a shock to see her laid out on a high bed, in traction for her leg and attached to drips and tubes. Her skin was a transparent grey and her eyes sunken and surrounded by shadowed bruises. Marielise confirmed what Zanele had said. It was better to be unconscious or in pain. Either state was better than knowing that Jo was dead. She was glad to see her friend however and Manda came each day with lots of news and information – anything to occupy Marielise's mind.

Zanele also delegated Manda to look after Charles and Margaret, and Sarah, Marielise's mother, when they came to visit Marielise. Charles talked of Marielise's injuries as the result of an accident and not a bomb, though he knew very well what had happened. Sarah just seemed rather confused and anxious though she hid it when she was with Marielise.

"The world is so different now," Sarah kept saying. "I hope it will be all right soon. I do hope so." But Manda could see that she loved her daughter dearly and that Marielise was soothed by the presence of her mother.

Manda was happy to see Margaret again. She had always liked her even when, back in Lusaka, she had thought Margaret rather conservative and old-fashioned. Margaret, surprisingly, seemed to have become rather a trendy figure in Harare with her Permaculture Cooperative Farm and Training School. Manda could see she was happy.

Margaret, always perspicacious, went to some trouble to find the time to talk to Manda and to ask her about herself and what was happening in her life. It was an emotional time for everyone and Manda found herself weeping into the cup of tea that Margaret had made for her.

"I don't know what to do," she snivelled, hideously embarrassed at crying over herself when everyone else was so sad.

Margaret listened as Manda recounted her problems.

"My dear Manda," she said, "it is much harder and therefore braver to leave your marriage and find a safe place for yourself and your children than to stay. What are you most afraid of – being poorer? I don't think so! Being thought badly of for leaving your husband? No! You are not the kind of person who stays married to please society or to have a good income. You are not even planning to leave Nick because you don't love him and because you want to have sex and affairs. There is nothing you can do to help Nick. We can't live life for our men. Each of us must do it for ourselves in the end. Marriage works in spite of that or because of it.

311

"You are a good person, Manda. You are not a failure because your marriage cannot be made to work. Don't be a victim, Manda. You are too intelligent and sensible."

Manda blew her nose.

"Thank you Margaret," she said. "Do you know – after leaving Nick, the very worst thing for me will be never staying in your beautiful cottage again."

Margaret smiled.

"I feel very sad about the cottage but we must sell it," she said. "Manda, one day you will find another such place and love it as much, because that is your nature."

"What do you think will happen to the cottage and the garden, Margaret? I can't bear to think of the garden dying or the trees being cut down," Manda asked.

"Perhaps a garden and a gardener have the same sort of relationship as a marriage and a married couple," Margaret said thoughtfully, "they are the work of the present moment and can't be done yesterday or tomorrow. A garden can't survive without the work of a gardener. A marriage can only survive if both people want it to work. I do miss my Siavonga garden very much but the only garden I can have is the one that I can work in at this moment in time.

"However," Margaret added with a smile, "when the cottage is finally sold, will you please, Manda, take care of the guest book and send it to me somehow? It is full of precious memories."

Sixteen

Circling

The Guest Book. The Cottage, Siavonga.
October 1989
Nick, Manda, Emma and James

'It was far too hot to do very much but we did all go to lunch and
to swim at Jacky's bar. The garden is lovely and green and we saw
a turaco and a pair of hornbills, also the usual fruit bats and a
special treat – fireflies. There were amazing and continuous storms
over the Matusadona Hills. Both sheet lightning and thunderbolts
and thunder. Far too many to try and count. Spectacular! We sat
on the veranda and watched for hour after hour. Charles and
Margaret have started the process of selling the cottage. It is a heart-
breaking decision but Nick and I will not be buying it. What we
will do when we can't come here anymore I can't imagine.'

Before she left Harare, Manda called Nick and suggested that he
and the children meet her at the Siavonga cottage so they could
have the weekend together. Nick was pleased. Manda could hear
him relax as soon as she spoke. He started at once to make plans
about what they would all do together.

From now on, Manda was going to have to walk a very
dangerous path. She knew that she was being duplicitous, but she
straightened her shoulders and pushed away any feelings of guilt.
She must escape from her marriage and she could not do so by

being straightforward, as was her nature, or simply by asking Nick to let her go. She was going to have to leave in stages, and with cunning. She was going to have to leave slowly, and with care. The most difficult thing that she would have to do was to behave as if her life was normal and happy. Sometimes though, she knew it would be just that – normal for her, and happy, but she must never let herself be fooled into thinking that she was safe. She would never be safe with Nick.

She must take great care of the children and of their safety too.

Now she had made up her mind, she felt that she could do it and could survive. Now she was behind enemy lines. The problem was that she loved the enemy.

As she made the long drive back to Zambia, Manda's mind revolved and resolved what she must do. *Roads are like that*, Manda thought, *all journeys are circular and one is always going home, yet the road that one returns on is always different to the road that one left on. The view going back is different to the view one sees leaving.*

She had left Lusaka on the ever-widening Kafue Road, jammed with lorries and minibuses and desperate traffic-dodging pedestrians, past the expanding ramshackle compounds and informal markets and the chalky stone-breakers with their heaped rocks of talc and limestone. She had passed the football players at Kafue, seen the new food outlets, crossed the Kafue Bridge – an old Bailey bridge that had once crossed the Thames River – and come through farmland to the Great Escarpment. She had wound her way down the escarpment, past almost stationary, overloaded lorries, past the deep valleys full of wrecked vehicles and dead memories. She had passed the rock cliff of the Four Ghosts, swung over the red splashes staining Blood Bend, crawled down the steepest gradient where a sign in Chinyanja painted onto a rock, advised her to 'go on all fours' by putting on her brakes. She had taken the road through the Fossil Forest towards Chirundu, and seen the children waving fistfuls of contraband currency outside the Customs Post. Once over the long, slow Chirundu Bridge and

314

the wide, bright Zambezi, her road took her through the game parks with elephant and lion, up the opposite escarpment and onto the long road to Harare in Zimbabwe, still a strange country to her.

Now on her return journey, Harare was behind her, with all its stylish, glossy smartness; its supermarkets, galleries, cinemas, gardens, tourists, aid workers, hospitals and its bitter, scarred memories of the Bush War. Manda would not go to Chirundu this time to cross the border. She would leave the Great North Road at Makuti and take the scenic road to Kariba through the valleys full of trees, rivers and wild animals. Every mile would take her closer to the lake and the cottage that felt like her real home in Zambia. She would go past Kariba Airport, along the lakeside drive and climb up to the Zimbabwe border on the south of the dam wall where a colony of hyrax or *dassies* had their home among the boulders. Once she had cleared customs and immigration, Manda would make that extraordinary transit over the arching concrete wall. On one side, she would see a 300 foot drop through air, empty except for flying swifts and swallows, to the bottom of the gorge where the Zambezi once again continued its muscled flow to the sea. On the other side, she would see and feel the pressure of almost 200 billion cubic metres of Lake Kariba water. Then she would be back at the cottage in Margaret's beautiful, green garden where Milimo would have magically arranged the household and her children and Nick would be waiting for her with smiles of greeting.

That hot evening, Nick and Manda sat together on the dark veranda mesmerised by the extraordinary stroboscopic light show exploding over the Matusadona Hills. Phosphorescent sheet lightning made the towering blue thunderheads continuously visible. Jagged gold streaks flashed and crackled across the sky and hurled themselves at the endangered earth. The constant noise of thunder rolled back and forth, above the savage din and crash of lightning strikes. The wet and fecund smell of rain reached their nostrils. The threatening storms made lush promises.

"Isn't this wonderful!" said Manda in awe, "Aren't you happy to see the lake filling up again Nick?"

Nick nodded.

"Yes" he said quietly. "It will be good to go out sailing again without the danger of clattering into those iron-hard dead trees and holing the boat."

"It's amazing that they haven't rotted away," Manda said, "I rather like their dramatic appearance and the cormorants like them too."

"Aquatic life generally likes them," Nick continued. "No one really knew what would happen to the *mupane* trees when the lake filled. Everyone calls them 'petrified' but of course they haven't turned to stone – they are just hard. The drought exposed many more of them even though vast areas were cleared of trees for the fishing industry.

"Do you know that the water from the floodgates has scoured out a plunge pool below the wall that is almost eighty metres deep? That was not expected and it is quite close to the dam wall foundation."

"Let's face it – in many ways the lake was a giant experiment. Just like our life is."

Nick turned with a smile to Manda.

Manda smiled back. She looked at her husband, wondering momentarily if his words signalled an awareness of his need to change. There was no sign of any self-knowledge. It was with a curious sense of relief that she turned again to watch the storms and see them reflected in the lake.

She said after a while, "I feel sad though, for the Zambezi River, lost and dispersed in the lake."

"No – it isn't!" Nick responded, "The Zambezi continues to flow through the lake as an identifiable current and so does the Sanyati River. The smaller rivers that dry up in the rainy season don't continue but the Zambezi is always there."

Manda looked up at her husband's face in the uncertain light under the storm lanterns. She wondered about the strong, dark and secret currents of his personality.

"So," she said softly, watching again the gentle ripples on the surface of the lake, "the drowned river is still there, flowing onwards through its valley."

Seventeen

Katanga

London 1991

"The Katanga crisis – Michael, what do you know about it?" Manda asked, digging her elbow into her lover's ribs by way of encouragement.

"Oh well it was particularly horrible from what I've read and been told," Michael said,

"Charles and Margaret talked about it a little – it really upset them. I did some research for my series of paintings on colonialism.

"The Belgian government decided to ditch the Belgian Congo very abruptly without making too many plans for the handover. The colony was extremely racist and the transfer of power was very abrupt. Belgium knew there was trouble brewing from African nationalists so they pretty much decided to cut and run, but – and there is always a 'but', in this case a bloody big 'but' – bloody being the operative word – there were these incredibly rich copper mines in the south in Katanga province. There was a lot of uncertainty generated by the mining companies and also the collapsing Central African Federation. Union Minière, the Belgian mining company, cooked up a plan for the Katanga Province under Tshombe to secede and maybe join up with the Zambian Copperbelt. The process of Independence was managed very badly – well hardly managed at all. Within days there was a mutiny in the Force Publique who were supposed to provide law and order. The usual story: racist white officers in charge of black troops for whom there was no possibility of advancement – in short it was a terrible mess. All hell let loose: murder and mayhem, and worse – basically the Belgians jumped into their cars and fled south from Katanga leaving everything and everyone who was vulnerable to be raped and looted and pillaged. Pet animals were abandoned and in some cases, it is reported, babies as well!"

Manda and Sebastian were silent for some moments. They had both researched the story individually but had not talked about it together.

It was a Sunday morning and Manda, Michael and Sebastian were having coffee in the lounge of Sebastian's London home. Manda and Michael, flopped side by side onto the plump sofa, had only recently started living together though they had been lovers for over two years. Their romance had not been straightforward because Emma and James were still unhappy about Nick and Manda's separation. It was Nick, however, who was the real problem.

Nick, as he had promised Manda, refused to discuss divorce with her, even though he had had several relationships with other women since she left. He had said he would never let her go, even if she was not living with him. Manda dared not try to force the issue. She was afraid of what he might do in revenge when the children went to visit him in the holidays. Nick and the children had been in a minor car accident once, but Manda was deliberately not told about it until the children arrived back for their school term and showed her with tears, their bruises and scrapes.

Manda had been traumatised by her decision to leave Nick and it took a while for her to recover. Meeting Michael again had helped her. She had been managing a complex of artists' workshops where he had a studio. A job she had acquired through Marielise's friend Eva. One day she had caught Michael throwing his canvases about in a storm of frustration and he had seen her amusement at his fury. They had ended up on the floor of his studio, covered with paint and shredded paper, and laughing together happily before going out for a Turkish meal in Newington Green. There they discovered in each other, passion, kindness and humour, and in a natural progression they became both lovers and good friends.

As Michael, Manda, Sebastian and Gerda didn't live far apart, they saw each other fairly often, in a relaxed way. Manda and Sebastian's children also spent time together in the holidays. At the moment, Sebastian's wife Gerda and their two children were visiting German grandparents in Munich and Emma and James were at the Natural History Museum with their grandparents, Frank and Helen.

"Hey little brother! How's life?" Manda asked, but started before he answered, on the questions that really concerned her.

"Look, we never do quite talk about this but I really do want to ask you – what do you know, as opposed to what Frank and Helen have told us, about our adoption – I mean how did it happen? I told Michael what I thought happened – then wondered if you might either know things I didn't, or confirm my guesses. I have asked the parents again, but they just say they weren't given our histories."

"Adoption is so difficult these days – sometimes I think that Frank and Helen just kidnapped us!"

They both laughed at the idea of their gentle and civilised parents doing anything so outrageous.

Then Manda said seriously, "They were pretty amazing for their time weren't they? Adopting two mixed-race kids from Africa was pretty daring then – of course they were a mixed marriage but they had obviously thought long and hard about it and I think they must have had a hard time often. So did we too from time to time though didn't we? It got easier as we got older.

"Do you remember poor Blanche at school? Her mother gave her that ridiculous name and said she was cute – like a *'picaninny'* –

was the word she actually used about her daughter – can you imagine – it was so awful!"

"Yeah and then Blanche got big and wild and wore an afro – wonder what has happened to her now."

"Actually," Sebastian said, "Frank and Helen never did give that many details. I don't think they knew very much about us because they weren't told very much. I think that's how it was then – it was the middle of the Katanga crisis – I think there just may have been a lot of nameless, abandoned orphans around."

"Funny the gaps that one has in family history. My parents never talk about Richard or his death," said Michael. "Sometimes I feel I have lost him twice because I can't remember him well enough now."

Manda squeezed Michael's arm, her head against his shoulder.

"So Mum and Dad were there in Zambia with the FAO, so I suppose they couldn't help but know all about Katanga," Manda mused,

"and us abandoned by who and why – is there really no knowing?"

"Well we were in a Catholic adoption scheme of some sort – in a home outside Lusaka I suppose. Being mixed-race probably made us unacceptable to both white and black Africans," Sebastian said.

"Yes you still see that prejudice, though only occasionally now," said Manda wrinkling her nose. "Younger people have no problems but I was told by an old Zambian man once that I must be 'dirty and a criminal' because I was one of those 'coloureds'! Weird hey?"

"So tell me more about what you know of your histories," Michael asked, "I did research the Katanga crisis but I didn't find any personal stories from individuals."

"Well," Sebastian said pulling a face, "I guessed long ago that I must be the result of the rape of a white woman by a black Congo soldier – or something like that. Reckon at the time that would have been the most likely reason for ditching a baby don't you?

Especially if the raped woman was a nun! Less likely at that date to be the other way around."

"I suppose so," Manda looked with concern at her brother. How did that make him feel? What should she feel? From time to time she asked herself that question.

"What about me? The same do you think?"

"It could be," said Sebastian, "but you are just that bit older so you couldn't be a product of that particular disaster. I think that your story must be a Northern Rhodesian or Zambian story. Perhaps you were just someone's mistake – an unwanted love-child?"

"Thank you very much!" said Manda, covering her face momentarily with her hands, "unwanted – result of rape – what an inheritance we have from Africa – thank God for Frank and Helen! We have had such love and such a good life, oh I do love our darling parents!" And she looked up again.

"This is a hard question," Michael asked quietly, "but what do you feel about your particular birth parents, Sebastian? I mean it must be so difficult to cope with your history. Does it make you angry? Who do you blame for it? Manda shrugs when I ask her how she feels."

"I suppose we would both be different people if we had been dumped on the streets as orphans," Sebastian replied. "We were rescued by love. I know that sounds like romantic mush but giving in to anger and blame would damage us most of all now. I guess that's why I am a doctor – I want to make things better where I can."

"We have just got to get on with it," Manda said. "Whatever the true facts are about our parents we cannot easily separate out who was to blame and who was an innocent victim. At an individual level it is so enmeshed and complicated. Survival has to be about forgiveness – it's just so hard to forgive. Oh Michael! With a history like ours – maybe you too should cut and run – leave me while you can!"

"Thanks for the vote of confidence my darling Manda!" Michael grinned in his lopsided fashion, "But it is you who should be afraid – I have a family history of generations of colonial exploitation!"

The three of them laughed but then Sebastian said more sombrely,

"I guess we are the children of the European colonisation of Africa. It has been going on for such a long time – there are whole tribes of mixed-race peoples in Africa. For me – I feel as if my African heritage is predominant and my sympathy is with the chaotic continent of Africa."

"That's because you're blacker than me," said Manda, smiling again and she hit out at her brother with one of Gerda's pleated velvety cushions.

"Young, black, beautiful and proud of it!" said Manda's short brother as he jumped up from his chair and started to rumba around the room. Manda and Sebastian were quite different in appearance: Manda taller, graceful and light-skinned; Sebastian short, wiry and dark. They were close together in age. As children they had felt, though not looked, like twins.

"I do not – I repeat – I do not feel white and European but neither do I feel African, even though I love Zambia and I was born there!" said Manda.

"Maybe we are just a completely new generation – what do you think? Perhaps we are the ones who can change the world – if only! Perhaps! What do you think?

"Oh by the way, Seb – do you think our ages are about right? No one can possibly know exactly when we were born?"

"Strange but true," Sebastian said with an ironic grin, "I think our birth registration is surprisingly detailed – almost to the hour in fact. That's why I think my mother was a white nun and you were the child of someone who cared about you. I think our births were both registered by white people because I assume such details would not have been a priority for Africans at the time.

I am only guessing though!"

Before Michael and Manda left, Sebastian asked them if there were any new developments with Nick and Manda's divorce.

"I know you two want to get married," he said. "Manda has been the victim of another kind of abuse. It happened but it wasn't deserved."

Manda just shook her head hopelessly. Michael put his hand on her arm gently.

"It will happen," he reassured. "Nick will want to marry one day himself."

Manda shook her head again.

"He'll never let me go," she said miserably.

EIGHTEEN

Overboard

Nick was down at the lake again.

This time he had gone down with his girlfriend Rita, to join even newer friends at a different villa on a different bay. Siavonga was now the place to go for weekends out of Lusaka. The affluent makers and shifters had taken up waterskiing and windsurfing in large numbers and there were several infuriatingly noisy jet-skis that circled around between Jacky' bar and the hotel at Manchinchi Bay, carrying grizzled older men doing their best to look lean and lithe.

Rita was enthusiastic about all water-sports. She looked gorgeous and trim in a short wet-suit and even better in her minuscule bikini with her firm, full breasts, slim waist and unblemished tan. Rita also knew all the new faces in Lusaka, those who had style, money, power and drive. She knew where the most fun was to be had and was always at the best parties.

Now that Apartheid was coming to an end, there were great opportunities in South Africa and an expanding appetite in Johannesburg for quality African crafts and curios. Rita was an exporter of such crafts. There was no real control of this market in Zambia and Rita could buy cheaply and sell for high profits. She was very knowledgeable about African crafts and well able to describe a basket or a drum or a fetish carving in terms that increased its desirability.

Rita had money but no husband at the moment and a husband was an asset that she knew would help her status enormously, especially if he was a social asset and reasonably well-off himself. Nick fitted the description very well. She sometimes found him a bit 'down and dour' but that was only at home when they were alone, he was never that way in company. When he was down she ignored him and went off to bed. She had her own room for these occasions and because she always insisted on having her 'beauty sleep'; she was quite happy to tell everyone about her beauty regime. Without adequate rest, one got wrinkles, and she wasn't having any of those.

This weekend they were going to join Heinrich and Estelle and two other old friends of Nick's, Andrew and Jessie, for a lakeside party weekend. The new influx of South African business interests into Zambia had produced an atmosphere that was more hard-edged, more 'Jo'burg-style', and more exclusively white expatriate again. Nick was happy enough about this difference for the time being as it prevented him from thinking of Manda. He didn't want to be reminded of her in the slightest. He didn't even mind that Heinrich was, in his estimation, rather a dubious character, who talked himself up a great deal, clearly had money, but was actually rather cagey about what his business was. Estelle was always talking about gems, and was usually wearing a new larger example of a stone in a particular cut or colour. It gave Nick a perverse pleasure to think that Manda would have very much disliked Heinrich and Estelle and it stopped him from admitting that he didn't like them much himself.

This evening a barbecue was planned on the patio above Bilharzia Bay.

"It isn't called Bilharzia Bay any more you know," said Rita, "the local residents are choosing a new name for the bay more in keeping with the new developments around it."

"Not Yeoville-on-Sea!" mocked Nick, naming a suburb of Johannesburg.

"No Nick! Don't be wicked!" but Rita laughed; she was even rather cynical about herself.

The evening was warm, balmy even, as they turned off the main Siavonga road towards the bay. There was some cloud about and a late diminishing moon was heading for the horizon. The tarred road turned east towards Eagles Rest and they swung onto an unsurfaced and corrugated dirt track that slowed them down. As they journeyed gently onwards, it happened that instead of raising a dust storm behind them, the soft speckled sand was disturbed ahead of them and it metamorphosed into literally hundreds of pennant-winged night-jars with metre long feathers at their silently fluttering wing tips; they were ghost-like and dream-like apparitions of exquisite beauty. 'Harbingers of death' according to the local Tonga. It was unique, one of the loveliest sights that Nick had ever seen and his heart cried out to share it with Manda, the wife that he loved, the wife that loved him, yet had left him forever. He imagined he could see her face reflected in the car's window, open-mouthed and smiling in wonderment and delight.

At Heinrich and Estelle's he leapt from the car, and without opening the door to help Rita, he reached behind his seat for the champagne he had brought.

"Come on! Let's party!" he said and not waiting to get onto the patio, he undid the twisted wire of the cap and pushed forcefully with his thumb to ease the cork from the bottle with the loudest bang possible.

Rita was most put out. As she climbed hastily down from the car, she caught her heel awkwardly and almost twisted her ankle. That made her really mad with Nick but of course she did not let her feelings show, except by being just that little bit too provocative with Heinrich, by flirting with Andrew just enough to make Jessie notice, and by buttering up Estelle with flattery about her latest gems.

Nick was determined to relax and enjoy himself, if that meant getting rather tipsy – so what! There were no police out late conducting breathalyser tests and he did occasionally drive under the 'influence' without coming to harm. He didn't care much about Rita's feelings right at that moment whereas he would normally have been a more considerate companion. Rita had no interest in the reason behind Nick's change of mood. She did not let him get away with treating her badly. Whatever the start to the evening, it progressed well. Heinrich had chosen the wine from the top of the range and the bottom of his pocket. There were tiger prawns from Mozambique for starters, the steaks were juicy and well-seasoned, and the dessert was sufficiently creamy, eggy and sugary to have the guests licking their lips and their spoons. Even Rita ate most of her serving.

It was still early in the evening when they finished eating and they settled into a silence that was not very convivial or comfortable. It didn't last; Heinrich would not let the party die. He leapt to his feet:

"How about a boat trip and a midnight drink on the beach near Banana Island. Come on everybody – let's have some fun!"

At first the women tried to pour cold water on the idea but Rita had upset Jessie by flirting with Andrew, and Estelle usually did whatever Heinrich wanted and then exacted payment in gems. Rita still wanted to pay Nick back, in her view he hadn't made up for his early neglect of her yet, so she decided to be very enthusiastic about the boat trip. She had always found that offering a physical challenge to a man was a good way of stimulating interest in herself so she kicked off her troublesome high heels and set off with Heinrich, ahead of the others to get to the landing stage where the boat was moored.

Jessie was the first to protest.

"Heinrich! For God's sake – there aren't enough seats for us all. How are we going to fit in?"

They all looked at the boat. It was true. It sat four people in shaped seats, one of which was for the driver. None of the men wanted to squash the planned excursion. They waited for the women to say no but Rita was not giving up

"Oh C'mon! Put the cool box between these two back seats for one of us and I'll sit on somebody's knee. Andrew? Nick?"

Estelle did not want to go.

"I'm afraid. It's got windy. Look how rough the lake is getting. It's dark – how will we see?" but she knew she would do what Heinrich told her to do in the end.

"Look at my searchlight," he said, "it's mega! You can see for miles. Get in girls, get in!"

So they all got into the boat and tried to squeeze themselves into the seats but the front seat would neither take Rita on Andrew's lap nor on Estelle's lap. The three women could fit very uncomfortably onto the two back seats and the cool box. Andrew looked at Nick and gestured that he take the front seat but Nick laughed.

"Not a problem! I'll go on the front of the boat and do some moon-bathing!"

"Yea! Good on you man!" said Heinrich, turning on the engine. "All aboard and away we go!"

"Hold on tight Nick!" Jessie called out. "If you fall off the front, dive down deep so that the propellers don't slice you up!"

"This is a jet-drive," said Heinrich, "all the dangerous bits are inside." And off they went.

It was an exhilarating ride. The boat was fast and sliced easily through the waves. Nick was splashed but not very much as the waves and the boat were travelling in the same direction. The light on the boat was superb and lit up the lake for a good distance so they didn't have to fear obstacles or getting too close to any rocks. It shone rather to one side however because Nick needed to be centrally positioned on the prow to keep his balance.

"How are you doing Nick?" Andrew shouted into the wind and Nick shouted back that he was fine and having the ride of his life.

They arrived very soon on the beach before Banana Island. It was a long level beach of the fine white sand that is common on Lake Kariba. They ran the boat aground with no trouble and were soon sitting on the smooth, unmarked surface and opening more champagne for the women and beer for the men. However, the same silence that had slowed down the party after their meal came over them again. Apart from the slapping of waves it was very, very quiet on the beach. That certain quiet that feels full of creatures listening and watching, the quiet of the wild and the bush and the lake; a lake that is also full of eyes watching. The quiet that is about being alone and loneliness, if you are the sort of person who cannot stand being alone. Not one of the picnickers was the sort of person who could stand to be alone. Their drinks went down faster than they needed to, considering that not one of them was thirsty or hungry.

Estelle and Jessie were more than ready to leave but hesitant to be told they were 'party-poopers'. Rita however knew her own mind and could usually get her own way. She wanted to go back.

"My God!" she said, "Would you look at the lake! It's getting so much rougher. We had better go – Jessie says she gets seasick when its rough – didn't you Jessie?"

Jessie was very glad to be called a wimp and climbed back into the boat while Andrew and Nick pushed it out and Heinrich started the engine up again.

The lake was rougher. Much rougher. They were now motoring into the wind and the seiche was heaping up the waves steeply against them. Every wave thudded into the boat and hurled spray all over Nick and the windscreen. The moon had set and outside the long searchlight beam it was black. They had not got far to go but they were not laughing any more. Each one of them focussed on reaching the landing stage and home. Andrew had his hand on the windscreen looking at Nick's back and wondering if he should have offered to swap positions with him. There was an extra hard thud from a wave against the boat, a second's quiet and then Nick was no longer there.

Nick was no longer on the front of the boat.

He was gone.

Nineteen

LAST RITES

"Are you thinking of floating wreaths on the water?" Jane asked Manda and then made a helpful suggestion.

"Mumbi and I have friends who grow flowers for export. Let us speak to them – perhaps you would like single stems of roses – or maybe only rose petals?"

They were speaking on the telephone about the funeral arrangements that needed to be in place when the family arrived.

When it was finally decided officially some six weeks later that Nick's body could not be found, a death certificate was issued. The chief of police at Siavonga had organised a police launch from Sinazongwe to make a search along the coast, and various local people had also spent time out in boats looking for any sign of the missing man. Chief Police Officer Phiri and Piet du Plessis agreed between them with some head-shaking that Nick must have been taken by a crocodile because he had not resurfaced or cried out when he fell from the boat. The next monster crocodile to be shot on the lake on suspicion of being a man-eater, would be sliced open and examined for human remains but that should not be mentioned to the bereaved. Officer Phiri and Piet both wanted, for the family's sake, to make sure that the matter was closed so that some kind of service could be arranged. It was nevertheless hard to decide what was best to tell the family.

"Tell the truth to Manda," Father Patrick advised, "I am sure that is best for the children too."

Father Patrick had held prayers for the missing man in the church at Siavonga the weekend after the accident. Now that the death certificate was signed there could be a memorial service in Lusaka at the Anglican cathedral but without a body or a graveside to visit there was an unhappy feeling that nothing had been concluded.

Sebastian had been in touch by phone with Manda from the first moment that she had heard the news and now came to see her.

"What are you thinking of doing for the children?" he asked, "And also for yourself, that is just as important."

"I have talked to Emma and to James," she replied. "We want to go to the place where it happened and say prayers and leave flowers – it's not very much, but somehow we need to mark it in a special way. Obviously we'll all be at the memorial service with Nick's parents, but I think that what we do on the lake has to be very private – just me and the kids.

"Father Patrick has offered to come out on the boat with us and read some prayers."

"Manda, please let me come with you," Sebastian said, "I don't like to think of you being alone at a time like this. How are the kids about it? They are so young to lose a father – Nick was so young."

Manda wept turning the phone sideways so it didn't fill up with her tears and so Sebastian couldn't hear her cry.

Finally she managed to say, "They blame me for Nick's death I think – they feel that this wouldn't have happened if I had not left him – it's not entirely rational but they never did really understand why I went – at times like this – it is a mess. I don't think they would believe me or understand my reasons for leaving Nick – it would take their father away from them twice – I didn't know what was right for me to say to them then and now it's even worse.

"It's difficult for us all, Seb. Oh gosh – I would be so grateful if you did come out with me. Michael would come but we both think that might complicate feelings for the kids. So it would be a comfort for us all if you came – really."

Manda found herself struggling with powerful, conflicting emotions. Sometimes it was sheer relief. Relief, that she was safe from Nick, but there was also terrible grief. Grief for Nick, the man that she loved.

Love, she thought with grief, *does not end. Will the grief also never end?*

Then she thought of Marielise.

It was arranged that the four of them, Manda, Emma, James and Sebastian, would fly out to Zambia together. Nick's friends in Lusaka chose a date for the memorial service to fit in with the family's arrival and Mumbi and Jane offered them the use of their own modern lakeside villa, and promised to keep their later plans a secret.

It was a miserable time for them all. Nick's parents ignored Manda, but clutched onto the children, then went back to the International Hotel and took the next plane to England. Their old friends, and Nick's friends and colleagues were kind and supportive but they had to meet with Heinrich and Estelle, Jessie and Andrew, all four of whom were still traumatised by the part they had played in Nick's death. Heinrich and Estelle offered long explanations of how it had happened, and longer accounts of what they done in their fruitless attempts to find Nick. Emma and James could not bear to listen, and walked away in tears, while Manda was forced to comfort people that she knew to have been reckless. Rita kept her distance though she did write letters of sympathy about Nick to the children. She had already moved out of Nick's house so that Emma and James were able to return there with Sebastian.

Eventually the family arrived in Siavonga and here they were at last, left alone with their grief. It was strange to be at Siavonga and not in their cottage, looking at the lake through the trees of their garden, but Manda was grateful for the distance that this gave her from the past. She didn't want to add this present pain to her memories of the cottage. The weather was good and the lake seemed at peace. They spent a day resting and preparing for the little ceremony.

Mumbi and Jane, thoughtful and efficient as ever, had also arranged for a motor launch for their use. Milimo was to be their boatman, a skill he had acquired since he was freed from his duties at the cottage. The family had driven down with the rose petals from Jane and Mumbi's friends, and placed them overnight in the chill of the large drinks cooler at the villa. While Manda and the children were in Lusaka, they had been back to Nick's house to collect a few precious symbols of his life to leave in the lake, together with their prayers and petals. Sebastian had found some of Nick's favourite wine to take on the boat. They would drink some as a toast to him and some they would pour into the lake as a libation.

Milimo took the boat out at a steady speed, fast enough to be comfortable, but not to be in a hurry. When they reached the bay where Nick had fallen overboard on that stormy night, they threw out an anchor and simply sat quietly, in the gently rocking boat looking around them at the white beach, the rocky shore and the green hills above. A fish eagle made its wild and haunting call from a perch on a dead tree and its mate responded. A large fish jumped nearby, then there were several more splashes and the circling ripples spread across the blue water towards them. A pied kingfisher made its astounding slap of a dive and rose again, hovering above the lake looking for another, better opportunity to catch a fish.

Eventually Emma and James said that they would like to begin their ceremony.

They each read out a letter that they had written to their father and when they had finished they torn up the paper and scattered it on the water. Manda and Sebastian followed, Manda with a poem and Sebastian with the verses of Chapter Thirteen of

Paul's Epistle to the Corinthians, then Father Patrick read out the prayers they had selected. Each of them had a small object that was weighted with a stone and they released them gently into the water. At the last they drank their toasts to Nick, emptied a bottle into the lake for him and then threw out handful after handful of rose petals.

Again they rested quietly for a while, each thinking their own thoughts and watching the petals swirl away. Sebastian looked at his sister, sitting in the middle of the boat with her children on either side of her, and Milimo and Father Patrick in the stern. It struck him that they looked like a family. The old priest with his white hair and distinctive posture, Milimo and Manda with their fine noses and almond eyes, together with the young boy James and young girl Emma, were somehow alike – perhaps it was grief that made them look similar.

Sebastian thought the old priest holding the prayer book might be Prospero, about to cast his magic book of spells into the deep water of the lake. Manda was of course, Miranda, and she had once said that Milimo was Ariel. Sebastian thought of Nick and what his sister had told him about his brother-in-law. So Nick was sometimes Caliban – or was Caliban sometimes Nick? Which of them held the other a prisoner?

Perhaps at last Nick was free and whole, and the slave that was Caliban had gone to join Sycorax, who in Sebastian's view, was a much maligned creature because of her colour. After all, the island had belonged to her and been stolen from her by Prospero.

When Sebastian was at school they had studied the *Tempest* in English literature. The class bully had tried to suggest that Sebastian, the smallest and blackest boy in the class, should play Caliban, but Sebastian, never easily intimidated, stuck out for the role he wanted, and insisted on being the smallest and blackest Prospero ever seen in any school performance.

Now he found himself reciting from memory the last verses of Prospero's final speech.

'Now my charms are all o'erthrown,
And what strength I have's mine own;
Which is most faint; now 'tis true,
I must be here confin'd by you,
Or sent to Naples. Let me not,
Since I have my dukedom got,
And pardon'd the deceiver, dwell
In this bare island by your spell:
But release me from my bond
With the help of your good hands.
Gentle breath of yours my sails
Must fill, or else my project fails,
Which was to please. Now I want
Spirits to enforce, art to enchant;
And my ending is despair,
Unless I be reliev'd by prayer,
Which pierces so that it assaults
Mercy itself, and frees all faults.
As you from crimes would pardon'd be,
Let your indulgence set me free.'

GARDENING

Miranda

1995

Manda clenched her teeth. She was not going to be beaten. She would take on the job bit by bit, piece by piece, square metre by square metre, until she had cleared away the brambles.

This was her choice and her decision. There was going to be one big flowerbed running the full length of the front garden.

Well – it wasn't a garden yet – just a plot of untended grass, weeds and brambles at the front of an old farmhouse with rotting shutters and grey mould on the outside walls.

At least the day was beautiful and warm. An early mist had lifted but not retreated so far that she could see the horizon. The garden was full of birds; their wings flashed with the light from the pale yellow sunshine as they stooped to the bird-feeders and then fled back to the bare fruit trees at the sight of a woman in jeans and coat stomping around in the cool morning air.

Manda parked the wheelbarrow, lifted the fork and drove the tines into the earth. They went in easily enough but when she pushed it down with her foot and twisted it to come up again it refused, held firmly in place by bramble roots. Manda pulled the fork straight back and worked her way steadily around this one root, loosening the earth until she could get a grip on the root with her gloved hands and tug at it. Sometimes the roots gave up and came away; often she had to chop at them with the spade and secateurs.

Manda smiled at her career path since leaving Nick. She had progressed from a Community Education Administrator to a Business Advisor on Lottery Art Projects. Finally she had become Michael's Studio Manager, with the end result that she was now labouring in an old French farmyard making a paddock into a garden and a house into a home. Most of the old farmhouse by the Adour River was still shambolic though the three half-finished bedrooms were at least warm and comfortable. Michael was converting the barn into a painting and print-making studio and guest wing, which would give them their income. Emma and James were at school, immersed in learning French and adapting surprisingly well. Manda lifted an eyebrow and bit her lip at the realisation that they would soon speak far better French than she ever could.

By eleven o'clock Manda had a wheelbarrow load of roots and clods of clay, and a square metre of dark damp earth ready for planting. This job was going to take weeks and then some more weeks, in fact, as Manda looked around her, she knew that the garden would take years and years to develop.

What did she know about gardening in this part of the world anyway? They had just recovered from snow and frosts that hardened the earth and killed the exotic shrubs she thought would be safe outdoors.

This is going to be a huge task, Manda thought, momentarily daunted, *I know nothing about gardening here. Everything is surprisingly different and differently the same. Gardens and plants are like children and husbands – you have to work with them and let them develop in their own way and tell you what they need. There is no compelling a garden – especially if you want its survival without becoming its slave.*

She stopped. A sense of loss and the memory of a little cottage and a shining lake troubled her, then somehow, she felt the quiet and comforting presence of Milimo and his timeless, patient smile with her in the garden. Manda shook herself, smiled too and whispered: "This is what I really want to do! Garden and share life with Michael!"

Moments later Michael appeared with coffee and croissants for a much-needed break. He gave Manda a light kiss on her lips.

"Take care my love," he said, his hand on her swelling belly. "Richard Joseph needs more growing time too."

Margaret

1995

Margaret rested on her spade and breathed in the wonderful, rich smell of damp earth, horse manure and newly turned compost. Such pleasure, such a moment, such happiness, she must keep this moment alive for ever and never let anything else intrude. She shut her eyes behind her dark glasses, folded her hat brim back and tilted her head up so that she could feel the sun's heat burning her forehead and cheeks.

Vimbai, working alongside of her, smiled and said, "It's a beautiful day Margaret – praise the Lord!"

"Praise the Lord indeed," Margaret responded smiling. "Praise the workers too, Vimbai – all of us."

"I pray you'll find faith and healing one day, Margaret," said Vimbai. Margaret reached out to touch Vimbai's shoulder. The generosity and kindness of Vimbai and her daughter, Chipo, were another of the good things about her present life.

Margaret wondered, if she was to find God, would it be in a garden? It seemed so clear to her that God had deserted the world – that he had gone – or never existed.

The world was a terrible place; unforgivable crimes had taken place in it and left it full of wounded and suffering people. Maybe it was okay for people to find some comfort in whatever way they could, in whatever church they felt safe but it didn't work for her.

Charles had also chosen to 'praise the Lord' with the Evangelical Church goers, but Margaret could not trust in anything except in the earth and the rain, and for sure the rain had never been reliable. If her plants would grow, if she could take handfuls of this rich, dark red earth and make it produce fruit and flowers, that would be enough.

If nothing and nobody takes this bit of earth away from me and if at last I can be buried in it – that will be enough goodness for me.

Margaret went on digging knowing that she must stop by mid-morning and let Vimbai and Chipo continue. Perhaps the physical work was her way of praying – it certainly made her as happy as Vimbai had promised that prayer would, but her sixty year old body refused to praise God by working outdoors all day. Soon she would go back into the shade house and make sure that the seedlings and young plants were watered and free of bugs and infections, then after that back to the office to see that bills were paid, seeds ordered, customers satisfied and the next lot of Permaculture students were on their way. It had been Margaret's idea to run this cooperative venture and resource centre to teach people recovering from the war how to grow nutritious and varied food economically without insecticides or much water, but Charles had helped make the project possible by donating some of his farmland.

Charles, Margaret thought, *has his own quiet and kind ways of showing faith in a material future, and without doubt, the news of his regular attendance at prayer meetings will please Father Patrick in his retirement home in Ireland.*

Marielise

1995

Marielise sat on her bottom in the garden and scraped away with her hand trowel at the friable, pebbly yellow earth until she was sitting in a small hollow.

The summer sun was pleasant and the garden was sheltered. None of her neighbours could see her digging with a bucket and spade like a little child. The hollow deepened slowly. She had placed her three buckets near her on the edge of the depression and she filled each of them to the top and then a little over. When the three were quite full she rotated herself onto her right side, bent her right leg under her and hauled herself up and out of her hole, until she stood up awkwardly and unfolded herself in stages. She then lugged the buckets of earth to the edge of the garden under the apple tree and tipped out the damp earth onto the pile of leaves and mould that was heaping up there. Marielise went back and looked at her work.

It looked as if she was digging a shallow grave. Marielise gave a quick glance up at the next-door's upper windows. The neighbours would wonder who she was going to bury here.

She knelt on the ragged grass lawn and lowered herself back into the egg-shaped basin with its crumbly edges. Last night a fox, drawn to the smell of damp earth, had left two paw prints in the soft gravel bottom. She hadn't wanted to scrape them away. Already she had removed several layers of clay and uncovered sand and smooth round pebbles – perhaps there had once been a small stream right here.

Marielise felt as if she was digging a little grave around herself, a comforting, warm gravelly pit in which to rest.

Marielise lay back in her hollow – it wasn't quite long enough for her body yet. She shut her eyes; the pain of losing Jo overwhelmed her. Pile the earth over her right now, right here, it was over, she had had enough. She could not bear to go back to South Africa next year and start over again, even though working on a project to empower women through education was exactly what she wanted to do. She thought of Zanele who was happy at last. She had an interesting and useful job in the developing media industry in Jo'burg.

Marielise had to move before she began to stiffen.

Some stiff you! she mocked herself.

Soon she would be able to place the butyl liner in the small basin and put in the water and pond plants. Soon she would have frogs, damsel flies and dragon flies.

My own tiny Kariba Lake, she thought smiling.

Natombi

1995

I have my place again at the house of my son, Milimo. I tell him to go and work alongside his daughter, Busiku, in the garden she is making. I tell him that if men can no longer go hunting for food then they must spend more time digging.

Busiku is a good girl. She has an education and she is going to learn agriculture at college. She has already been to Zimbabwe to learn from Mrs Beaumont about how to grow things well with little water. I watch her and see that she understands how to look after her crops. She explains to me how she collects the rain in a large plastic tank and keeps it for the dry weather. Here there is no Zambezi to bring silt to the garden so she showed me how she has made a compost heap and how she collects the dung from the chickens. I understand very well what she is doing. All of my people are gardeners. She has asked me also to keep the Rain Ceremony each year. We have need of our beliefs she says and also of education.

I do not sit idle while my son and my granddaughter are working. I am a basket maker and I weave the wide patterned Tonga baskets that my people used for collecting grain. Each one has a traditional pattern that has its own name. We do not keep our food in them anymore but I can sell each basket to a co-operative in Lusaka.

My life is good.

I am Natombi.

Glossary

A luta continua! The fight continues! (Portuguese).

ANC: African National Congress.

badza: Hoe.

bakkie: Pick-up truck. (Afrikaans).

boer/ boere: Literally Afrikaner farmers; used for White South African Nationalists.

boma: Fence or enclosure around a hut or group of huts to keep out wild animals. Also a local administration centre.

braaivleis: Barbecue – the process and the grill. (Afrikaans).

broer: Brother. (Afrikaans).

bwato: Dugout canoe.

CAPCO: Central African Power Corporation.

Chimurenga: The war of liberation in Zimbabwe.

choka!: Scram!

CITES: Convention on International Trade in Endangered Species.

dambo:	Marsh. A shallow seasonal lake or marshy area.
dassie:	Hyrax.
donga:	Gully made by soil erosion (Zulu)
duiker-berry:	Tree, Mukunyu Pseudolachnostylus Maprouniafolia.
fundi/fundis:	Expert/Experts.
gombe gofu:	The chinspot batis. Batis Molitor.
hakata:	Divining sticks or bones used by an nganga.
hazeku ndaba:	Without a fuss, no problem, no discussion.
hamagutu:	Whip scorpion. Damon Variegates, Order Amblypygi.
insete:	Traditional string skirt made from the roots of the musanta.
jirre:	Afrikaans slang for 'Jeez' as in Jesus. Expression of shock.
kabwalala:	Thief – one who makes the dogs bark.
kaffir:	Originally Arabic meaning unbeliever and used to describe Africans, it became a derogatory word used by whites.

kaffir-boetjie:	Little brother of a kaffir – insulting term for whites who befriend Africans.
kapenta:	Lake sardine. Kapenta is the Bemba word for sex workers – ladies who paint their lips.
Katete:	Place name.
katundu:	Belongings or goods.
kraal :	Thorn fence to keep domestic animals safe.
Kwacha:	Zambian currency. Bemba for dawn.
laager:	Defensive enclosure made by a circle of wagons.
leguvaan:	Monitor lizard.
marula:	Tree, Sclerocarya Birrea.
MK:	Umkonto we Sizwe abbreviated to MK. Spear of the Nation, the armed wing of the ANC in South Africa.
mpande:	Flat end of a seashell from a Conus snail used as ornament or currency. Pottery copies were also used.
mujenje:	Tree, Diospyros Kiirkii.
mukwa:	Tree, Pterocarpus Angolensis, kiaat.

muli bwanji:	Greeting (Chinyanja).
munt:	From the Bantu word 'muntu' for 'man' or person – used in a derogatory way by whites.
mupane:	Tree, Colophospermum Mopane.
musanta:	Tree, Kirkia Acuminata.
mushi:	Good or pleasant: Chilapalapa – European pidgin version of Chishona used to talk to employees or people thought inferior but also became part of white Rhodesian language.
muzungu:	White person or ghost or unappeased spirit.
nganga:	Witchdoctor or traditional healer.
nshima:	Mealie meal, staple food from corn.
pata-patas:	Plastic sandals.
sikatongo:	Ritual leader recognised by the neighbourhood.
solifugid:	Solifugae. Neither a spider nor a scorpion. Called a sun spider or a hunting spider.
SOMOFCO:	Solomon Mahlangu Freedom College.
stoep:	Literally 'step' but means veranda (Afrikaans).
terr:	Short for terrorist.

uhuru:	Freedom (Swahili).
UNIP:	United National Independence Party, President Kaunda's party.
UNZA:	University of Zambia.
veldschoens:	Bush shoes (Afrikaans)
vlei:	A shallow seasonal lake or marshy area (Afrikaans).
water dikkop:	Water bird, Burhinus Vermiculatas.
yendani:	Go, leave.
ZANC:	Zambia African National Congress.
ZANLA:	Zimbabwe African National Liberation Army. ZANU's military wing led by Herbert Chitepo and latterly Robert Mugabe.
ZANU:	Zimbabwe African National Union. The party of Sithole and Mugabe.
ZAPU:	Zimbabwe African People's Party. Led by Joshua Nkomo.
zikomo:	Thank you (Chichewa).
ZIPRA :	Zimbabwe People's Revolutionary Army. ZAPU's military wing.

TIMELINE SOUTH AFRICA

1948 Apartheid set in law

1950 Population classified by race

1960 Sharpeville shootings ANC banned

1961 South Africa declared a republic. Mandela heads new ANC military wing

1960s International pressure against Apartheid government begins

1964 Nelson Mandela sentenced to life imprisonment on Robben Island

1976 Soweto uprising

1984-89 Township revolt. State of Emergency

1990 ANC unbanned. Mandela released

1991 Multi-party talks. Apartheid laws repealed. Major fighting between ANC and Zulu Inkhata movement

1994 ANC wins elections

TIMELINE ZIMBABWE

1890 Pioneer Column of White settlers arrives

1893 Ndebele uprising crushed

1922 British South Africa Company administration ends. White minority self-government

1930 Land Apportionment Act

1930 – 1960 Black opposition grows. Emergence of ZAPU and ZANU

1953 Central African Federation formed by Britain. Northern Rhodesia (Zambia), Southern Rhodesia (Zimbabwe) and Nyasaland (Malawi)

1963 Federation breaks up

1964 Ian Smith's party, the Rhodesian Front comes to power

1965 Unilateral Declaration of Independence

1972 Guerrilla war intensifies

1978 Smith's attempted settlement. Zimbabwe-Rhodesia under Bishop Abel Muzorewa not recognised

1979 Lancaster House agreement

1980 Independence. Robert Mugabe and ZANU win elections.

TIMELINE ZAMBIA

1898 British indirect rule established over Northern Rhodesia

1920s Discovery of copper

1953 Federation of Rhodesia and Nyasaland formed

1960 UNIP formed by Kenneth Kaunda

1963 End of Federation

1964 Independence under Kaunda

1972 Zambia a one party state under UNIP. Nationalisation agenda. Border closed between Rhodesia and Zambia, first by Smith, then by Kaunda.

1975 Tan-Zam railway opened. Help for Liberation struggles in region

1976 Zambia declares support for Zimbabwe liberation war

1990 Food riots

1991 Multi-party constitution adopted.

TIMELINE KARIBA DAM

March 1955 Decision to proceed with Dam

July 1955 Contract for preliminary works. Main civil engineering contract Contracts for turbines and generators

February 1957 Floods

July 1957 Diversion of river through tunnels. Start of cofferdam

November 1957 Cofferdam dewatered, river bed exposed

February March 1958 Exceptional floods. Main cofferdam overtopped

June 1958 Main cofferdam dewatered after floods

1958 Uprising at Chisamu Village against resettlement of Tonga.

December 1958 Dam closed. Impounding of lake

June 1959 Last concrete poured in dam excluding road.

1971 North Bank Power Station begun. Completed 1976

1965 – 1973 Kafue Dam begun and completed.

TIMELINE FOR LIBERATION WARS IN REGION

MOZAMBIQUE

Liberation war 1964 – 1974

Independence 1975

Civil War Proxy Cold War 1977 – 1992

Multi-party Elections 1994

ANGOLA

Liberation war 1961 – 1974

Civil War Proxy Cold War began in 1975 ended in 2002

At one point South African forces fought against Cuban forces.

NAMIBIA

Occupied by South Africa in 1915 from Germany as a fifth province and known as South West Africa.

The guerrilla war began in 1966. South Africa withdrew in 1988.

Acknowledgements

John Corley for allowing me enough space and time to write and for his unfailing patience and efficient help with editing.

Tanvir Bush for her generous encouragement and for rescuing the Guest Books from the 'Cottage' for me.

Ilse Mwanza, Gabrielle Stubbs, Lesley Bower, Colin and Jenny Carlin, for reading the drafts and giving invaluable advice and support. Lucy McCann of the Bodleian Library, Rhodes House, Oxford for finding for me the '1958 Report of the Commission into the use of firearms in Gwembe District'. Professor Elisabeth Colson for her books on the Tonga people and the Gwembe Valley in the Kariba Series. (Also Barrie Reynolds). John Hudson, Hugh Macmillan, Guida Bell-Cross, Patrick Mweemba and many old friends in Zambia for help and details about places, names and birds.

A very special acknowledgement must go to Anne and Peter Hyatt, original owners of the beloved 'Cottage' and to Dominic Hamalengwa.